PRAISE FOR
OPAL COUNTRY

'Classic Hammer, with the heat and the small town obsession with secrecy and past grievances. A crime novel that will stay with me for a long time' **Ann Cleeves**

'A complex, twisty thriller, with nuanced characters and a winding plot all set in the oppressive Australian heat' **Lisa Hall**

'A clever and compelling small town mystery, with an evocative setting and a brilliant cast of characters. This slice of Australian noir sparkles like an opal in the blistering sun' **Lisa Gray**

'*Opal Country* is a top-notch Aussie noir with real heat coming off the pages' **Christopher Fowler**

'A brilliantly atmospheric mystery' *Heat*

'This novel - tighter, tougher, tenser - is Hammer's best work yet' *The Times*

'Keeps you stuck to the story like an Outback miner's shirt to his back' *Sun*

'A sharp thriller' *Woman's Own*

'Chris Hammer is regarded as one of Australia's best new noir crime writers, and this immersive and lyrically written thriller copper-fastens this well-deserved reputation' *Irish Independent*

'Gold-standard Outback noir [. . .] Chris Hammer's best writing to date' *Crime Fiction Lover*

'Nobody does Australian outback crime better. Hammer nails it again' *Peterborough Telegraph*

'*Opal Country* is richly rewarding. Hammer is quite brilliant' *Shots Magazine*

PRAISE FOR
TRUST

'A thoroughly entertaining thriller' *Mail on Sunday*

'Once again Hammer provides a gripping, complex mystery' *Sunday Times* Crime Club

'You won't want to put it down. Hammer is superb' **NB Magazine**

'A dark and brilliant thriller, one that lingers in the mind' *Mail On Sunday*

'Stunning . . . *Scrublands* is that rare combination, a page-turner that stays long in the memory' **Joan Smith,** *Sunday Times* **(Crime Book of the Month)**

'A heatwave of a novel, scorching and powerful . . . Extraordinary' **A. J. Finn, author of** *The Woman in the Window*

'Incendiary . . . A rattling good read, ambitious in scale and scope and delivering right up to the last, powerfully moving page' **Declan Hughes,** *Irish Times*

'Atmospheric, utterly gripping and written with devastating beauty. *Scrublands* is as scorching as wildfire and as hard to look away from' **Gytha Lodge, author of** *She Lies in Wait*

'Well-rounded characters, masterful plotting and real breadth; this is an epic and immersive read' **Laura Wilson,** *Guardian*

'Set in the parched Australian landscape, *Scrublands* is a brilliantly plotted thriller which reveals a town full of brooding secrets. I couldn't put this compelling debut down' **Sarah Ward, author of** *The Shrouded Path*

Chris Hammer

OPAL COUNTRY

WILDFIRE

FOR GWYNETH, BRENDON AND INGE

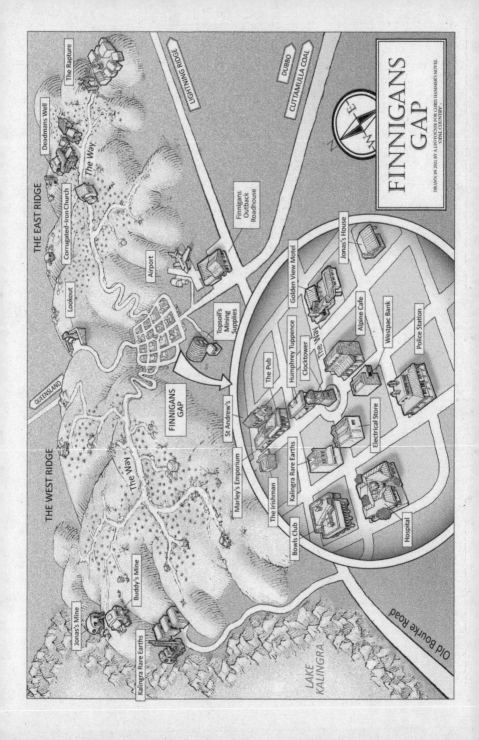

FINNIGANS GAP

DRAWN IN 2021 BY A LOVE'S CHILD FOR CHRIS HAMMER'S NOVEL 'OPAL COUNTRY'

prologue

THE NIGHT IS PERFECT FOR RATTING. A LAYER OF HIGH CLOUD HAS SPREAD across the sky, blocking out the moon and the stars, sucking light from the world. Only the night-vision goggles—military grade—allow for progress, the driver careful in a landscape rendered luminous, easing the old truck between trees silhouetted against the radiant earth. It's like a video game, glowing and hyperreal, bleeding light at the edges. And yet this is life, unmistakably authentic. Here, the stakes are not theoretical; here, there is no respawning, no second chances. Get caught ratting and there is no coming back. It might be possible to evade the violence and avoid the courts, but the shame would follow, leper-like, to other opal towns: Lightning Ridge, White Cliffs, Coober Pedy. Exile inescapable, reputation irredeemable, humiliation irreversible.

So the four men proceed in silence, ratters united by greed and needs unspoken, by quiet desperations, and divided by mutual loathing for who they are and what they've become, the engine the only sound. At the top of a rise above the far end of the opal fields, the driver slows the truck to a stop. This far along, The Way, the road linking the West Ridge to the town, the only access, the only egress, has splintered into multiple tracks. They drop the cockatoo, with his goggles and army surplus walkie-talkie. From here, he can look back at The Way as it undulates along the ridge line from Finnigans Gap ten kilometres away. The town itself is hidden in its hollow, its aura glowing through the night-vision goggles, but the intervening path is clear. The town is not so far, fifteen minutes, but far enough that he can alert them at the first flare of headlights, far enough for them to get clear in time. Or so they hope.

The truck moves forward, grinding down a gear, slowing even more as they leave the remnants of the track, moving cross country, the driver's caution overriding his desire to get there, to get started. Through the thermal-imaging goggles, the bonnet of the truck glows obscenely bright, its heat making it shine like a beacon. He knows no one else can see it, no one without the goggles, just the cockatoo on the ridge, but it makes him nervous all the same. And yet he can't afford to go any faster; the landscape is too treacherous, with its exposed mine shafts and ventilation holes, its mullock heaps and fallen trees and rusted-out machine parts. There's been no rain for four or five days, and yet he's concerned about lingering mud, the potential to skid, to lose control. He needs to avoid any mistakes. A puncture would leave them temporarily vulnerable; a broken axle would be disastrous. Finally, their destination comes into sight, marked by the darkened caravan.

Next to the driver, the leader is experiencing a kind of calm, settled now that the operation is underway, the sort of tranquillity that used to visit him before combat. The preceding few hours are worse, hiding underground on his own barren claim, waiting for the opal fields to empty, his fellow ratters nervous and edgy, unable to sleep, unable to speak, forbidden by him from drinking or taking drugs. Four men, trapped together, bound by circumstance.

Two hundred metres from the mine shaft, the truck stops. The driver cuts the engine—pivoting on the point of no return—and the leader climbs out. It's his operation; he's the one who must take the risks. They've been watching the mine for a week or so, on and off, through the rain, through the mounting heat, more diligently these past two nights. There has been no sightings of Jonas McGee; not today, not yesterday. The intel must be right: he's out of town, living it up on his windfall, squandering his fortune. Hundreds of thousands of dollars, according to the rumour mill. Maybe even millions. But gone for now, careless in his wealth, stupid in his luck, almost deserving of looting. Almost.

The leader approaches the caravan. McGee has been staying out here, guarding his hoard against ratters, so said the grapevine. But not tonight. There is no sign of life. His truck is here, which is concerning. But it sits pitch-black against the glowing earth, its engine cold. The leader approaches the caravan, itself black, registering no heat signature whatsoever, apparently devoid of life. Nevertheless, he removes his goggles, places them carefully in his backpack, operating by touch alone. He pulls out a small flask of whisky and, still operating by feel, removes the cap, spills a little down his front, then takes a swig, swirling it around his mouth before spitting it out. It's his cover story: that he's drunk and lost.

Barely plausible, but hopefully enough. Should he be discovered, should Jonas be here, he will start to sing and carry on, loud enough to alert the others. But for the moment he is quiet, standing motionless, hoping his eyes may yet adjust to the absence of light.

As he waits, he listens. The night is silent, as if in anticipation. There is no wind, not even up here on the ridge, nothing to animate the darkness, nothing to rustle the leaves on the sparse ironbarks and box gums. A dog barks in the distance, kilometres away, emphasising the void. It is so very dark without the goggles. It's all he can do to perceive the edge of the van against the clouded sky. He feels his way to the door, knocks once, knocks again, the sound like gunshots, holding his breath, the whisky sharp on his tongue. But there is no sound from the van, no response, no movement. It's all okay, McGee is gone; the recent rains have put a hold on mining and he's taken off to enjoy his spoils. The leader breathes again.

Goggles back on, he moves towards the mine. At the top of the shaft, all looks good: it's covered by its steel lid, padlock in place. Good. No one would be underground with the only exit locked down. He pulls out his radio, hits the button in three long dashes. The all clear.

He hears the truck engine fire, watches it rumble towards him. Then the driver is out, together with the third member of the crew, his lieutenant, pulling the tarpaulin from the back, exposing the gear. Everything is there in readiness: the electric winch, silent and effective; the padded buckets; the nylon ropes. There is no talk. They know their roles: the leader will go down the mine, dig for opals, extract the gems from the walls with his handheld excavator, not risking the heavy machinery any honest miner would use: the diesel generators and air compressors, the vacuum pumps. Here, stealth is all-important. His second-in-command will collect the rubble, take it to the bottom of the shaft and fill the buckets; the driver will winch them to the surface, load the back of the truck. They'll be gone an hour before dawn, collecting the lookout along the way. Later in the day, mining the leader's own claim, the ore will be mixed with his. They will take it to the wash site, clean it, hidden in plain view, extracting the opals, downplaying their discoveries.

The leader checks the lock, is relieved to see the brand. No need for the hacksaw then; boltcutters will suffice. A fortune in gems and the man can't be bothered buying himself a decent lock. The leader slices through the hardened steel and raises the lid, flipping it back on its hinges. Too easy.

He hesitates only long enough to ensure he has what he needs, then starts down the shaft, a metre in diameter, a 'three-footer', straight down. He clings to the steel ladder, strung section by section from the framework of the lid, hanging free, swaying slightly. The shaft is ghost-like, hazy and dark, emitting little light, even using the goggles. Thirty metres down he reaches the bottom. He removes his backpack and stows the goggles, replacing them with a conventional torch, a miner's headband. He flicks it on, the brightness flaring in the still of the mine, lighting the walls, the roof supports casting shadows through the mined-out cavern.

He's in an open space, two and a half metres high, more than enough to stand. A ballroom. The roof is propped up by pine trunks, thirty centimetres in diameter, bark still in place. Off in one corner, he can spy where these bolsters are taking the strain, bent and squashed at the top where the earth is trying to fall in on itself. He shrugs it off: the potential for a cave-in is the least of his worries, even after the rain of the previous week.

The mine is tidier than most: empty water bottles are stacked in a pile by the bottom of the ladder, ready to be lifted to the surface. Next to the bottles is a pile of wood, four-by-twos: not new but scavenged. McGee must have been shoring up the roof. Next to the wood is a large silver toolbox, padlock undone. More complacency. Carefully, he examines the footprints left in the dust, finds the uppermost impressions and starts to follow them, confident they will lead to the most recent digging, to McGee's lucrative new discoveries.

As he proceeds, the smell grows worse. What was merely a suggestion, a vague taint at the bottom of the ladder, steadily becomes insistent. What the fuck has the bastard been up to? So desperate to plunder the opals that he can't be bothered to bury his shit? No, the smell is worse than that. The smell of roadkill, the smell of repressed memories. Maybe a wallaby has come to grief, fallen down one of the blower shafts. Not that that will stop him.

Spider webs brush his face. He ignores them. Behind him he can hear the faint noise of the winch, the buckets thudding against the steel ladder on the way down. His deputy must already be at the bottom.

He comes to a cordoned-off passage, orange plastic webbing strung across its entry, the sort used on roadworks. The tunnel is supported by a roughly made wooden framework. There's a piece of cardboard, ripped from a carton, with one word scrawled: UNSTABLE. He moves past it, past a blower hole, the vacuum tube still hanging from it where McGee has been sucking out his fill. He must be getting closer.

Past the hole, the smell grows markedly worse. His stomach turns and the hairs on the back of his head come alert. Something is wrong here. Very wrong. He knows this smell, from another time, another land, an endless war.

He passes a mining machine, an excavator. He's close now.

And then he sees it. Sees him. Jonas McGee, dead eyes staring, something small and black crawling from the corner of his mouth. The man is not just dead, he's been crucified, nailed to a timber frame, metal spikes through his wrists, black blood congealed around them, a ratter's drill placed by his feet like an offering. Crucified. Christ-like: except here the face holds no ecstasy, the eyes no rapture.

The leader fights back an urge to vomit, pushes it down, disciplines himself. He knows he must leave no trace here. He hits the radio button, three short bursts, followed by another three. The warning: the message to get out fast, to get out now. He looks about, sees what he needs. A piece of loose sacking. He lifts the drill, makes the snap decision: he needs to take it with him. He can leave nothing that implicates ratters. And then he slowly backs out, using the sacking to erase his footprints behind him. They need to get away; they need to have never been here.

Chris Hammer was a journalist for more than thirty years, dividing his career between covering Australian federal politics and international affairs. For many years he was a roving foreign correspondent for SBS TV's flagship current affairs program Dateline. He has reported from more than thirty countries on six continents.

Chris's non-fiction book, *The River*, published in 2010 to critical acclaim, was the recipient of the ACT Book of the Year Award and was short-listed for the Walkley Book Award. *Scrublands*, his first novel, was published in 2018 and won the CWA John Creasey Debut Dagger Award, as well as being shortlisted for Best Debut Fiction at the Indie Book Awards, and Best General Fiction at the ABIA Awards. It has also been longlisted for the Ned Kelly Best Crime Novel of the Year. *Scrublands* was optioned for television by Easy Tiger (a Fremantle-Media company). The sequels, *Silver* and *Trust*, were published in 2019 and 2020. *Opal Country* is his fifth novel and the first in a new series.

Chris has a bachelor's degree in journalism from Charles Sturt University and a master's degree in international relations from the Australian National University. He lives in Canberra with his wife, Dr Tomoko Akami. The couple have two children.

SUNDAY

chapter one

DETECTIVE SERGEANT IVAN LUCIC IS SITTING IN THE BACK OF THE POLAIR Cessna, staring out the window. There is nothing to see, just an endless plain of clouds stretching to the western horizon, glowing white below the morning sun. Beneath the clouds it will be raining; it was bucketing down when the plane left Sydney, fighting the roiling squalls of greyness, dipping and fighting, engines whining against the weather. But up here the sky is blue and empty, tranquil above the never-ending whiteness. Like a blank page, inviting inscription.

He glances across at the others. The crime scene investigator, Carole Nguyen, is working assiduously at her laptop, tapping and frowning and tapping again, too engrossed to notice his attention. Behind her the forensic pathologist, Blake Ness, is asleep and snoring, the sound harmonising with the engines, earplugs in, eyes shielded by an old airline mask. Ivan doesn't bother to look behind

11

himself: he knows the seat is empty. His boss, Detective Inspector Morris Montifore, should be there, should be leading the investigation, but he called at the last moment, said he couldn't make the trip. So Ivan is on his own, heading towards a murder scene: an opal miner crucified at some hellhole called Finnigans Gap, up near the Queensland border, miles from anywhere. And that's all he knows. There was nothing waiting for him at Bankstown airport: no brief, no Montifore, no explanation.

His head throbs, a residual hangover generated more by lack of sleep than too much alcohol. Sunday morning and here he is, woken at five thirty, ordered to the airport by Montifore, only to be left to take the assignment solo. Sunday. He should be in bed, nursing his head and regretting his losses. Or, at the very least, he should be emulating Blake and trying to catch up on sleep. It's bound to be a long day, draining and confronting. It will be hot at Finnigans, probably very hot; in January, seven or eight hundred kilometres inland, that's a given. And yet his mind is restless. There was something strange in Montifore's voice, something troubled. He tries once more to identify it, but the more he tries to recall the conversation, turn it over in his mind, the more nebulous it becomes.

The co-pilot wanders back to tell him they're going to land at Dubbo, to fuel up just in case. He says Finnigans Gap has an airstrip, but that's all. No refuelling, no control tower, no services. 'Paved runway, though,' the aviator says, approval in his voice.

On the ground at Dubbo, the rain is a gentler variation of the coastal torrents, soft and soaking, the landing smooth by contrast with the stomach-churning take-off from Bankstown. Ivan walks across the tarmac, through the drizzle, to the commercial terminal, seeking caffeine and information. The place is deserted, but there's a cafe open, preparing for the day's flights. He orders a long black and a pre-prepared ham-and-cheese croissant. It's given a minute in a sandwich press to impart some warmth, but not enough to melt the cheese. He taps his card, and for a moment his heart does a double beat. But it's okay, the transaction is approved: there's enough in the account. He takes his breakfast to the windows overlooking the runways. A couple of backpackers are asleep on the floor, dead to the world. He walks further along, finds an isolated seat, sets his piping-hot coffee to cool and scoffs half his croissant. It tastes surprisingly good; he must be hungry.

The first thing he does is check his bank account. It's fine. Well, not in the red. He checks the withdrawals from last night: just three of them, three hundred bucks a throw. Not so bad, then. Within the boundaries. He transfers more money across from the other account, the one he's meant to use for gambling. He knows he should be more disciplined, knows he squanders too much of his own money. Then he takes another bite, sips some coffee and rings Morris Montifore.

'Ivan? Where are you?'

'Dubbo. Refuelling. What happened?'

'The deputy commissioner. She overruled Homicide. I was on the way to Bankstown when Plodder rang me, told me I need to stay in Sydney.'

Out on the tarmac, Ivan can see the avgas truck making its way towards the police plane. He glances at his watch. They've already been on the ground fifteen minutes. He looks at his croissant, but his hunger has abandoned him, replaced by a bad feeling.

The deputy commissioner and Detective Superintendent Dereck 'Plodder' Packenham, head of Homicide, both up before dawn on a Sunday, ringing Montifore.

He attempts to make light of it. 'Up for another medal then?'

Montifore chuckles at that, dry and humourless, the laugh he knows so well. 'No, my friend. I think our days of gongs and glory are a thing of the past.'

'What does that mean?'

'Means I'm being investigated. Professional Standards.'

'Bullshit. How is that even possible?'

'Good question. No idea.'

'Sorry, I don't get it,' Ivan says.

'Neither do I. I haven't even been told anything officially as yet. Just back channels.'

'Friends in high places.'

'Something like that.'

The truck has pulled up next to the plane. The driver is attaching the fuel line. Montifore's words make no sense to Ivan. For the past six months, he and his superior have been feted: photos in the paper, a distinguished service medal, even a pay rise. They'd solved a slurry of murders: three judges, an undercover cop, a newspaper editor, an American gangster, an infamous standover man. And in so doing, they helped to expose a cabal of influence and corruption centred on a private dining club; the repercussions lasted for months, are still being felt. Montifore has been touted as a future head of Homicide, even a deputy commissioner, Lucic a senior sergeant.

'What's changed?' he asks.

'Blowback. The revenge of the old guard.' Montifore's voice is remarkably matter-of-fact. 'They resent how we've been lionised and they're reasserting their influence. They want me out.'

'But how? We did nothing wrong. We played everything by the book.'

'Best we don't talk about it. Not now. You don't know who might be listening.'

The man refuelling the plane is waving his arms at someone over by the terminal, pointing at the back of the truck, as if there is some problem.

'Is that a joke?'

'No. It's not. I'll call you tomorrow, when I find out more. Good luck up there.'

'Wait—what can you tell me about this case?'

'You haven't received a brief?'

'Not yet. None of us have.'

'Who's with you?'

'Carole Nguyen and Blake Ness.'

'You don't have another detective with you?'

'No. I think they're giving me a local.'

'In Finnigans Gap? Hell. Good luck with that.' Montifore chuckles again, the same irony-laden sound.

Above the downpour, the view is unchanging: radiant blue above, a field of white below. Finally, the clouds begin to fray, then dissolve altogether, confirmation that the plane is indeed making progress. Ivan is presented with the earth, spread out before him, the great expanse of the interior, out past the last of the hills, where the land is flat and forever, too far inland for the rains to persist. Last time he flew this far inland was in the PolAir chopper, a couple of years back now, out to a small town called Riversend in the Western Riverina. Back then the earth was bleached, barren and bone-dry, in the grip of a terrible drought. Now some mighty switch out in the Pacific has altered its orientation and the rainclouds have returned, sweeping in week after week, painting the flatness with variations of green, even this far from the coast. Water is spread across the landscape, the sun flashing back at him from farm dams and ephemeral marshes, rivers and creeks. For a moment it captures him, this panorama of life renewed. He's reminded, with this aerial perspective, of Aboriginal paintings, the land from above, imbued with spirit, replete with hidden meanings, of unspoken significance. For a moment, the magic of it resonates within him, the magnitude. But only for a moment. He shakes off the idea; he's a policeman, not a philosopher. There is a job to be done. There's nothing special to be read in the landscape; painting it a different colour doesn't alter its essential emptiness.

He returns his mind to his assignment. He tries to look at the positives: he's been hoping to emerge from Montifore's shadow, to lead his own investigation, to make his own name. He just wishes he had more warning. And more resources. In Sydney, such a murder would attract a whole team: up to a dozen professional and experienced Homicide detectives, with admin support and scientific expertise. Instead, it's just him, Carole and Blake, with whatever help Ivan can muster locally—hopefully someone competent enough to run errands and complete the paperwork. To expect anything more, real insights and investigative flare, would be foolish. He knows. He started in uniform, spent two years paying his dues in a country town in the state's Central West:

petty crimes, pub brawls and domestic violence. Sexual assaults, car crashes and quad-bike accidents. Not exactly a whetstone for the forensic mind. No, this case is his and his alone; he will wear the success or bear the failures.

He's run cases before, murder inquiries, but only simple ones: the husband or boyfriend covered in blood, literally or metaphorically, and soaked through with guilt. He hates those cases: so simple to solve, so grim and sad and tragic. So wasteful and unnecessary. Lives taken needlessly and heedlessly, benefitting no one. Pathetic. Maybe this case will be different. A challenge, where bringing a killer to heel will deliver satisfaction and pride, the community protected, justice served. Nothing compared to what he and Montifore achieved last winter, but maybe enough. Maybe enough for him to start establishing his own reputation. It occurs to him that there will be those who would like to see him taken down a peg, jealous of the success he's enjoyed working under Montifore. Now, should he fail, he can imagine the whisper campaign: *It was Montifore all the time; Lucic was just a passenger.*

If Professional Standards are coming for Morris, then they might be after him as well. He hadn't thought of that. Instead of glory, he should be thinking of keeping his head down and covering his arse. Lord knows, he can't afford to lose his job. Even suspension would be catastrophic, given his gambling, given his lack of savings or assets. The pay rise was good for his self-esteem but has done nothing for his bank account: the more that comes in, the more goes out. He realises he needs this case: get it right, get it done, do it by the book. His big opportunity, but it might be gone before he knows it. He could be implicated in Montifore's transgressions, without even knowing what they are, without even being in Sydney to defend himself.

A new thought comes to him: why was a murder way out in the sticks even allocated to Montifore and himself in the first place? Was it a set-up, the old guard conniving to get them out of Sydney while they moved against Montifore? Or was there a more benign reason: the detective inspector's reputation for getting results while remaining politically astute? Is there something complex or sensitive about this case, something requiring Montifore's skill set? Or maybe the brass wanted to send a message to the two detectives, not to get above their station. Was that the idea: assign them a shit investigation, out beyond the interest and budgets of the media? But why the last minute change of plan, why keep Montifore in Sydney? The deputy commissioner involved, the head of Homicide acquiescing, Professional Standards investigating. Has Lucic himself been sidelined without even knowing it, sent so far west he's beyond relevance? He stares out the window. He can't know the answers to these questions, but he knows one thing: he needs to demonstrate he is not merely an adjunct to Montifore, that he's his own man, with his own skills. This isn't an opportunity, he realises, this is a test.

His attention is drawn back to the landscape. A gash has opened in the great plain, black against green, like an infected wound. The pilot seems to take it as a hint; Ivan hears the engines change pitch, feels the nose dip ever so slightly. As the plane moves closer, he can see it's an open-cut coalmine, vast and deep, with Matchbox trucks wheeling their way to and fro, servicing a line of giant excavators and conveyor belts. A railway snakes away from the mine, heading east to some distant port. From this height it looks like a model, some toy set from a rich kid's playroom.

A few minutes more and the plane starts to bank. Ivan catches a glimpse of a long ridge stretching west to east, rocky and barren, pale brown and dun above the green of the plain, dotted with sparse trees as if to emphasise the lack of ground cover. As the plane tracks around, losing height as it goes, he can see a small town nestled in a hollow where the ridge dips. Finnigans Gap, dividing the ridge into two. Now a lake appears to the west, vast and empty, almost completely devoid of water but shimmering with salt, glowing white and shades of pink, ringed by a halo of dark soil, nothing growing, in contrast to the verdant land stretching to the horizon. The ridge grows closer, more defined, like an ants nest: he can see no ants, but he can see their burrows, the piles of rubble extracted by miners. Now he sees the airport, on the flat of the plain but hard up against the town, the runways a skewered cross: the main tarmac runway running east–west, crossing a shorter strip of red gravel at an angle.

The plane dips lower, propellers changing pitch, coming in on its final approach. There's a small building, presumably the terminal, not much more than a shed, one car parked next to it, a four-wheel drive. Hopefully it's his assistant. The plane starts to buck in the thermals, and from the window he can see a willy-willy sweep the mine shafts beyond the airport fence.

chapter two

SHE SITS IN HER FOUR-WHEEL DRIVE, ENGINE IDLING, AIR-CONDITIONING
engaged. The dash says the outside temperature is thirty degrees; it's
nine thirty in the morning. The forecast is for forty or more. The
memory of the past few weeks, the respite of unseasonal rains, is
fading. There are still reports of storms and floods along the coast,
but that might as well be another country. Out here the fronts
have passed, the fluky coalition of a wayward monsoon and the
remnant of a cyclone are gone, the ground is already dry, the mud
cracked into mosaic and returning to dust. It's almost a week since
the rain stopped, and summer is reasserting itself with a careless
brutality. Through the airport fence, above the runway, the air is
bubbling with heat, conjuring mirages, turning dirt to water and
tarmac to sky. She scans the heavens: few clouds, no plane.

She feels alert, not in any way tired after the two-hour dash
from Bourke. She drove it in record time, heedless of speed limits,

eager to get here, eager to be at hand when Ivan Lucic arrives, to make a good first impression. She still can't quite believe her luck: a murder investigation, seconded to one of the force's rising stars, and here in Finnigans Gap, scene of her own career-defining success. Somehow, mysteriously, the stars are aligning once again. She can feel the thrill in her blood.

She returns to her phone, reads another newspaper account thrown up by her Google search for Ivan Lucic, another report of the scandals still rocking New South Wales, of high-level corruption and conspiracy, of murder and skulduggery. This particular article is a few months old, written by Martin Scarsden, the journalist who led much of the media coverage, but it mentions Morris Montifore and Ivan Lucic by name, praising their bravery and integrity, their professionalism, their relentless pursuit of the guilty. She can't quite believe it: she will be working with *the* Ivan Lucic.

Now, in the distance, she sees it, the black dot of her future, the PolAir plane tracking in from Dubbo. A movement catches her peripheral vision: a man appears, as if from nowhere. The airport manager, shuffling across from the terminal, wearing a bathrobe, thongs and a three-day growth, looking like he's just climbed out of bed. Probably has; from memory, there are no scheduled flights into or out of Finnigans on weekends.

He sees her and walks towards the police car. She lowers her window as he approaches, the warm breeze breaching the vehicle's cocoon. The man doesn't bother with a greeting, as if resenting every effort of this Sunday morning intrusion. 'Wait until he pulls up, the props have stopped. Then drive up next to the plane. No point in making 'em walk,' he says gruffly.

'Cheers,' she says.

But the man is already ambling across to the gate. He unlocks it, swings it open, then shuffles back towards his bolthole, not looking back, half-heartedly swatting flies as he goes.

The plane comes in, bucking slightly in the wind, a kick of smoke as the tyres touch the tarmac. The pitch of the engines steps up as the pilot reverses the thrust, before powering them back down as the plane slows. It swings around and taxis back towards the terminal, coming to a stop fifty metres away, one engine cutting out, then the other. She drives through the gate, stopping next to the aircraft, getting out, is there when the door opens and a set of steps fold down. First out is one of the pilots, making sure the stairs are secure, followed by a youngish-looking man, maybe in his thirties, wearing a charcoal suit, white shirt, no tie, a messenger bag slung over his shoulder; a slender man with a lean face and thick dark hair. Ivan Lucic, looking less substantial than the on-line photos. The suit coat lasts until he has his feet on the ground, his head turned momentarily to the sky, as if disbelieving the power of the sun. He needs a hat; that fair skin will burn in no time. At least he's brought sunglasses, expensive-looking wrap-arounds. Make him look like a wanker, but at least he'll be able to see.

'Hello. Detective Constable Narelle Buchanan,' she says to him. 'Call me Nell.'

'Ivan Lucic. Pleased to meet you,' he says, shaking hands with a slow confidence, tilting his head to indicate the two others following him from the plane. 'This is Carole Nguyen, crime scene investigator, and Blake Ness, forensic pathologist. Give us a hand loading the gear, will you?'

'Of course.'

She greets the other officers, helps load the back of the Nissan Patrol. By the time they're finished, Lucic is sweating.

'You want to check into the motel first?' she asks as they climb into the vehicle. 'Clean up? Change?'

'No. Let's go straight there. The poor bastard has been hanging long enough.' With his glasses off, she sees his eyes are an icy blue, a contrast to his dark hair.

'Sure,' she says. She likes that, his urgency. And his respect for the dead.

— —

The body is stinking, leaking, a horrible parody of Christ. Ivan Lucic stares at the man, the former man, attempting to look beyond the obvious, to see past his own revulsion. The face has taken on a waxen complexion, shiny in the harsh light of the LEDs. One side is discoloured, bruised, an ugly colour turned more ugly by death. In front of Ivan, Carole Nguyen is taking photographs, shielded by her professionalism and a disposable body suit, latex gloves and a face mask. She's moving in close to capture the finer details of putrefaction. The pathologist is at one side, standing silently with his mask off, looking on as if mesmerised. The only sounds are the shutter of the camera and Carole's plastic feet coverings shuffling through the dust. Ivan wonders if he'll even refer to her images; maybe eventually, if and when he prepares a prosecution brief. But for now, the scene is embedding itself into his retinas, imprinting on his mind, another to add to his ghastly vault, another inerasable memory of lives taken, of violence and injustice. The body is a husk; the man who inhabited it, Jonas McGee, is long gone.

'Look,' says Blake Ness, coming back into the present. The pathologist points to the ground. Extending out from the base of the cross is a furrow, etched into the earth.

'What is it?' asks Ivan.

'My guess? The cross was lying flat. He was nailed onto it. Then it was lifted, dragged, with him on it, and pushed up against the wall. What do you reckon, Caro?'

The crime scene investigator lowers her camera, considers Blake's assertion. 'Yep. I reckon that's right.' She frowns. 'We'll need to weigh the cross. Maybe re-enact it. Work out whether you'd need two people to lift it up like that or just the one. Right now, I'm thinking one could do it.'

'Based on what?'

'That gouge in the ground. It looks like it was dragged up, not lifted.'

The three of them stare, imaginations mulling possible scenarios.

Ivan looks again at the body, the desecration. The man is well muscled, lean. He's wearing a blue singlet, tough canvas pants. His feet are covered in socks, encrusted with black blood, with holes at the toes. 'Where are his boots?'

'We've got 'em,' says Carole. 'Boots and gloves. Already bagged. His wallet was in his pocket, but we can't find a phone.'

'It's been taken?'

'Either that or he didn't have it with him.'

'Apart from the obvious, any sign the body has been interfered with?' Ivan asks.

'Not at this stage,' she replies.

'Right. Thanks. Let me know when you're done.' He walks back towards the entry, back into the darkness, his torch lighting the way. The mine is not as claustrophobic as he'd feared; he'd imagined crawling through tight spaces, like caving. Instead, the roof is high, the floor even, the walls, the colour of caramel fudge, diffusing the light. Not so bad, if it wasn't for the smell. There is a machine, an excavator, cables running back and up one of the ventilator holes, some sort of flexible vacuum tube emerging from another shaft.

Further on, he turns a corner and sees Nell waiting at the bottom of the access ladder, bathed in light flowing down from above, as if she's on a stage with the spotlight on her. Her hair is brown, cut short, practical, her face open and friendly, smile lines radiating from brown eyes. There is something compact about her, self-possessed, that appeals to him. Like she's happy in her own skin. And she seems cheery and positive and not overly respectful. She's dressed in cargo pants and a lightweight cotton shirt, sleeves rolled up, holstered gun sitting on her utility belt. Some detectives look uncomfortable wearing a weapon; she looks as if she's grown up with it. There's a uniformed constable with her, in the shadows, a chubby young fellow sent to guard the crime scene. Short red hair and an unconvincing beard struggling to cover the acne emblazoned across his cheeks. He looks dazed, as if someone has whacked him.

'Who discovered the body?' Ivan asks Nell.

'Anonymous tip-off. Crime Stoppers.'

'So not a call to the local station?'

'No. Here, listen.' She pulls her phone from a pocket and swipes at the screen, selecting an audio file, playing it. *'Jonas McGee. He's dead. Murdered. Down his mine, outside Finnigans Gap.'*

The recording lasts less than ten seconds, a male voice, no particular accent. Calm. Rehearsed.

'When was it received?'

'Yesterday afternoon. Twelve minutes past three. The locals got it from Crime Stoppers around four, dispatched Constable Ahern at about five to check it out.'

Ivan turns to the young man. His face is set. 'Garry, isn't it? Ivan Lucic. Thanks again for your work on this.' That elicits a weak smile. 'You're a probationary constable?'

'That's right, sir.'

'How long for?'

'Six months.'

'You've done a good job here. Thank you.'

The young man nods, grateful for the acknowledgement.

'How you holding up?'

'Fine, thanks, sir,' the young man replies, acting as if the question is unnecessary.

'Pretty confronting,' suggests Ivan.

'Yes, sir.'

'You came down by yourself?'

'Yes, sir.'

'What can you tell me?'

'There were no footprints,' says the young officer. He points at the ground, where their own prints have left impressions in the dust. 'It was all smoothed out, as if someone had wiped them away after themselves.'

'What with? Any ideas?'

'No. I looked. Couldn't find anything. They must have taken it with them.'

'I see. So how did you know where to find the body? It's quite a labyrinth down here.'

'It was like a trail. Everywhere else, there were footprints, but between here and the body, they'd been smoothed away. And as I got closer, you know—the smell.'

'What did you do?'

'I didn't touch anything. I took a photo with my phone. Went back up. Called the sarge, sent her the image. She got me to wait here, protect the scene.'

'Right. You been here all night?'

'Most of it. Not down here. Up above. Making sure no one came down.'

'Get any sleep?'

'A bit. Not much.'

'Is this the only entrance?'

The young man blinks, as if caught out. Then: 'I'm not absolutely sure, but most mines have only the one. Expensive to drill a second. But I can find out for you.'

'Thanks, that would be useful. You see anybody?'

'A few trucks this morning. Miners heading out to their claims. But this is pretty much the end of the road.'

'Recognise any of them?'

'Not really. Buddy Torshack came over, wanted to know what I was up to.'

'Buddy Torshack? Who's he?'

'Has the neighbouring claim. His shaft is only a couple of hundred metres or so away. Saw the police car.'

'What did you tell him?'

'That McGee was dead. I asked him about his movements, whether he'd seen anything. He said no. He lives in town, came out this morning.'

'Thanks, Garry. Anything else?'

'Yes, sir. The top of the shaft, where we came down. There's a steel door, a kind of a lid. All the mines have them. There was a padlock. It's been cut. Looks like boltcutters.'

'That's useful. Thank you. Do we have the lock?'

'Yes. In an evidence bag.'

'Prints?'

'I thought I'd leave that to the experts.'

'Good thinking.'

They're interrupted by Carole Nguyen, emerging from the shadows. 'I'm almost done. You want another look before we take him down?'

'No. I'm good. Constable?' Ivan asks Nell.

'I've seen enough,' she says.

'Any idea how long he's been dead?' he asks the investigator.

'We'll know more once Blake has him on the slab, but my guess is somewhere between four and six days. The temperature down here is pretty constant; he'll be able to get a good estimate.'

'Excellent. Thanks.'

'But there is one more thing you should know. McGee was dead well before he was nailed up. At least four hours. Rigor mortis had set in.'

That causes him to reconsider what he has seen. 'So, if that didn't kill him, what did?'

'Too early to say. Blake is taking a closer look, but so far, there's nothing obvious.'

'What about his face? It looks like it's bruised.'

'Well spotted. But I can't see that killing him.'

'So what are you saying?'

'Maybe he wasn't murdered. Maybe he died of natural causes.'

— —

The heat above ground is ferocious. The sun is almost directly overhead, pouring its unfiltered energy onto the rocks and gravel, with little or no vegetation to diffuse it. Such is its power that the metal framework at the top of the shaft burns Nell's fingers through her latex gloves as she scrambles the last few metres up and out, grabbing Ivan Lucic's outstretched hand as she climbs the last two rungs.

'Thanks,' she says, peeling off the gloves.

'How the fuck does anyone live out here?'

'Beer and aircon,' she replies. 'C'mon. Let's get in the car.'

Inside, she fires the engine, gets the air-conditioning going. It blows hot and dry. She can see that Ivan is almost holding his breath, waiting for the relief to come.

She climbs out, fetches some water from the back, hands a litre bottle to the Sydney detective as she gets back in. He accepts, silently grateful, and takes a sustained swig. She can see the sweat on his brow, his face flushed, his business shirt sticking to his torso, its white cotton turned grimy from the mine, his suit coat abandoned on the back seat. She waits until he's had more water before speaking again.

'How long before we know how McGee died?' she asks.

'That's up to Blake,' says Ivan. 'If it was an act of violence, he'll figure it out pretty quickly. There'll be marks, incisions, fractures. But if it was something else, something less obvious, we won't know until he can examine the body thoroughly. He'll need to open him up, look for internal bleeding. Run toxicology tests. Maybe X-rays and other scans.'

Nell shakes her head. 'The hospital here is just a clinic, more a glorified triage centre than a proper hospital. Anything serious, they drive the patients to Dubbo; anything life-threatening, they fly them to the coast. I seriously doubt they'll have the equipment he needs, unless he brought it with him. We might have to drive the body to Bourke or Moree. Or Dubbo.'

'Shit. How far?'

'Bourke's two hours west, Moree's three hours east. Dubbo is bigger, has a base hospital, four hours south.'

He sighs. 'Fuck me.' She can see he's frustrated, not knowing precisely what it is they're investigating.

'What do you think?' she asks. 'Murder or not?'

He looks pensive, almost pained. 'Nailing him up. That's such a violent act, such a deliberate act. Such a desecration. Why kill him in a non-violent way, then nail him up like that?'

'Why nail him up at all, if he was already dead?'

'Exactly.'

There's a pause. The aircon is starting to work. She drinks some water herself before resuming. 'Maybe they were scared to confront him physically?' She can feel his eyes upon her.

'Go on,' he says.

'The killer was a coward. They wanted him dead, wanted to inflict pain. To harm him. But they were too scared to face him. So they poisoned him, or drugged him, then meted out the violence once he was dead.'

'Maybe,' he says. 'Pretty muscly-looking guy, by what's left of him. How old was he?'

She checks her phone, a police-issued MobiPol, for the information Garry has sent through. 'Forty-three.'

'What else have you got?'

'Not a lot. He's a long-time resident. Criminal record if you go back far enough. He did time in prison, starting eighteen years ago. Dangerous driving causing death. Sentenced to seven years, out in four. Good behaviour. Clean slate ever since, except for an apprehended violence order—taken out by his own daughter, Elsie McGee, eight years ago.'

Ivan frowns. She can see him trying to extract meaning from the information. 'So he could be violent. Where is she now?'

'I'll check. But the AVO lapsed years ago.'

'We need to speak to her. When we get to town, can you find her? And pull up the records. See who died in the car accident, who was affected. Probably nothing, but we can tick a few boxes while we wait for Blake's findings.'

'Revenge?' she asks.

'Why wait eighteen years?' he counters.

They fall back into silence, both drinking more water.

'Why you?' asks Ivan.

'Sorry?'

'Why send you? Why someone from Bourke, not Moree or Dubbo?'

'Finnigans Gap is part of the Bourke Area Command. And Bourke's the only place in it with detectives.'

'Makes sense then. And any reason you in particular? Draw the short straw? Rostered on for Sunday?' His voice is light, almost banter.

'No. The boss thought I might be useful. I was stationed here for almost three years. In uniform. I only left three years ago. He thought my local knowledge might come in handy.' She smiles. 'And, of course, I was keen.'

'You spent three years here? Wow. How did you survive it?' He returns her smile, making sure she knows he's at least half joking.

'It's not so bad, once you get used to it.'

'Right. Like herpes.' Then the humour eases out of his face, replaced by concern. 'How long have you been a detective?'

'Bit more than a year.'

'Your first homicide?'

'First one where the killer isn't sitting there with blood on his hands.'

He nods. 'You'd still know people in town here then?'

'Some.'

'Did you know McGee? Ever run into him?'

'Not that I remember.'

He frowns, as if choosing his words carefully. 'I know I don't need to tell you this, but we need to keep the details to ourselves for the moment.'

'Won't be easy. It'll already be the talk of the town.'

'Really?'

'Shit, yeah. Cop car stationed here all night. What do you reckon?'

Ivan absorbs this. 'Okay. They know he's dead, possibly that he's been crucified. But not that he was already dead for hours before that. Let's keep that to ourselves for now.'

'Of course.'

The car is getting cooler now, the air-conditioning taking effect. Their attention is captured by the constable emerging from the shaft, spitting on his hands afterwards as if it might offer some relief from the burning metal. He walks over and Nell cracks the window. 'I'm calling the ambulance. They want to bring him up. Maybe use the winch on his truck.'

'Right,' says Nell. 'You need a hand?'

'Nah. I reckon the three of us can handle it. But they said you have some body bags in the back.'

'You didn't bring any with you?'

'No.'

Nell jumps out, goes round the back, helps ferret out a sealed bag from the pathologist's equipment.

'Hey, Garry,' says Ivan, joining them at the back of the truck. 'Buddy Torshack. Where do I find him?'

The constable points across to a caravan a few hundred metres away. 'That's him. His truck is still there, so he must be too.'

'Is that where his shaft is?'

'Yep. Right next to it.'

'Thanks. Are you able to help some more after you finish with Carole and Blake?'

'Sure. The sarge said I should stay as long as you need me.'

'Good. I'll talk to Torshack, but I need you to canvass the other miners out here. Get their names and contact details, find out their movements. Monday, Tuesday and Wednesday. Ask them if they've seen anything unusual out here. Find out when was the last time they saw McGee.'

'Okay. Got it.'

'And, Garry, don't volunteer any information about the crime scene, okay? Nothing.'

'Absolutely.'

The young officer moves away and Ivan turns to Nell. 'C'mon, let's go talk to Torshack.'

'Okay. Jump in. We'll drive over.'

'Let's walk. It's just over there.'

She laughs, before realising he's serious. 'You kidding? We'll cook in this heat.'

'Okay. You drive, I'll walk. Meet you there.'

She watches him go, wondering why he could possibly want to go on foot. And if she'll wear the blame if he gets sunstroke.

chapter three

IT'S JUST TWO HUNDRED AND FIFTY METRES OR SO, BUT BEFORE HE'S EVEN
halfway to Buddy Torshack's caravan, Ivan concedes Nell was
right: he should have let her drive him over. He likes to walk
whenever he goes somewhere new, to get a sense of the space. For
Morris, it's always about the people, but Ivan likes to feel the world
around him, to listen to it, to let it make suggestions. But all it's
telling him right now is that the day is unbearably hot. It's as if
the sun has picked him out, like a malevolent schoolboy with a
magnifying glass. It comes from above and it comes from below,
bouncing back up at him from the barren earth. When he puts a
hand to his hair, it's hot to the touch.

He swills the last of his bottled water. All around him, the
ground is naked rock; a few shoots of green, lifted by recent rains
among the crevices, appear to be dying before his eyes, shrinking
from the solar assault. This is a desert, no matter how much rain

might fall: the land is too hard, too rocky, there is not enough soil. Everywhere there are small piles of rubble, mullock heaps, lifted from the ground by exploratory drilling, the stones chalky and crumbled, like fine sandstone or hardened clay, bleached blond and caramel. He passes a hole covered haphazardly by a mesh of rusting metal, the sort of steel grid used to reinforce concrete. It's about thirty centimetres wide, maybe some sort of ventilation shaft, rocks piled next to it from when it was drilled out, left there like an explorer's cairn. He catches the faint smell of death: perhaps he's above the body. He looks around him. Sure enough, not more than a dozen metres away he can see a tube running from a similar hole. So not for ventilation but extraction, a blower hole where Jonas had sucked out his ore. He wonders if that is the right word; it doesn't seem like ore to him, just rocks. Rubble that may, if luck and geology have cast their spell, contain riches.

Small flies, silent and insistent, have found him in this no-man's-land, settling on his face, crawling under his sunglasses and into his eyes, seeking moisture wherever they can, not easily swatted away. He keeps his mouth shut, blows hard as one crawls into a nostril. He uses his empty water bottle to slap his back, lifting a swarm of blackness. How can they bear the heat? He removes his sunglasses to flick one away, can barely keep his eyes open amid the glare. Do they sense his vulnerability, these flies, out here in the midday sun? Have they descended upon him as his own personal plague?

He comes across a rusted piece of derelict equipment, some sort of sieve, and squats to examine it, but it tells him nothing, confides no secrets. Then, as he stands, he feels woozy, blood rushing from his head, and for an instant the horizon shifts and he fears he may faint. The idea comes to him that this land is insubstantial, hollowed out, held aloft by nothing more than pillars of crumbling rock and the narrow trunks of pine trees, as if the whole lot might collapse, taking him with it, pulling him down. He knows it's an illusion, the sun toying with him, insinuating danger where there is none. Ahead of him he can see Nell's car waiting next to the caravan. The only thing the land is suggesting is that he's an idiot.

An old man is sitting outside in the shade of a tarpaulin, watching with keen eyes as Ivan approaches. 'You'd better get in out of the sun, young fella,' he says by way of greeting. 'Before you fry your fucking brains.'

Ivan joins the man under the tarp. The air is no cooler, but the shade is like a benediction.

The old fellow is wearing shorts and sandals, his torso naked. He's scrawny, no fat, as if the heat has melted it off him, leaving only muscles, bones and sinews, and a small beer belly. Even it looks hard, like a fossilised football. A tattoo of a fish and anchor adorns one shoulder. He's sucking on a tinnie, the beer clad in a foam holder with the faded maroon of Queensland rugby league. A couple of pairs of work boots sit nearby, socks strewn across the top, airing.

'Here.' The man holds out a can of fly spray to Nell. Ivan stands still, feeling at a disadvantage as she circles him, engulfing him in a cloud of pesticide.

'You want a drink?' says the man.

'Got anything soft?'

'Nup.'

Nell hands him a bottle of water. 'There's more in the car.'

'Thanks.' He takes a long, long slug of water, conscious of the other two watching him.

'So you found him then,' says the scrawny man. "Bout time. Was beginning to stink.'

Ivan's mind lurches, suddenly alert, lassitude gone. He exchanges a glance with Nell before addressing Buddy Torshack. 'You knew the body was down there?'

'Nah. Thought it was a roo or something. Couldn't work it out.'

Ivan thinks of the small shaft he just passed with the steel grid covering it, wonders how an animal of any size could fall into a mine. 'When was this?'

'Yesterday. When I got back down there, after the rains.'

Ivan frowns. 'Back down where? You could smell the body from your mine?'

'Sure. Didn't think much of it.'

'How could you smell it down there?' Ivan persists.

Buddy takes a swig of beer. 'They're connected. The mines.'

'How's that?'

Buddy shrugs. 'Happens often enough. Our claims, they're fifty metres by fifty metres. All the government will let us have at a time. So you work 'em all the way to the boundary. Sometimes you break through to the other side. No big deal.'

Ivan is recollecting the mine, the area shored up with a wooden framework, closed off by orange plastic and the sign UNSTABLE, not so far from where Jonas was crucified. He'd thought it was a cave-in risk. 'This boundary, where the mines join, there's a barrier? Orange webbing?'

'That's it.'

'Any sign of anyone coming through the gap, from one side or the other?'

The old man shrugs. 'Wouldn't know. Haven't looked. Haven't worked that section for months. Years.'

'Can you take us down? Show us?'

'What? Now?'

'If you could.' Ivan turns to Nell. 'Can you go back down McGee's shaft, fetch Carole? Tell her we want her to come down Buddy's mine with us; tell her I want her to examine the boundary. She should take a look on that side first.'

'Of course,' says Nell.

The two men watch her move to the car, start driving across to the other mine. The miner takes another swig of his beer and begins to put his socks and boots on. 'It's true, then? That someone crucified him?' Buddy sounds almost gleeful at the prospect, as if it's nothing more than a juicy piece of gossip.

Ivan nods. 'Yeah, it's true. Any idea who would want to do something like that?'

'Apart from me? No. Maybe one of his God-bothering mates.'

He's been standing, but now Ivan takes a seat on a rusted metal trunk. 'What do you mean apart from you? Why would you want to harm him?'

The opal miner looks at Ivan for a long moment, studying his face. 'He killed my wife. His own too.' It's a statement of fact, apparently free of emotion.

Ivan squints, detecting nothing. 'The dangerous driving charge? Eighteen years ago?'

'Eighteen years this past September—the bastard,' he spits, then takes a slug of beer as if upset at squandering moisture. 'He was pissed, drunk as all fuck. Killed them both.' The voice remains dry, matter-of-fact, but beneath it Ivan can hear the bedrock of emotion. Buddy is now staring into the distance. Eighteen years and he's not over it, no matter how hard he tries to disguise it.

'You don't sound upset that Jonas is dead.'

'I'm not. Pity it didn't happen sooner.'

'What happened? Back then?'

Buddy Torshack shrugs, as if this is ancient history, but his eyes betray him. 'We mined together, me and Jonas. I'd taken him on when he was a drifter and didn't have anywhere else to go. We ended up as partners. Mates. Got married to sisters. He was my best man, I was his. We were like the one family.'

Ivan waits, but Buddy seems to have come to an end, as if he has explained all that Ivan might need to know. The detective is forced to prompt him. 'And then?'

'And then, one Sunday, we went over to Lightning Ridge. Picnic races. Took our wives and our kids. He drank too much, way too much, but insisted on driving. He crashed on the way back. End of story.'

'Where were you?'

'Driving my car. I was first on the scene.' Buddy drinks more beer. 'The women were dead. Nothing I could do. Both of them, gone just like that. Sisters, they were. And the bastard barely had a scratch on him.'

'And the kids?'

'In the back of my car. Asleep. Thank God for that. His daughter Elsie. My son Kyle.'

'Did you testify against him? In the trial?'

40

'There was no trial. He pleaded guilty, owned it. He wanted jail time, he wanted punishment. Practically demanded it.'

'Atonement.'

'That's a big word.'

'What happened to his daughter?'

'Elsie? Went and lived with her mum's brother in Adelaide. Came back when Jonas got out of prison.'

'How did that go?'

Buddy shrugs. 'All right, far as I know. I had as little to do with them as possible. I know he gave up the grog, became a bible basher, did a lot of good works. Charities, service clubs. Lot of people ended up liking him, or at least respecting him.'

'But not you?'

'Nah. Not me.'

'His daughter. She took an AVO out against him. An apprehended violence order.'

'I wouldn't know anything about that.'

'Nothing?'

'Only that there was one. Not why.'

Ivan changes tack, brings the conversation back to the present. 'When you smelt the body, you didn't check?'

'Nah. I guess I should have, but I didn't. As I said, I thought it was a wallaby or some such.' He shrugs. 'Hoped it might get a bit more rank before Jonas got down and had to deal with it.'

'So it wasn't you who rang Crime Stoppers?'

Buddy shakes his head. 'Not me.'

'They got an anonymous call yesterday afternoon. Said that he was down there, crucified. Who could know that? Who else would go down Jonas's mine?'

'Ratters.'

'Ratters?'

Buddy looks perplexed. 'How long you been here? In Finnigans?'

'Couple of hours. Why?'

'Fair enough.' Bootlaces tied, Buddy returns to his beer, but the can is empty. He looks mildly surprised, pulls it from the stubby holder and chucks it onto the growing pile of empties. There are three or four dozen cans, none of them old enough to have rusted. 'Ratters are thieves. The lowest of the low. They come down into mines, usually at night, when no one is about. They dig. They steal opals.'

'Doesn't anyone hear them? I thought all these machines would make a racket, even thirty metres down. Especially at night.'

'Nah. The big excavators do. Powered by diesel generators up here on the surface. Then the rubble is sucked out by the blowers. You can hear them a country mile away. The ratters use handheld tools, big ones, battery-powered. Winch the ore up by hand. All very stealthy.'

'Doesn't sound very efficient.'

'Nah, it's not. They need to know where to dig. So they get wind of someone who's had a strike. You know, made some money—bought a new car, or is pissing on at the pub, that sort of thing. Then they go down, find the freshest excavations and go for it. Over the course of a few hours, they can get quite a haul.' He looks at the pile of empties. 'The cunts.'

'Did Jonas mention anything to you about ratters?'

'To me? Nah. We rarely spoke. But word is that he was getting a bit of colour, some good rich blacks, some deep reds. Making dough. I know he was spending a lot of time out here.

Guarding the place, as it were. Even last week when the rest of us were in town, waiting out the rain.'

'You don't work when it's raining?'

'Nah. Too dangerous with the generators, all their cables. But it's prime time for ratters, when no one else is around.'

'So when did the rain stop?'

'It was real heavy last weekend, then started easing up after that. Fizzled out by Wednesday.' Buddy scratches at his hair. 'Yeah, pretty sure it was Wednesday.'

Ivan takes the information on board, making a mental note to check the rainfall during the past week. But already he's building a mental picture. Jonas out here alone, guarding his mine, the other miners holed up in town, with only ratters out and about.

'What about you?' he asks Buddy. 'You finding much opal?'

'Me? Nah. Not that I'm looking that hard. When I'm finished here, I might pull up stumps.'

'Retire?'

'Find something else to do. Something easier. It's a young man's game, mining opals.'

'How old are you, Buddy?'

'Fifty-eight. But this work, keeps you fit.'

To Ivan that seems half true: the man's arms and shoulders are muscled and well defined, his gut small despite the beers. Yet his face is lined and creased, his teeth cracked and tinged by yellow. His hair is thin and grey. The overall impression is of someone older, more like mid-sixties than late fifties; someone who has done it hard.

He does the arithmetic: Buddy is fifty-eight; Jonas was forty-three. A fifteen-year gap, yet married to sisters. Eighteen years ago, Jonas would have been twenty-five, still young, drunk driving back from Lightning Ridge with the sisters; Buddy, already forty, the responsible older man following in his own car, safeguarding the children.

'You work the claim by yourself?'

'Mostly. My boy gives me a hand every now and then. But he's useless. Lazy, like all the young 'uns. Runs hot and cold with the mining. Wants us to move on, stake a new claim. That's where he is now, out prospecting. Thinks the grass is greener. He'll learn.'

'How do you do that? Prospect? Thirty metres down?'

'Test drilling. What do you reckon?'

Ivan looks out at the landscape he walked across, seeing the mullock heaps, recalls their various sizes: the biggest from access shafts, medium-sized from ventilation and blower holes, small ones from test drilling. 'Fair enough.'

He drinks more water. Fuck, it's hot, even under the shade of the tarpaulin. It's as if his skin is a sieve: the more water he pours down his throat, the more it flows from his skin. He feels simultaneously parched and sodden. In the distance, he can see Nell and Carole emerging from Jonas's shaft. Buddy is watching them too. Ivan realises the opal miner must have been sitting here observing the comings and goings all morning.

'How many miners are out here? Must be a few, if the size of your claims is so limited.'

'Out on this spur? Seven or eight. Five or six are full-time, the others on weekends.'

'And you keep your mines locked at night? There seemed to be some sort of cap or lid above Jonas McGee's access shaft.'

'Yeah. We all have them. Keep it locked down whenever I'm not here.'

Nell and Carole are in the car, the constable taking it slowly, careful to negotiate her way past rock piles and blower shafts.

'Apart from ratters, is there anyone else who would have access to Jonas's mine?'

'Not since he arseholed Stanley Honeywell.'

'Who's Stanley Honeywell?'

'Used to be his offsider. Up until about three months ago. Then he sacked him.'

'They have a falling-out?'

'Wouldn't know.'

'What can you tell me about him?'

'Not a lot *to* know; not a lot to him. The size of a mountain, but slow. Brain damaged, so they say. Good worker, though, strong as an ox. Pretty shrewd move by Jonas, if you ask me: get a willing worker on the cheap, dress it up as charity. London to a brick he wasn't paying award rates.' The contempt is written all over the miner's face. 'My guess is that's how the ratters found out that Jonas was on to something. Stanley. Unable to keep his mouth shut.'

'So you know for a fact that there've been ratters down that mine?'

'Nah. Not for a fact. But they've been down my hole, the stupid bastards. And I haven't found fuck-all for months.'

— —

Nell is the last down the mine, following Buddy, Ivan and Carole. It's the same set-up as at McGee's: a vertical shaft, another three-footer, with the same hook-and-hang steel ladder connected to the steel framework at the top of the shaft. She drops to the floor and moves across to a large open space just away from the shaft, maybe twenty metres by fifteen, the roof propped up every few metres by the same pine trunks as in Jonas's mine. Someone must run a concession, trucking them in from the east, the Pilliga Scrub or somewhere, selling them to the miners. In the combined torch-light, the cavern opening up around the trunks looks almost airy. It's certainly cooler.

'This way,' says Buddy. 'Other side of this ballroom.'

Nell smiles, remembering the turn-of-phrase from when she was stationed here, finding it fitting.

'Be careful, though—stay away from over that side,' Buddy warns, pointing with his torch. 'Risk of cave-in.'

She can see where the pine trunks have bent and distorted from the weight of the ceiling, their tops splayed and cracked, the risk of collapse seemingly imminent.

He leads them around the other side of the open space, threading his way through the pine trunks and into a wide passage. They follow it for about fifteen metres, and then the space opens up again. Passages lead off in several directions. A real maze, it seems to Nell. Buddy waits until they have caught up.

'The roof, the floor—they all seem pretty much at the same level,' says Ivan.

'Correct,' says Buddy. 'We're all mining the same strata. Theory is it's an ancient lake bed, millions of years old. Compressed clay, turned to rock. There's hard rock above and harder rock below, but we're not interested in that. The opals are here, in the mudstone.'

'Do they run in veins, like gold?' asks Ivan.

'Nah. Wish they did.' Buddy looks around him. 'Here. I'll show you.'

Buddy takes them down another tunnel that again opens out. He points to a line in the wall: a thin layer of grey, glass-like substance is embedded there, glistening in the torchlight. 'This is potch: a type of opal, but pretty much worthless.'

Ivan takes a closer look. 'Why worthless?'

''Cos there's no colour in it. It's the colour that's valuable. Greens and blues. Purples and reds. Here and Lightning Ridge, you get black opal. That's the most valuable. Not the black by itself; it just highlights the colours embedded in it. They stand out more than they do against white or grey opal. I found one once, deep black, but cut through with reds and blues, the red so bright it seemed to glow. That one stone was worth two hundred grand.'

Nell can hear the wonder in Buddy's voice, the fervour in it. She's heard it before in this town, in the pubs and the shops and the dealers. Opal lust, like gold fever, lighting up the eyes of the desperate and the dreamers.

'So are the coloured opals found with the potch?' asks Ivan.

'Nah. Not that simple. They don't come in layers like the potch. More like individual stones. We call 'em nobbies. They can gather together in the clay, like they were washed together millions of years ago and settled in the mud, so if you find one, you might find more.'

'And what are they? How are they formed?' It's Carole, perhaps her scientific curiosity overcoming her deference to Ivan.

'Little sea creatures,' says Buddy. 'Fossilised. But fossilised in a special way. With silica, from the sand. But water gets trapped in the silica, moisture, and forms the colours.'

'Oh, I get it,' says Carole. 'Refraction.'

'Look here,' says Buddy. He points to a narrow cleft in the wall, a shallow excavation maybe fifteen centimetres high, running horizontally for about two metres at head height. 'Ratters. Using a handheld excavator.'

'Really?' says Lucic. 'Is it recent?'

'Nah. Couple of years old.'

'Okay. Can you show us where the mines meet?'

Buddy leads the way again, backtracking and then heading down another tunnel. Nell feels herself becoming disorientated, wondering if she could find her way out without a guide.

'It's just along here,' says Buddy up ahead.

They move into another open space, another 'ballroom' with pine tree props shoring up the ceiling. On the far wall, Nell can see the orange plastic mesh covering the access to the neighbouring mine.

'That's it there,' says Buddy. And the smell is there as well, that horrid and tenacious stench.

'Hold up,' says Ivan. 'I want Carole to have first look.'

Nell, Ivan and Buddy wait as the crime scene investigator moves across the space, torch in one hand, camera in the other. The odour of death imposes silence upon them.

'So this is the only access point between the mines?' Ivan asks Buddy.

'Yep.'

They stand without speaking until Carole is back. 'Sorry. I can't be definitive. There are plenty of footprints, but it's like the surface of the moon down here. There's no way of telling if they were left last week or last year. There are no signs of anything being dragged, though, a body or anything else.' Her sentence ends with an upward inflection, as if there is more she wants to say.

'What is it?' asks Ivan.

'There's plenty of dust, but no spider webs, no cobwebs.'

'Should there be?'

'Dunno. But you'd imagine there would be a flow of air between the mines. Good place for a web.'

'Could someone have moved through between them recently?'

She shrugs. 'Someone has, but I can't say when.'

They stand for a moment longer. Nell looks at Ivan's face, sees the concentration there, stark in the torchlight. She wonders what he might be thinking, what significance he's reading into the link between the mines. But she finds herself unable to ask, to break his train of thought. There is something solitary about him, something that forbids intrusion.

chapter four

THE SUN IS WAITING FOR IVAN AS HE CLIMBS FROM THE MINE. THE SMELL IS gone, but the air is full of heat and dust and flies. Now he feels a sudden urge to piss. Little wonder; he's been drinking water ever since he got here. A good sign, though; shows he's not dehydrated. He walks off behind the four-wheel drive to relieve himself, mind working as he sprays the rocks. Ratters, down both mines. The possibility they moved between them. But the padlock on Jonas's mine was cut, indicating someone broke in. Jonas wouldn't lock it, not if he was going down. Which suggests someone crucified him, locked the mine when they left, then the ratters or whoever it was who found him removed the lock with boltcutters. The idea of the ratters makes sense: who else would cut their way into a mine; who else would find a body, ring the police but feel compelled to remain anonymous?

Over at the camp site, a young bloke is sitting drinking beer, shirtless, body lean and muscled and tanned, his left arm a sleeve of tattoos. His hair is long and black, a broad-brimmed hat resting on one knee. There is something languid about him, like he's been poured into place, as if nothing has the potential to bother him. A roll-your-own cigarette is hanging from his lips; the pose of a French film star. He draws upon it, letting the smoke waft from his mouth and nose, as if he's been waiting for someone to witness it.

'You're here,' says Buddy, emerging from the shaft. 'Wasn't expecting you.' He turns to Ivan. 'This is Kyle.' And almost as an afterthought, 'My son.' Then he turns to the young man. 'How'd you go? Any luck?'

'Nah. Nothing yet.' The lad checks out the three police officers, his eyes settling on Nell. 'You're back.'

'Just visiting.'

'Where's your uniform?'

'Got promoted. Don't wear one anymore.'

'That right? Good for you,' he says. 'Is it true? Someone crucified him?'

'Yeah, it's true,' says Buddy, answering for them. 'Is that why you're here?'

'Yeah. Wanted to know.' Kyle turns to Nell. 'Why you going down our mine?'

Ivan answers. 'We thought ratters might have been down, used it to access Jonas's claim.'

Kyle shrugs. 'I guess it's possible.'

'You seen any sign of them?' asks Ivan.

Another shrug. 'Nah. I don't spend much time out here anymore, not if I can help it.' There's a challenge in the words, a taunt.

Buddy is frowning as he responds. 'Nothing down our mine worth ratting. Not now, anyway.'

'Not for yonks,' says Kyle, and Ivan hears the niggle in the youth's voice. Or maybe surliness is just his default, part of the cigarette-enhanced bid for coolness.

'So you haven't seen anything else unusual round here lately?' he asks.

Kyle breaks into a grin, like he's just heard a good joke. 'Sure as shit have.' He turns to Buddy. 'You tell 'em about the limo?'

'Limo?' asks Ivan.

Kyle laughs. 'This big black limousine. Shiny as shit. Red carpet job, like something from the movies. Tinted windows. It's been crawling around up here, trying not to lose its muffler. Dumb cunt. Headed past here up to the bluff, to the turning circle overlooking the lake. Full of Japs. Or Chinks. Wearing suits, the fucking idiots.'

Ivan just stares at him; if the young man is cutting snide about his own suit pants and business shirt, he's way past that. 'How do you know they were Asian if the windows were tinted?' he asks.

'They stopped up there, got out. Binoculars, cameras. Like they were on fuckin' safari.'

'A black car. Suits. Out here. Lunatics,' says Buddy.

Ivan ignores the father, addresses the son. 'When was this?'

'Weekend before last—last time I was over this way. One of those Chryslers with the chrome don't-fuck-with-me grilles. Second time I saw it. Might have come back again. I don't know.'

'Can you show us where they stopped?'

'Why?'

'Could be interesting.'

'Sure.'

Ivan turns to Buddy, leans down and shakes his hand, makes a point of thanking him. And thereby dismissing him. He wants to speak to Kyle without the father, probe the son free of their mutual antipathy.

'Jump in with us,' says Ivan to the young miner. 'In the back. Constable Buchanan can drive.'

The truck is hot as Hades; Nell hasn't left the engine running. She apologises and gets the aircon going, but once again the initial blast is hot and dry. They start moving, Kyle giving directions.

'You see much of Jonas these last few weeks?' asks Ivan.

'Not much. I haven't been here.'

'You get on with him okay?'

'Depends what sort of mood he's in. Better than with my old man, put it that way.'

'How's that?'

When the lad answers, his voice is cautious. 'Buddy tell you what happened? With my mother and the car crash?'

'Yeah, he did.'

Kyle shrugs. 'It fucked 'em up, both of them. Sometimes Jonas would be kind to me, when he was feeling guilty, next moment he'd have a go at me, like it was my fault, like I was an unwelcome reminder. At least old Buddy-boy is consistent.'

'You don't get on with your father?'

'Not the first time that's happened.'

'But you operate the mine with him?'

'With him? More like for him. I do the work and he sits there sucking piss all day.'

'So why hang around?'

'I'm not. I'm drilling. Prospecting. I'm gonna start my own claim.'

'How does your dad feel about that?'

'Who gives a fuck?' And this time there is real spite in the words, real anger.

'What about Jonas's daughter? You see her?' asks Ivan.

Kyle looks away, out the window, frowning. 'Elsie? Nah. Long gone. Moved back to Adelaide years ago.'

'You knew her?'

'Sure. She's my cousin.'

'Still in contact?'

'Sometimes. But only when she wants something.' More bitterness; Kyle is sounding more and more like a bloke with a chip on his shoulder. 'Jonas was always on about her. How she went to uni, got married, had a kid. Must have been grateful that he didn't fuck her up, that he didn't ruin her life as well.' There's a frown. 'I wonder if she knows. You know—about Jonas.'

'We'll be in contact with her,' says Nell from the front seat. 'Part of the job, telling next of kin. But maybe you should try giving her a call as well.'

'Me? Why?'

'She'll have questions. The answers might come easier for her from someone she knows.'

'You reckon?' There's hesitancy in his voice.

'Yeah, I reckon.'

They drive on, pass a clump of ironbarks. 'Just along there,' says Kyle. 'You can see a bit of a track.'

There's a moment's more silence before Ivan resumes his questioning. 'And what about Stanley Honeywell? Has he been about?'

'I haven't seen him for months, but I've been out prospecting. No one wants to drill in summer, so it's lots cheaper to hire a rig at this time of year.'

'You know where we might find him?'

'Lives in a shed on the other side of town. Squatters camp called Deadmans Well.' He addresses Nell. 'You know it?'

'Yeah. All too well.'

Kyle speaks to Ivan. 'He might be there. Or at the coalmine. I hear he's been pulling shifts.'

'That big open-cut operation? I saw it when I was flying in,' says Ivan. 'What's it called?'

'Cuttamulla Coal,' says Nell. 'You want me to check it out? See if I can find him?'

'Please,' says Ivan, before turning again to Kyle. 'Any indications of a falling-out between Jonas and Stanley?'

Kyle laughs. 'Are you kidding? No one could fall out with Stanley. He's a gentle giant. They tried to get him playing footy, but he was hopeless. Couldn't bring himself to thump anyone.' Kyle chortles at his recollection, then lets the humour drain away. 'I don't know who killed Jonas, but it sure as shit wasn't Stanley. No way he could do that to anyone, let alone to Jonas.'

'So if Stanley wasn't around much, who else might be out here at Jonas's mine?'

'No one I know of. Worked it by himself.'

'You can do that?'

'Yeah. But he wasn't here the whole time. Before this latest little strike, he was doing it hard, just like us. He did a bit of part-time work about the place. General handyman. Carpenter.'

'Carpenter?'

'Yeah. Nothing fancy. Formwork, house frames, that sort of thing. I used to help now and then when I was younger. Cash in hand. Until I worked out he was ripping me off.'

Ivan takes that on board. 'When was the last time you saw him?'

'A couple of weeks ago. I wanted to borrow some gear. I thought he might be more agreeable than Buddy-boy. Told me to keep an eye out for ratters. Said they'd been down his mine.'

'You tell anyone about that?'

'Sure. The old man. Of course.'

'Of course.' Ivan moves on. 'Apart from Buddy and you and Stanley, who else would Jonas see on a regular basis?'

'Out here? No one much. But he lived in town. He was a churchgoer, so you could try there. Not sure which one, but there's only two: Church of England and Catholic. And I'm pretty sure he sold his opals through the Irishman. Not sure if it was business only, or if they were mates as well.'

'The Irishman? Who's he?'

Kyle laughs again. 'Don't know his real name. Sean someone, I think. But everyone knows him as the Irishman. Fuck knows why. Doesn't even have an accent. His shopfront is on the highway, up from the crossroads. You can't miss it.'

'Anyone else?'

'He was mates with Trevor Topsoil. Runs a machinery shop. Mining supplies. Same bloke I've hired my rig from. He's single; wife left him. They used to go fishing together, up in Queensland.'

Ivan addresses Nell. 'You know where all these places are? Topsoil? The Irishman? The churches? Deadmans Well?'

'Yeah, I know 'em,' she replies. There's something in her voice, something dry. He wonders what it is. Maybe Deadmans Well has unpleasant memories.

'Just up ahead,' says Kyle. 'By that outcrop.'

Nell stops the car by the rocks. The land has opened up, a vast vista, overlooking the lake. Climbing out, Ivan gets a sense of altitude, just how far the ridges have been thrust above the surrounding plains. This must be the only high ground for hundreds of kilometres in any direction. He scans the horizon, believing he can see the curvature of the earth, like looking out to sea. Out on the plains, there are swathes of green contrasting with the red soil. Closer to the rock, he can see it's patchy: undergrowth interspersed with gravel and rock. It makes a contrast with the lake bed stretching out below: a vast expanse of white and pink, ringed by grey, a plain of salt encircled by dead soil. It shimmers in the heat, bouncing the sun back at them as if angered by their presence. Even behind his sunglasses, Ivan is forced to squint, feeling the radiant energy coming off the lake. If it's forty up here, it must be close to fifty down there, like the surface of a hostile planet. There is a little water pooling by the eastern shore, but nothing growing.

'Lake Kalingra. First time it's had any water in it for years,' says Kyle. 'Must be more than a decade.' He's standing a little apart, bare-chested but wearing his felt hat, wide-brimmed and shaped by sweat and use. He must have been out prospecting for weeks; you don't get a tan like that digging underground.

'How long will the water last?' asks Nell.

'With these temperatures? A few more days, tops. It's as shallow as shit.'

'This black limo: why come up here?' Ivan asks. 'Is it a tourist thing? Sunsets? Birdlife?'

'Nah,' Kyle scoffs, again that self-amused chuckle of his. 'Down there. Can you see?' He points.

Ivan follows the line of the ridge, sees where it splits into two spurs, running down towards the lake shore. Between the spurs, partly obscured by one of them, is a section of land, still elevated above the lake but relatively flat. Ivan can see a gantry, some demountables, a drilling rig. There's a dam, not large, but brimming with water, evidently a more efficient storage for the run-off than the shallow lake.

'A new mine,' says Kyle. 'Rare-earth minerals.'

'Not much to look at,' says Ivan.

'Not yet,' says Kyle. 'But word is that it's the next big thing. Worth more than Cuttamulla and the opals and the whole shitshow put together.' Then he points down towards where the ridge meets the plain. 'There's an access road to the mine, runs round the shore of the lake. See it? But it's been flooded. You'd get bogged, for sure. I reckon that's why they've been coming up here in the limo. Just to get a look at it. Close as they could get. You could walk down, if you were desperate enough.'

'So, the mine is cut off?'

Kyle shrugs again. It's a habitual gesture, nonchalant and uninterested. 'Another day or two and it'll be fine. Not that it matters. It's not operating yet. Just prospective.'

The heat is getting to Ivan. He looks at the youth, bare-chested, face shaded by his hat, apparently unaffected. 'Let's get back in the car. Too hot out here for a city cop.'

'Sure,' says Kyle, smiling as if he's won some small victory.

Back inside the cool of the car, Ivan swivels in his seat so he can look Kyle in the eye, gauge his reaction. 'Do you believe your father could have killed Jonas McGee?'

Again, the sardonic smile, a snicker, as if the idea appeals to him. 'Sure. Hated his fucking guts. But I can't see why he would wait until now.'

'Because Jonas is finding opals and your father is skint?'

Again, the shrug. 'Wouldn't know. Couldn't say.'

'We'll need to know your movements too, this past week. Monday, Tuesday, Wednesday.'

'Me? Why?'

'Process of elimination. Part of all Homicide investigations. We rule out known contacts. Helps us focus our efforts.'

'Sure,' says Kyle. 'Happy to help. I'll see if I can write it down for you. Most of the time I've been in town or over on the East Ridge.'

'Where's that?'

'Other side of town. Where I've been prospecting. This is the West Ridge, that's the East Ridge.'

'Can you drill when it's raining?'

'Shit, yeah. Provided it's not too heavy. Better than in this heat.'

Ivan looks out across the shimmering salt lake, pulsing with heat, and listens to what it's telling him: that it's such an isolated spot, this far end of the West Ridge, with no through traffic and very few people in the immediate vicinity. It's telling him to follow the rule of proximity: suspicion must fall most heavily on those who come out here. Buddy and Kyle and the other miners who work this spur. Stanley Honeywell will need to be eliminated. And, yes, the Asians in their black limousine. He shakes his head. They'll need to be checked out, of course, but for now the hierarchy of suspicion is clear, dictated by proximity. Checking alibis will be essential. He also needs to speak to the daughter. And find the ratters, the ones who discovered the body.

chapter five

NELL CONCENTRATES ON DRIVING, NEGOTIATING THE FOUR-WHEEL DRIVE ACROSS
the rocky terrain, moving forward at walking pace, the car rocking
from side to side on the uneven ground. Beside her, Ivan Lucic
is silent, eyes averted, staring unseeing at the landscape. They've
dropped Kyle back at his father's mine and left Carole, Blake and
Garry to retrieve Jonas McGee's body.

'Motel?' she suggests, reaching the beginnings of The Way and
getting the car out of second gear. 'Shower? Something to eat?'
Ivan is looking pretty ordinary, clothes smeared with dirt. The
sleek young officer who stepped from the plane a couple of hours
ago has lost his gloss.

He shakes his head. 'How can anyone eat in this heat?' But
there is more to it than that; there is an intensity in him. She can
sense it, can imagine those blue eyes, engorged with concentration

behind the sunglasses. He glances at his watch. 'Can we arrange a meeting with the local cops first?'

'We can try. It's Sunday. The sarge won't be rostered on.'

'With a man crucified on his watch? Can you call him?'

'Her.'

'Sorry, her.'

'Sure. Shall I do it now? I'll pull over.'

'Nah. Let's get to town first.' His voice softens. 'You were good back there. Professional.'

'Thanks.'

'What's she like? This sergeant?'

'Don't really know her. Her name's Cheryl Pederson. Appointed just as I was leaving.'

They're travelling more quickly now, the road improving as they move closer to town, but they come to a patch of corrugation and she needs to concentrate, the vibrations coming through the steering. 'What's next?'

'As soon as Blake gives us a time of death, a window, we'll need to establish the whereabouts of the miners up on that spur. Check their stories. Priority on Buddy and Kyle Torshack. And we definitely need to interview Stanley Honeywell.'

'I said I'd find him.'

'Good. We also need to locate the daughter, Elsie McGee, and see if there is any way of identifying the ratters or whoever it was who made the Crime Stoppers call.'

Now that they're not hurrying to the crime scene, Nell has the opportunity to look about them, refamiliarise herself with the location. The road is growing more defined all the time as smaller tracks from the outlying spurs join it, like tributaries flowing into a river. The Way follows the top of the ridge line, curving with the contours, dipping and rising. All around are the signs of mining: mullock heaps, trucks, diesel compressors, caravans and shacks. Nothing looks new, nothing looks modern. It all looks rusty, second-hand, jury-rigged. She can see two men wrestling with a blower tube, shirts off, hats on, like an image of war, the sepia landscape lending the appearance of an aged photograph. For a place reputed to yield millions of dollars of precious stones annually, it looks more like some battlefield, with rusted-out wrecks strewn about the landscape. And off in the distance, on either side, the sense of space, of air, out where the ridge line falls away to the plain.

'Before we check into the motel, let's try this Topsoil character,' says Ivan. 'You know him?'

'Yeah.'

'He runs a mining supply company. Will it be open on a Sunday?'

'Let's see. If it's not, I know where he lives.'

'How's that?'

'Small town.'

She can feel his eyes on her, that lingering regard behind the sunglasses. He's used to it, she realises, licensed as a police officer to rest his eyes on someone's face far longer than politeness and social mores would normally permit. She finds it disconcerting, as if she is under suspicion.

They're getting closer to town now and The Way is wide and well graded. She accelerates, confident on the dirt, happy to see Ivan grab hold of the Jesus handle, the city cop uneasy on the vagaries of the gravel road. A pothole here and there just adds spice; the big Nissan is well set up for it. Another five minutes and she's forced to slow as the ridge dips and The Way starts to wind down from the heights in a series of switchbacks into the hollow of the town.

Finnigans Gap looks little changed to her: the same erratic collection of housing, everything from neat kit homes through converted shipping containers to shanties patched together from corrugated iron, plastic sheeting and second-hand scaffolding. They pass a collection of car wrecks, a dozen or so, corrosion brown at the bottom of the hairpins, as if someone has pulled them together with the intention of starting a business, only to think better of it and head to the pub instead. Other towns put on their best face, compete in 'tidy town' competitions, window-dressing their welfare class and shining with civic pride. Finnigans Gap can't be bothered; cars, trucks, mining machinery and old white-goods lie scattered randomly. Here's an iron bedframe, there's a railway bogie, beyond it the bucket from an earthmover. Nell wonders if it's deliberate, not so different from those tidy towns, putting on a show for the tourists: look at us, see how tough we are, how hardscrabble.

Only at its core does it conform to the norms of a country town, just for a block or two where it rubs up against the tourists: the streets are sealed and guttered, and the footpaths are made of concrete instead of dirt. On the left, as the road beneath their wheels turns from gravel to bitumen, she sees the bowling club, the 'bowlo', the biggest building in town, its social hub, dwarfing the low-rise hospital on the other side of the street. She passes by and comes to the exact centre of Finnigans Gap, the crossroads, where The Way, linking the western and eastern ridges, meets the north–south Dubbo–Queensland highway. The crossroads is the one place the town could be mistaken for somewhere else, if you discounted the absence of trees. For a block in all four directions, the shops are well-enough aligned, mostly attached to each other, sharing an awning. There's the Alpine Cafe, famed for its hamburgers, a combined post office-cum-newsagent-cum-sports store; a drive-through bottle shop, a branch of the Westpac bank, another drive-through bottle shop, a boutique hotel, a chemist, a pub, a clothing emporium, an electrical goods outlet, a supermarket and a bric-a-brac and second-hand bookshop. For the tourists, there's an art gallery, three or four opal shops, an opal museum. But the order begins to peter out after a block. Then there are vacant lots, and the buildings in between become freestanding and haphazard, some set back from the road, some almost encroaching upon it. There is brick and there is board and there is fibro, often painted ludicrously vivid colours as if to grab the wayward attention of the grey nomads, colours bright enough to penetrate the fog of cataracts.

The town has no traffic lights; the only intersection of any real significance is the crossroads, which is in fact a roundabout. In the centre of it sits a squat brick clock tower; the town is too recent for a war memorial. Approaching from the north or the east, the clock tells the correct time during the winter, but at this time of year it lags an hour behind, so that it's telling Queensland time instead of summer time. Coming from the west, it is perpetually five thirty, and coming from the south, forever ten past ten. That hasn't changed since Nell was stationed here; she doubts much else has changed either.

She swings the Nissan around the clock tower then heads south along the highway. The land dips again and flattens out onto the plain proper. To the left is the turn to the airport and then, a few hundred metres further along, well before they get to the Finnigans Outback Roadhouse—notorious among locals for overpriced fuel and overcooked food—she turns right into an optimistically signposted industrial park. It's a slapdash jumble of corrugated-iron buildings set back from the road: two engineering and steel fabrication businesses, a truck dealership, a stock and station agent, a rudimentary hardware store, a fuel depot and Topsoil's Mining Supplies. Trev's big dick RAM truck sits outside, covered in dust. There's a trailer with a boat gleaming in the sun, placed where all can see.

'What's with the boat?' asks Ivan.

'Fishing. It's big here. Waterskiing too. Up in Queensland. There's a dam there, only about an hour's drive.'

'I see.'

The heat seems to have gathered in the hollow of the town, flowing down into the industrial park, warping the corrugated iron and melting the bitumen of the car park. Nell pulls the Nissan in as close as she can to the double glass doors leading into Topsoil's. The flies are waiting for them, swirling around, trying to hitch a ride on their backs into the shade of the interior. They take turns spraying each other with repellent. She wonders if it might be a bonding ritual, likes chimps grooming.

If anything, it's hotter inside, despite being out of direct sunshine. Large fans hang from the ceiling, revolving slowly, moving the heat around without dispelling it. Trevor Topsoil is sitting on a stool behind the counter and looks up as they enter, a barrel-chested man, just as she remembers him, with a tuft of hair jutting from his Everlast t-shirt and an impressive chin protruding from his face, the sort of chin perpetually darkened, no matter how recently he's shaved. She touches her own face, an involuntary gesture, remembering his bristles against her cheek.

He just grins when he sees her, the same big dopey grin he always used to wear, back when she fancied him, back when she hoped there was more to him. He ignores Ivan, the grin breaking wider as he checks her out, unashamedly scanning her from top to bottom and back again. 'Well, fuck me. Look what the cat dragged in.'

'Yeah. Good to see you too, Trev.'

Ivan frowns at the banter and cuts through it. 'Trevor Topsoil?'

'That's me.'

'Detective Sergeant Ivan Lucic. This is Detective Constable Narelle Buchanan. I'm assuming you've met before.'

'Met? That's one way of putting it.' And the grin continues.

She glances at Ivan, realising she should have told him. Too late now.

'Strange reaction,' says Ivan to Trevor. 'Two detectives walk into your business and all you can do is smirk like a loon. Most people would be concerned.'

'I'm just pleased to see the constable.' He winks at her, and she can feel herself blush, eliciting a wider grin from Topsoil. 'Hey, Nell, I got a couple of new tatts. You want to see?'

'Not now, Trev.' She feels her face burning like a minor sun, Ivan's ice-cold gaze doing nothing to cool her.

Trevor turns back to Ivan. 'Why would I be concerned?'

'You're a friend of Jonas McGee?'

'I am.'

'He's dead. Crucified.'

'So I heard.'

'You don't seem too perturbed.'

'Why would I be?'

'Because he was your mate?'

'Yeah. True.'

She sees the furrow carving through Ivan's forehead as he tries to get a grip on Topsoil's laconic lack of interest, trying to work out if it's for real or for show. She knows it's genuine: the most carefree bloke you'd ever meet, the laid-back larrikinism that makes him simultaneously so attractive and so frustrating.

'When did you last see Jonas McGee?' asks Ivan.

'Last week. Let me check.' Topsoil moves along the counter and taps away at a computer. 'Here it is. Monday. He was in ordering some equipment.'

'He had money?' asks Ivan.

'He did. Told me he'd found a good little pocket of nobbies.'

'How much did he spend?'

'Nothing upfront. About three hundred bucks on order. Cash on delivery.' Topsoil thinks it over. 'Pity about that.'

'Doesn't sound like much.'

'Nah, but he was talking about updating his excavator. That runs into thousands.'

'Right. How big was this new strike of his then?'

'Couldn't tell you. That wasn't Jonas. Kept his cards close to his chest. But word gets out. You know—people see things, hear things. Ask the Irishman. He was Jonas's buyer.'

'Did Jonas seem anxious at all? Worried?'

'Nah, mate. He'd been a bit strung out about his daughter, I know that much, but that seemed to have worked itself out.

He was even talking about getting back into a bit of fishing, once the weather cools down a bit. Been months since we threw a line in together.' He smiles again, that same dopey grin. 'If anything, he's been happier than I've seen him in a long time. Excited. You see it in their eyes, the miners, when they're on a run. Like gamblers.'

'Did he have enemies? Any feuds?'

'Nah, mate. Too quiet. Kept to himself, mostly. He could be quarrelsome, for sure, but nothing to deserve that.' Trevor frowns. 'Is it true? They actually nailed him up? I thought people were bullshitting.'

'It's true. Any idea who could have done that?'

'Nah. Fuck me. Who'd do something like that?'

'What about Stanley Honeywell?'

Topsoil laughs. 'Nah. He's soft in the head. Like a big puppy. Wouldn't hurt a flea.' The store owner rubs his formidable chin. 'Although . . .'

'Although what?'

'He's a former crim. Jonas told me they met in prison.'

'You know what he was in for?'

'Jonas didn't say.'

Ivan turns to Nell; she nods her understanding. She'll check Honeywell's record. He returns his attention to the man behind the counter. 'Did they have some sort of falling-out? We're told Stanley hasn't been working at the mine.'

A shake of the head. 'Nah. That was last year. They were on a lean run. Jonas was worried about him. Spoke to me. I helped get Stanley a job out at Cuttamulla, something regular. I think it was a load off Jonas.'

'The coalmine? They a big client of yours?'

'I wish.' Topsoil looks towards his computer, as if checking his inventory. 'Nah. They come in for bits and bobs, little things here and there, but a big corporation like that, they truck in their own stuff from the coast.'

Ivan waits until they're outside, in the four-wheel drive with the air conditioner pumping, the air acrid with fly spray. 'You want to tell me?'

She shrugs. 'We were a bit of an item, back when I was stationed here. That's all.'

'What does that mean, "a bit of an item"?'

She bristles, wonders whether or not it's any of his business, before conceding maybe it is. 'We'd hook up every now and then. He's fun. Cruisy. Relaxed.'

'But?'

'But that's all he is. The emotional depth of a mullet. It never went anywhere.'

Ivan laughs. 'Hell of a town.'

She frowns as she drives away. She's not sure how to take this Ivan Lucic.

chapter six

THE MOTEL IS CALLED THE GOLDEN VIEW, EXCEPT THERE IS NO VIEW. IVAN IS happy to ignore the lack of a vista: it's modern and well maintained, somehow incongruous in the jumble-sale aesthetic of the town, sitting on The Way, east from the crossroads, where the road is still sealed. With its barbecue area covered with shade cloth, a swathe of artificial turf and a gleaming, if small, swimming pool, it looks like it's been misplaced, as if it belongs somewhere closer to the coast.

Ivan's room is large and clean, with exposed brick and a high skillion ceiling of lacquered wood. It has an impressively large television, satellite channels, an air conditioner and a ceiling fan, even the promise of wi-fi. There's a bar fridge with iced water and milk, and it has one of those pod coffee makers with a selection of capsules ranging from mild to intense. In the shower, the pressure is good and the water is cool, surprisingly so. He lingers under the stream for an extra moment, lets it beat on his face, eyes closed, willing it to wash the heat of the day from him. He emerges refreshed and gets dressed. All he has with him is a second suit, some black jeans, three or four business shirts, a couple of t-shirts and underwear, his running gear, all thrown in at a moment's notice, not thinking through where he was heading. He opts for the suit pants, a fresh shirt. The pants feel too fragile, too stylish, but the black jeans would be intolerably hot, only suitable for after dark.

He's just finished when there's a knock at the door. It's Nell, outlined by a blast of baking light and the rush of heat. She hands him a wrap: chicken, avocado and spinach. He feels a little awkward. 'Thanks, that's considerate.'

'It's too hot to stand here. I'll wait in the car.'

He follows her out, carrying his message bag and his food. Inside the vehicle, he takes a bite of the wrap, then asks what she has for him.

'I got in touch with Sergeant Pederson. She is working today but she's over in Lightning Ridge, some joint operation. Back later. Says she can meet us at the station about five.'

'Good. Thanks.'

'Also, I've found Jonas's church. The minister runs a Sunday evening service out at the coalmine but can fit us in before he leaves. Says he knew Jonas quite well. He'll meet us at the Anglican church.'

'Excellent. What about the opal dealer? The Irishman?'

'Can't get hold of him, but his store is on the highway, just up the slope from the crossroads. Round the corner from the church. We can have a look on the way to the church.'

'Tell you what, it's not far—I'll walk over, see what I can find out there.'

She glances out her side window at the sky. 'Jesus, you really like this walking caper, don't you?'

'I know. But we can't spend all our time in cars. I want to get a feeling for the place, I want to acclimatise.'

'Good luck acclimatising.' She looks doubtful. 'Take a bottle of water with you. They're in the back.'

'Thanks. I might leave my gun there. Not sure I need it for a clergyman.'

'What else do you want me to do?'

'How'd you go chasing down Elsie McGee and Stanley Honeywell?'

'Elsie McGee lives in Adelaide. Garry has a number for her; I've left a message. Stanley is at Cuttamulla. I rang the mine. He's been rostered on all week. They have their own accommodation.'

'He's staying there?'

'That's what they say. Beats driving back and forth every day. Beats staying at Deadmans Well.'

'Right,' says Ivan, impressed by her initiative. 'How far is Cuttamulla?'

'About an hour's drive.'

'And he's been there all week?'

'So they say.'

'That would be useful, ruling him out as a suspect. We'll need to confirm it, find out how they can be sure. But let's leave it until tomorrow. Maybe we take a run down to see him first thing, when Blake has a better handle on the time of death. In the meantime, can you get Stanley's record? Everyone reckons butter wouldn't melt in his mouth, but if Jonas met him in prison, he must have done something bad.'

'Anything else?'

'I want to get phone tracking data for Buddy and Kyle Torshack, and for Stanley as well. Monday through Wednesday. We need to know where they were.'

'You got it. For Jonas as well?'

'Good thinking. And let's find where Jonas lived in town here. That caravan at the mine looks one step up from camping.'

'You want me to have a snoop around, talk to the neighbours?'

'Please.' Ivan can foresee a problem: if Jonas was staying out at the mine, guarding against ratters, chances are he would have locked up his house. 'What do you do for search warrants? Is there a courthouse?'

'There is, but only just. Open a couple of mornings a week. The magistrate gets here a day a month, if she's lucky. There's a part-time registrar, a local bloke, Humphrey Tuppence.'

'He can do warrants?'

'Yep, he's an authorised justice. Warrants and bail.'

'That's handy. Let's get warrants for the phone records and to search Jonas's house.' He double-checks the location of the Irishman's store with her, before climbing out. 'See you soon.' He watches her drive away, then walks towards the crossroads.

Finnigans Gap is like no other town that Ivan Lucic can recall. It feels somehow incomplete. Perhaps it's the lack of trees, perhaps it's the mishmash of architecture, the strange mix of working town and tourist destination. Beyond a few hundred metres or so out from the clock tower, there is no rhyme or rhythm to it.

The Irishman's store is standalone, made from large concrete bricks and painted a lurid green with huge shamrocks, three- and four-leaf. There's a sign mounted on the roof: THE IRISHMAN—OPALS BOUGHT AND SOLD. A smaller sign above the door identifies the proprietor as Sean McGrath, together with his mobile number. Other signs are bolted to the door. OPENING HOURS 7 AM TO 2 PM. VIEWING OTHER TIMES BY APPOINTMENT. A sign to the left of the door says: STONES BOUGHT—ROUGH AND RUBBED. Amid all the hoardings, Ivan doesn't see the paper note pinned to the door until he's tried to open it and found it locked. NIPPED OUT. BACK IN FIVE.

Ivan rings the number on the sign.

A gruff voice answers: 'Yep?'

'Sean McGrath?'

'Yep?'

'This is Detective Sergeant Ivan Lucic. I'm outside your store. Are you close by?'

'No. Dubbo.'

'Dubbo? The sign says back in five.'

'That's right. Don't want some fucker coming in through the roof while I'm away.'

'That happens, does it?'

'It's Finnigans Gap, mate, not Double Bay.'

'When are you back in town?'

'Tomorrow. What's the problem?'

'Jonas McGee. He's dead. Murdered.'

That silences McGrath for a long moment, and when he does respond his voice has lost its combativeness. 'My God. Really?' Another pause. 'You're investigating?'

'That's right.'

'Fuck. What happened?'

'He was found yesterday, dead down his mine out on the West Ridge.'

'How do you know it was murder?'

'He was crucified.'

There's a sharp intake of breath. 'Fuck. That's appalling.' To Ivan's ear, the shock sounds genuine. 'What's it got to do with me?'

'I'm told he sells his opals through you.'

'Yeah. Not through me, to me. But I haven't seen him for almost two weeks.'

Ivan takes that on board. 'I was told he'd been having a lucky run this little while.'

'Yeah, pretty good, but nothing extraordinary. Don't believe everything you hear.'

'Could he be selling through someone else?'

'Nah. Why would he do that?' And then: 'It's a pretty small town. I reckon I would have heard.'

'Fair enough.'

'I treat my miners well, mate.' The assertive tone is back, the initial shock dissipating. 'Some of them are awful shits, to be frank with you, but I keep them onside. Jonas was a gentleman compared to most of them. Honest and decent. Look how he's supported Stanley Honeywell all these years.'

'Have you seen Stanley recently?'

'Nope. I deal with Jonas.'

'Are you friendly with Stanley?'

'Are you kidding? No.'

Ivan finishes the call and checks his watch. There's half an hour before the meeting with the priest. He brings up Google Maps, double-checks the location of the Anglican church, is relieved to see it's about fifty metres away. He looks up from his phone, but there's no sign of a spire. One thing's for sure: he's not waiting outside in the sun.

Across from the Irishman's opal store, just up from the pub, is the oldest building he's seen so far, maybe fifty years, a big barn of a place, like an airport hangar except with walls of brick instead of steel. MARLEY'S EMPORIUM says the sign, with others indicating it sells everything from clothes and kitchenware to cricket bats and car-seat covers. He walks across, enters. The emphasis is on price, not quality or choice. What you see is what you get. He buys some dun-coloured chinos, loose-fitting and made of cotton, and a few short-sleeved shirts, plus a lightweight bucket hat. It's completely devoid of style, something he wouldn't be seen dead wearing back in Sydney, but it will do the job out here. He's tempted by some tough-looking work boots to compensate, but goes for lighter hiking boots instead. He doesn't want to get blisters.

— —

Nell waits in the car outside the church, watching Ivan walk round the corner, amused by his hybrid dress: fashionable suit pants and business shirt from the city, topped with a bucket hat. Another day or two and he'll look as daggy as any local.

St Andrew's is neat as a pin, surrounded by gravel that has been painted green and neatly raked, a vague facsimile of a lawn. Behind the church, she can see the start of a graveyard. The building itself is made of brick up until about waist height, then continues with white weatherboard, as if the congregation ran out of money halfway through construction. The shape is traditional enough, with arched windows and a high-pitched roof of corrugated iron. A few of the windows have air conditioners mounted beneath them. There is no steeple, just a large cross at the apex of the roof.

She climbs out as Ivan reaches her, sweating under his new hat. 'Been shopping?'

'Going local.' He places his bags inside the car. 'Tell me: I asked the Irishman if he was friendly with Stanley and he sounded almost offended. Why would that be?'

'Stanley's an ex-crim with more tatts than teeth, and he's thick as two short planks, and he's black. Take your pick.'

'Stanley is black?'

'Apparently. Islander, Chinese, Indian, Aboriginal—Garry Ahern checked him out for us.'

'Jesus. Is that an issue?'

'Out here? Sometimes yes, sometimes no. There's a divide.' She softens. 'Stanley is a former prisoner who lives at a squatters' camp; the Irishman is a small businessman who lives up in the dress circle. Rotary Club, the Chamber of Commerce, National Party.'

'Okay. I get the picture.' He regards St Andrew's and its green gravel yard, seemingly unimpressed. 'How about Stanley's record?'

'Long as your arm. Everything from armed robbery to assault. But nothing since he got out of prison fourteen years ago, a few months after Jonas. I'll get a printout once I can access a computer.'

'Excellent work.'

She feels an inner glow at his praise, tamps it down, tells herself not to be stupid.

'Anything else?'

'I found Jonas's house. All locked up. Nothing to it. Most impressive thing about it is the cactus hedge.'

'That's a thing?'

'Very popular.'

'Worth the trip in itself. Neighbours?'

'One side is an empty house. For rent. The other side, there's a young couple with a tribe of kids. The woman spoke highly of Jonas. Said he was very considerate, always happy to help out. Fixed their toilet just the other week. But they haven't seen him for at least a fortnight.'

'Maybe he was camping out at his mine all that time then. Even in the rain.'

'Sounds like it.'

'Okay, good work. Let's talk to this priest.'

She was hoping for cool, but is disappointed: only one of the three fans hanging from the ceiling is revolving, and then so slowly it can't possibly have any effect. The air conditioners under the windows aren't operating. The windows themselves look like they were built to house stained glass, but contain frosted panes instead.

The priest is seated at a card table, transistor radio broadcasting the cricket. There's a clear plastic jug with orange cordial or juice with ice cubes, some plastic glasses and a plate of biscuits. Fruit slices, the ones Nell used to call 'dead-fly biscuits' when she was a kid. The man is old and shrivelled, as if the climate has dried him out, reminding her of a picture she once saw of an Egyptian mummy. Not dead yet, just pre-embalmed.

'Aussies are on top,' says the priest, nodding his head at the transistor, his voice like sandpaper. He's addressing Ivan, not acknowledging her.

'Good to know,' says Ivan. 'I'm Detective Sergeant Ivan Lucic, this is Detective Constable Narelle Buchanan. We're Homicide detectives.'

'God's work,' says the priest. 'I'm Reverend Oscar Vale. Please be seated.'

They sit, side by side in a pew, while the priest pours them each a drink, hand shaky. Ivan, still sweating from walking, accepts gratefully. Nell sips cautiously: it's some sort of artificial orange flavour, overly sweet; like the gravel outside, it bears only a fleeting resemblance to the genuine article. But it's cold and wet and has ice cubes.

'How long have you known Jonas McGee?' asks Ivan.

'I married him. Twenty-five years ago.'

'You knew him well?'

'Not back then. He was a drinker and a fighter and a sinner. Pumped up with pride and engorged with opal lust. His wife was the one who insisted on the church wedding.' The priest nibbles at the dead-fly biscuit, as if trying to ration it, make it last. 'She was already pregnant at the time.'

'You think he was forced into marriage?' asks Nell.

The priest looks a little surprised, as if he isn't expecting her to be allowed to ask questions, but he answers readily enough. 'No. He loved her all right. That much was clear. He mightn't have thought much of me or this'—he gestures about the building—'but he was all for the marriage.'

'And after they were married?'

'Nothing for years. I'd see her a bit about the town. Annie. Nice lass. Bit wild, but essentially solid. She had their daughter baptised here, Elsie. I'm not sure Jonas even turned up for that, but I might be wrong. Fair while ago now. Next time I saw Jonas was at Annie's funeral.'

'He was there?'

'Yeah. Police gave him bail for it. It was pretty awful. Her parents came up from Adelaide. Their two daughters, both dead. And him, on the periphery.'

'Jeez,' says Ivan. 'What did you make of that?'

The priest frowns. 'Language, please. This is a house of God.'

'I'm sorry. Please continue.'

'I think he caused unnecessary distress attending their funeral. But it took guts, I'll give him that.'

'And after that?'

'He went to jail. I didn't see him for another five years, or however long he was inside. When he got out, he came to see me, said he'd changed.'

'What did he want?'

'To make amends. I advised him to move away, start over somewhere else; told him that it would be better for him and better for the girl. But he refused. Said he'd thought it through. He wanted to stay.'

'Did he? Make amends?'

The priest takes another nibble of the biscuit. 'I'll leave it to a greater authority than me to make that judgement.'

Ivan scowls. 'Right now, that greater authority is us,' he says, voice even, but Nell likes the way his eyes are boring into the priest. 'We want to catch whoever killed him. Put them before a court. They can go to heaven or they can go to hell, but we get first crack.'

The priest smiles for the first time, apparently taking no offence. 'Of course. I apologise.' And then, nodding, 'Yes, I'd say he made a pretty good fist of it, for a layman. Always came to church, donated money when he could, helped the less fortunate. Always joined in any working party, active in the service clubs.'

'You've heard about his death?'

The priest glances past Ivan towards a crucifix mounted on the wall. 'I heard he was crucified. Is that correct?'

'It is. Nailed to a homemade cross.'

'Sweet Jesus,' whispers the priest, crossing himself. 'That's appalling.'

Ivan gives him a moment. 'When was the last time you saw McGee?'

'Me?' The priest looks surprised, as if he's being listed as a suspect. 'This time last week. Sunday. He came to the morning service. He rarely missed one.'

'He was genuinely religious then?'

'I'd say so. Ever since he returned from prison. He told me he'd had an epiphany there. He'd found God.'

'You believed him?'

'Yes, I did. There are two types of Christians: the showy ones and the pious ones. He was one of the pious ones.'

'And how did he seem to you, that last time you saw him?'

Father Vale shakes his head, as if the memory saddens him. 'We didn't talk, not properly. Not on that occasion. Shook hands after the service, exchanged a greeting, that's all. He seemed a little tense, a little preoccupied.'

'How so?'

'Nothing in particular. Usually he was quite chatty around the church, but these last couple of months he was restless, like there was something on his mind.'

'Any idea what?'

'If I had to guess, I'd say it was his daughter. He was very fond of her. Devoted.' The priest is studying the plate of biscuits, like he's trying to hunt down a memory. 'But that would only be a guess.'

Nell senses a subtle change in Ivan; he seems more focused as he continues his questioning.

'We've been told they were estranged.'

'Yes. She wouldn't talk to him.'

'Do you know why?'

'No. He was quite guarded. Very private. The more something meant to him, the less likely he was to talk about it. Some people are like that.'

'She didn't come to church here?'

'The daughter? No. Never.'

'Some years ago, she took an apprehended violence order out against him. Do you know anything about that?'

'No. They had a big fight, he was very distressed, but he never told me what it was about. I only knew because he spent a lot of time here. Praying.'

Ivan looks at his notepad, as if deciding where to take the interview next.

Nell fills the gap. 'Do you know of anyone who might have intended to harm Jonas?'

'Like that? No. Of course not.'

'Not just like that—like anything?'

'No.'

Ivan takes a deep breath. Nell takes it as a sign and defers, letting him resume his questioning.

'Father, the crucifixion of Jonas is deeply disturbing on many levels. It may demonstrate some deep hatred of Jonas. Or maybe he was simply the wrong person in the wrong place and the perpetrator was experiencing a psychotic episode. Maybe even religious delusions.'

The priest's expression is serious. 'Yes. I understand. It's common enough, people becoming delusional, hearing voices. Believing they are receiving divine guidance. But violence is rare.'

'Are there any people you know of in Finnigans Gap who suffer in this way?'

The question appears to trouble the priest. He looks at his hands, considers his position before answering. 'Yes. Perhaps.'

'Perhaps?'

The priest selects a second biscuit, takes a sizable bite, chews before responding. 'There is a cult here. A self-styled sect. The Rapture. They call themselves a church, but they're far from it. Led by a man who has proclaimed himself a prophet. Calls himself the Seer.' The look on the man's face suggests the biscuits really are filled with dead flies. 'A complete charlatan.'

'Is there any particular reason you're telling us about them, other than their religious beliefs? A reason to link this sect to Jonas McGee?'

'I believe there is some history there, but I can't say what exactly. You must understand, I'm just telling you what I've heard, not what I know.' The priest has placed the remains of his biscuit on a plate, and is wringing his hands now, as if wrestling with conflicting thoughts. 'I don't approve of this sect. People know, they come to me, tell me things. I don't know what is true and what isn't. Not that it matters; to me the whole idea is blasphemous. It's bad enough having the Roman Catholics in town.'

'The Catholics?' asks Nell, exchanging a glance with Ivan. 'What have they done?'

'Papacy,' spits the priest, gobbling the rest of the biscuit, chewing it with force.

'Right,' says Nell, eyeing the Kool Aid jug with suspicion.

'Back to this sect,' Ivan continues, shifting his weight. 'Have they demonstrated any violent behaviour? Does the Seer or any of his followers display psychotic tendencies?'

'There is one thing I've heard . . . There's a church out in the diggings, up on the East Ridge, just before you get to Deadmans Well, not so very far from the Rapture's compound. Not a real church; a film set, never consecrated. Purpose-built for a moving picture, constructed entirely of corrugated iron. It's a shell, no interior; I'm told they filmed the inside scenes in Sydney. It's an eyesore, a heresy, and it should have been dismantled long ago, but it's become a tourist attraction, so the chamber of commerce wants to leave it there. There have been some disturbing reports.'

'Such as?'

'Animal sacrifices.'

Ivan becomes completely still, attentive. To Nell, the wattage of his gaze seems to have stepped up. 'When was this?'

'Past year. A few occasions. A cat. A goat. A wombat. Where the altar would be, if there was one.'

'A wombat? Who'd kill a wombat?' whispers Nell, appalled.

Ivan persists. 'And what makes you think this is connected to the Seer and the Rapture? Do they use the place?'

'It's close by their compound.' The priest glances at Nell. 'The local police should know more.'

chapter seven

THE POLICE STATION IS DESERTED WHEN THEY PULL UP OUTSIDE. NO OTHER cars, just them. Beside him, Nell leaves the engine running, not even asking: the air conditioner is essential. It's past five, but there's no sign of the day cooling. Here, in the hollow of the town, the sun will soon dip behind the West Ridge, promising some relief. The dashboard says the outside temperature is still thirty-eight degrees. Nell is checking her phone, but Ivan is restless, unwilling to sit and wait lest the exertions of the day catch up and impose their weariness upon him. He can feel it starting to gnaw at his concentration.

'Back in a mo,' he says, and climbs out into the heat, like a frogman leaving a diving bell.

It's a strange-looking building for a police station; it lacks the solid brick of so many country stations. It appears more like a community hall, clad with corrugated steel, the corrugations smaller and denser than standard and painted a creamy yellow. He walks through the low steel gate, thigh-high, like something from a school playground. There's a statue beside the path: an opal miner winching up ore. It's been vandalised; the bucket is gone and so is one of the miner's arms. The plaque remains, noting the twenty-fifth anniversary of the station, now ten years ago, and the thanks of the local community. There's a verandah of wood, a domestic front door with a steel security door, a noticeboard behind glass. He checks it out. A Neighbourhood Watch flyer—meeting first Tuesday of the month at the bowling club—a Crime Stoppers ad, a schedule of sitting times for the local court and the one in Lightning Ridge, and a list of after-hours phone numbers. Even in the shade of the verandah, the colour has bled from the notices and the paper looks curled and brittle, as if it might spontaneously catch fire. He retreats to the cool of the car.

'Anything?' he asks.

'Text from Sergeant Pederson. She'll be here in ten.'

'So what's the set-up?' asks Ivan. 'How many officers?'

'Four when I was here. A sergeant, a senior constable, a constable and a newbie.'

'A newbie? That was you?'

'Yeah. That was me.'

'And Garry now. Good kid.'

'I think so.' She smiles. 'He'll remember today.'

'Won't we all,' says Ivan gently. 'Four officers; it seems quite a lot for a town this size.' He remembers his year in the country: just him and a senior constable in a town twice as big.

'It's not your average town. Too many men, not enough women. Too much grog, too many crims, too much opal lust. Too bloody hot.'

'Sounds like fun.'

'Friday nights, Saturday nights, it's cowboy country. The lock-up is overflowing. Bar brawls and domestics. Full moons are worst.'

'Seriously?'

'Yeah. It's a thing.'

'Where's the lock-up?'

'Shed round the back there. All right for overnight; too hot for days like this.'

He can't help but think how he might fare out here, handling drunken brawlers. It was something he'd hated in his years in the bush, the threat of physical violence, when his words weren't enough, when he found himself reaching for his taser or baton, even for his gun. Hats off to her, surviving three years here. She seems so small compared to most cops, yet appears to take it all in her stride. Three years. And Bourke is no holiday camp; full of ice and racial tension.

She fills the gap in the conversation. 'Lightning Ridge has eight officers. Bigger town, more tourists. Bigger area. They can help out if necessary.'

'Happen much?'

'Not really.'

A police four-wheel drive pulls in next to them, windows tinted. Nell and Ivan climb out to greet the sergeant. But it's not her. It's two male officers, in uniform.

'What the fuck are you doing here?' demands the larger of the two, a big bloke in his late fifties, the beer-and-burger gut of the outback straining against his shirt, his face red, veins bursting: too much sun and too many beers. His question is directed at Nell, full of venom.

'Hello, Carl. Good to see you too.'

'Who's the suit?' The fat cop flicks his head in Ivan's direction.

Ivan removes his sunnies, lets his smile register with the burly officer for just long enough, drilling him with his eyes, before speaking. 'Detective Sergeant Ivan Lucic. Homicide,' he says, emphasising his rank ever so slightly; just enough to penetrate. He can see from the man's uniform that he's a senior constable.

The big bloke looks momentarily confused. Then: 'Homicide? Jonas McGee?'

'That's right.'

The officer calms down visibly. 'She's with you?'

'Detective Constable Buchanan has been seconded from Bourke to assist, that's correct.'

The senior constable called Carl takes another disdainful look at Nell, and then bursts out laughing, a rich baritone, full of joy and malice. 'Fuck me. That's perfect.' His companion is just staring, mouth open, taking it all in, not even pretending to know what's going on. The senior man continues: 'So you'll be here for a few days?' His tone has switched from belligerence to amusement.

'Most likely,' says Ivan noncommittally, not wanting to surrender any of his superiority.

'Terrific,' Carl responds, smiling, before the underlying aggression returns. 'You stay out of our hair and we'll stay out of yours. Detective.' And then to Nell: 'Detective.' And then he laughs again, turns and leads his junior colleague into the station, shaking his head as he unlocks the door, as if entertained by the randomness of the world.

'Tell me,' Ivan demands, voice quiet.

'Senior Constable Carl Richter. Known as Scaley. He was here during my three years.'

'So I gathered. Not a fan of yours?'

'You could say that.'

'What about the other one, the constable?'

'No idea. He's new.'

But before Ivan can ask anything more, another car swings in, another police Land Cruiser. It has a carbon-fibre aerial so tall it looks like a repurposed fishing rod. It continues to sway back and forth even after the vehicle has stopped.

This time it is the sergeant, a woman in her late forties, hair a low-maintenance bob, with friendly eyes and a tanned face. 'Sorry, I was longer than I thought. Cheryl Pederson.'

They shake hands, introduce themselves.

'How was Garry today?'

Ivan likes that this is the first question she asks. A senior officer concerned for her young charge. 'Excellent. It was very confronting, but he's cracking hardy. Was a real help out at the scene. Made some astute observations. We've got him canvassing the surrounding mines, looking for witnesses. I hope that's okay.'

'Of course. Good to hear he's been useful. Maybe you can take him for a beer one evening. Make him feel part of the team.'

'Sounds good,' says Ivan, silently admonishing himself. He hasn't thought of drinking with the locals; he's been too focused on the investigation. He knows people skills aren't his strong suit, the interpersonal touch that makes officers like Morris Montifore such effective team leaders.

'C'mon, let's get inside—too hot to be out here,' says Cheryl.

The station has a small foyer, a waiting room for the public, with seating to the right and an unattended counter to the left. There's a door straight ahead. She leads them through it into a corridor running left to right along the spine of the building.

'This way,' she says, entering a room to the right, more of a meeting room than an office. 'We can set you up here. Phones, computers. Wi-fi. Whatever you need.'

'Thanks. I'm pretty self-contained. Mobile and laptop. Nell?'

'I'm good.'

'Just the log-on for the network then.'

'Too easy. We don't have a lot of manpower to spare, but let us know if there is anything else we can help with.'

'Just a couple of things,' says Ivan. 'Is there any CCTV in town? Particularly anything that might capture vehicles heading up onto the West Ridge?'

Sergeant Pederson looks doubtful. 'Not that I know of. We have no traffic cameras or anything official. A couple of businesses might have cameras. The only one I can think of is the bowlo. It's on the road that heads up onto that part of the ridge. They might have an angle looking across the car park to The Way.'

Ivan looks at Nell; she nods, making a note to check it out. He turns back to the sergeant. 'We're working on the theory that it might have been ratters who found the body. Is there any way of finding out who they are?'

'Hang on,' she says. She leaves the room, calling out down the corridor as she goes, returning with the two uniformed officers trailing in after her. Suddenly, the small room seems crowded. 'This is Senior Constable Carl Richter and Constable Vince Kantor,' she says. 'Detective Sergeant Ivan Lucic and Detective Constable Nell Buchanan.'

'We've met,' says Richter dryly.

Cheryl Pederson seems to pick up Richter's lack of enthusiasm. 'It's Sunday. We all want to get home. The detectives just need a bit of guidance.'

Ivan takes up the invitation, addressing Richter. 'We think McGee's body was discovered by ratters. Any idea how to find them?'

Richter gives a derisory snort. 'Good luck with that.'

'Can we get a message to them?'

'Saying what?'

'That we're interested in what they found and nothing else. I will personally assure anonymity. They can talk to me. A few days and I'll be back in Sydney.'

Richter shrugs. 'I can try, put it out there on the grapevine, but if they get back to you or not, that's up to them. I can't make any promises.'

'Fair enough. Thank you.'

'Anything else?' asks Cheryl.

'What do you know about Elsie McGee, the victim's daughter?'

Cheryl shakes her head. 'Sorry. Never heard of her. Carl?'

'Shot through years ago,' says the burly senior constable.

'What about Stanley Honeywell? He used to help Jonas McGee mine opals.' Ivan asks the group as a whole.

Richter snorts again. 'Yeah, I know Stanley. Harmless. A couple of sandwiches short of a picnic.'

'But with an extensive criminal history,' counters Ivan.

'That's true,' says Richter. 'Extremely violent in his day. But we've never had any trouble from him. Not in more than ten years.'

'But you know who he is?'

'Sure. Lives out at a miners' squat. A place called Deadmans Well. You know it, Nell?'

'Of course,' says Nell, sounding rueful.

Cheryl explains to Ivan: 'We get trouble out there from time to time. Rough men, sleeping rough, living rough. They police themselves for the most part, but this time of year, with the heat, you can imagine. Tempers get strained; throw in some grog and you get fights. But from what I've heard, Stanley is a peacekeeper.'

'So you can't imagine him nailing up his boss?'

The sergeant shakes her head, as if saddened by the idea. 'Sorry, I can't imagine anyone doing that.'

'Well, we need to find him. Nell is on to it, but if any of you have any ideas, let us know. Okay?'

'Check,' says Vince.

Richter merely looks at his watch. 'Long day, boss.'

Cheryl looks surprised, turns to Ivan.

'Sure,' he says. 'Thanks for your help.'

'It's nothing,' says Richter, leaving, trailed by the constable.

'The heat,' says Cheryl apologetically.

'Not to worry,' says Ivan.

'I'd like to take you out for a meal, your first night here. Talk you through the lay of the land. But, you know, Sunday night, family commitments. Anyway, I'm sure Nell knows her way about town.' She smiles warmly. 'Anything else before I head off?'

'What can you tell me about the Rapture?'

Cheryl blinks. 'The crucifixion. You think there's a link?'

'More of a matter of eliminating possibilities rather than any real suspicion,' he replies.

'I don't know of any connection between them and Jonas. Doesn't mean there isn't one, of course. But they don't work the same area; the Rapture's mines are out along the East Ridge, about as far from him as you could get.'

'Mines? Plural?'

'Yeah, it's the cause of a lot of ill will.'

'Why?'

'Most mines are one-man bands, or partnerships, or family affairs. The regulations say you can only work one claim at a time, a small area. Work it or lose it. The Seer has a team of about a dozen, including people prepared to front for mining licences. Allows them to operate more than one claim. The other miners reckon it's unfair, allege he's not paying award wages. Not a lot we can do about it.'

Ivan frowns. 'Explain this to me: what's with all the small claims? Why doesn't some big mining company buy them out, mine commercially? If the opals are only thirty metres down, they could open-cut the whole area.'

The sergeant smiles. 'I'm told it's been tried; people starting companies, private and public, to do just that. It's never worked out. They can't get the economies of scale. The way the law is written, it favours the little bloke. You can only stake a fifty metres by fifty claim.'

'Sounds like they've legislated for the Wild West.'

Cheryl laughs. 'Yeah. You're not wrong there. It must be what the nineteenth-century gold rushes were like, all these prospectors out staking individual claims. I'm told that back in the seventies, when Stewie Finnigan found his first black opals here, there was a genuine rush. People poured in from all over: South Australia, the States, Russia. Lightning Ridge all but emptied; this was the next big thing. People staking land left, right and centre with no idea what was underneath, not even doing exploratory drills. There were fist fights and knife fights and gun fights. A complete madhouse.'

'Glad I wasn't here,' comments Ivan, before bringing the conversation back on point. 'So there's a lot of resentment then, towards the Seer and his so-called cooperative?'

'It runs deeper than that for some of the old-timers,' says Cheryl. 'Nowadays, his adherents come from the city. Lost souls for the most part, looking for meaning, somewhere to belong. They keep to themselves. But Carl reckons it used to be different. Worse. Local kids were being caught up in it; people called it a cult. It got close to outright confrontation apparently.'

'So, what changed?'

'Don't know. I've only been here three years, and we've had no trouble at all in that time.'

'No violence?'

'No.'

'Police records?'

'Not the Seer or his family. Some of his followers have low-level convictions: drugs, break and enters, resisting arrest—but almost all of it back in the city, not here. Here, they behave themselves. That's the Seer's argument: that the sect is turning their lives around.'

'Tell me about this old church of theirs—the movie set.'

She grimaces, shakes her head. 'I can see where you're heading. Yes, there's been some weird shit there. A couple of animals tortured, killed. But it's not their church; they've got their own. As far as I know, they have nothing to do with it, except proximity.'

'These animals . . . sacrificed?'

'You could call it that.'

'Crucified?'

'No. More like disembowelled. We've taken it seriously, but there is nothing to link it to the Rapture. They've never used the place, as far as we can determine, although there's plenty in the community who dispute that.'

'How frequent are these animal sacrifices?'

'There were two or three incidents in the past year. But we've had nothing for a couple of months.'

'Any idea why not?'

'Not really. Maybe it's kids. Found out we were investigating and backed off. Or they've moved on, getting their kicks out in the bush, where there are no witnesses.' The sergeant shrugs. 'So as far as I know, there is nothing to link the Seer and the Rapture to Jonas McGee's death. If he hadn't been nailed up like that, we wouldn't even be talking about them.'

——

Nell drives them the few hundred metres to the bowling club. The town is in shade, the sun having fallen behind the West Ridge, but the sky is luminous. Pink clouds are arrayed like scallop shells against the blue. There's a sign outside, stating its official name: THE FINNIGANS GAP EX-SERVICEMEN'S BOWLING, CROQUET, CRICKET, RUGBY AND ANGLING CLUB. And underneath: INCORPORATING THE FINNIGANS GAP BRIDGE, CANASTA, MAHJONG, BACKGAMMON AND CRIBBAGE CLUB.

Before they get out of the car, Ivan, who has been silent since leaving the station, says, 'You were quiet back there.'

'Was I?'

His eyes are upon her, reading her face, those penetrating blue eyes. 'Richter. Tell me.'

Her heart skips a beat. She knows exactly what he's asking but hedges her answer. 'Sorry?'

'Senior Constable Richter. He hates your guts. Why?'

'He thinks I'm a rat.'

Iván says nothing, but his eyes are unwavering. They look like they've been backlit, the same luminous quality as the sky itself.

Unnerved, she fills the gap. 'I liked working here. It was a dream come true. I was a good cop,' she says, immediately feeling clumsy in her assertion, knowing she hasn't addressed the question. 'Richter looked after me. A mentor, a surrogate uncle. So was the sarge, Desmond Ottridge. Sexist shits, of course, old school, but also protective. We'd go into a bar fight, a domestic violence situation, they'd always have an eye out for me. They shielded me, taught me things, explained how the town worked, how policing worked. How people worked. There was a junior constable, Elliot, who was insecure, could be a real shit, but nothing I couldn't handle.'

'What happened?'

'Drugs. There were always a lot about. No surprise in a town like this. I got a tip-off, uncovered a sizable stash out at Deadmans Well. I wanted to dig into it, find out where they were from. A bit naive, I guess, but I was keen. Proper investigative work, a step up from drunken brawls and domestics. The sarge hosed me down, said it wasn't a job for a newly minted constable. He told me the Drug Squad knew all about it, that the drugs were coming in from the coast via Lightning Ridge, that they wanted to leave it operating while they chased down the Mr Bigs. He said they had them under surveillance on the Gold Coast.' Nell realises she's been staring out the windscreen, following the progress of a young family making its way into the club, not making eye contact with Ivan. She turns, looks him in the eye. 'I would have left it there. Maybe I should have. But a source, an informer, told me the supply lines were working the other way around, that the drugs were being manufactured here and sent to the coast, with a sideline into Lightning Ridge.'

'So what did you do?'

'I told the sarge, of course. He thanked me for the information, said the Drug Squad were on to it, were running surveillance here as well, undercover—a long-term operation, together with the Crime Commission. Told me it was above my pay grade and his as well, to keep my mouth shut and let them do their work. Said my three years would be up in a month or two and I could transfer back to the city.'

Ivan is nodding, comprehension on his face. 'Go on.'

'But my sources were telling me production was stepping up. And they were adamant: there was no surveillance. So I took the initiative. I rang the Drug Squad in Sydney to check. Took a few days, but soon enough they confirmed my source was right. There was no surveillance, there was no undercover.'

Ivan takes a deep breath, face set. 'Shit. How did it go down?'

'The Drug Squad enlisted my help. I tapped into my informants and learnt the location of a meth lab working down an abandoned mine, another one growing a field of dope underground. They came in at night. Raided the mines, arrested the locals running the operation. An opal dealer called Paxton Barret and a couple of brothers, the Longfers, from out at Deadmans. Sent them to prison, shut down the operation.'

'And Sergeant Ottridge? What happened to him?'

'Took leave, then retired to Queensland two weeks later. Six months short of twenty-five years in the force. I never saw him again.'

'You informed on him? Spoke to Professional Standards?'

'No. It didn't come to that. But . . .'

'But?'

'Well, I'd already told the Drug Squad what Ottridge had said to me: his claim that they were running surveillance and an undercover operation when they weren't.'

'So what happened to you?'

'Honestly? I thought I was fucked. Richter wouldn't give me the time of day, Elliot was practically dancing on my grave. They were close to Ottridge, thought I'd shipped dirt on him to advance my own career. I considered quitting, getting out. I might have done it if my three years weren't almost up. As it was, I applied for an early transfer.'

'And got it, I'm guessing.'

'No. Before the panel could deliberate, I was invited down to Sydney to train as a detective. The Drug Squad had put in a good word for me, the officer who led the raids out here. Faith Basheer. She said what I'd done took guts and street smarts.'

'She's right. It did. And integrity.' Ivan Lucic turns down the intensity of his stare and smiles. 'I was wondering how you got fast-tracked as a detective. Good for you. Just rewards.'

'Or, according to Richter, thirty pieces of silver.' She grimaces. 'I thought I was acting against drug dealers. I didn't realise I was destroying Ottridge's career.' She holds back the emotion. 'He'd been very good to me, Ivan. Him and Richter both. I thought Richter would have moved on by now, been pensioned off as well. I wasn't expecting to see him.'

Ivan reaches across, places his hand on hers, a surprisingly intimate gesture of support. 'You didn't destroy Ottridge's career. He did.' He gives her hand a squeeze and then removes his own. 'C'mon, I need a beer—and a steak.' He opens his door, then turns back to her. 'And don't worry about Richter. Leave him to me.'

— —

The club seems huge to Ivan, so much bigger than he'd anticipated. He'd be impressed, if he didn't know what was funding it. Past the foyer, with its slow fountain of marble and glass, plastic greenery and self-serve sign-in—bona fide travellers welcome—he can see a passage leading to the pokies to the left, a bar straight ahead with pool tables, another upstairs with a cafe, and a bistro to the right, a vast area of tables and chairs, a dance floor with a mirror ball.

Blake and Carole are already in the bistro waiting for their food, sitting at a table under the honour roll for the Anglers Club. They exchange greetings, then he and Nell line up, order at the counter. Steak for him, crumbed calamari and salad for her. He pays, collects the receipt and a blue plastic disc, the sort that will vibrate and flash when their meals are ready to be collected.

There's a screen, big enough for a small cinema, broadcasting the cricket. The test is over for the day, replaced by a pyjama game from Melbourne. A few diehards are watching down the front, drinking beers and barracking. Cricket has never made sense to Ivan, raised on a steady diet of European football, indoctrinated by his father. Cricket was for the Anglos, not for sophisticated Europeans. Sophisticated. His father. What a joke. A wicket falls, a spectacular catch, eliciting a howl of approval from the watchers. Ivan looks at the replays, understanding the batsman is out, appreciating the skill involved in the catch, but not comprehending the significance, why the audience is cheering so loudly, how it affects the state of the game. He wishes he did.

Dinner conversation starts small: the oppressive weather, trivia about opals, wonderment at how people can live this far from the coast. But before long, inevitably, conversation turns to the case, to Jonas McGee.

'Here's what I can tell you,' says Blake, slicing into his filet mignon, pink juices mixing with pepper sauce. 'Time of death was sometime between midnight and six am on Tuesday. That's about as accurate as I can be for now. A six-hour window.' He forks the meat into his mouth, chewing appreciatively.

'That fits,' says Ivan. 'We're still trying to find who was last to see him alive.'

'My guess is he was dead for at least four hours before he was crucified. After rigor mortis had fully set in, between four and eight hours,' says Blake. He slices more steak. He hits some gristle and concentrates on it for a moment, sawing through. 'So he was crucified between four am and noon, Tuesday.' He takes another mouthful, chews hard.

'Right,' says Ivan, eyeing Blake's steak uncertainly. 'So he was lying like that, dead, in that Christ-like pose, arms outstretched, perpendicular to his body, his legs straight and crossed at the ankles?'

'Yes, I would say so. It's difficult to rearrange limbs after rigor mortis. If they'd done that, there would be obvious signs—tearing of the muscles and whatnot.' Blakes takes more steak onto his fork, knifes some mashed potato and gravy onto it, and inserts the whole lot into his mouth, chewing appreciatively.

Ivan looks to Carole, who simply lifts an amused eyebrow. 'So what's the suggestion here?' he asks Blake. 'That someone found him already in that pose, and that gave them the idea to nail him up like that?'

'Possibly,' says Blake. 'Or that they killed him then arranged his limbs like that and waited for rigor mortis to set in. That it was all premeditated.' As if to demonstrate, Blake pushes the remains of the filet about his plate, edging the boiled peas to one side.

Ivan and Nell exchange a look. Ivan wonders what sort of killer might sit next to a body for hours, waiting. Knowing.

'I'm not sure it was premeditated,' says Carole, the crime scene investigator. 'While Blake was looking at the body, I was looking at the cross. I think it was purpose made.'

'Go on.'

'I pulled it apart. The wood matches the pile sitting at the bottom of the access shaft. All the necessary tools are there as well, in the metal storage bin. The cross was held together by two bolts. I'd say the holes were drilled within the past week or two.'

'So made there and then?'

'Yes. I found wood shavings near the crime scene, suggesting the wood was carried there, the holes were drilled and the cross bolted together on the spot.'

Ivan thinks of Jonas, working part-time as a carpenter. And he thinks of Kyle. The young man had volunteered the information that he'd helped his uncle when he was younger. 'The cross, was it well made?' he asks Carole.

'What do you mean?'

'Jonas was a carpenter. He would have had some skill.'

'No. Very crude. The cross arm attached by two bolts. There was no attempt at making a proper joint. No cutting of the wood, no recessing it to make a better fit or to strengthen the joint.'

'Can we draw any conclusion from that?'

Carole gives an uncomfortable smile. 'Nothing definitive. Anyone could have made it. Either someone killed him, then arranged his body, made the cross and crucified him. Or someone found him lying like that, rigor mortis already setting in, and that gave them the inspiration to make the cross.'

'I can't see Jonas being involved,' says Ivan.

'Why say that?' asks Carole, clearly intrigued.

Ivan can feel Nell and Blake studying him. 'He was very religious; I thought maybe he'd planned it. Some strange self-sacrifice. But he was also a carpenter. He wouldn't want to be nailed up to a shabby piece of workmanship.'

'I guess,' says Carole doubtfully, then speaks with more conviction. 'Crucifying someone is an act of violence, of deep emotions. Whoever did it must have truly despised McGee. There was no rush; they had plenty of time to think it through. On one level, it's about framing McGee's death, to send a message about him, who he was, what he deserved. On another level, it's all about the perpetrator, what they wanted, what they felt they needed to communicate.'

'Maybe,' says Ivan. He turns to Blake. 'What actually killed him?'

The pathologist shakes his head. 'Don't know. Not yet. The hospital here has very basic equipment.' He rests his cutlery on his plate. 'It took me a couple of hours just to set up a temporary examination position in the morgue, so I only had time for a preliminary investigation. So far, there is no obvious sign of death. There is pre-death trauma to the face, possibly from a punch. I place that as happening shortly before death. Highly unlikely to have killed him, but might have been enough to knock him out. I'll open him up tomorrow. Should know more then.' He returns to his steak, slices another piece. More juice flows, mingling with the sauce. 'But I have to warn you, if the evidence is equivocal, I'll have to drive the body down to Dubbo or fly it to Sydney.' He puts the meat in his mouth, chewing with contemplation.

'So you can't rule out natural causes?'

'Not at this stage.'

After that, the conversation drifts. Blake demolishes some apple pie with ice cream, and Carole and Nell have a coffee before the two·forensic experts take their leave.

Over at the bar, it's getting rowdy. There's a big bloke shouting drinks, maybe a miner who's struck it lucky. Except he doesn't look like a miner. His face is rough enough, with its lines and bursting capillaries, but he's dressed more like a grazier from central casting: moleskins, riding boots, thick belt supporting his belly like a sling, chambray shirt straining. He towers over the crowd around him; he must be close to two metres tall. A chant goes up—'Bullshit! Bullshit! Bullshit!'—as the man sculls a schooner in one go. He waves his hand around, orders more beer, and the crowd cheers.

'Who's the big man?' asks Ivan. They're still seated under the Anglers Club honours board, away from the bar. 'Opal miner on a streak?'

'Not one I recognise. Doesn't look like a local, though. Not in clothes like that.'

'Seems popular enough.'

'Shout the bar and you will be too,' Nell observes.

A waitress appears with a tray supporting a dozen small glasses. 'Free shots,' she says. 'Vodka this side, tequila towards you.'

'What's the occasion?'

'No idea, but he's buying.' She flicks her head back towards where the big man is holding court.

'Who is he?'

'Don't know, but his credit is good.'

The waitress continues on her rounds. More patrons are beginning to filter in as news of free booze penetrates into the far reaches of the club.

Nell sighs. 'I hope this doesn't get out of hand.'

'Not our problem,' says Ivan. 'Leave it to the locals.'

'Lucky it's Sunday,' she says. 'There would have been three times as many people last night.' She sips her wine. 'What's the plan for tomorrow?'

'We can't just wait for Blake and Carole; we need to press on. Now we know McGee died early Tuesday, we can start checking movements, alibis. If he died between midnight and six in the morning, that's got to narrow down the number of suspects. First thing tomorrow, check the CCTV from this place. And push on with getting the phone tracking for the Torshacks and Stanley. Once Garry has a list of miners out there, we'll check them as well. There can't have been that many people out on the West Ridge at that time of night.

'After you've checked the bowlo, I want you to drive to the open-cut mine, find this Stanley Honeywell character. Interview him, check his movements, see if you can verify them with the mine. Find out if he's missed any shifts, what the window of opportunity might be for him to drive up here and out to McGee's claim. Last Tuesday morning is key; if we can place him at Cuttamulla all day, then we can rule him out.'

'Is he a suspect?'

'Has to be. But if we can eliminate him as the killer, then he becomes a valuable source of information. Ask him about enemies, about the mine, about rumours that McGee had been on a run with the opals.'

'You trust me to do that by myself?'

He smiles. 'Sure I do. Just remember to record the interview.'

'What will you be doing?'

'I want to check out this Seer and his followers.'

Nell smiles. 'Thanks, Ivan. Thank you.' She raises her glass, drains the remaining mouthful. 'C'mon, I'll give you a lift back to the motel.'

'You go,' he says. 'I'm going to walk. Clear my head.'

'More walking? Get a feel for the town?'

'Something like that.'

But it's not like that. Maybe that was his intention, or maybe he always knew he was fooling himself. He goes to the gents before he leaves, and there he sees it, the entrance to the grotto, the gaming lounge, running off the other side of the foyer.

The passageway is decorated like a theme-park impression of an opal mine, with papier-mâché rocks forming a tunnel and LED party lights embedded in the walls, pulsing red and green, blue and yellow, opals there for plundering, fake treasure in fake dirt. He walks through, rounds a corner, and there they are, waiting for him, their lurid lights flashing, their mesmeric enchantment calling to him. He knows what he's doing even while he doesn't; knows he shouldn't even as he can't help it. They lure him in, sap his will and fleece his wallet. They have him.

MONDAY

chapter eight

HE CAN'T SLEEP. THE CEILING FAN IS REVOLVING, THE AIR-CONDITIONING IS running, the bar fridge is grunting. A dog barks, a car passes, a light plane flies over. Sleep becomes fragmentary, then elusive, then impossible. His mind is working, the early morning remorse, the self-flagellation at weakening, of letting the gambling machines penetrate his skin, stripping his wallet and his self-respect. He knows he needs sleep, needs to be fresh for the new day, but the more he tells himself this, the harder it becomes.

So he runs. He dresses in his shorts and singlet, and heads out of town, not up the dirt roads but along the highway, ascending the hill out of the amphitheatre town, heading north, up towards the pass that bisects the twin ridges, the road to Queensland. He pushes himself hard, lactic acid burning, a punishing pace. The lights of the town glow about him, the low grumble of the occasional truck as miners head out before dawn to beat the heat. Three cyclists dressed in lycra, tail-lights flashing red, puff their way past him like escapees from the city.

Beyond the town the road continues upwards under the slowly lightening sky. A wallaby bounds across in front of him, seemingly oblivious to his existence. In the distance, the cyclists have melded into the gloom, only their tail-lights visible, bobbing like red fireflies. He's settled into a steady pace now, breathing rhythmically, a two-part inbreath followed by one quick exhalation: in, in, out; in, in, out. His legs are no longer complaining and his arms are moving more easily, his motion self-contained, correctly calibrated. The day is approaching; the last stars are dissolving into the incipient blue. The cyclists return, moving at speed down the slope, the riders a blur, crouched low to cut the wind, their headlights bright.

At the peak, where the highway swerves to the right and hugs the ridge line before starting its descent towards the border, he finds a lookout, a turn-off on the right side of the road. There's enough light for him to make out the space before him. He can see room for half-a-dozen cars and, past that, a paved area ringed by a low wall of local rock. The elevation must not be much more than a hundred metres, but in a land without altitude, it's enough. He looks out, north towards Queensland. There's a sign mounted above the wall, angled and curved, explaining the view. He uses his phone, lights it up, but it points to sights unseen, out beyond the horizon: the Cape, the Gulf, Darwin, Cairns. There are no distinguishing features within sight, no landmarks. He wipes his hand across the steel, collecting the morning dew. Out on the plain, a farmer is night ploughing, lights carving into pockets of mist.

Ivan had thought they were too far west for cropping; perhaps it's some opportunistic grazier putting in some hay, exploiting the recent rains. Another gambler: without more falls, such a crop must surely die, stillborn in the January heat. But for now, the earth is breathing, opening itself to the moisture of the night, before the onset of the stifling day. He sits on a bench. High in the east, pink strata clouds are catching the first rays of the rising sun. They look so very far away, emphasising the magnitude of the land, making him feel his own insignificance.

He's still sitting there by the time the sun flares along the ridge line, setting the rim on fire. It stops him, stops his thoughts, makes him watch, to witness. Two cockatoos pass, moving from silhouette to glowing white, their feathers tinted gold by the rising sun. The air enters his lungs, full of purity. For a small moment, he is alone and tiny and okay. The night is gone, its anxieties and its recriminations, and the new day beckons. Down below, in the town, there will be coffee. Suddenly, he desires nothing more. He starts to jog back down into the hollow of Finnigans Gap.

—–—

Nell heads for coffee at the one place she knows will do a reasonable job: a van parked outside the town's information centre. She's thinking a good-quality espresso might put Ivan Lucic in an amenable mood before she heads off to Cuttamulla Coal. She can't quite work him out: on edge, focused, not quite comfortable with her or anyone else. A lone wolf forced to tend a flock; considerate one moment, distant the next; always thinking, never relaxing. But he's given her responsibility, hasn't talked down to her, listens to what she says. That she likes. For that, she will forgive him his intermittent coolness and periodic silences. For that, she will offer up a coffee.

She texts: *Coffee?*

He replies: *Thanx.* Then: *Long black. No sugar. Large.*

There's a long line at the coffee van. A squadron of grey nomads has got in first. They have their own networks, she knows, their own way of learning what's good value and what isn't. So she's standing there, wondering at this city-length queue in the middle of nowhere, thinking of how to approach her interview with Stanley Honeywell, when she sees the black limo cruise past. A big fat Chrysler with a chromed-up grille and tinted windows, shiny and washed, the only car in the Gap not covered in a thin layer of dust. It has to be the one Kyle Torshack saw up on the ridge—a ridiculous car, a movie-prop car, a car for red carpets and football players, wedding receptions and school formals. She watches as it eases around the corner, heading south. She abandons the coffee queue and dashes to her Nissan; she'll need to move quickly if she wants to find out who's driving it, what they've been doing here. There's not much to the south: the airport, the industrial zone, the roadhouse—the driver might well be leaving town.

She gets to the eighty-kilometre speed zone, where the buildings retreat from the road, and she starts accelerating, thinking her quarry is already out on the plain. Then, as she looks this way and that, she sees it off to the left on a side road, emerging from behind the cover of low buildings, heading towards the airport. She brakes, pulls over, planning a U-turn, but is delayed by oncoming traffic, a B-double lumbering into town, followed by a couple of motorhomes, more grey nomads. She considers flicking on the lights, giving the siren a thrash; instead, she tells herself to relax, to calm down. The road to the airport is a dead end; the limo is going nowhere fast.

By the time she gets up alongside the airfield, the manager is opening the gate, allowing the Chrysler to sweep onto the tarmac. Nell pulls up in the lee of the Flying Doctors shed and climbs out. Quickly, she texts Ivan: *Found black limo. Following.* And then, as an afterthought: *Coffee delayed :).*

Out on the tarmac, there's a corporate jet, a Gulfstream. She reaches back into the car, into the glove compartment, retrieves a set of compact binoculars. As well as the plane and the black limousine, there's a big four-wheel drive, a top-of-the-range Land Cruiser, painted desert tan. It has something painted on its door, but the angle is too extreme, she can't quite make it out. She scans the jet: it's a polished white, with no logos or corporate insignia, just the VH registration. She opens her phone, takes down the number. Then, as she watches, a large man steps from the front passenger seat of the Land Cruiser. Through her glasses she recognises him immediately: the oversized bloke who was shouting the bar at the bowlo the previous night. From the black Chrysler emerge two men and a woman, all dressed in dark suits, all East Asians by their look, thin and dapper. The men's only concession to the climate and the location is an absence of ties. The woman has a briefcase, the men have laptop bags. They mill about, shaking hands with the big man, bowing, as he towers above them, bowing back. She can see smiles, the body language of laughter. A man in a suit is out of the Chrysler, the chauffeur by the looks, busying himself taking luggage up into the jet. He finishes, bows, and returns to the driver's seat. On the tarmac, there's another round of handshakes and bowing between the big man and the others, and then they separate. The three Asians mount the short gangway into the plane as the man gives a final wave and climbs back into the front of the Land Cruiser, in the passenger side. God, she wishes she had her camera, the one with the long lens.

The cars pull away, heading back out the gate, even as the engines on the jet fire up. The limo comes first, shining in the morning sun; it has hire-car plates. She transcribes the number onto her phone. Then the four-wheel drive comes past. She catches a glimpse of the big man, laughing out loud as he shares a joke with his driver. She can read the signage on the side of the vehicle now: KALINGRA RARE EARTHS. Kalingra, like the lake; the car must belong to the new mine that Kyle Torshack showed them. It's local then; there'll be plenty of time to chase it down later. She decides to follow the limo instead. There are no hire cars in the Gap, not like that. It must have come from somewhere else. So she trails the Land Cruiser, but her real quarry is the Chrysler.

Sure enough, when the airport road rejoins the highway, she sees it turn left, heading south. She's held up at the intersection for what seems like an eternity, waiting for the Kalingra Land Cruiser to make its right-hand turn back towards town. By the time she's on the highway and heading out of Finnigans Gap, where the speed limit climbs to one hundred and ten kilometres per hour, her prey has vanished, blending into the heat mirage of the road. She opens up the throttle, fighting to keep the four-wheel drive straight. The engine is large enough, a big six, but the car is set up for the dry creek beds and bulldust pans of the outback. She's not used to high-speed pursuits, not in a vehicle like this. She tries to call it in, wanting information on the licence plate, but no one is answering at the station. It must be too early in the day.

— —

There is no one at the police station when Ivan gets there, freshly showered and keen to get cracking. No one. Seven thirty on a Monday morning and the place is locked up. He looks at his MobiPol phone, but it knows no more than he does. He examines the statue, with its pilfered bucket and the miner's missing arm. Vandals. At the police station. His phone trills. An SMS, Nell offering coffee. He's already consumed two cups at the motel, but the pod machine has left him wanting more. He orders a long black, and resumes waiting. His irritation is rising with the temperature, the power of the sun already challenging the morning cool. There is no wind and the flies are gathering with intent. He sorely needs his own supply of repellent; wishes he'd thought of it when he was clothes shopping yesterday. He swats them away, checks the weather app on his phone. Twenty-four degrees. The forecast is thirty-three by eleven, topping out at forty from three to five pm, lingering above thirty-five until nine o'clock. Forty degrees. Forty fucking degrees. Again.

One of the local police four-wheel drives pulls in, but it's not the sergeant. Richter climbs out, smirk locked and loaded.

'Nice threads,' he says by way of greeting.

'Nice morning,' says Ivan, voice studiously neutral.

Richter gives an amused snort. 'She abandon you, then? Didn't take long.'

'Getting coffee.'

'Lucky you.' Richter eyes the sky, as if assessing an enemy. 'C'mon. Let's get inside.'

'Listen, Carl, maybe you can help me.' Ivan's voice sounds more conciliatory than he feels.

'Sure,' says Richter. 'Of course.'

'I reckon we'll need another car. Nell has hers, but the forensic team needs to get about and so do I.'

The senior constable shrugs, shaking his head. 'Ask the sarge, but I doubt we can help. We only have three cars between the four of us. You might be better off hiring one.'

'Any suggestions?'

'Garage on the highway, just down from the crossroads. Don't go near the roadhouse, it's a rip-off. If the garage is out, try Trevor Topsoil at the mining supply place. He might give you a sweetheart deal.' And Richter grins, his expression taunting. With a smirk like that he could run for prime minister. The senior constable unlocks the door to the station and moves inside.

Ivan is about to follow, when a new text from Nell vibrates his phone: *Found black limo. Following.* He stares at it, annoyance sweeping him. *Coffee delayed :).* Who the fuck is running this investigation? Slowly, deliberately, he centres himself; tells himself she is doing the right thing; tells himself that he wants to know who's been out near Jonas's mine site just as much as she does. He knows he can't let such pettiness cloud his judgement; it's the first full day of the investigation.

Instead of entering the station, he turns and starts walking towards the garage, before the heat arrives in earnest. He doesn't want to be left waiting for her, and he does need a car.

—•—

The limousine is really moving. It'll be a V8, perfect for eating up the kilometres out here where the roads are straight and the traffic is thin. She's going as fast as she dares, but still it takes Nell twenty minutes to close the gap. When she gets close enough, she flashes her lights, then gives the siren a touch. Finally, just as she's deciding he's deliberately ignoring her, the driver of the Chrysler gets the message. The black car begins to slow, indicator flashing. It eases off the road onto the verge. She pulls in behind it.

The driver is out of the car immediately; a man in dark slacks and a white business shirt. She reaches around to the back seat, gathers her gun and some handcuffs, and as she steps out of the car, attaches her holster to her belt, where the driver can see it. But the man is holding his hands wide, indicating he has nothing to hide, that she has nothing to fear. They are alone on the plain, on the dead flat: two cars and two figures beside a long tenuous strip of bitumen. There is nothing else, save a couple of curious emus staring at them from the saltbush beyond the fence line. She walks towards him.

'Morning, officer. Can I help you?' he says.

'Going a tad fast, mate.'

He smiles, self-confident. 'You don't look like highway patrol.'

'The law is still the law.'

He again spreads his hands wide, a conciliatory gesture. Non-threatening. 'I'm guessing you're Detective Constable Narelle Buchanan, right?'

She's disconcerted by his knowledge, but keeps her voice even. 'That's right.'

'Merv Claxton. Twenty-seven years in the force.'

She can see it now. In his stance, in his face. In his confidence. Once a cop, always a cop. 'Nice car, Merv.'

'A beauty. Wish she was mine.'

'What's your business in Finnigans Gap?'

'Sorry, can't say. I've signed a confidentiality agreement.' Merv smiles with mock sincerity. 'Court enforceable.' He shrugs. 'But I saw you at the airport. You can run the rego of the plane. Of the other car. You'll work it out soon enough.'

She sees the patronising grin, feels her ire rising.

'Sorry, Merv. Your commercial-in-confidence agreement doesn't cut it—we're investigating a murder.'

The jokiness disappears, the hands fall to his side. 'Murder? Jeez. Why didn't you say so? I thought you were after me for speeding.' He looks at her hard. 'Tell me what you want to know.' Now his hands are gesturing again, emphasising his contrition. 'Not that miner? The one who got crucified?'

'You heard about that then?'

'Whole town is talking about it. Ivan Lucic investigating, you back in town. Can't see what it has to do with me.'

She wonders who he's been talking to. Maybe Richter. 'This car, or one very much like it, was seen close by the mine.'

'What mine?'

'The opal mine where his body was found.'

'Where's that?'

'Out at the far end of the West Ridge.'

'Up the end there, overlooking that dried-up lake bed?'

'That's the place. Kalingra.'

'Yeah, we were there. A couple of times.'

'Doing what?'

'I don't really know. I was driving these three Chinese. The only time they spoke English was to give me instructions.'

'Were they interested in the opal mines?'

'No. Couldn't give a shit. They wanted to see the lake and they wanted to see the site of a new mine being developed nearby.'

'The rare-earth mine?'

'That's the one. But I have no idea what their interest is. Investing would be my guess, but I couldn't understand a word they said.'

'What days were you up there?'

'Early in the week; Monday, I think it was. Again on Saturday.'

'Can you check for me?'

'No problem. I'll run through my records when I get a chance.'

'You say they're Chinese. Is that a guess, or you know for sure?'

'Sounded like it to me.'

'So a guess. Did you get their names?'

'No. I'm the driver, that's it. I just called them "sir" and "ma'am".'

'Where did you get the car?'

'Dubbo. Hire car. Taking it back now.'

'I'm guessing you're not from there.'

'Fuck, no. Sydney. Flew in, picked up the car. I'll fly back after I drop it off. Four-hour drive between here and Dubbo; it's nine to go all the way to Sydney.'

'How long were you in Finnigans?'

'Ten days all up. The Chinese came, they went, they came back.'

'You got your driver's licence there, Merv?'

He hesitates for no more than a heartbeat, then reaches into his pocket. He pulls out his wallet, shows her his licence. As he moves, she can see an impression on his shirt where the fabric has lifted slightly on his left-hand side. It looks like the sort of scuff mark that might be left from wearing a shoulder holster. 'You just the driver, or security as well?'

'Personal protection is what they call it.'

'A bodyguard?'

He shrugs. 'If you like.'

'Open the boot, will you, Merv?'

She sees him tense. 'No. You'll need a warrant for that.'

'Not sure I do, Merv. Open it.'

He spreads his arms, as if acknowledging he's overstepped the mark, that all is well. He leans back in through the driver's door and springs the boot. It's huge. There's a suitcase, a medical kit and a dozen bottles of mineral water in their plastic wrap, but that's not what catches her attention. There's a gun case, and next to it a holster bearing a Smith & Wesson insignia. She looks at Merv.

'They're licensed,' he says before she can ask. 'I'm licensed.'

'Show me.'

He does, pulling the cards from his wallet.

'Who do you work for, Merv?'

'Sydney Security and Chauffeurs. They're on the web. Here.' He extracts a business card. 'Call 'em if you like, Nell. I can wait.'

She doesn't fall for that one; even if she can get a signal this far from town, she doesn't want to be standing out in the heat while some robotic voice says her call is important to them and that she has advanced in the queue.

'I might do that,' is all she says. She looks at the card: it has contacts for the company, but not for Claxton. 'What's your mobile number, Merv?'

He smiles. 'You going to track me?'

'If I get a warrant.'

'No problem.' He recites a number.

She copies it into her phone. 'Thanks, Merv. You've been most cooperative, so I'll forget about the speeding. But one thing before you go . . . The other man at the airport, the big bloke in the Kalingra Rare Earths four-wheel drive. Who's he?'

'Seriously? You didn't recognise him?'

'No.'

'Bullshit Bob Inglis.'

'Sorry?'

'Robert Inglis, better known as Bullshit Bob. The billionaire.'

'A billionaire? What's he doing up here with the Chinese?'

'Negotiating ownership of that mine, would be my guess. But that really is above my pay grade.'

chapter nine

IVAN HIRES A CAR, A KIA SUV, NEW ENOUGH AND BOASTING ALL-WHEEL DRIVE.
The engine sounds tinny, and it's on the small side if he needs to
drive the forensics team, but they'll be heading back to Sydney
soon enough. He gets it from the garage; apparently demand is
not so strong in midsummer. He's glad: getting fleeced by the
roadhouse doesn't appeal to him, and neither does dealing with
Trevor Topsoil. He's just signing off on the vehicle when Nell
rings, full of apologies.

'Don't worry about it,' he replies curtly. 'What did you learn?'

She recounts her encounter with Claxton, the Asian investors
leaving town on a private jet.

'Okay. Good job,' he says. 'And he confirms he was up there,
on the West Ridge?'

He can hear her sigh even through the phones. 'He does. But
nothing to do with Jonas, nothing to do with opals.'

He thinks about it. There's nothing to link the Asian investors with the death and violation of Jonas McGee. He'd like to discount them, but remembers the rule of proximity. 'What do you suggest?'

'Low priority, but I still want to find out who they are, what they were doing here,' says Nell. 'Claxton reckons he was there on Monday, not Tuesday, but I might crosscheck if I can.'

'Good. But first priority is Stanley Honeywell. Can you still get down to the coalmine and speak to him?'

'What about the bowlo and the CCTV?'

'Vince or Garry can do that.'

'Sure. I'll get going then. Should be back by lunchtime. What about you?'

'I've got a car. I'm going to check out the Rapture. Hopefully, by the time you return, Blake and Carole will have more for us.'

Ivan's about to drive off when the garage owner approaches, handing him a refillable cup full of steaming coffee. 'Looks like you could do with this, love,' she says. 'Give the cup a wash and leave it in the car when you bring it back.' And then, even better: 'There's fly spray in the glove compartment if you need it. They're shocking right now. All this rain; it's not natural.' Suddenly, the day seems more promising.

The corrugated-iron church sits slightly off The Way, a sheet-metal mimicry, rusting and groaning in the sunlight, a loose sheet banging in the wind. The set designers, long gone, have done their job well: the dimensions are perfect, a close rendition of what a real church might look like. The pitch of the roof is steep, the windows, three each side, are suitably arched, and there's an entry vestibule. There is no cross to be seen; maybe it's been souvenired.

A couple of city sedans have pulled up, tourists circling the building with their cameras. Someone has put a drone up, and it's hovering above the church like a giant blowfly, reminding Ivan to give himself a good coating of the car's repellent. He walks around the other side of the church, away from the tourists, only to find a bride and groom having their photographs taken. Moving closer, he sees their clothes are ripped, their faces are covered in fake blood and their eye sockets are blackened. A zombie photo shoot. A lizard watches, remaining perfectly still, as if bamboozled by the unlikely nuptials.

He tries the door to the vestibule, but it's been wired shut. He moves along the side of the building, peering through a glassless window. There is nothing to see inside; just a dirt floor strewn with empty bottles and discarded fast-food wrappers, a couple of old mattresses and the remains of a smashed guitar. The sharp smell of urine is the only indication anyone has been inside anytime lately; the only sounds are the swarming flies and the creaking of metal.

He leaves the church to the tourists and the undead and continues driving along The Way, the track hard and corrugated, the steering wheel juddering with the vibrations, the Kia lacking the solidity and road-holding of Nell's big Nissan.

Half a kilometre past the church, the road fractures into three. Off to the left, he can see a collection of caravans, shacks, lean-tos and campervans, together with trucks, kombis and rusted-out mining equipment. This must be Deadmans Well, the squatter camp where Stanley Honeywell lives. Ivan checks his watch, wonders if it's worth a visit, decides to call in.

It's a *Mad Max* scene, deserted, a rising wind singing off a broken windmill, the distant sounds of the Rolling Stones. 'Sympathy for the Devil'. A stray dog sidles towards him before collapsing onto the dirt and licking its balls. He's wondering which way to go, where he might find someone, when he hears voices. Laughter. He follows the sound, realises it's the same direction as the music. There's a larger place, a more permanent-looking home: it's a repurposed railway carriage with a deck bolted on and an impressive array of solar panels rising above the roof line. Next to it is parked an armoured personnel carrier, an antique from last century. He recalls an eccentric farmer down in the Central West who used a restored tank as a poor man's bulldozer to clear trees. But the APC doesn't look like it's going anywhere: there is a tarpaulin attached to one side and a clothes line stretching out from the other. Under the shade of the tarpaulin, someone has welded a barbecue to the vehicle's metal plating.

Again he hears the voices coming from the railway carriage, but as he approaches he realises they're originating from somewhere beyond it. He walks around the side of the carriage, past a chicken coop and a greenhouse, its roof opened up to let the heat out. Above it, there's a squat windmill, pumping water into a pond boasting water lilies and a couple of fat carp. Beyond the carriage, there's a raised platform, topped by a large hot tub, sheltered by shade cloth. He climbs the stairs and finds three men, apparently naked, sitting in the tub, drinking beer from long-neck bottles. All are well into middle age, all have impressive beards, one of them plaited. With their earrings and tattoos, their beards and their bottles, they look like pirates. Ivan checks his watch: ten thirty, Monday morning. Early in the day to be drinking, even for Blackbeard.

The laughter stops and the three men eye him cautiously.

'Not a place for tourists, mate,' says the biggest of the three.

'I'm not a tourist. I'm a cop. Looking for Stanley Honeywell.'

'Not here, mate. Working at the coalmine. Cuttamulla. Back in a few days.'

'Thanks. Which is his place?'

There's no response. Then: 'Who's asking?'

Ivan pulls out his wallet, shows the badge. 'Ivan Lucic. Homicide.'

The big man nods his comprehension. 'Jonas McGee,' is all he says.

'That's right,' says Ivan.

'You got a warrant?' asks the man.

'No.'

The big man smiles. His two front teeth shimmer in the light, catching Ivan off guard. They're made from opal, colours shifting on white. 'It's the green shed, over that direction. A hundred metres.' And then he adds, 'Just stick to the homicide, okay? Leave the rest to us.'

'Sure,' says Ivan. 'Who are you?'

'I'm the mayor.'

'Of Deadmans Well?'

'Correct.' The man takes a chug of his beer, smiles his opalescent smile. 'It's unofficial.'

'No kidding. When was the last time you saw Honeywell?'

'Not for a couple of weeks. He reckons the tucker is better at Cuttamulla.'

Ivan looks about him, wondering if there is any more mileage to be had talking to three pirates in a tub. 'Okay, thanks again.'

'Bring yer bathers next time.'

✳

There's not much to Stanley Honeywell's home. It is indeed a shed, a small prefabricated building clad in some sort of artificial weatherboard, dyed green, sited under the boughs of what looks like an oak tree, its leaves incongruously verdant against the bleached stone of the ridge. Ivan walks under the shade of the tree, squats, places his hand on the ground. It's moist; water is coming from somewhere.

He returns his attention to the shack. There are two windows and a sloping iron roof. The door is sealed by a large padlock. A small cactus garden grows by the door, enclosed by a circle of bricks, painted white. He walks around the back, finds an outhouse, leaning precariously, as if the next strong wind will collapse it, and a goat on a long rope, grazing happily amid a patch of lush grass. And there's another windmill turning slowly in the breeze, another rock pool. Ivan runs his hands through the water. It's cold to the touch, refreshing. He puts his hand to his lips; it bears a chalky taint, almost pleasurable. He gets it now: Deadmans Well, artesian water.

He considers the lock, contemplates breaking in. But it's the man who's important, not his home. If Nell places him near Jonas's mine at a time even close to last Tuesday, they can get a warrant and come back, or bring the man himself back here. Ivan takes a last look. The place is neat, modest, peaceful, with the sound of cool water and the shade of an oak tree. For just a moment, he feels a touch of envy: life looks uncomplicated for Stanley Honeywell.

— —

Nell is back in her car, out on the highway, heading south once more, the same road on which she chased down Merv Claxton and his shiny limousine. Recalling her pursuit, it occurs to her she'll soon be out of phone range. The thought slows her. Another half an hour before she gets to Cuttamulla Coal, an hour back. What if Stanley Honeywell is not actually there? What would Ivan Lucic think of her then, wasting so much time on this critical first full day of their investigation? 'Shit,' she whispers aloud, hitting the brakes and pulling the car over onto the gravel verge. Just in time: her phone shows just one bar.

She looks up the number for the coalmine, rings it. There's the usual bouncing around: a receptionist, a PA then, finally, the shift manager, a man called Penuch.

'Not here,' he says. 'Didn't show for his shift.'

'What time was that?'

'Midnight.'

'You're twenty-four seven?'

'Of course.'

'When was he last seen?'

'Finished his previous shift at noon yesterday. That's all I know.'

'Is there any way to determine if he's left the mine site?'

'Yeah. From what I can tell, he's not here. Give me your number; I'll double-check and get back to you.'

'Thanks for that. And if there is some sort of record of comings and goings, can you check if he was at the mine all day on Tuesday?'

'Tuesday last week?'

'Yes. Between Monday night and Tuesday night.'

'I'll see what I can do,' says the manager. 'There should be a digital record of who comes and goes through the gate. All staff swipe in and out.'

She gives the man her number, thanks him, then ends the call. She rings Ivan, but he doesn't pick up. So she texts him: *Honeywell not at Cuttamulla. Didn't show for midnight shift.* And then, as an afterthought: *Returning to station.*

— —

The gates to the compound of the Rapture have been fashioned out of black iron. Not actual gates, nothing that can be opened or closed, but an archway, a declaration you are entering the church's territory, that past here, it's their beliefs that hold sway. Each pillar is adorned with a cross of polished steel, with another at the centre of the archway itself, above the driveway. They flare brightly in the sun; three crosses, like Calvary. The size of the gate is impressive: high and wide, large enough to accommodate a bus or a truck. To Ivan's eye, there is something austere about the structure, slightly forbidding, as if it defends a rigid faith, not a loving one. That's reinforced by the fence that adjoins it: two metres high, supported by galvanised-steel posts, giving the compound more the look of a low-security prison than a religious retreat. It's the first fence he can recall seeing on the ridges. The miners use pegs to mark territory; there is nothing to stop people, trucks and wildlife from roaming freely. Except here, at the Rapture.

He parks the Kia by the fence outside the gates, puts his gun in his messenger bag and locks it in the car; no need to appear confrontational. He puts on his hat as he climbs out, adjusts his sunnies and holds his breath as he sprays himself with repellent. This is one to do on foot, for unshielded assessment. He walks through the gate into a large open space, buildings arranged facing him in a semicircle. There is no one to see, nothing to hear, just the wind coming in from the west, hot and parchment-dry. At the centre of the open space is a fountain, not working, an ugly thing, amateur in construction, melding two garden-centre nymphs. They hold aloft not pitchers but another metal cross. Presumably, if the fountain were working, the cross would be spewing water. As he walks closer, he sees some green-tinged puddles in its base, as if the fountain might run every few days. Maybe only on Sundays. He watches as a couple of wasps dive and dip, scooping water for the construction of some nearby nest. The wind is blowing through, lifting dust, but the wasps hover and adjust expertly.

There is a church, made of weatherboard, painted a luminous white. There are more burnished crosses: one each on its double doors, another above the lintel, a fourth at the peak of the roof. Next to the church, to the left, is an area paved with concrete flagstones. There's some sort of baptismal font, a repurposed plunge pool, complete with its own altar. Flies swarm around it, attracted by the moisture. To the left again, towards the perimeter fence and separated from the rest of the buildings, is an imposing home, made of brick, painted the same glowing white as the church, with a terracotta-tiled roof and twin white pillars holding up a portico, like a McMansion that has calved off from the suburbs and drifted westwards. Back the other way, about halfway round the semicircle, on the other side of the church, is a hall, clad with fibre-cement sheeting, adorned with neither crosses nor paint. To its right are two low huts facing each other, accommodation at a guess; washing is hanging from lines on their verandahs, catching dust.

Beyond this, across a patch of open ground, the buildings grow larger. There's a machinery shed, two storeys high, made of steel, professionally constructed. Past it, at the end of the row, is another metal shed, wide rather than high. The hall, the barracks, the work sheds all have solar panels on their roofs. They'll be generating a lot of power on a day like this, possibly a lot of money. After the ad hockery of Deadmans Well, the Rapture's compound looks neat and orderly, well planned and well cared for. The turning circle where Ivan is standing has been raked. But to him, it doesn't seem like a happy place; it feels more functional than joyous.

He can smell cooking wafting on the wind, maybe coming from the accommodation huts. Onions frying, and garlic. And now comes the sound of hammering, metal on metal, and then a mechanical rumble, clanking to life from the direction of the machinery shed. He goes there, seeking the source of the noise, seeking people, but there is no movement in the dark interior. He can still hear the hammering, the clanging and scraping, and the low hum of electricity. The medley is coming from behind the shed.

He walks around, following a vehicle track that runs through the vacant land between the machinery shed and the accommodation huts. As he walks, he finds himself looking out into space, the blue sky with little to hold it up: the Rapture's land sits on the very edge of the ridge, before it falls away to the plain. Rounding the shed, he sees a cement mixer revolving, the sort that turns slowly on the back of concrete delivery trucks. This one has been transplanted onto its own stationary steel chassis. A young man and woman are working together, shovelling rocks into the maw of the rotating cylinder. Both have tattoos on their arms: crosses. They're dressed in shorts and singlets, deeply tanned limbs aglow with perspiration in the heat of the day, only their hats, gloves and work boots offering protection. Another couple stand looking on, one holding a lever, presumably controlling the mixer, the other a fireman's hose.

The scene is somehow silent, an animated tableau, no one talking, just the rumble of the machinery, rocks clanging inside the metal drum. Ivan sees cables running off into a shed: solar power. One of the young women—the hose holder, not the shoveller—sees him. She stands erect, arching her back, somehow defiant, looks at him long and hard, then returns to her work, ignoring his presence, opening up the hose nozzle, directing water into the slowly spinning drum. She too has a cross tattooed on her arm.

He walks closer, but still they take no notice of him, intent on their work. As he stops to watch, the youth controlling the lever removes a glove, places his fingers in his mouth and issues a whistle, shrill and penetrating, bringing the diggers to a halt. He pulls a lever, stops the cylinder from revolving. The four of them take hold, swinging it across and down, before stepping back. The man starts working the lever: the cylinder starts to tilt down towards a tower of huge sieves. He lowers the drum further and it begins to rotate again. It lowers again and a slurry starts to pour out and onto the sieves. The others gather around, raking at the mix with their shovels as it runs out across the wire mesh. Ivan understands what they're doing: breaking down the mudstone, straining out the nobbies on the sieves, looking for opals. He can see the waste water running off the side of the ridge, down towards the world below, like effluent from heaven. He watches as they continue to work the sludge down through the strainers, clearing it of potential finds one by one. When the cylinder is empty, he walks up to them, too close to ignore.

'I'm looking for the Seer,' he says.

The young woman who first saw him answers. 'In the house, or in the church. He won't be anywhere else.'

'Thanks.'

'No phones,' says the woman. 'No phones allowed in the compound.'

'Right. Understood.'

Ivan walks back the way he came, deciding to try the house first. It looks so clean, pristine compared to the muddy work of separating treasure from dirt. There is an iron doorknocker, a Christian fish symbol, hanging vertically, the hinge at its nose. He gives it a brisk bang. There is no response, just flies, testing his protective cloud of repellent. He knocks again.

The door is answered by a pretty young woman with crinkled blonde hair, modestly dressed in a white smock dress, with crucifix earrings that match the tattoo on her arm. When he identifies himself and inquires after the Seer, she asks him politely to wait just inside the door, then she moves further into the house.

A few minutes later she's back. 'He'll see you. This way, please.'

The Seer stands as Ivan enters. He's small and wiry, wearing a white Western shirt with seams of black thread and a black string tie held by an opal-faced clip. His belt buckle is large and silver, depicting Christ on the cross. The crucifix is also fashioned from opal, shimmering in the light. The image seizes Ivan's attention, a flashback: Jonas McGee hanging, his blood black. The Seer's hair is dark with streaks of grey and oiled back, his face weathered, his eyes like deep brown pools. He moves his hands in a gesture of benediction; they look soft, his nails clean. 'Bless you,' he says. To Ivan, he looks more like an ageing country and western star than a preacher; Willie Nelson with better teeth. There is an assumption of superiority in the man's body language, in the confidence of his movements and the authority in his eyes. But to Ivan, the size of the room emphasises the Seer's diminutive size rather than enhancing his stature. It's spacious and opulent and impeccably clean, furnished with lounges of white leather and glass-topped tables, a gilded chandelier and a cream carpet of deep pile. It makes Ivan feel scruffy; he resists the impulse to remove his shoes. There are picture windows, looking south, out across the plain, a view that goes forever. A celestial view. There's a large woman sitting on one of the white sofas, back straight, wearing an old-fashioned dress, about the same age as the Seer; Ivan would place them in their sixties.

'Please have a seat,' says the Seer. His voice is sonorous and deep, much deeper than might be expected to issue from such a small frame.

Ivan sits and the young woman in the smock dress returns, carrying a tray of drinks. As she lowers the tray, Ivan's attention is again drawn to the tattoo on her left arm. He takes a small glass, surprised to smell strong alcohol. He looks from the girl to the Seer to the older woman, wondering what the relationship here is, what control the man might exercise over his followers.

The holy man takes a glass from the tray, quaffs it. 'Please,' he says to Ivan. 'Join us in celebrating the spirit.'

Ivan takes a sip. It's strong, like vodka, but with a raw edge, possibly homemade. The others are watching him expectantly. He sculls the shot, resists coughing, the liquid flaring on his tonsils, even as he questions why he is complying.

'How can I help you, officer?'

'I'm investigating the murder of Jonas McGee.'

'I heard. The miner who was crucified. Quite a ways from here. Why would you ask me about it?'

'Did you know him?'

'Once upon a time I did, yes. Before he strayed.'

'Strayed? From here?'

'He used to visit. Him and his wife. They were attracted, but they never fully committed. They wanted to take what we offered but not to give in return.'

'How so?'

'They kept their own business, their own mine. Their own lives.'

'That's not an option?'

'Part-time Christians can go to part-time churches. There are plenty of those.' There is an edge to the man's voice, not of anger or irritation, but of judgement.

'You don't approve?'

'Hate the sin, love the sinner,' says the Seer. The man stares at him. There is a flickering in his eyes, as if they are juddering of their own volition. Ivan feels disconcerted. The Seer continues: 'He lapsed. He failed to commit. Little wonder those women died; it was upon his head.'

Ivan bites his lip, taken aback. Keeping an open mind is vital to criminal investigations, remaining willing to entertain new possibilities. Perhaps that's why he feels affronted by this man's closed mind, his righteousness. Ivan has spent enough time in courtrooms, seen juries wrestle with questions of guilt, labouring for hours, for days, conflicted as they declare guilt or innocence, unsure whether they have reached the right decision. And yet here is this man, condemning with lazy self-assurance, with entitlement. Ivan keeps his voice even, professional. 'McGee's crucifixion suggests religious belief may have played a part in his killing.'

'So you think of us? What about the churches in town? That desiccated old heretic at St Andrew's? Or the Catholics?'

'I spoke to Father Vale yesterday.'

'I'll bet you did.'

The Seer signals to the girl, takes another glass of moonshine, this time sipping a little instead of downing the lot. He sucks the liquid back and forth through his teeth. If the man is drunk, there is no sign of it.

'I'll be talking to the Catholics as well.'

'Good. But I don't see how I can be of help.'

'When was the last time you saw him?'

'Jonas McGee?'

'Yes.'

'Years ago. Five years, eight years, ten years. A long time.'

'That's hard to believe, small town like this.'

'We keep to ourselves up here. This is consecrated land. Protected. I seldom leave. I don't mix with sinners; it's important I keep myself pure.' He sips a little more alcohol; maybe that's the point of it: a prophylactic, guarding against Ivan inadvertently contaminating the house with his unholy presence.

'Jonas was a sinner?' asks Ivan. 'You sound very sure.'

'We're all sinners, officer. You included.'

'And you?'

The Seer avoids the question. 'I see people's auras, you realise. I see into their hearts.' His eyebrows are raised now, almost taunting Ivan, while his voice resonates as if addressing his congregation. 'But people like you, you are all grey. Grey people believe in nothing.

Your auras are pale and hazy, lacking light and colour and definition. Without value, like potch. Jonas was quite different. His aura
was vivid, like a rare opal.'

Ivan keeps his scepticism at bay. 'How so?'

'He was a believer. Always a believer. But troubled. Fated.
Volatile.'

'Believing in what?'

The Seer replies in a voice falling into the patterns of preaching,
as if reciting from the scriptures. 'For he saw salvation, but rejected
it. For he might have walked with angels, yet he spurned them.
For he could have entered the kingdom of heaven, yet he turned
the other way.' The Seer holds his position for a moment, apparently for effect. 'That is worse, so much worse, than a grey man
like yourself, a non-believer, forever denied paradise. He saw it,
he knew it, and still he rejected it. He drank and he gambled
and he fornicated. He crashed his car, he killed his wife, he killed
her sister. And it was in his aura all along, I saw it there, I foresaw
it: the bright red streak of the damned. Like a black opal streaked
with blood.'

Ivan chooses his words carefully, not wanting to antagonise the
man or incite more nonsense. 'Father, could someone else know
that about him? See his aura? Decide that he deserved crucifixion?'

'Oh no. It is a rare gift, a precious gift.' The Seer leans forward.
'And he did not deserve crucifixion. That's for saints, not for the
damned.'

Despite himself, Ivan takes a sip of his poteen, giving himself
time to think. Its rawness burns at his tongue. He chooses his
words carefully, as he broaches the same line of questioning he
put to Reverend Vale. 'Every ministry takes in lost souls. Troubled

people come to churches, seeking solace, seeking guidance. Seeking salvation. It's a great service to the community that you render, taking them in, caring for them. Sometimes, those people struggle with psychosis. I'm sure you know what I mean.'

The Seer's mouth has curved into a sneer. 'I'm not sure I do.'

'Do any of your disciples experience such issues? Violent tendencies, or psychotic episodes? Hearing voices, that sort of thing?'

The Seer stares, eyes flickering more noticeably. There is a touch of menace in his voice as he answers. 'Hearing voices is a sign of divinity. I myself have heard the voice of God.'

Ivan stares into the shimmering eyes, feels momentarily trapped by their logic, before turning it back on the Seer. He drops his voice, almost to a whisper, imbued with import. 'But the devil can also talk, can also whisper into the minds of the unrighteous, the vulnerable, the weak—those who lack your piety.'

The brown eyes go wide. 'You believe he is here? Beelzebub? Here, at Finnigans Gap?'

'A man has been crucified,' says Ivan, straight-faced.

The Seer rises to his feet, arms outstretched, voice stentorian. There are marks on his hands, brown circles, like the remnants of stigmata. 'I will cleanse! I will exorcise him! If there are demons here, I will find them. If they lurk in the shadows, in the hearts of the unworthy, then I will banish them!'

The Seer sits again, eyes flaring and darting as he sculls more alcohol, as if to safeguard his soul, before falling to his knees, praying aloud. The two women also kneel, demonstrative in prayer. Ivan glances at his watch, wonders how long the show will go for, and stands.

'Pray!' commands the Seer. 'On your knees and pray!'

Ivan says nothing. Just gives him an icy stare, long enough for him to read his aura. Then he turns, walks to the door and lets himself out. He doesn't like fundamentalists, he doesn't like this place, he especially doesn't like the Seer. But he needs to keep his balance, to keep his perspective. He stands in the shade of the portico, trying to regain his centre, trying to suppress his distaste. He's still standing there, looking at the garden-centre fountain, when the door opens. It's the older woman. She steps out to join him. Now, as he meets her eyes, he can see intelligence there, the sort of pragmatism the Seer so patently lacks.

'My husband had nothing to do with the death of Jonas McGee. We have had nothing to do with that man for decades. But he did come back here, once. Years ago.'

'McGee?'

'His daughter was here, seeking shelter. He attempted to take her away.'

'What happened?'

'She left. Not with him, but she left. We never saw her again. And we never saw him again.' She lets that sink in. 'The Seer hasn't left the compound for years. His followers seldom do. Only to mine for opals. All of our mines are close by, here on the East Ridge. I go to town once a week, take some helpers, do the shopping, get supplies, sell our opals. I can assure you, no one from here has been anywhere near the West Ridge for many, many years.'

She doesn't wait for Ivan to respond, but re-enters the house, shutting the door behind her. It closes with a pneumatic wheeze, as if sealing off the outside world. He's left alone in the burgeoning heat. The flies descend and he can hear the rumble of the opal extractor in the distance. The encounter with the Seer has left him feeling a quiet anger, but he can see little justification in investigating the Rapture any further.

chapter ten

IVAN RETURNS TO THE POLICE STATION, FINDS NELL TYPING AWAY FRENETICALLY on an old-fashioned computer, punching the keys with intensity. A takeaway coffee cup is on the table. 'This for me?' he asks.

'Yep.'

'Thanks.' It's stone-cold, but he takes a sip nevertheless, just to show his gratitude. It tastes surprisingly good. 'You seem fired up. What's happened?'

'Cuttamulla. They just got back to me. Confirmed that Stanley Honeywell didn't show for his shift last night, that he drove out of the mine around nine pm and hasn't been seen since. But get this: they also reckon he left the mine last Tuesday.'

Ivan lowers the coffee, eyes meeting Nell's. 'And he's on the run?'

Her face says it all; their most important lead, their only suspect, has disappeared. 'Not answering his phone. Shall I put out an alert?'

'How far's the Queensland border?'

'Forty-five minutes.' She nods her comprehension: a statewide alert throughout New South Wales is routine; an interstate request requires paperwork.

'Everyone we've spoken to reckons he's a gentle giant, incapable of violence,' says Ivan, throwing the statement out, inviting debate.

'So they say. But he wasn't in prison for fare evasion. He has a record of criminal violence as long as your arm,' Nell responds. 'Something might have pushed him over the edge, made him regress. Or maybe it was an accident. A big guy like that, a bit simple-minded, doesn't know his own strength. One blow. That bruise on McGee's face. So not murder, maybe manslaughter. But if he killed him, he killed him.'

'Doesn't really matter, does it? We need to find him.'

'I've just done a rego check. He owns a kombi van.'

'A hippie coalminer?'

'It means he's mobile. He can sleep anywhere.'

Ivan is still staring, realises his eyes have rested on her face for too long. A bad habit of his. 'Ask the mine for the times he was absent on Tuesday. When he left, when he got back. That's critical.' He's already doing the mental arithmetic: an hour from Cuttamulla to Finnigans Gap, possibly longer in an old van, another fifteen or twenty minutes out to Jonas's stake. The same going back. That's two and a half hours at the very least. Plus another half-hour to kill McGee. So he'd need to have been away from Cuttamulla for three hours or more, in the early hours of Tuesday morning. And if he killed McGee and then waited to crucify him, he'd need at least seven hours away from the coal mine.

Ivan takes a seat, again locking eyes with Nell as his mind whirls. Now he understands why she was buzzing when he entered; he feels it too, the case coming together. 'I called in at Deadmans Well. His place is all locked up. Hasn't been seen there for a week or more, according to the bloke who calls himself mayor. So if he left the mine Tuesday, there is no evidence he went to Deadmans.' He can feel the conviction strengthening within him: Stanley is their man. Either that, or he's going to have vital information. 'Okay. We need to find him. Issue the alert. Queensland as well.'

'On to it.'

'But first, tell me about the limo.'

'It's a hire car out of Dubbo. Driver is Sydney-based, a former copper called Merv Claxton. You heard of him?'

An image comes to him, a vague memory of a large man, full of himself, but he can't place the memory. 'Maybe. What did he tell you?'

'He's been driving a group of Asian investors around. Thinks they're Chinese but isn't sure. He took them up to the ridge near McGee's mine a couple of times. They've been checking out that rare-earths mine that Kyle Torshack pointed out.'

'Sound legit to you?'

'Yeah. It does. Sounds like they've cut a deal with that bloke we saw shouting the bar at the bowlo. His name is Robert Inglis, a billionaire. Here, I found this.' She hands him a sheet of A4, a printout of a story from the *Australian Financial Review* website. The time stamp indicates the story was published less than an hour ago.

BOB'S RARE-EARTH COUP: NO BULLSHIT
By Larry Griggs

In a spectacular twelfth-hour manoeuvre, Australian mining magnate Robert 'Bullshit Bob' Inglis is set to take control of the highly fancied Kalingra Rare Earths prospect near the opal-mining centre of Finnigans Gap in northern New South Wales.

Kalingra is a private company, but excitement was ignited late last year when it announced its intention to float on the stock market. At the time, it was widely rumoured Chinese investors were taking a cornerstone stake, but in a statement to the stock exchange before the opening of trade on Monday, Inglis declared his private holding company, Bulldust Investments, is set to acquire a 100 per cent stake in Kalingra.

It is not yet known whether Inglis intends to float the company through an initial public offering (IPO), listing Kalingra as a company in its own right, or whether the billionaire intends folding it into his majority-owned Wide Valley Resources. A third option would be to run it as a separate, private entity.

The investment at Kalingra represents a major change of direction for Inglis, diversifying away from the base metals strategy that has seen Wide Valley emerge as a leading second-tier producer of iron ore and copper.

It's also a geographical repositioning, with all of Wide Valley's existing assets located in Western Australia.

Rare-earth tenements have become highly desirable during the past decade, after China first imposed export restrictions in 2010. Although those trade embargoes were later lifted, China's increasingly aggressive trade posture under President Xi Jinping has renewed the international scramble for the sought-after metals.

China currently controls 80 per cent of global rare-earth extraction and close to 100 per cent of downstream processing, sparking strategic angst within the United States Administration and Congress, as well as the wider western defence community. The metals are used in a number of sensitive high-tech applications, including aerospace, computing, ceramics, high-performance magnets and weapons systems.

The recent increase in Sino–US tension has led to a tripling in the share price in the past twelve months of Australia's only significant existing rare-earth producer, LikeUs Pty Ltd, based in South Australia.

Should Kalingra become operational, it has the potential to provide a much-needed boost to the nearby opal-mining town of Finnigans Gap, where gem production is rumoured to be in decline. The town has long been seen as the poor cousin of nearby Lightning Ridge, with smaller, lower-quality opal deposits.

It's likely that, in the future, the local community will become increasingly dependent on the fortunes of Kalingra and Delaney Bullwinkel's nearby Cuttamulla Coal. It could make for an entertaining time at the town's bowling club, given the chequered history between the two billionaires.

'Bullshit Bob,' says Ivan, finishing the report. 'Explains the chant as he was sculling beers in the bowlo last night. Explains why he was shouting the bar.' Ivan gestures with the printout of the newspaper story. 'It's interesting, but where exactly does this leave us?'

'Nowhere significant, if you ask me,' Nell replies. 'The Chinese had a legitimate reason to be up on the ridge overlooking Kalingra. And it fits with what I saw at the airport this morning: Inglis and the Chinese shaking hands, bowing and smiling. He must have bought them out. All very merry. There's no obvious connection between them and Jonas. Put it this way: why would a bunch of Chinese suits climb down an opal mine and crucify an opal miner?'

Ivan can't help but agree. 'Yeah. I think we can put it on the backburner. Stanley Honeywell has to be our priority.'

'Agreed. How about you? How was the Seer?'

'A whacko. A waste of time, crapping on about reading auras. Claims he never leaves the compound.'

'So rule him out?'

'No. Not entirely. He reckons he knew Jonas from years ago. Gave me chapter and verse about his aura. And according to his wife, Jonas's daughter Elsie sheltered there at one stage. Did you ever get hold of that AVO?'

Nell turns back to her computer, works at the database. 'Yeah. Here it is. Eight years ago. Jonas was prohibited from going within a hundred metres of her. No record of him breaching it. It lapsed after six months.'

'We still need to speak to her. Have we heard anything?'

'I'll check with Vince,' says Nell.

'He around?'

'Think so.'

'What about Garry? He was checking out the miners.'

'Yeah, I've got his list here.' She waves a piece of paper. 'Names and mobile numbers. Now Blake has given us an approximate time of death, I've asked Garry to get back to them, see if any of them were out there Tuesday morning.'

'Excellent. But we'll need to double-check. Run the phones through tracking.' He grimaces; the phone companies aren't always prompt in their cooperation. 'Anything from Richter on the ratters?'

She shakes her head, expression neutral. 'Nothing yet.'

'Right.' Ivan doesn't like being dependent on the senior constable but can't see any immediate alternative. 'I'll be right back.' He walks out, down the corridor to the other end of the building, enters the open-plan squad room. Richter and Vince are at their desks.

'Morning, gents,' says Ivan.

'Morning,' says Vince. Richter merely grunts.

'Vince, have you been able to speak to Elsie McGee?'

'Only by text. Turns out she's in Los Angeles. She's married, goes by her husband's name. Claremont.'

Ivan swallows his irritation. Vince should have told him this; he shouldn't have to come asking. 'Does she live there now?'

'No, just visiting.'

'What did you say in your text?'

'Asked her to contact us. That it's important, concerning her father. I texted your name and details. Yours and Nell's.'

'Good work. Did she share any other contact details? A US number, email?'

'No. You want me to ask?'

'Please.' Ivan turns to Richter. 'Any news on the ratters?'

The veteran policeman shrugs. 'I've put the word out. But don't hold your breath.'

Ivan is just thinking how to respond when the probationary constable, Garry Ahern, comes in. 'Oh. Sergeant Lucic. You're here.' He reaches into his breast pocket, extracts a post-it note. 'There was some crank on the phone just now, says he has an anonymous tip for you. Insisted it was important.'

'How do you know he was a crank?'

'Because he was banging on about contrails, QAnon and the vaccine. I told him I'd let you know.'

'Thanks, but I've had my fill of loonies for one day.'

'Here.' Garry hands him the note. 'I promised I'd give you his number.'

'Mission accomplished, then,' says Ivan. He glances at it as he starts to crumple it in his hand. A number. And a line of text: *The revenge of the old guard.* He carefully smooths it out. Reads it again. Sure enough, it's the exact same phrase Morris Montifore used the previous morning. 'When did this bloke call?'

'Ten minutes ago. Says he'll only speak to you. Why, is it important?'

'Nah, just some loony.' He places the post-it note in his top pocket, refocuses, thanks the uniformed officers and returns to the office he shares with Nell.

'You okay?' she asks, seeming to pick up on his disquiet.

'Yeah. Fine.' He rests his eyes on her as he pushes thoughts of Montifore into the background and assesses their position. They can't just sit here, wait for someone to find Stanley Honeywell, wait for the ratters to get in contact, wait for Elsie McGee to call. They need to progress, to get out of the station, to find evidence. 'We need some warrants. Where can we find this registrar you mentioned?'

'Near the crossroads. I can do it—just let me get these alerts out.'

'Goodo. I want to access metadata from Stanley's phone: his list of contacts, calls and messages for the past two weeks, and tracking data, if it's there. See if he's been at the coalmine for the past nine days; if Tuesday was the only time he left there. If we can place Stanley up on the West Ridge last Tuesday, that might be the clincher. Do the same for Jonas's phone while you're at it, and the Torshacks. Plus the miners Garry interviewed.'

'Got it. Okay if I run Merv Claxton as well? The chauffeur?'

'Yes. Good thinking.' Ivan smiles, impressed. 'Also, bank accounts. Stanley and Jonas. Let's see if it's true Jonas was enjoying a windfall from his opals. Money might be a motive.'

'Will do. Mind you, some of these miners, it's strictly cash.' She jots down a few notes to herself. 'The registrar is a good guy. Shouldn't be a problem this early in the day.'

'How's that?'

'Likes a drink. Always playing golf.'

'Terrific.'

'What are you going to do?' asks Nell.

'I need to talk to Carole and Blake,' he says. Which is true enough, as far as it goes.

But he doesn't go searching for the forensics team, not straight away. Instead he walks to the crossroads, turns left onto The Way, finds the electrical goods store. This time of day, there is no one on the streets; mad dogs and Homicide cops. And flies. By the time he gets to the store he is covered in them. He needs more repellent; they seem to be developing resistance to the stuff the garage owner gave him.

The temperature inside the shop feels twenty degrees cooler, a potent advertisement for the air conditioners that crowd the display windows and present like an honour guard along the aisle down the centre of the store. Them and fridges, large, small and portable. The top-load washers, the dishwashers, the stoves and the widescreen TVs are further back, the second division. There are a couple of people casually examining the wares; Ivan wonders if they're genuine customers or merely refugees from the heat. There's a woman behind the counter applying nail polish with focused intent.

'You sell phones?'

'Yep. Androids, iPhones, the lot. All the latest models.'

'Actually, I'm after a cheap one. A dumb one. Pay as you go. Phone calls and SMS only.'

The woman looks up from her polish application. 'You the Homicide cop? Don't they give you a phone?'

'Of course. But only for work-related purposes. MobiPol phones. They're very strict about it. Taxpayers' money. And security.'

'Is that so?'

'My girlfriend is overseas. I've copped a slap on the wrist for calling her too much.'

The woman smiles. 'Overseas? You'll need plenty of credit then. You can load up here.'

'Yeah. Maybe. We thought it might be cheaper if she calls me.'

'Where is she?'

He takes a stab. 'Singapore.'

'Yeah, that makes sense then,' she says, grinning like a shit-house rat, making sure he knows she doesn't believe him. But that doesn't stop her selling him the phone, once her nails are dry enough for her to fossick one out from a locked cabinet. He realises the whole town is going to know he bought a burner, but can't see what he can do about it. He could request confidentiality, although that might make his purchase all the more gossip-worthy.

Back on the street, he's thinking of finding a park, somewhere with shade. Every town has one, with lawn, picnic tables, a playground, a toilet block, public barbecues, maybe an Anzac memorial with a flagpole and rocks with plaques. He checks his phone, the official one, but Google Maps gives him nothing. No park. What sort of town doesn't have a park? The sort of town that doesn't have trees.

He sits under the awning of an opal shop. He gets the phone out, inserts the sim. It has five dollars credit. It takes him a moment to set up, then he draws a deep breath and sends a text to the number on the post-it note. *The new guard.* A minute later the burner rings, overly loud and chirpy.

'Ivan Lucic,' he answers.

'Ivan. Morris.'

'So I guessed. What's with all the cloak-and-dagger?'

'I wanted you to know I'm now officially under investigation. Professional Standards. They might be tapping your work phone—and wanting to interview you.'

Montifore's voice is matter-of-fact, a briefing, just like they're working a case. It takes Ivan a moment to recalibrate. Around him the town is glowing, sunlight pouring down, bouncing off the hard surfaces, all the concrete and bitumen. It doesn't look quite real, like a floodlit stage. 'What is it, Morris? What's the allegation?'

'Talking to the media. Leaking. Compromising prosecutions.'

'What?' Ivan can't suppress his laugh, the expression of disgust. 'You're kidding? Feeding the media is part of the job description.'

'Only if the brass like what you're saying.'

'That's it? That journo, Martin Scarsden. The shitshow last year with the Attorney-General and his corrupt mates. Surely you'll beat it.'

'Not if they don't want me to. And I'm pretty sure they don't want me to. They want to make an example of me. Chances are I'm going down, but I want to make sure you aren't collateral damage.'

'This is bullshit, Morris.'

'If I go, I want it to be on my terms, not theirs. That's what I'm angling for now. A package, a good one, not a sacking. If they want me gone, they can pay the freight.'

'So you're reconciled to it?' There is incredulity in Ivan's voice; he can hear it, so Montifore must. The guy lived and breathed his work; Ivan can't imagine him as a civilian, retired. Where could he possibly direct that intellect, that passion, that commitment?

'I wouldn't say reconciled, but there's not much I can do. The writing's on the wall. The important thing is this: if they interview you—*when* they interview you—you have to tell the truth. That's how you inoculate yourself. No point in putting your career in jeopardy when I'm already a dead man walking. Deny knowledge, or blame everything on me. Just don't lie.'

'Can't you fight it?'

'No, I don't think I can. But I don't regret any of it. I knew what I was doing. What we did, the result we got, that was worth sacrificing a career. We did more in a couple of weeks than others have managed in a generation. I'll never get the chance to do something so important again.'

'Scarsden. That's why you always kept me out of the room when you talked to him. I thought it was because you didn't trust me.'

'Don't blame him, Ivan. He's done as much as anyone to drain the swamp.'

'Yeah, if you say so.' He thinks about the journalist. He never liked him, never trusted him. Just like all journos, in it for what they could get, ethically absent. 'Okay. Well, thanks for the warning.' He thinks it over. 'I guess that's why they sent me out here. To get me out of town.'

There's a momentary silence. 'No, I don't think so. Coincidental. They had me slated for it. I was on my way to the airport when Professional Standards pulled the pin.'

'You? Out here? Why?'

'I've been there before.'

'What?'

'It's a long story, Ivan. A wild-goose chase. Young bloke wandered off and died. Death by misadventure. Seven years ago.'

'What happened?' But as Ivan looks up and along the street, he can see Nell running. Running. In this weather. 'Listen, Morris. I'll need to call you back.'

'Sure. Anytime. But not the work phones.'

Now Nell sees him, changes direction, stops running, walks briskly across the street to him. Her face is awash with sweat and urgency. She is grasping something in her hand.

'Are they the warrants?'

She looks momentarily perplexed. 'Uh, yeah. Got 'em.'

'So why are you running?'

'The hospital. Stanley Honeywell is there. Checked himself in last night.'

chapter eleven

THE HOSPITAL IS MUCH AS SHE REMEMBERS IT: A SINGLE-STOREY BUILDING, modern and purpose-built, exuding the gloss of government money. She leads the way, flipping her badge at the receptionist, getting directions to the ward. Ivan is tailing along, seemingly distracted, the piercing blue eyes unfocused for once. She wonders what he was doing, sitting talking on the phone in the heat, why he isn't more switched on. Surely this is the critical moment, when their investigation could pivot from guesswork towards prosecution.

Stanley is massive. It's the first thing that strikes her: just how huge he is. He dwarfs the narrow hospital bed, threatening either to tip out of it or collapse it. He's not just tall, but big with it. Not muscle-bound big, not the sculpted definition of a gym junkie, but softer and rounder with curved shoulders, carrying weight, suggesting great strength and ponderous power; the sort of strength that could seriously damage a lesser man. One of his feet is draped over the railing at the foot of the bed, another hangs out the side. He is too large for the bed. Right now, he looks passive enough. And sorry enough. He has a black eye, purple against his dark skin, left hand bandaged and arm in a sling.

Ivan introduces himself and Nell as police officers, eliciting apprehension in the big man's face. It's a reaction Nell knows well: the panic of the habitual criminal, the reflex action, the look of guilt, not knowing what the police want but assuming it's something he's done. Ivan glances at Nell; she takes it as a prompt. She sits down on the one chair beside the bed, brings her eyes level with the patient, even as Ivan stays standing. 'Who did this to you, Stanley?' she asks gently.

'An accident.'

'What accident?' Nells asks.

'It was an accident. At Cuttamulla.'

She keeps her voice soft, non-confrontational. 'When was this?'

Stanley frowns. 'A pallet came off a truck. I got hit by boxes.'

'When?'

The frown deepens. 'Yesterday, I guess.'

'Isn't there a clinic at the mine?'

'Sure. It's good.'

'So why come here?'

'The union guy told me.'

'Why?'

'Workers comp. That's what he said.'

'To have an independent record?' asks Nell.

Stanley doesn't seem to grasp her point. 'I guess,' he says, sounding noncommittal.

'Right,' says Ivan, voice no-nonsense. 'You know what happened to Jonas McGee?'

The man's one good eye widens, then his face falls. There's something childlike about the wash of emotions, the lack of guile. 'Yeah, they told me.' There's grief there, sadness mixed with confusion, the suggestion he might start to cry, then an idea blooming. 'You after the killers?'

'That's right.'

'Wow,' he says. 'Like on TV.'

'Like on TV,' says Ivan, frowning as if struggling to assess the man. 'When did you find out?'

'What?'

'That Jonas was dead.'

'Oh.' That causes Stanley to frown again, as if pondering some difficult problem. 'Yesterday,' he says, and then repeats it, perhaps to reassure himself. 'Yesterday.'

'You think that's what distracted you? When the pallet hit you?'

Stanley looks confused, seemingly not able to connect the cause-and-effect Ivan is suggesting. And then, again, the blossoming of an answer. 'The union said it wasn't my fault.'

Nell takes over the questioning, voice soothing. 'Stanley, when you are on a shift, do you always stay at Cuttamulla?'

A smile breaks, revealing happiness and sporadic teeth. 'Shit, yeah. Good bed. Grub. Showers. It's all free!' And now he's beaming.

'And you've been rostered on, up until now?'

'Ten-day shift; I work ten-day shifts,' he says, pride in his voice. 'Last day tomorrow. Union says I still get paid, even if I'm here.'

'Good for the union,' says Nell, offering a supportive smile. 'Stanley, this is important. Last Tuesday, you left Cuttamulla. There's a record, when you swiped your card at the gate. You were driving your car, your kombi van. You remember that?'

Stanley shifts in his bed. To Nell, his discomfort is obvious. 'That was before the accident,' he says.

Nell looks to Ivan, whose eyes are still locked on the patient, still assessing. She turns back. 'It's not about your accident, Stanley. It's about the death of Jonas McGee. Where did you go last Tuesday when you left the mine?'

A glint comes to Stanley's eye, as if he's remembering a good joke. 'Home. I went home. To feed the goat. Harry the goat.'

Ivan has been holding back, but now he interjects. 'Did you go anywhere near Jonas McGee's mine?'

Stanley says nothing, just stares at Ivan, looking perplexed that his answer hasn't sufficed.

'Last Tuesday, when you left Cuttamulla, did you go to his opal mine?'

'No.'

'Did you see him?'

'No.'

'You call him?'

'I . . .' It's all he can get out.

Ivan leans forward, bringing his authority to bear, like a schoolmaster to a wayward pupil. 'I asked you a question. Did you phone Jonas McGee?'

Nell now can see sweat breaking out on the injured man's brow, wetting the edge of his bandage. 'I tried,' says Stanley. 'I tried.'

'He didn't answer?'

'No. But I tried.'

'Yes, you tried. And why were you calling him, Stanley? Why?'

The man is shaking his head, and now a tear does come to his eye. 'I don't know. I don't.' And he sobs, loud and clear; strong enough to make the bed shake.

Ivan leans back. Nells takes over. Despite herself, she reaches out, holds the man's hand. He doesn't hesitate, squeezing back, accepting its comfort. Her voice remains gentle. 'Do you have your phone with you?'

He nods, unable to speak for the moment.

'Can I see it, please?'

He releases her hand, reaches across to a bedside table, but can't manage the drawer with his bandaged hand. 'In there,' he says.

She swivels around, opens the drawer, finds the phone. It's an old model, cracked screen, seemingly held together by sticky tape and its Disney-character case. Mickey and Pluto. 'May I?' she asks.

'Uh-huh,' he agrees.

The phone is locked. She hands it to him. He opens it with fingerprint recognition, hands it back. She scrolls through it. It shows several calls made to Jonas during the week, none of them answered. Not just on the Tuesday, but in the days before and since. She hands it to Ivan so he can see for himself. If it's a ploy, an attempt to establish an alibi, it's a simple one. She looks at Stanley, wonders if he possesses the cunning to attempt such a thing.

Ivan keeps hold of the phone. 'Who are these other calls to? Who's Penuch?'

Stanley looks terrified. Nell answers for him. 'He's a shift manager at Cuttamulla. He's the one who told me Stanley was absent last Tuesday.'

Ivan dips his head in understanding, then addresses Stanley. 'He's your boss?'

'Yeah.'

'Don't mind if I take his number, do you?'

'Why?' Again, the sense of unrest in the big man.

'Why not? Is there a problem? I can always look it up.'

'Please don't.'

'What is it?' asks Nell. 'What are you afraid of?'

'The union told me not to speak to him. They will fix it.'

'I see.' She makes a quick decision, hopes Ivan will go with it. 'We won't call him then, okay? Not until the union says it's okay. But can I get his number, just in case?'

She has the impression he hasn't followed, that she has been talking too quickly, linking too many things. But he answers in the affirmative. 'I guess.' Maybe it's his go-to answer when he's unsure of what is being asked of him. *I guess.*

'Thank you,' she says, and forwards the mine manager's number to her own mobile, thereby giving her both Penuch's mobile and Stanley's number.

Ivan again inserts himself into the conversation. 'You still haven't told us why you left Cuttamulla last Tuesday. It wasn't just to feed the goat, was it?'

Stanley says nothing. He looks like a roo caught in the headlights, waiting to be run down. Ivan's eyes linger, his intimidating stare, but there is nothing from the man.

'We can find out,' says Nell, careful not to sound confrontational. 'Do you know how?'

Stanley shakes his head.

'Your phone can tell us. Wherever we take them, there's a record. If you fed your goat last Tuesday, your phone will tell us you were at Deadmans Well. If you were here in town, having lunch at the cafe, it will tell us. And if you went up to the West Ridge, to visit Jonas, it will tell us that as well.'

Stanley looks up at Ivan, as if for confirmation Nell is speaking the truth. Ivan nods his affirmation.

'So why not tell us, Stanley: where were you?' asks Ivan, voice reasonable.

'Not telling,' says Stanley, thrusting his lower lip out like a petulant schoolboy.

Ivan shakes his head. 'Either you tell us, or your phone will.'

'Still not telling.'

Nell reaches out again, takes his hand. He almost pulls it away, but then lets her. She speaks softly. 'If you weren't with Jonas, you can trust us. We promise we won't tell anyone else.'

'Cross your heart?'

'And hope to die.'

He looks up at Ivan, back at her, as if unable to come to a decision.

'Please, Stanley,' she says.

'I was here. In town.'

'Doing what?'

'Nothing much. Lunch.'

Ivan sighs. 'You sure? We can check your phone.'

'It's true,' says Stanley.

Ivan's eyes bore into him. 'And you swear you didn't see Jonas? Or go to his mine?'

'I swear.' And then, sweeping across his face, as if a nightmare has seized him, a look of abject terror. He pulls his hand back. 'You're not going to send me to prison, are you?'

'Not if you didn't kill anyone,' says Ivan.

'Promise?'

'Promise.' Ivan waits a second, maybe to let the message sink in, before continuing. 'Can you tell me, did Jonas have any enemies?'

Any remaining terror has gone, leaving as quickly as it came. Now Stanley appears surprised. 'Jonas? No. No enemies.'

'You were close to Jonas, weren't you?' Nells asks. 'You were friends.'

'Yes.'

'He helped you?'

'Yes.'

'How did you become friends?'

Stanley stares. Again, emotion washes through his eyes. 'In prison. I got bashed. They said my brain was bleeding. Not outside, inside. In here.' He touches his temple. 'He helped me get better. He nursed me.'

'And later?' asks Nell. 'When you got out?'

'He picked me up. Drove me here. Gave me work in his mine. He said I was a good worker. Strong.' Now there are definitely tears in his eyes. 'I never had a dad,' he says, as if that explains everything. Nell looks to Ivan, but can't interpret the stillness in the sergeant's eyes.

Nell returns her attention to Stanley, feels his vulnerability. She's afraid she's going to tear up, embarrass herself in front of Ivan.

Ivan, by contrast, remains resolute as he resumes questioning. 'What about Buddy? Were Jonas and Buddy friends?'

'Buddy? Nah. They don't talk. Kyle does the talking for them, backwards and forwards.'

'You know why they didn't talk?'

Stanley frowns with concentration. 'No. Kyle told me. Something sad. But I can't remember.'

Nell reaches back into the conversation. 'You and Jonas were very close. Almost family. But a few months ago, he told you that you could no longer work with him. Is that right?'

'Yep. That's what happened.' This time Stanley is not emotional; he sounds upbeat.

'What happened?'

'He got me a job at Cuttamulla. He and Trev. Good money, good food.'

'You didn't miss working with Jonas?'

'I did. But he said we were running out of opals, there weren't many left.'

Ivan cuts back in. 'You were working down the opal mine. Working hard. Did it seem like it to you, that there weren't as many opals?'

'I don't know. I guess.' To Nell, it seems that the question is too hard for the man, that making such an assessment is beyond him.

'So you are happy working at Cuttamulla?' she asks.

'Yes.'

'And you stay out there when you are working?'

'Yes.'

'And when it's not your shift, when you're not at Cuttamulla, you stay at your shed at Deadmans Well?'

'Yes.'

'So why all the phone calls, Stanley?' She holds his handset up so he can see it. 'Why are you always calling Jonas?'

'Because he's my friend.' He looks at her, his good eye pleading. 'I heard he found some new opals. I wanted to see if he needed me back. To help him. I've plenty of money. I could work for free.' And the truth of his answer is again reinforced by the moisture in his eye.

Nell and Ivan come together outside the ward, ready to swap impressions. The sergeant looks like he's thinking, recalibrating. Working through it. She's doing the same. She feels for the big man, but she also harbours a lingering suspicion he's trying to hide something. About the accident at the coalmine, about his reason for coming to town last Tuesday. Why so secretive about having lunch? Why the story about the goat? Like a schoolboy fearing detention. Maybe it's just the reflex action of a lifelong crim: telling the police the truth only gets you into trouble. Even so, she can't help it: she's starting to think the prime suspect is no longer so prime. It's not the facts, it's something more intuitive: the impression of a gentle and lost soul.

'Is what you said about the phone tracking true?' he asks. 'It's not going to work if there's only one tower covering the whole town. There won't be triangulation.'

'No, we're good. There's a tower in town, but it's in a dip, so there's one at the far end of the East Ridge, another a fair way along the West Ridge. Up on the high ground, to give maximum coverage out across the plain.'

'Good. So between the gate records at the mine and the phone tracking, we can rule him in or out. We don't need to rely on what he told us.' She's about to respond, when Ivan steps around her. 'Excuse me,' he says to someone behind her.

She turns. A doctor is approaching.

'Can I ask you about one of your patients, please?' He shows his badge. 'Stanley Honeywell?'

The doctor sighs, exasperated, her voice challenging. 'What? Why?'

Nell recognises her straight away: young, East Asian, plenty of fun when she's off duty. Right now, however, she has bags under her eyes and testiness within them. 'Mary. What sort of shifts they got you on?'

'Hey, Nell. Good to see you back.'

'Listen,' says Ivan, taking the cue, addressing Nell, 'I've got to make a call. I'll see you outside.'

Nell waits until he's out of earshot before speaking again, voice low. 'It's a murder investigation. Jonas McGee.'

The doctor grimaces. 'Jeez, Nell. You haven't heard of doctor–patient confidentiality?' The statement seems to weary the medico, as if it's a protocol she learnt back at med school, when issues like ethics were intriguing puzzles rather than workplace irritants. 'I can tell you Stanley has said nothing that would incriminate him.'

'What *can* you tell us?'

The doctor frowns, looks undecided.

'What is it?' asks Nell.

Mary looks about them, as if making sure no one can over-hear them, before speaking. 'His injuries. He's lucky they're not more serious. Could have easily detached a retina or copped a bad concussion. Or fractured his skull. He's well on the way to recovery, though.'

'He says he was injured yesterday. That timing sound about right to you?'

The doctor thinks for a moment, then nods. 'Yeah. About then.'

The timing seems important to Nell: well after the death of Jonas McGee. 'And the injuries themselves?'

Mary shakes her head, looks around, again checking they're alone. 'I don't think it was an industrial accident. I think he was beaten up.'

'Can you be sure?'

'No. But his balls are black and blue—the size of oranges— and yet there's no bruising on his thighs. Think about it, his story. A pallet comes off a truck, spilling containers. It's falling towards you. You duck, cower, turn your back, cover your head. So injuries to your hands, your back, your scalp. But he's got injuries to his face and front as well. And his testicles. I reckon someone beat the shit out of him.' She raises her eyebrows, shrugs her shoulders. 'But that's your concern, not mine.'

—◆—

Ivan approaches the hospital reception. 'Where's your morgue, please?' he asks pleasantly, as if seeking the gift shop or cafeteria.

'Pardon?'

He flashes his badge. The receptionist points the way.

He's just heading down the corridor when a door at its far end swings opens and Blake Ness emerges. 'Ivan. Good timing. I was just about to call you.'

'What news?'

'Confusing news,' says the pathologist.

'How's that?'

'I still don't know how he died. Not yet.'

'Really?'

'The only sign of violence is the blow to the face you're already aware of. I doubt that killed him. Could have been a heart attack. And as you know, he was dead a good while before he was nailed up.'

'Yes. The killer and whoever crucified him could be totally different people.' Ivan says it more as a statement to himself than a question to the pathologist.

'Ivan, aren't you listening? There may not be a killer.'

'Yeah. I heard you. You say you can rule out any additional violence. Can you say if he died at the mine or somewhere else?'

Blake shakes his head. 'Almost certainly at the mine. Carole agrees. But facilities here are primitive: good for storing bodies but not much else. I could only conduct the most basic autopsy. I'll have to get the body to somewhere bigger to run proper tests. Dubbo, or Sydney if you want it. There are some post-mortem abrasions and bruising, but well after death. They can be explained by the body being manhandled into position when it was nailed up.'

'And time of death—still early Tuesday?'

'Yep. Same as I told you at the club.'

'If you're ruling out violence, what about poisons?'

The pathologist shrugs. 'I've taken blood, some organ samples. They'll need to be tested in Sydney. No equipment here.'

'I see. What's your plan?'

'I'll head back to Sydney first flight I can get. Take the samples with me. The body can stay here on ice. If anything suspicious comes up on toxicity, we can always ship it down for further tests.'

'Right. Can you give it priority?'

'Sure. Along with everything else.'

'Seriously. The brass will want to know. If he died of natural causes, they may want to pull me out, reassign me. Leave it to Nell and the locals to investigate the crucifixion.'

It's only later, as he considers what he's said, that he realises he doesn't want to leave. Somehow, crucifying a dead man seems almost as bad as killing a living one. He wants to resolve this case, catch the perpetrators. Yes, it's important for his career, but it's more important for the townspeople of Finnigans Gap. There may be a killer on the loose; there may be worse.

chapter twelve

THE ALPINE CAFE ON THE MAIN STREET HAS ONE WALL ENTIRELY COVERED WITH
a mural of the Matterhorn, a startlingly clear photograph taken
on a startlingly clear day, spoiled only by the Coke fridge parked
in the foothills and a black-light bug zapper mounted on the wall
above the summit. As Ivan regards the vista, the zapper fizzles
and spits, like a storm cloud, exterminating yet another insect.
He's eating a toasted cheese-and-tomato sandwich so cold and
tasteless he could be on the upper slopes himself. He and Nell
are in one of the booths that line the wall opposite the mural.
Next to the mountain, deeper into the cafe, is the counter, with
a couple of tired cuckoo clocks mounted behind it to suggest
altitude. Or Europe. Or something. There's an air conditioner
above the entrance and beside it a jukebox—not a real one with
real records, but a facsimile with a video screen depicting a 45-rpm

record being selected and placed on a platter. It's chosen Buddy Holly. New tech, old music.

'What do you think?' he asks her.

'The food?'

'No. Stanley.'

'I don't think he killed Jonas,' she says. 'I don't think he's capable.'

He takes another bite of his sandwich, providing himself with time, if not taste. 'So you buy the gentle giant schtick?'

She looks hard at him. 'I don't think it's schtick.'

'So not premeditated. Not deliberate. But you saw the size of him. Hands like ham hocks. One moment of anger, one punch.'

She looks reluctant to agree. 'Possibly. But not the crucifixion; I can't imagine that. That would take an entirely different mindset altogether.'

'Maybe,' he says. 'The data will settle it. The phone tracking, Cuttamulla's records. We need to get them ASAP.'

'He's still a suspect?'

'Until he's not.'

She purses her lips. 'The doctor I talked to, she reckons he was bashed. That it wasn't an industrial accident.' She recounts Mary's description of the pattern of injuries, how they don't match Stanley's claims of a pallet of boxes falling from a truck. 'I guess that would explain why he wanted to get away from the mine. He didn't feel safe there. That'll be why the union is involved.'

'It also demonstrates he isn't so simple,' says Ivan. 'He's capable of telling a lie. And convincingly so.' He frowns, wondering what it could mean. 'Stanley Honeywell gets beaten up at Cuttamulla yesterday, Jonas McGee gets murdered and crucified six days ago at his opal mine. What's the connection?'

'I can't see one. Chances are the bashing is unrelated.'

'Okay, let's not worry about motive; let's just get the data and either eliminate him or put him in the frame.'

'I've already asked Cuttamulla for the precise times he left and returned. And Vince is getting the phone tracking and metadata from Telstra.'

'Telstra? What about the other carriers?'

'Out here, there are no other carriers.'

He smiles. 'Of course.' He takes another bite of his sandwich, chews, swallows, repeats. 'But we also need to keep moving, consider other possibilities.' Part of him wishes that the phone records do place Stanley on the West Ridge. The man has a criminal record, a record of violence, years in prison. And he's the sort of man any halfway competent prosecutor would tie in knots; the sort of man, big and threatening-looking, that any jury would find it very easy to convict. A man who, if he was up on the West Ridge, has lied to investigators. They would have opportunity, association, possible motives. And yet Ivan agrees with Nell: it doesn't feel right. His gut is telling him that Stanley Honeywell is not the killer.

'The one thing that didn't ring true was that stuff about feeding the goat,' he remarks. 'Since when do goats need feeding? And the blokes at Deadmans said they hadn't seen him for weeks.'

'I'd trust them as far as I could throw them,' she says. Then, more thoughtfully, 'Maybe he's ashamed of something. You know, visiting a hooker or something like that.'

'Doesn't matter. If the phone tracking shows he was here in town, that's all we need to know. He'll be in the clear.' Ivan looks at his plate; the sandwich has gone. He must have eaten it. The faux jukebox flips another facsimile disc. Roy Orbison. The bug zapper zaps more bugs; the Matterhorn remains aloof. 'The warrants. How'd you go? You got access to the bank accounts, not just the phone records?'

'All done. And we can search Jonas's house here in town and Stanley's shack out at Deadmans.'

'Excellent. Let's split up then. I'll take McGee's house, you do the banks. We can leave Deadmans for later. How many banks are there?'

'Just the one. Westpac.'

'That makes it easy. Let's see what we can get, then regroup.'

Over on the Matterhorn, an errant grasshopper flies too close to the sun, hits the zapper and bursts into flames, spiralling like a Messerschmitt over London. Roy Orbison croons on, oblivious.

— ▪ —

There are no customers in the bank, just a teller behind plexiglass. Nell flips her badge and asks for the manager.

'You're lucky. It's her first day back,' he says.

'From where?'

'Maternity leave.'

Inside her office, an exhausted-looking woman remains behind her desk, doesn't bother standing. A name plate on the desk identifies her as *Janelle Provost, Branch Manager*. She looks at Nell's badge, and then at the warrants. She squints, like she has never seen one before and has missed the training.

'When would you be needing these?' she asks, her voice a soft lilt.

'Right now would be good.'

'I'm not so sure I'm authorised, you know.' There's definitely an accent there. Some obscure pocket of England.

Nell smiles. 'You are absolutely authorised. That's what these warrants do. Indeed, they don't give you the choice to refuse. So they absolve you, provide absolute cover. No one in management or in court or anywhere else can ever accuse you of doing the wrong thing, because all you are doing is obeying a legal instruction.'

'I see.' The manager smiles, relieved. 'Is this to do with the murder?'

'That's right. If you like, I can wait while you call the court registrar, Humphrey Tuppence. He can explain it to you.'

'No, we're good. How do you want the statements? Electronic or printed?'

'So both Jonas McGee and Stanley Honeywell have accounts here?'

'That's right.'

'Can I get printouts now, please? And electronic versions sent here.' She hands the manager her business card with the email address.

Janelle Provost starts typing away at her computer. On her walls, there are pictures of cats and kids. A baby, newly framed, tiny in the arms of a large man in high-vis, standing in front of mining equipment. A local then.

'Okay. Looks pretty simple. Mr McGee has two accounts: a savings account and a home loan.' She taps a few more keys. 'Mr Honeywell has just the savings account.' She stares at the screen, a frown carving into her forehead. 'Sheesh,' she exclaims softly.

'Sheesh?'

'I'll print them out, the past year. You'll see.' She scans the screens. 'I'll email the electronic accounts, back as far as we've got.'

Nell scans the printout of Stanley's account. At first glance, it's a straightforward record of daily life. A year ago he was scraping by, his account almost inactive, nothing going in or out for weeks. This must have been when he was working for Jonas, receiving cash in hand. There is one deposit, cash, of three thousand dollars. Maybe a bonus, a good haul of opals, too much cash to stick under the mattress. Maybe a parting gesture from Jonas. Then, about three months ago, the salary from Cuttamulla kicks in, a regular fortnightly income. Nell is impressed . . . and irritated: Stanley earns more than she does.

And then, she reaches it, the sheesh moment. A week ago. A deposit. Twenty thousand dollars. Last Tuesday: the day Jonas McGee died. She looks at the manager, who is sitting next to her, eyebrows raised. 'Is there any way of knowing where this money came from?' Nell asks, even as she knows the answer.

'No. A cash deposit.'

'Deposited by whom? Stanley?'

'Let's check.' The manager smiles, getting into the swing of it, fatigue lifting. She turns to her computer, but finds no answers. 'Just give me a moment, Detective. We should still have the deposit slip.'

Nell waits, imagination firing. How would Stanley get hold of that sort of money, in cash? Not working shifts at the coalmine; his salary is going straight into his bank account. Payment for killing Jonas? Would he be so simple-minded as to put it in his bank account? She thinks of texting Ivan, but the manager is back with her. 'Here's the slip, and a photocopy for you. It was Stanley Honeywell himself. He deposited the money.'

Nell looks at the slip. The signature is like a child's handwriting, large and laboured. *StanleyH*. 'This is his signature? You're sure?'

The manager's eyes are bright. 'I asked the teller. He remembers it clearly. We get a lot of cash coming through here—opals are that sort of business, big dollops of money. But you remember something like that.'

'Can I speak to the teller, please?'

'Of course.'

The manager walks out, returns. 'He's got a couple of customers. Won't be two shakes.'

Nell nods, moving on to Jonas's accounts. They reveal a more complex life. Rates, insurance, utility bills. There are cheques and EFT deposits going to the church, to charities—small amounts but regular. Three months ago, though, the patterns changed. She crosschecks: it's about the same time Stanley started drawing a salary from Cuttamulla. The payments to charities ceased. Then a large deposit, a month ago: $36,600. Cash. And the same day, two more deposits, electronic transfers: $120,540 deposited from something called CommSec, and a bank transfer from his other account for $130,000. And then he drew a bank cheque: $287,000. All on the same day.

'Where is this deposit from?' asks Nell. 'The hundred and thirty thousand dollars?'

'His home loan. It's a redraw facility. Here . . .' The manager hands over the home loan statements. 'He just about had it paid off, then whack, he draws down a hundred and thirty thousand and puts it across to his savings account. The same day there's a deposit of a hundred and twenty thousand from CommSec, plus the thirty-six thousand in cash. Then he withdraws the lot, more than a quarter of a million dollars, in the form of a bank cheque.'

'CommSec? What's that?'

'Share trading. An online broker owned by the Commonwealth Bank. Linked to his account. Here you can see over the past six months or so, there is money going out at a steady rate from his account into CommSec.'

'Signifying what? Buying shares?'

'I'd say so. Then the hundred and twenty grand is him selling the shares, cashing in.'

Nell studies the figures, does a few quick mental sums. 'Looks like he made quite a profit, wouldn't you say?'

'I would indeed.'

'And do you know if it was him? Can we confirm that?'

'Not the online transactions, no. But we can check the cash deposit and the bank cheque. The teller should be free by now.'

In fact, the teller is just finishing up with a customer, an old man, keen for a chat. Janelle Provost politely but firmly escorts the elderly conversationalist out, locks the door behind him and puts up a sign to say the bank is closed for ten minutes. Her initial reluctance has evaporated like a cold beer in a desert town; she's clearly enjoying herself.

The manager addresses the teller, his eyes widening as she explains. 'The detective here is investigating the death of Jonas McGee. She's interested in his activities here a month ago. She has warrants and we are compelled to disclose the information. Were you on duty?'

'I was. I remember it well.'

The manager is about to continue, but Nell holds up a hand. She wants to be the one asking the questions. 'What's your name?'

'Josh. I'm not in trouble, am I?'

'Not at all. But I want to get your recollections as clearly as I can.' Nell sets the audio app on her MobiPol phone to record and places it on the counter.

The teller looks at it nervously. He's young with neat hair, the collar on his company shirt a couple of sizes too big.

'The recording is for accuracy. You okay with that?'

'I s'pose.'

Nell runs through the formalities: names, time, location. 'Josh, tell me what you remember from the day Jonas McGee made all these large transactions.'

'He came in here—Jonas—sat over there, and waited till the place was empty. He had a backpack. He pulled out a bin liner full of cash and told me he wanted to deposit it. Took me a good half-hour to count it.'

'How much, can you recall?'

'It was just over thirty-six thousand dollars.'

'And were the bills new? Old? Large denominations? Small bills?'

The teller frowns. 'A real mix, if I remember. He had them all counted out, bound in rubber bands. I had to double-check, of course. Lucky we have a counting machine.'

'And did he say where the money was from?'

'I reckon it must have been from selling opals.'

'Did he actually say that?'

'No, but some of the larger notes were bound with red rubber bands.'

'Signifying what?'

'The Irishman. He uses red rubber bands.'

'And by the Irishman you mean the opal dealer?'

'That's right. Sean McGrath. He banks here.'

'Okay, thanks. That's very useful. And Jonas made a withdrawal as well?'

'He did. He'd gathered a lot of money into his transaction account. There was over a hundred thousand he'd withdrawn from his home loan, and money transferred in from somewhere else. He pooled it all together and withdrew it as a bank cheque.'

'You remember the amount?'

'Two hundred and eighty-seven thousand dollars.'

Nell looks at the statement. 'You have an excellent memory. Can you recall who the bank cheque was made out to?'

'The bearer.'

Nell blinks. 'So whoever held the cheque, they could cash it?'

'That's right.'

'And you have no idea who it was intended for?'

The teller shrugs. 'No. I guess that was the point.'

Nell turns to the manager. 'If that cheque has been cashed, would that generate a record of who cashes it?'

The manager nods. 'Yes. It should do. Certainly if the person who cashed it deposited it into an account.'

'Can you do that for me then? Determine if it's been cashed? And if so, by whom?'

The manager shakes her head. 'No. It wasn't cashed here; we'd know that. If it's been cashed elsewhere, we won't have access to that information. I'll have to put a request through to head office.' She frowns. 'Will the warrant cover that? Headquarters is very careful about privacy issues. They may feel constrained from releasing the identity of the person who cashed the cheque. They might need to deal with another bank.'

'Fair point. Would you like to scan the warrant and send it through to your superiors with the request? Emphasise that this is a murder investigation and the information is vital—and urgent. If they require a new warrant, let me know. I'll organise it for them.'

'Very good.' The manager looks at her watch. 'I'm not sure I'll have anything for you today, but I'd be hopeful we could have something by tomorrow.'

'Excellent.' Nell turns back to the teller. 'Were you also here last Tuesday, when Stanley Honeywell came in?'

'Oh yes, I remember it well. He's quite memorable.'

'Could you tell me what happened?'

'He came in here with this shopping bag—like from the supermarket, but it was stuffed full of money. He wanted to deposit it in Jonas McGee's account but wanted to make it anonymous. I said he would have to sign the deposit slip and that I would need to tell Jonas where it was from.'

'What did he say?'

'He was a little confused. I suggested he deposit it into his own account while he thought about it. So that's what we did.'

'And this money: was it similar to the cash that Jonas deposited?'

The teller shakes his head. 'No. It was all loose. He hadn't counted it out. No red rubber bands or anything else. I ran it through the counting machine.' The young man frowns. 'I seem to remember a mixture of denominations, but that might have been a different miner.'

'But you're sure about the fact it wasn't counted and there were no rubber bands?'

'Yes.'

'And yet it came to exactly twenty thousand dollars?'

'That's right. I remember I was surprised at it being such a round number.'

'And how long do you think this whole transaction took?'

'Hard to say,' Josh replies. 'But probably fifteen or twenty minutes.'

'Here,' says the manager, pointing to a copy of the printout. 'The deposit was made at eleven twelve am.'

'Thanks,' says Nell. She realises the potential to build a timeline. If Cuttamulla can give her a precise time Honeywell left the mine, she and Ivan will be able to see if he had time to get out to the West Ridge before or after making the deposit. Together with the phone data, they should be able to work out if the bank was his sole destination.

'Thank you both very much,' says Nell, taking back her phone, switching off the recorder and handing the teller a business card for good measure before addressing the manager. 'Let me know who cashed that bank cheque from Jonas McGee. Call me if you have any problems. And please keep all of this information to yourselves. Don't tell anyone outside of head office what we have discussed here.'

As soon as she gets outside, she takes a seat in the shade of the awning and calls Ivan, but it rings out. She tries again with the same result. She sends a text: *SH was at bank Tuesday. Deposited $20,000 cash. See you at hospital.*

She gets into her car, sits for a moment, considering what she knows. At first glance, twenty thousand dollars is a hell of a motive to murder Jonas. But, then, why try to deposit it into a dead man's account? It doesn't make sense.

She tries Ivan again; same result. She needs to act on her own authority. She decides she's going to arrest Stanley Honeywell. The lock-up, the prospect of prison, that'll get the big man talking. It brings her no joy, but she can't see any other option. Ivan can hardly complain, not after what she's learnt. But she won't interview Stanley; that would be a step too far. He can sweat it out in the lock-up, then Ivan can interview him, with or without her, extract whatever it is that the former prisoner knows.

At the hospital, she doesn't bother with reception. She knows the way, she has her handcuffs. He may be big, but she's confident she can handle him. Put all that martial arts training to use. But when she gets to the ward, the bed is empty. Her first thought is the toilet, or maybe showering. Or getting food. But as she retraces her steps, she encounters Mary, the young doctor.

'Stanley Honeywell—he's not in his ward.'

'Checked himself out,' says the doctor.

'When?' Nell feels a surge of adrenaline. And of dread.

'As soon as you two left.'

'Really?'

'Yeah. Congratulations. He looked absolutely terrified.'

Nell bites her lip. 'Do you know where he went?'

'No.'

— —

Ivan finds himself in the closest thing Finnigans Gap has to suburbs. Like most towns, prestige increases with elevation. Above him, on either side of the Queensland highway as it winds up in the direction of the lookout, there's a sprinkling of dress circle homes, pretensions borrowed from Sydney or Melbourne, with large decks and barbecue settings. The only residential views for hundreds of kilometres.

Jonas McGee's home has no views, no decks and no pretensions. His house is lower down, practically on the flat. It's made of treated logs, some sort of kit home, possibly built back in the seventies during the first opal rush. Up under the eaves, the wood is still green; on more exposed surfaces it's turned grey and started to splinter. The yard is gravel and dirt, but neat enough. A lizard stays perfectly still, as if sensing Ivan's approach, with only its blue tongue flickering. Separating the yard from the street is a cactus hedge, the plants growing haphazardly, twisting this way and that at strange angles, impossible to tame. The neighbours are as Nell described: an empty house on one side, clearly deserted, one window boarded up and a FOR RENT sign, faded and leaning precariously. The house on the other side is teeming with kids; he can hear shouts and laughter and yelps coming through the thin walls. An air conditioner on the side wall is pumping away, dripping water. There is a trampoline in the backyard, but it's too hot to use at this time of day, even by kids. Fairy lights, left over from Christmas, are strung along the verandah, awaiting nightfall.

McGee's house is locked, with no sign of life. Ivan can sense its emptiness and wonders about that; how it's always so apparent when no one is at home. Or perhaps it's his subconscious at work; he knows it's empty, he knows the owner is lying cold and motionless in the hospital morgue. He should break in, he knows he should. He has the warrant, he has the authority. Instead, he walks to the single-car garage at the side of the house. Another kit job, the same cheap construction; not even a concrete slab, just treated pine walls, a flat tin roof. The drive is dirt and dried mud, twin runnels showing where a vehicle has parked outside, but the recent rain has erased any tyre marks.

Ivan tries the swing door; it opens up with a token protest, hinges squealing for lack of oil. He finds the light switch, flicks it on. A bare bulb hangs from the rafters, hardly making an impact against the glare of the outside world. Flies swarm, as if they've been waiting for him in the dark. He thinks of the repellent, still in the rental, but can't be bothered. There is room in the garage for a car, but no evidence of one being parked here anytime recently. Jonas's truck was up at the opal mine, possibly up there for some time. Hanging on one wall is an unused hose, still in its store packaging, and an unopened sack of grass seed, evidence of more optimistic times. There's a bench at the end, with a small window above it. It's neat and tidy. There's a large silver toolbox, tradesman's size, just small enough to be manhandled onto the back of Jonas's truck, similar to the one Ivan recalls from the opal mine. It's secured with a padlock. Ivan tries lifting it, can feel its weight, the shifting of tools inside, the sound of metal. Power tools, at a guess. Cheaper hand tools, old but sharp, hang from shadow boards mounted each side of the window. Nothing to see here, Ivan decides. He borrows a crowbar from the shadow board. Enough procrastination.

The doors to the house are locked, front and back, but somehow it seems more respectful to break in through the back door, less intrusive. He should have police tape to seal off the scene, to protect it from intruders. He'll need to send Garry over, get him to do it. Maybe he should have brought Carole along; it's not a crime scene as far as he knows, but her eye for detail is unsurpassed.

Too late now. He slips on plastic shoe covers and pulls on some latex gloves. Show time.

The door is cheap, the lock cheaper. It takes him a pathetically short amount of time to break them open. Inside, the house is spartan, hot and musty under the tin roof, dust motes floating. It's old-fashioned; at a guess, not much changed since it was built. The kitchen is small: a chipped formica benchtop, burnt orange, the lino squares on the floor starting to lift at the corners. A basic electric stove, four rings, the cooktop scrubbed clean, scratches left in the enamel. There's no dishwasher; plates have been washed and left to dry in the rack beside the sink. The fridge has a litre container of milk, eggs, a tub of no-name margarine and not much else. Ivan smells the milk; it's beginning to turn, the use-by date a week ago. In the freezer there are jumbo bags of frozen vegetables: peas, beans, corn kernels. White bread. Four'n Twenty pies, mince from a Dubbo supermarket. Anglo food; old man's food. Ivan has to remind himself that McGee was only forty-three, the house built around the same time the miner was born.

He walks on. The lounge is sparsely furnished. There's a sofa, springs sagging, with a coffee table separating it from a modest television. A pile of old magazines sit on the table, *Fishing Monthly*, and a bible. Not King James, but one of the new ones: *The Good News Bible*. He picks it up. The pages are well thumbed, the spine cracked from use. Some passages are underlined. Ivan can imagine Jonas eating here alone, microwaved pies and vegies in front of the telly, watching the news. Then afterwards, dishes done, reading his magazines, studying the bible.

On the mantelpiece, there are signs of humanity: framed photos of his wife; of his daughter as a young girl; of his wife and daughter together. One of a family group, in front of an ancient Holden, the glimpse of a beach in the background: Jonas in shorts and a polo neck, short back and sides, holding a beer; his wife in a sundress and sunglasses, smiling, a pretty woman; the girl in swimmers, zinc spread across her face. It looks anachronistic, like something from the 1970s: the age of the car, the fashion, the faded colour, but it has to be more modern, this century, not long before the wife died. Annie. That was her name. Annie. He puts the picture back, noting that it carries no dust. Neither do the others. Well cared for, then. Loved. At the end of the row are two pictures in pink plastic frames: a young girl, hair plaited, laughing at the camera as she is piggybacked by a huge man, face split with a smile exposing irregular teeth. Elsie and Stanley Honeywell, radiating joy. The second photo: Stanley beaming in the background as the girl blows out birthday candles, the cake the same pink as the picture frame. Ivan counts the candles. Her eleventh birthday.

There's little else in the room: faded curtains on the window, a dusty two-bar radiator, a couple of armchairs, a small cabinet of pressed wood, almost an antique. He opens the cabinet; it's a bar, a cocktail cabinet. Bottles of spirits, covered in dust despite being inside the cabinet, standing on a mirrored shelf. A bottle of Campari, the label dated, like a prop from an old film set. There's a bottle of tonic water with a use-by date that expired almost two decades ago. He opens the bottle; there is no fizz. The drinks cabinet, never opened, never cleaned out. But kept there, a constant reminder.

He walks through the rest of the house: the bathroom unremarkable in its simplicity and cheap plastic fittings; the master bedroom with its sad double bed, neatly made up. Ivan thinks on that; imagines Jonas making it every morning before heading to his claim. Back in Sydney, Ivan doesn't bother making his; why bother if there's no one to share it with?

The sadness deepens in the second bedroom. A single bed, soft toys, posters on the wall. The girl has been gone eight years, is an adult now with a child of her own; this is the room of a teenager. And yet it still seems relatively modern, more up to date, put on hold just eight years ago, when she left, and not eighteen years, like the rest of the house.

The third bedroom is different: a home office. A metal filing cabinet. A wall calendar, last year's, still showing December. A corkboard with mining forms, permits, utility bills pinned to it. On the desk, a tax return, half completed. Jonas did his own, still used paper. And yet, right next to the forms is a laptop, shiny and new, out of place in this antique house. Ivan knows he can hand it over to Carole; she has the training to crack it open, to log on. And if it's unusually obstinate, she can take it with her to Sydney, get the geeks to do it. But on a whim, he sits, starts it up. It's password-protected. Of course it is. He wonders what the password might be. Opalstrike? He resists trying. This is no poker machine gambit; there are no endless plays. Instead he disciplines himself, opens the desk drawer. Pulls it out, holds it aloft, hoping to find the password taped to the bottom. No luck. He's about to close the computer down when he sees the photo of Elsie on the shelf above the desk, a girl on the brink of adulthood, eyes shining. He picks it up, looks at the back, and there it is: her name—*Elsie*—and eight digits. At a guess, her birthday. He tries typing it in. He's in luck: the computer complies, boots up.

The laptop is spartan and as well ordered as the house. There are folders, aligned carefully on the screen. One is marked *Elsie*. He opens it, the sense of trespass strong. There are photos. Old ones. And new ones. Jonas might have been estranged from his daughter, but he clearly remained devoted to her. All that was left of the life he once had.

Ivan's thoughts are interrupted. There is a sound; a disturbance. The empty house doesn't feel quite so empty. He stands, looks around, walks to the room's doorway. Nothing. It must be the metal roof, bending in thrall to the sun.

He moves back to the computer. Another folder: *Shares*. He opens it to find more folders. There are contract notes recording the buying of shares. He opens one, then another. All in the one company: LikeUs Pty Ltd. He scans the screen, remembering the newspaper report. Australia's largest rare-earth mine, located in South Australia. He looks at the contract note. Ten thousand dollars on this purchase alone. He looks at the date. Just three months ago.

And in the quiet of the house, among the dead man's relics, Ivan smiles, a grim and knowing expression. He recognises this pattern. Jonas was a gambler. Not poker machines, not horse races, but the share market. Mining stocks. He considers the house: neat and tidy but worn out, needing money and getting none. Money coming in from opals, a new pocket of valuable gems, but not enough money to keep his friend Stanley in work. Ivan recognises these traits and recognises Jonas. A fellow addict, a fellow sinner. It explains the neatness of the house; it explains the dedication to good causes, the need for penance, the churchgoing. He'd given up drinking, kept his grog in its cabinet as a demonstration of his will, his self-discipline. But here was the secret. Gambling. And where there is gambling, out of control and addictive, there are always debts. And where there are debts, violence lurks. Was this the motive for the crucifixion? Not religious, not psychotic, but grubby and deliberate and mercenary: a loan shark sending a warning, letting other clients know what might become of them. Ivan can imagine it: the lender of last resort heading out to teach McGee a lesson, finding him already dead. And then the crucifixion. Not personal at all, just business. Sending the message.

It fits well enough, feels right. He returns to the computer, to the evidence. He opens all the contract notes and starts going through them. He's expecting to see buys, when the urge to gamble seized Jonas, and he's expecting to see sells, when the miner needed to feed the circling shark. But something's askew, something doesn't fit the narrative. There are no sells; just one sizable sale at the end. Ivan doesn't understand: it looks like Jonas was making money, not losing it. And then he hears it again, the sound of floorboards creaking, enough time for him to start to turn, not enough time for him to see what's coming.

His head explodes in light and pain, the sound of his own skull rattling under the blow, the force knocking him sideways, enough to throw him from the chair. And then, on the floor, the smell of dust, the darkness descending, even as some remnant of consciousness admonishes him for his own carelessness, his own stupidity.

chapter thirteen

DEADMANS WELL IS AS SHE REMEMBERS IT: A RAMSHACKLE COLLECTION OF caravans, corrugated-iron and fibro shacks, a railway carriage with solar panels, a clapped-out troop carrier. She knows she's not welcome here. Not after the drug busts. She wishes she'd brought Garry along, or Ivan, but there is no backing out now. She has her gun, her pepper spray, her handcuffs; there for all to see, hanging from her utility belt.

She walks up to the railway carriage, the mayor's place. She knocks, preparing for a rebuke, a confrontation. But it's not the mayor who answers the door; it's a vacant-looking woman in cut-off jeans and a tank top, about forty, with a lean build save for a compact beer belly. 'You a copper?' asks the woman.

'Good guess. And you are?'

'Lydia. Mayor's wife,' says the woman. 'If you want him, he's out back in the tub. Can't get him out of it in this weather.'

'Actually I'm searching for Stanley Honeywell. You seen him?'

'Big Stanley? Nup.'

'Where's his place?'

The woman points. 'Over that way. Cute little green shack. Just look for an oak tree. Can't miss it.' And then, as an afterthought, 'Be careful of the goat—it gets stroppy with strangers.'

Nell thanks Lydia, walks off to find Stanley's shack. Up here on the ridge, the wind is up, but it's bringing dust, not relief. Bits of rubbish are blowing through the camp, pieces of paper and wrapping. Postcards and cut-outs from magazines. Some people have no pride. And then she sees it: the green shed, door off its hinges, its contents strewn about. That's what's blowing in the wind—not rubbish but Stanley's possessions. The shed has been totalled, its windows smashed, cactus garden levelled. Someone has emptied it out, tossed his belongings everywhere. It must have been recent; wasn't Ivan up here just yesterday? She looks about. Clothes, food, kitchenware, broken furniture. Like a mini hurricane.

She bends down, starts sifting through it, not so much searching as thinking. She scans the windswept rubbish. Was this a real search, or was it something more? A message, intimidation, punishment. What was it Mary said? He'd looked terrified as he fled the hospital. She examines more of the detritus: the torn pages of a magazine, a never-sent postcard from Lightning Ridge, one half of a map of New South Wales. Underneath, there's a birthday card, a child's drawing on its front: a round face drawn in brown pencil, three lonely teeth lost within a broad smile. *Happy Burthday* scrawled in a child's hand, a different colour for each letter. Nell opens the card. *I luv you Stanly!! Luv Elsie Xxx Ooo.* It holds her attention for a long moment before she moves to place it gently back amid the rest of Stanley's keepsakes, but can't bring herself to abandon it to the elements. She folds it, places it in one of the pockets of her cargo pants, convincing herself it might be evidence. She feels bad, bad about what has happened here. She contemplates the papers blowing about her feet, the mementoes and the mundane, and something else catches her eye—the flash of the state coat of arms. A business card. She picks it up. Detective Senior Sergeant Morris Montifore. She stares at it, bewildered. The famous Montifore, his business card. Here, at Deadmans Well.

She makes her way back to the mayor's house. Her hesitancy is gone; she wants answers. The sun is just as fierce, but now it powers her, lifting her. She strides around the back of the carriage. The mayor is not in the tub but sitting in the shade, hairy-chested and tattooed, a ring through his left nipple. He's wearing a pink tutu and smoking a joint.

'Stanley Honeywell,' she says. 'Where is he?'

'Search me, luv. Haven't seen him for yonks.'

'It's important. He may be in danger.'

The mayor takes a drag, holds it for a long moment, breathes out a long smoky sigh. 'I don't see much. People come and go, things happen, but I don't see much. That's why I'm the mayor. My platform is very laissez faire.'

'We're talking about murder.'

'Then we're talking about the wrong bloke. Stanley wouldn't harm a fly, let alone nail someone up and leave 'em to die.'

'He knows things.'

'That'd be a first,' says the mayor, but she can see he's taking her seriously. 'Nothing to do with me,' he repeats. 'Laissez faire.'

'His place has been trashed. Who did that?'

'I wouldn't know, officer. I wouldn't know much.' Then, as if reconsidering, he shakes his head. 'You sure it's trashed?'

'Go see for yourself if you don't believe me.'

'Well, in that case, I'd say it was the cunt from the coalmine. No one here would do that. We like Stanley.'

'Who are you talking about?'

'Red-headed bogan in a company truck. Big bloke.'

'Company? What company?'

'The coalmine. Cuttamulla.'

'When was this?'

'Half an hour ago. You just missed him.'

'You let him take Stanley away?'

'Don't know that he did. But if Stanley's gone, then chances are he's with the bogan. If I'd known about the shack, we would have stepped in.' He takes a quick toke of his joint, his mouth turning down. 'Bring us the ranga—we'll sort him out.'

'No. You see him, you tell us. No vigilante shit. You got me?'

'You're awfully pretty when you're angry, you know that?' And he laughs.

'Fuck you,' she says.

But when she gets back to her truck, she finds the back left tyre has been slashed. She walks around, checks the others, but they're fine. It's just the one. So she can fix it and move on. Some sort of warning, she guesses. Fuckwits. Who do they think they're dealing with? She considers returning, arresting the mayor for the dope, searching his house. But then what? Wasting hours taking him into town, processing him. What would Ivan say about that? She stares at the ruined tyre a moment longer, long enough for the flies to gather. She swats them away and gets to it.

She has the jack in place, is just starting on the wheel nuts, when a battered Toyota truck pulls up. She doesn't bother looking up: if they've stopped to help or they've stopped to gloat, it makes little difference. She's more than capable of changing a tyre.

'You right?'

She looks up. It's Kyle Torshack. 'Yeah, I've got it.'

'Puncture?'

'Screwdriver.'

'Right.' His eyes look away, off towards the gathered shacks and lean-tos of Deadmans. 'Not very welcoming. You need a hand?'

'No. Thanks for stopping though.'

'I'll leave you to it then.'

'Hang on,' she says, getting to her feet, brushing the dust from her hands. The cloud of flies rises with her. 'You prospecting up here?'

'Yeah. The rig's a bit further along. Up on the north-east spur.'

'You haven't seen Stanley Honeywell about, have you? With a big red-headed bloke from Cuttamulla?'

'In a Cuttamulla ute?'

'That's it.'

'Yeah. Down in town. Almost collected them near the roundabout.'

'Which way were they headed?'

'South.'

'Towards Cuttamulla?'

'I guess.'

Nell swats at the flies. She can't remember them ever being this bad. It must have something to do with the rain. Then she thinks of the birthday card, still in her pocket. 'Did you manage to speak to Elsie?'

'Nah. Tried last night,' he says. 'No luck.'

'We heard she's in Los Angeles.'

'Is that right?' He looks around the rock-strewn landscape. 'Lucky her.' He brushes away the flies with a casual flick of the wrist. 'You making any progress?'

'Early days.'

'Let me know if you want any help with the locals.' He tilts his head in the direction of Deadmans. 'If they start getting too stroppy.'

'Thanks, I can handle them.'

'If you say so.' He gives her a loose smile. 'See you round then.' He looks at the jack and the wheel brace still hanging from the wheel nuts. 'Have fun.'

'Sure. You too.'

But the young man has already moved away. Before he's started his car, she's on the phone, leaving the tyre for the moment. She tries Stanley Honeywell's number, but it rings out. Still in range then, still close enough to Finnigans. She tries again, but this time, one ring in, the phone cuts out, as if it has been turned off. She tries Ivan, but his phone rings out as well. Where the fuck is he?

She returns to the task at hand, fixing the wheel. There's nothing complicated about it: the four-wheel drive is heavy, but the jack is good, never used; the spare wheel is cumbersome, but she takes pride in wrangling it into place, enjoying the physicality of it, her own competence. It takes her ten minutes, tops. Job done, the damaged wheel stowed, she tries to call Stanley once more. This time the message from the carrier is clear: *The number you are calling is not available on this service.* The phone has either been turned off altogether, or is out of range. In her mind's eye, she imagines it out on the plain, beyond the reach of the Finnigans Gap towers, speeding towards Cuttamulla.

She starts the engine, then gives Ivan one last try. She's just about to give up when he answers.

— —

It's the sound that stirs him towards consciousness: the screeching of a cockatoo, somewhere nearby. Or perhaps it's the smell that first penetrates: the odour of blood and dust and all it invokes, scenes of murder and violence, of lives cut short. The twin sensations send a charge through him, pushing him upwards. The cockatoo screeches once more, so loud and so shrill that pain bursts upon him, like a screwdriver inserted behind his ear. His eyes jolt open; he wants to silence the bird, wring its neck. The moronic thing must have landed on the cactus hedge. And with that thought he is fully awake, fully aware of where he is: lying face down on the floor of Jonas McGee's study.

He touches the back of his head, oh so tentatively, feeling the wetness on his hand, right at the epicentre of the throbbing pain. He brings it around to where he can see it: bright red, his own blood. He heaves himself into a sitting position even as his pounding skull screams in protest, appealing for him to stay still, telling him that movement will hurt. He rejects it, looking around the room, processing his situation. Blindsided. Some arsehole crept up from behind and laid waste to him. A sucker punch. He touches the back of his head again. More than a punch, something much harder. A shudder runs through him. Blows like that can kill people, or leave permanent damage. He knows; he's seen the aftermath, cold and blue and covered with a sheet. He takes a moment, waves his hands in front of his eyes, holding up one, then two, then three fingers. His focus seems fine, no blurriness. He recalls his name, his date of birth, his street address, the name of the prime minister. His opinion of the prime minister. He knows where he is, why he's here, what he did this morning. All good: he remembers right up until he was in this house, examining Jonas McGee's laptop. If he's forgotten anything, it must be mere seconds, minutes at most. Another promising sign. He reaches out, holds on to the chair at the desk, pulls himself up. The pain is no worse; maybe the elevation helps. He looks at the floor. A few drops of blood but nothing too bad. No pooling. He's relieved. Even minor head wounds can bleed profusely, so the cut can't be too serious. He looks at the desk. The laptop is gone. Of course the laptop is gone.

A sense of anger captures him. An intruder has entered, belted him, stolen the computer. Or the aggressor was already there, waiting for him to turn his back, provide an easy target. The anger is joined by humiliation. They must have seen him enter, followed him in, silent enough that he didn't hear. How stupid of him, how negligent.

And how stupid of them. How desperate. The laptop must hold incriminating evidence, something someone doesn't want a Homicide detective to see. A conviction comes to him then, a belief, before his mind can run through all the alternatives: a certainty that Jonas McGee didn't just drop dead of natural causes, and that his crucifixion wasn't some random act by someone suffering a psychotic episode. Someone killed him, someone crucified him, and Ivan is going to find out who—and make the bastards pay. Them and whoever the hell belted him in the back of the head. And, God willing, he's going to shred that fucking cockatoo.

Only now does it occur to him that he might have been unconscious for some time. He checks his watch, but he's not sure. He can't quite remember when he entered the house. He knows it's not like sleep, where you somehow have an idea of how long you've been under. This is more like an anaesthetic, where all sense of time is lost. He checks his phone. Sure enough, there are missed calls from Nell. And a series of text messages. *IMPORTANT! Check email—bank statements for JM & SH.* And then, fifteen minutes later. *Stanley out of hospital, on the run!* And almost immediately afterwards: *Where are you?* And then: *Going to Deadmans Well to arrest SH.*

He stares at his phone. Arrest? What the fuck has been happening? Frowning makes his head hurt. The cockatoo screeches again, but now it's not just one of them, a whole flock has landed to torment him. His phone rings; the screen says *Nell Buchanan.*

'Nell?'

'Where have you been?' There is urgency in her voice, irritation.

'Unconscious. Some fucker knocked me out.' Talking sets off more ringing in the back of his head. He tries to keep his sentences short. 'Jonas McGee's house.'

A delay before she responds. 'Shit. I'm sorry. You okay?'

'I'll live. Why are you arresting Stanley?'

'We need to find him, Ivan. Have you seen the bank statements?'

'No. What's in them?'

'Okay, let me fill you in.' She tells him of Stanley Honeywell depositing the twenty thousand dollars the same day Jonas McGee died, how he fled hospital, how she found his shack ransacked, that he has possibly been abducted by the mine manager from Cuttamulla.

'Right,' says Ivan. It's a lot to comprehend. 'So he lied to us about what he was doing in town last Tuesday.'

'Looks like it.'

He sighs. There is still a slight muddiness in the way he is thinking. 'His shack was pristine when I was there yesterday afternoon, so chances are it's the mine manager who took it apart. We need to get to Cuttamulla, detain Stanley. Make sure he's safe. I'll see you there.'

'I'm on my way. But, Ivan, there's something you need to know.'

He can hear the trepidation in her voice. 'What's that?'

'At Stanley's shack. There was a business card. Morris Montifore. Homicide.'

That stops him. He blinks. Was the blow to his head worse than he thought? Has he awoken in a parallel universe? 'What? That's not possible.'

'Stanley's stuff was strewn all over the place and it was just lying there in among it. I recognised the coat of arms. Detective Senior Sergeant Morris Montifore.'

'Senior sergeant? Are you sure?'

'Hang on, I've got it here.' There's the briefest delay. 'Yep, that's what it says. Looks genuine to me.'

'Morris is a detective inspector. Hasn't been a senior sergeant for years.'

'Right. Must be an old one then. But what's it doing here?'

'He was up here a few years ago, investigating an unexplained death.'

'What death?'

'A young bloke wandered off and died out on that salt lake beyond the West Ridge.'

'I remember hearing about that. Before my time.'

'Might be worth double-checking the records, but you go ahead. Getting to Stanley is far more important. I'll see you at Cuttamulla.' And then he adds, 'But I might be a while.'

'You sure you're okay?' Now there is concern in her voice.

'Never better.'

chapter fourteen

SHE DRIVES ALONG THE WAY AS QUICKLY AS SHE CAN, FLICKING ON HER LIGHTS and siren to get past a convoy of dawdling tourists, inexplicably stopped in the middle of the road, gawking at the corrugated-iron church. She gulps water, conscious of the time she's spent in the sun. She knows that she should pace herself, that a few minutes here or there isn't going to make a difference, that it would be sensible to make allowances for the spare tyre. And yet a sense of urgency has come over her. The wheel should be fine: the pressure looked solid once she'd dropped the jack and it took the full weight of the vehicle. And it's a rear wheel; it won't affect the steering. It's Ivan's words that are prodding her to speed: *We need to get to Cuttamulla, detain Stanley. Make sure he's safe.* It hadn't occurred to her that the big man could be in danger; she'd been thinking of him entirely as a suspect. But she remembers the bruising, the extent of his injuries, the image of him as a gentle giant, Mary at the hospital asserting he'd been assaulted. And now the old birthday card, sitting in her pocket. He's been taken, taken by a man who has demolished his shack. A dark thought comes to her: if someone really wanted to harm Stanley, Cuttamulla is the last place they'd take him. From the elevation of The Way she can see out across the plain: such a very, very big country; too many empty kilometres, too few witnesses. If the two men are out there, then there is no way of finding them. Not now, not ever.

She's starting to wind her way down from the West Ridge into Finnigans Gap, yet she's still high enough to see a plane approaching the airport. She thinks it might be PolAir, come to pick up Carole and Blake, but soon sees it's moving too fast: a jet, small, white and streamlined, landing at speed. The road drops lower and she loses her line of sight. Perhaps it's the Gulfstream back for another visit. But why would the Chinese be returning now the Kalingra deal is done? Her curiosity is piqued, but she needs to get to Cuttamulla, she needs to get to Stanley Honeywell. There'll be plenty of time for plane spotting later.

— —

Ivan shuts the door to his motel room after him, takes off his sunglasses and moves straight into the bathroom. He swallows painkillers: first a couple of ibuprofen, followed by some codeine-laced paracetamol from his emergency supply, reserved for the worst of hangovers. Then he strips off, gets the shower going and tentatively washes his hair. The water runs pink, but not for long. He's relieved to see it. The wound is small, and has all but stopped bleeding. No need for stitches. He probably should report it, just in case, but the thought of filling out forms only sets his headache flaring. So he gets half dressed, just his underwear and a shirt, sits on the bed and texts Morris on the burner. The disposable phone feels small and foreign in his hands. *Need to talk. ASAP.*

Almost immediately the phone chirps in response.

'Ivan, I was just thinking of you,' says the distant voice.

'Can you talk?'

'To my heart's content. I'm now officially on gardening leave. Talk away.'

Ivan is disconcerted by the jocular tone; this is not the focused intensity of the detective he knows. 'Morris, you said you'd been to Finnigans Gap before—seven years ago. You started to tell me about it.'

There's a delay in his former boss's answer; when he speaks, the joviality has disappeared. 'Yeah. This bloke was found dead out on a salt pan. Forget its name. We investigated, but didn't come to any solid conclusions.'

'Kalingra? Lake Kalingra?'

'That's it.'

'Who's we? Who was assisting?'

There's a laugh. 'Me, mate, I was the assistant. Reg Montgomery took the lead.'

'You and Reg Montgomery?' That surprises Ivan. Montgomery was a legend, only recently retired. Old school. Tough as nails, with a high resolution rate, despite overseeing only the most challenging cases. And seven years ago, Morris Montifore had moved well beyond rising star to be a highly respected crime solver, already a detective senior sergeant. 'You and Montgomery? Hell of a team for a death by misadventure.'

'There was more to it than that.'

'Tell me.'

'Someone somewhere called in a favour and wanted it investigated. Reg and I pulled the short straw.'

'But you found nothing?'

'Ultimately, yeah. But it was curious; things didn't quite add up. The most likely conclusion was the simple one: the kid had wandered off, got disorientated, dehydrated and died. End of story.'

'So what didn't stack up?'

'Well, as I said, we reckoned he wandered into the middle of the lake by himself. We couldn't find any evidence that anyone had taken him out there. There were no tyre marks, no other footprints, nothing like that. But we never established how he got to the lake in the first place. It's miles from anywhere. There was no abandoned car. He was living kilometres away. So we suspected death by misadventure, but not necessarily death by accident. Someone must have known what he intended, or taken him there, or witnessed it.'

'What was the victim's name?'

'Zeke someone. I forget his surname, but it'll be on record. Something Eastern European.'

Ivan plays devil's advocate. 'I've seen Lake Kalingra. It's pretty brutal, but it's not the Simpson Desert. You could walk across it in a day.'

'Bullshit. Not in forty-degree heat. Not without water. We were out there for an hour and it almost did us in. Worst headache I've ever had. And it almost blinded me.'

Ivan touches his own head. The pain is receding. Is it an illusion, or is the medicine starting to work? 'Anything else strange about the case?'

'Yeah, as a matter of fact. There were no marks on the body, no sign of violence, nothing to suggest he'd been physically coerced in any way. The autopsy found nothing like that. But it did find he'd ingested all sorts of drugs, which explains how he could easily have become disoriented out there. And one more thing: there was a ring of scars circling the head, small scabs on his forehead.'

'Caused by what?'

'Well, we never found it, but Reg and I speculated he might have been wearing a crown of thorns when he wandered off across the lake.'

The hairs on the back of Ivan's neck stand on end. 'What? Like a religious thing? Like Christ in the wilderness?'

'Maybe.'

'You say he was living miles away. Where exactly?'

'He was a member of this whacko sect. Christians. At the far end of the mining leases.'

'The Rapture?'

'That's it.'

'And he was high? Under the influence?'

'You name it, he'd swallowed it. Uppers, downers, opiates, analgesics, hallucinogens, party drugs. Even had some Viagra mixed in there for good measure. Amazing he got as far as he did.'

'So that's why you were assigned this time around? Because Jonas McGee was crucified?'

'I guess. Packenham sounded me out. I said yes, in case there was some connection.' Ivan can hear the hesitation before Montifore continues: 'I was never satisfied with the case. I always felt we had overlooked something.'

Ivan nods to himself. Plodder Packenham, the head of Homicide. Straight as a die. 'Right. So back then, did you ever come across a man called Stanley Honeywell?'

'Not that I recall. Why?'

'He has your business card—and he's a suspect in McGee's death.'

'Who is he?'

'You wouldn't forget him. Giant of a bloke, a man mountain. Mixed race. Islander and Aboriginal, Indian and Chinese. Tattoos.'

'Yeah, I reckon I know who you're talking about. Does he work out near the lake, in one of those opal mines up on the ridge?'

'Yeah. He did.'

'Well, that explains it. We canvassed the whole area up there, asking if anyone had seen this bloke wander off onto the lake. Handed out our cards like confetti. You know the deal.'

'Let me guess: no one saw anything.'

'I wouldn't read too much into that, mate. Middle of the day, forty-degree heat. Makes a lot more sense to be underground.'

'So why has he kept your card all this time?'

'You'd have to ask him that.'

Ivan thinks it through. Morris's explanation of how Stanley came to have the card is logical enough. But why did he keep it? Just in case something came up and Stanley could help? Or just part of the flotsam and jetsam of life? He thinks of his own desk back in Sydney, one drawer with a couple of hundred cards, most of them useless and out of date. 'Morris, if the victim was living at the Rapture, I assume you interviewed the Seer, the self-proclaimed prophet?'

'Of course. Reg and I tag-teamed him. But he had nothing useful to say. Just a whole lot of malarkey about how the kid was in heaven, among the righteous.'

'Nothing about why he was full of drugs?'

'No. I wanted to put him in the can, sweat him, but Reg reckoned that was because I didn't like him, not because he was a suspect.' Montifore chuckles. 'I was still a bit of a bull at a gate in those days. Reg was more nuanced.' And now the humour leaves the inspector's voice. 'A few days later, we still didn't have much to go on and they pulled us out.'

'You sound pissed off.'

Montifore doesn't respond straight away. When he does, his voice is sombre. 'I can't put my finger on it, but I reckon we weren't sent to find a killer, we were sent to appease the powers that be.'

'What do you mean?'

'We were pulled out too early. Someone wanted a line drawn under it. Reg wasn't happy; neither was I.' Montifore lets out a long breath, an elongated sigh. 'That's when it started.'

'When what started?'

'Off the record? Between you and me?'

'Of course.'

'First time I got the shits badly enough to background a journo.'

'They wrote it up?'

'They tried. Story got spiked.'

— —

Nell is almost at Cuttamulla, sitting on one hundred and forty on the dead-straight road when she sees, in her rear-view mirror, a large white Range Rover looming behind her. She's driving thirty kilometres per hour above the limit, so how fast has this joker been going to get behind her? And who in their right mind tailgates a speeding cop car? She's got half a mind to pull him over, but she knows she can't. Her time, Stanley's time, is too precious. She strikes a bargain with herself: if the Range Rover stays behind her, she'll overlook it, but if the arsehole overtakes her at this speed, she'll take the plate number and give him grief when she has more time.

She's almost at the mine when her phone starts pinging through the console with missed calls and text messages. It makes sense: the mine has its own mobile phone tower. So many miners, so well paid, out in the middle of nowhere with nothing to do. Probably one of the most lucrative mobile phone towers in the country. Up ahead, she can see the piles of coal, like a range of black hills rising above the horizon. She's close, but she decides to check her calls. As she starts to pull over, the white Range Rover roars past, followed by an identical vehicle. Not one car, but two. They brake aggressively and turn off into the mine. Stopped beside the road, she scrolls through the last hour of calls, making sure she hasn't missed anything vital from Ivan. But it's another number that catches her attention, another message. *Finnigans Gap bank. Stanley H was just here.* Stanley Honeywell at the bank? When? Now? And here she is, stranded an hour away. *Shit.*

She rings the number.

'Hello, Westpac, Janelle speaking.'

'Janelle. Detective Constable Nell Buchanan. What have you got?'

'Stanley Honeywell came in and withdrew the money—all of it.'

'What? The twenty thousand dollars?'

'I'm sorry. It's his money. I had no authority to refuse him.'

'Understood. Not your fault. Tell me, how was he? How did he act?'

'Like he was stressed. Kind of cowed.'

'What did he say?'

'Nothing. But he wasn't alone.'

'Go on.'

'Ray Penuch was with him. From Cuttamulla.'

'Big guy? Red hair?'

'That's him. He's in here at least once a week. Does their payroll.'

'And you're suggesting what exactly? That Stanley was acting under duress from Penuch?'

'He wasn't smiling, that's for sure.'

'So what was Penuch doing? Looking over his shoulder? Telling him what to do?'

'No. Just standing by the door, arms folded, like a pub bouncer.'

'And did they leave together?'

'Yes. I watched them go. They got into a Cuttamulla truck.'

'And when was this?'

'About an hour and a half ago.'

'Right. Thanks, Janelle. Anything else?'

'No, that's it. I thought you would want to know.'

'Absolutely. Thank you. You've been incredibly helpful.' Nell is about to end the call when she remembers her own visit earlier in the day. 'I guess it's too early to have an answer back from headquarters about who cashed Jonas's cheque?'

'Sorry, not yet.'

The call over, she does her maths. If Stanley and Penuch left the bank an hour and a half ago, there's still a chance she's in the right spot, that they've returned to Cuttamulla. That, or they're somewhere out there on the featureless plain.

She rings Ivan. This time there is no delay; he answers on the second ring.

— —

'Okay, let me know if he's at the mine as soon as you can,' Ivan tells Nell, standing on the verandah of the police station, looking at the vandalised statue. 'I'll come out if he's there. Him or this Penuch geezer.'

He ends the call. How much has he missed, those lost minutes he was laid out cold on Jonas McGee's floor? And how much time has he wasted, going back to the motel, showering, washing off the blood, changing clothes? He touches the back of his head. No more blood, but he can feel an enormous lump. Hopefully no one inside the station is going to start asking questions. But when he gets inside, it's all but empty, just Garry down in the squad room.

'Where is everyone?' Ivan asks.

Garry stares, mouth open, before responding. 'Lunch. They're at lunch.'

'Right. Bit late in the day, isn't it?'

'Busy day,' says Garry.

'How'd you go with the miners up on the West Ridge? I forgot to ask.'

'All on your desk. I checked eight mines, but only three of them say they were up there on the Tuesday, none of them before noon. The others said it was still too wet to be working.'

'No one before noon?'

'There was a meeting of the miners' co-op Tuesday morning. Most of them were there.'

'So they all have alibis?'

'Yes.'

'Good work. We'll track their phones, just in case, see if anyone's story doesn't match.' But his mind is already moving on. If someone knew about the miners' meeting, knew Jonas was alone up on the ridge, it would provide the perfect opportunity.

Garry interrupts his speculation. 'You know the phones won't register if they were underground.'

'True. We should be able to piece it together, though. Did any of them have anything interesting to say?'

'A couple of them saw the big black car, but weren't sure precisely when. My impression was that it was up there several times.'

'Okay, thanks. That's useful.'

Ivan leaves the constable and moves back to the work room assigned to him and Nell, now being referred to as the detectives' room. He gets inside and closes the door. He wants to get to Cuttamulla, but he wants to be up to speed first. The last thing he needs is to go off half cocked. On his computer he checks the emails, opens up the bank statements that Nell has sent through. He sees almost immediately what she was referring to: the twenty thousand dollars deposited last Tuesday, now withdrawn. He stares at the figure on the screen. It wants to tell him something, he knows it does. Twenty thousand dollars in cash, the day Jonas McGee died. His eyes drift further down. Nothing, just regular wages going in from Cuttamulla, the usual living expenses, nothing fancy. Stanley Honeywell is a man who lives well within his means. With a grimace, Ivan realises that, even with the twenty thousand gone, Stanley Honeywell has more to his name than he himself does. Stanley may be slow-witted, but not so slow-witted as to toy with poker machines.

He flips to Jonas McGee's accounts. The first thing he sees is the huge whack of money being withdrawn: $287,000. That's a lot of opals. But as he scrolls backwards, he sees something else: the money going into CommSec, then a large payout coming from the online broker. He pulls up the CommSec website just to make sure, confirming it is a share-trading platform. It's big, lots of customers, the biggest online broker in the country. Everyone from day traders and speculators to investors. Not the big players, not the hedge funds and whatnot, but retail. Mum and dad investors. A memory comes to him of looking at Jonas's laptop. What did he see there, before he was knocked out? He does a couple of quick calculations, adding up the money going in, the money coming out. A little over $50,000 into CommSec, roughly $130,000 out. In three months. A remarkable return on investments. So maybe not a gamble after all. Maybe that's the definition: if you're winning, it's investing; if you're losing, it's gambling.

He closes his eyes, tries to recall McGee's computer. There were documents, a company. He grasps at the tendril of memory. It's there, just out of reach. Amazing he can remember anything at all, given the blow knocked him out. Again he touches his head. A little local soreness, but the headache has all but receded. An image floats before his closed eyes, he almost has it, it's on the tip of his tongue. He remembers that it was somehow familiar, that he already knew the company. And now he has it. He stands, scrambles around on the table, finds the *Financial Review* story that Nell showed him just that morning, locates the relevant paragraph.

The recent increase in Sino–US tension has led to a tripling in the share price over the past twelve months of Australia's only significant existing rare-earth producer, LikeUs Pty Ltd, based in South Australia.

LikeUs. That's it; that's the company where McGee made his money. Ivan googles it. Rare earths. Lots of reports about its booming share price, so hardly a state secret. But it's based in South Australia, up in the middle of nowhere near Woomera, fifteen hundred kilometres from here. The headquarters are in Adelaide. That makes Ivan think of McGee's daughter, Elsie, living in the same city. Maybe she was feeding him inside information? But that thought leads nowhere: $130,000 is chickenfeed in the context of the stock market. ASIC, the regulator, doesn't bother investigating unless insider-trading allegations run into millions. And there's no need to have insider information to invest in rare earths: they're the flavour of the month, splashed all over the papers. So all he's left with is Jonas making money mining opals, investing it in a rare-earth company and making a sizable profit. Nothing dodgy, nothing illegal. Nothing to get killed for. The man then pooled his windfall with some cash and a draw down on his home loan, and withdrew the lot via a bank cheque. Intriguing, but nothing that would explain how and why he died, or why anyone would want to crucify him.

Ivan runs a hand through his hair, an unconscious gesture, unintentionally touching his head wound, setting off a sharp dart of pain. He stares at the bank statements, wonders if they can tell him anything more. He goes back through Jonas's account. There are a couple of deposits from Kalingra Rare Earths, one for a thousand dollars, one for eighteen hundred. About three months ago. What was it Kyle Torshack said? That Jonas had picked up extra income from carpentry?

Ivan ponders the rare-earth mine, what connection it might have to LikeUs. Two things: they both target rare earths and they are now both owned, in part or in whole, by Bullshit Bob Inglis. He googles Kalingra. The website confirms it's a private company, but there is no reference yet to Robert Inglis or his corporate manoeuvres. The site is simple, almost amateurish. Jonas worked at Kalingra. Maybe it's what sparked his interest in rare earths. Maybe that's all it was. Even if he gleaned some inside knowledge about Kalingra's prospects, that could hardly have informed his decision to invest in a mine halfway across the continent.

It occurs to Ivan that the mine is next to the lake, close by Jonas McGee's own mine. The rule of proximity comes to mind. He'd been thinking of its application to the other miners, the ones working close by, the ones who might have had the opportunity to kill Jonas or to desecrate his body. But now it's suggesting something else. He knows he should get going, but first he decides to check the details of Morris Montifore's old case, the young man who died out on the lake bed.

— —

Nell is growing more and more frustrated, cooling her heels in the reception of the admin building, a large demountable linked to other demountables. She's already been waiting for more than half an hour and still there's no word from the company. She wants to get out there, into the mine, search for Stanley, make sure he's unhurt. It's a stupid impulse, she knows. The mine is huge, a massive entity, more like a principality than a business. She'd always known Cuttamulla was here, of course, but she'd never comprehended its scale. She could look for a hundred years and not find him. So she's forced to sit, to wait. She doesn't even know if Stanley Honeywell is here; she's totally reliant on the company to confirm that. And so she waits, watching the clock tick, pacing back and forth, pretending to read the wall displays. One describes the mine's mission: taking energy to the world, lifting millions from poverty. Another spruiks its environmental credentials: the total rejuvenation of the land once the coal is removed, and the use of carbon-offset programs to ensure production is carbon neutral. A carbon-neutral coalmine. Terrific. The displays lack finesse, like a school project printed on better paper. The room itself is similarly low-key, functional and practical, leaving any glitz for the big-city headquarters. She eyes the receptionist with growing antipathy, feeling the badge itching in her pocket. She wants to do something, but she has no idea what.

A man enters, a man in an immaculate suit. He looks about fifty, tanned face and a too-white smile, with salt-and-pepper hair, as if he's stepped from a luxury watch advertisement. 'Constable Buchanan, I assume?' He's holding her card and smiling. His teeth are perfect.

'Detective constable. I'm here to interview Stanley Honeywell,' she states.

'So I understand. And let me assure you, we are doing everything possible to locate Mr Honeywell. The good news is I can confirm he is onsite. However, he isn't answering his phone and he's not wearing his pager. Nor is he at his accommodation.'

'But he's definitely here?'

'We can confirm he returned just over an hour ago.'

'With Ray Penuch?'

'That is correct.'

Nell feels relief; better here than out there somewhere. 'And you are?' she asks.

'Cyril Flange. At your service.'

She eyes his clothes. He's wearing cufflinks. Who wears a suit at a coalmine? With cufflinks? 'You're based here?'

He smiles, a superior smirk. 'No. I'm counsel to Mr Bullwinkel, the chairman and chief executive of Cuttamulla Coal. We're based in Sydney.'

Nell thinks of the twin Range Rovers out on the highway, of the corporate jet coming in to land as she descended from the East Ridge. 'Delaney Bullwinkel? He's here?'

'Indeed. He's extremely hands-on. Prides himself on it. Comes up at least once a month.'

Nell shakes her head, signalling her confusion. 'So why are you involved in this investigation? Surely finding Penuch and Honeywell is below your pay grade?'

He returns her look of confusion. 'What investigation?'

'Into the murder of Jonas McGee.'

'I'm sorry, Constable, I have no idea what you are referring to. I just arrived here. I heard you were seeking to interview one of our employees and I offered to help out.' He offers a patronising grin, triggering irritation in her.

'In that case, I'm very grateful for your assistance,' says Nell, suppressing her annoyance. 'While you locate Stanley Honeywell, I'd like to speak with Mr Penuch. Could you page him for me, please?'

Mr Smooth spreads his arms in apology. 'Alas, we are also having difficulty locating Ray Penuch. We suspect they're together.'

The thought of it, of Stanley at the mercy of Penuch, reignites her sense of urgency. 'Mr Flange—Cyril—I have reason to believe that Ray Penuch has assaulted Stanley Honeywell. *Seriously* assaulted. Yesterday and perhaps again today. It's urgent that we find them. That *you* find them. I hold fears for the safety of Stanley Honeywell.'

The lawyer's face loses some of its gloss. 'I'm sorry. I didn't realise the situation was so time critical. Please stay here. I'll redouble our efforts.'

And so Nell finds herself waiting once again. The clock, the posters, the pacing. She walks over to the receptionist, for the first time noticing a number of video monitors aligned below the woman's counter. She tries to keep her voice light as she engages. 'Great set-up you've got. Wish we had this at the station.'

The receptionist looks glad for the distraction. 'Good, isn't it? You should see the real nerve centre, in operations. They've got hundreds of screens, run the whole mine from there. Lot of it's remote control. The same in the security block; dozens of screens. This is nothing. Just people coming and going.'

'I get it. When I called from the gate, it came through here. Was that you I spoke to?'

'No. Security. But I could see you.'

'Can you show me?'

'Sure. Come round the back here.'

Nell walks around behind the receptionist, where she can see the three monitors. One has a mosaic of six camera angles, the other two each have one view, a larger version of two of the angles on the first monitor. 'Can you show me the gate?'

'Here it is.' The receptionist uses a remote control, a domestic television hand unit, to switch channels. 'There's two views. This one's front on. Captures the whole vehicle, including number plate recognition. Security knows which vehicles are onsite and which have left.' Just as the receptionist finishes explaining, a truck appears in frame. Presumably, somewhere in security the number plate is being registered. But the wideshot makes it difficult to see through the windscreen. She watches as an arm extends from the window and the driver swipes a card against the sensor. The boom gate rises and the truck moves through.

'Very neat,' enthuses Nell. 'I love the number plate recognition. But you don't really get to see the driver, or if there are passengers.'

'Here.' The receptionist punches up another camera angle. Nell has difficulty determining what it's showing; it just looks vacant. The sky, a fence, some road, the corner of a building. Then a car moves into frame and she comprehends that it's a driver's-side view. This angle is wide as well; the car is towards the bottom of the screen; presumably a truck would be closer to the top. As she watches, the window comes down, the driver breaking his air-conditioned seal for long enough to swipe his card. It shows his face clearly, although his passenger is largely obscured.

'Are they recorded, these videos of comings and goings?'

'Not here, but I think security does.'

'You can't access the recordings from here?'

'Me? No. Why would I?'

Nell shrugs. 'I'm just amazed at how clever and well resourced this company is. So cutting-edge.'

'Thank you,' says the receptionist.

Nell returns to her seat, mind full of questions. If Penuch was driving, if Penuch was the one who swiped at the gate, how does Cyril Flange know Stanley Honeywell is here?

Another fifteen minutes and Cyril is back, wearing an expression of apology like face paint at a kids' party. 'Constable Buchanan, I am so sorry for the delay. Our entire security team, plus other staff, are now out looking for them. Security is going back through CCTV recordings to see if we can track where they have gone. We'll find them, but it could take some time.'

'Thank you.'

'While we wait, I wonder if you might fill me in on what's happening here? I understand the urgency in finding the two men, the physical danger, but I'm still none the wiser as to what has actually transpired.'

Nell's not sure if she believes him, but knows she needs his cooperation. She keeps her explanation as short as possible. 'Last Tuesday, Stanley Honeywell deposited twenty thousand dollars in the Finnigans Gap branch of the Westpac bank. The same day, his former employer, Jonas McGee, was murdered. We wish to speak to Mr Honeywell in relation to the death of Mr McGee.'

'He's a suspect?'

'We want to speak with him urgently.'

'How does that fit with the allegation he has been assaulted by Raymond Penuch?'

'Shortly before returning to Cuttamulla this afternoon, Honeywell withdrew the money from the Westpac bank. Raymond Penuch was with him. We have reason to believe Honeywell was acting under duress from Penuch, and that Penuch had already assaulted him at least once.'

'That's shocking,' says Flange, oozing sincerity. And then, as an addendum: 'Constable Buchanan, can I take you into my confidence?'

'Of course.' Nell isn't sure if she trusts this man, but isn't about to decline an offer of information.

'This matter obviously concerns us. These two men, at loose on our mine site. We really do not want this to get out. To the media, I mean.'

Nell considers him. 'You find them for me and you have my word: the media won't hear a thing.'

'That is most professional of you. Thank you.' Flange studies her, as if making a decision. 'In return, I have something for you. Here.' He hands her a folder.

'What is it?'

'Printouts from our security team. I believe you requested them.'

She opens the folder. An A4 page, headed: *Stanley Honeywell. Employee 5154. Movements, week 3, January.* And beneath it, time stamps of Stanley leaving Cuttamulla last Tuesday and returning later the same day, then leaving again on Sunday morning. There is also a handwritten note: *Re-entered with Raymond Penuch, employee 2435, Monday.* She flips the page. There are four photographs, stills taken from CCTV frames: three of Stanley, one of Ray Penuch, swiping their cards at the boom gates, all time-stamped.

'Thank you. That's a great help. But the last entry, Ray Penuch returning to Cuttamulla: how can you be sure Stanley Honeywell was with him?'

'His swipe card was used, shortly after they returned, to open his accommodation, among other things. It's part of the trail security is following.'

'Can you be sure he was the one using it? Not Penuch?'

Flange nods, as if appreciating her attention to detail. 'He's here, all right. Security has found CCTV of him after his return. They're following the recordings, trying to work out where they've gone.'

'Can I see that vision?'

'No, not immediately. Security is throwing all their resources into tracking the men and finding them. You'll understand, they accumulate thousands of hours of recordings in a single day. But, of course, all vision will be kept and we can supply you with the relevant material.'

'Do you know if the two of them are together?'

'They were on the most recent recording, but that was some time ago now.'

Nell sighs. 'I would like to help if I could. I feel a bit useless just sitting here.'

Flange oozes empathy. 'I'm sorry. This site is huge. And dangerous. No one can move about without undergoing induction. And even then, only with a qualified guide.'

'So I wait.'

'You can, although we'll be closing up soon.'

'I thought this was a twenty-four seven operation?'

'The mine is, of course. But reception and administration work office hours.'

'Is there somewhere else I can wait? In security, perhaps?'

'I'm sorry, Constable. You don't have the clearance. I'm not sure even I can go there. There are constant concerns about industrial espionage, protection of intellectual property and industrial processes. No outsiders are allowed.'

'I'm a police officer, investigating a murder.'

'Even so.'

'So what are you suggesting I do?'

'Return to Finnigans Gap. I will personally let you know as soon as we locate the men. Security are under instructions to detain both of them, to keep them separate, to ensure the safety and wellbeing of Stanley Honeywell and to hold them in custody until you can return or we can deliver them to you in town.'

'In custody?'

'We have our own holding cells.'

'That's legal?'

'Absolutely. Part of the workplace contracts; workers consent to a number of conditions when they sign on. I assure you the holding cells are seldom used, apart from locking up the occasional drunk for their own good.'

'No,' says Nell. 'I'm not going anywhere. I wait here until you find them.'

Flange sighs. 'Suit yourself.' He shakes his head. And then he smiles, flashes those perfect teeth. Nell feels like rearranging them.

chapter fifteen

THEY EAT IN SILENCE AT THE PUB; THERE'S NOT A LOT TO SAY. THE MENU IS primitive, as far from fine dining as Finnigans Gap is from the Pacific Ocean: burgers, steaks, schnitzel, microwaved pizzas, fish and chips. Ivan looks at Nell's meal, sitting on her plate, largely untouched: two pieces of identical fish, perfect triangles. He wonders if they're real or reconstituted, whether they're from China or the North Atlantic or a mixture of the two. Triangle fish. There are chips. They come with every meal. Compulsory carbohydrates. And the salad of country Australia: iceberg lettuce, half-ripe tomatoes sliced into quarters, topped with shaved carrots, cucumber circles and dressing out of a bottle, full of sugar and MSG. It's as if the last seventy years of immigration never happened.

Around them patrons drink quietly, as if respecting their mood. It's Monday night, the place is almost empty. It's not the sort of pub Ivan remembers from his uniform days in the Central West.

Down there, the pubs were old, two-storey affairs, built last century or the one before that, small rooms full of character and charm. This place is just one big room: cement-block walls, steel girders, industrial air-conditioning. The tables are plastic, the chairs cheap aluminium, the only decorations promotional material supplied by the breweries. Soulless. Even so, on this night, Ivan prefers it to the club. On an evening like this, with the investigation going nowhere fast, he doesn't want to be anywhere near the poker machine grotto. There'll be machines here, too—there are machines everywhere—but they won't be as numerous, they won't be as new, they won't be hermetically sealed from reality. Now that he thinks of them, he can't help looking. Sure enough, beyond the bar, Ivan can see the flashing lights: VIP ROOM. He averts his eyes, thinks of the case. The critical first full day of their investigation has passed, full of sound and fury signifying very little indeed. He feels flat, exhausted. He glances up at Nell; she looks the same, picking at her food, sipping at her second wine. He's not drinking. The headache from the blow to his head remains contained, but he doesn't want to risk a breakout.

The printout from Cuttamulla, detailing the movements of Stanley Honeywell on the day Jonas McGee died, sits on the table, examined and re-examined and now discarded. The timeline is conclusive: Stanley was absent from Cuttamulla for less than three hours, leaving at just before ten in the morning and returning at twelve twenty. Enough time to get to town, deposit the money at the bank at eleven twenty, then return to Cuttamulla. Leaving no time to get anywhere near Jonas McGee's opal mine at the far end of the West Ridge. Up on the East Ridge, the goat fed itself. They've double-checked: the times provided by Cuttamulla align with the time stamps on the deposit record at the bank. They'll check the phone records, the metadata and tracking information generated by the network masts, but Ivan has no doubt they'll corroborate what they already know: Stanley didn't kill his old friend and benefactor, he didn't crucify him, and he was nowhere near the mine last Tuesday.

Nell tries a bit more fish, then pushes the plate away, drinks some wine, looks at the files. 'They couldn't be fabricated, could they?'

'I don't think so. No. Not and line up so accurately with the bank records.'

'I guess not. It just sucks, that's all.'

'Fair summary,' says Ivan, returning to his schnitzel. Somewhere between the kitchen and their table, it has lost its crispness.

'Did you know? About the phone call? Did they give you advance warning?' Nell asks.

'No. I got mine straight after yours.'

'From the deputy commissioner?'

'From her office.'

'Saying what?'

'That I need to keep a tighter rein on my subordinates.'

'And what did you say?'

'Nothing. I didn't get the chance. It was a very short phone call.'

She pulls the plate back towards her, stabs at the fish idly with her fork, but doesn't lift any to her mouth. 'Yeah. Same here. I was only there for another ten minutes after Flange left when they rang. Told me to leave before five, before the office shut. That smarmy fucking lawyer didn't even have the guts to put in an appearance.' She pushes the plate away again. 'I've never been so fucking humiliated. I reckon the arsehole was sitting up there in security, laughing at me, watching on CCTV.'

Ivan nods in sympathy, but his words are blunt. 'It doesn't matter, Nell. Look at the printouts. Stanley can't have killed McGee. He was still at the mine when he died. And he didn't have enough time to get up there when McGee was crucified.'

'Is that meant to make me feel better?'

'Yes. As a matter of fact.'

'We've left him out there, Ivan. Doesn't that bother you? They're probably pummelling the shit out of him, while we sit here and eat our dinner.'

He feels a tinge of anger; he's not the one at fault here. 'Of course it bothers me, but what exactly are you proposing I do about it? Disobey a direct instruction from the deputy commissioner? How could I do that? Stanley isn't even a suspect anymore.'

'So we just lap it up?'

He looks her in the eye. 'Yes. That's exactly what we do.'

He can see her own anger, see it rising. She's about to say something, to verbalise it, but before the words can form, they're interrupted by Carole Nguyen and Blake Ness. 'Oh, here you are. We looked for you at the club. We reckon the food's better over there.'

'Thought we should sample all that Finnigans Gap has to offer,' says Ivan, trying and failing to keep his tone light.

'Right,' says Carole, sounding a little unsure of her footing.

'Join us for a drink?' asks Nell.

'No. Early start tomorrow,' says Blake. 'There aren't any scheduled flights until Wednesday, so they're sending a PolAir plane up first thing. We're heading back. Dawn flight.'

'Lucky you,' says Ivan.

'We've accomplished all we can up here,' says Carole.

'Well, thanks for everything, as always,' says Ivan, making the effort to stand, to give the investigators that much respect, shaking their hands. 'Blake, is it possible for you to take McGee's body with you?' he asks.

'Perhaps,' says Blake, sounding unsure.

'I appreciate it's a lot to ask, but without knowing what killed him, it's hard for us to progress. Can you really check him out thoroughly—toxicology, the works—find out exactly what killed him?'

Blake looks at his watch. With the early start, he'll need to prepare the body for transport this evening. 'You want to persist?'

He doesn't hesitate. 'Absolutely.'

Blake nods, as does Carole, as if acknowledging Ivan's commitment.

'Sure,' says Blake. 'I can do that. I'd like to find out myself.'

'Let me know if there is anything more I can do,' adds Carole. And then, as if to emphasise which side she is on: 'Anything.' Ivan wonders if they've heard about the deputy commissioner's reprimand.

The four of them shake hands a second time, a sign of solidarity, while they tell each other what a pleasure it has been to work together, how they look forward to meeting again. Blake and Carole make an effort to praise Nell. For a moment, collegiality bonds them, but once the two forensic scientists are gone, silence returns. At least Nell's anger has subsided. The place around them is quiet, nothing more than a low hum. There is Big Bash cricket on television, screens mounted around the walls and above the bar, but the sound is down and no one is paying attention. The lights from the VIP room beckon. He returns his attention to his increasingly limp schnitzel.

It's Nell who speaks first. 'Do you want to get back to Sydney? Leave me here to mop up?'

He looks at her. 'No. I want to know if he was murdered or not. And if he was, I want to find the killer.' And then: 'It really is that simple.' He doesn't mean to put it there, but there is needle in his voice.

'So you're fine with that lawyer snapping his fingers and giving us our marching orders?'

'No, of course not. I know how you feel, but we're Homicide detectives. We can't right every wrong the world throws up. People like Cyril Flange, Delaney Bullwinkel, they're influential. Connected. You've just experienced how much. If we go after them without good cause, then there will be blowback. I guarantee it. And we don't have good cause.'

She shakes her head. 'That shits me.'

Ivan gives up on his food, pushing the plate to one side as well, and makes a decision. 'You remember that case Morris Montifore and I worked last year? The big one, the one in all the papers—all those Sydney murders? The one that journo, Martin Scarsden, claimed all the credit for?'

'I could hardly miss it.'

'Right. Big-city power, a ring of influence, a dining club. Heavy hitters, one and all.'

'What's your point?' she asks, expression surly.

'Delaney Bullwinkel is a member. Was a member.'

'What are you saying?'

'What I'm saying is this: it is not in our interest to antagonise them. They've been helpful. They've provided crucial evidence of where Stanley was and when on the day McGee died. The bank records corroborate it, and we can double-check with Honeywell's phone records. Without that help, we'd still be chasing him, finding him, interrogating him, maybe even building towards a prosecution. Wasting time, only to eventually get the phone tower info and realise we were on the wrong track. Sure, Cuttamulla want to cover up the assault. It's bad publicity. But it's small beer. Honestly. And it's got fuck-all to do with our investigation. It's a dead end.'

Nell says nothing, just glares at him.

'It happens all the time in murder cases. The most promising lead fizzles out. Ultimately, that's a good thing. Eliminating possibilities. You need to be resilient, reposition, move on.' He can see she's still not convinced. 'Case in point. I spoke to Cheryl before. Those animal sacrifices at the fake church up on the East Ridge? She took another look, realised they were only happening during school holidays.'

'Kids?'

'Yeah. She and Richter found the culprits. Nothing to do with the Rapture. Not everything is connected. But we persist.'

'I guess.'

'And sometimes, you don't get there. You don't get the breakthrough; it doesn't all come together. The killer gets away with it and the file goes into the cold case cabinet.'

She bites her lip, but the words come out anyway. 'Is that what happened with Montifore? His investigation up here?'

Ivan closes his eyes for a second, decides to tell her. 'Yes. That's exactly what happened. Two of the finest detectives in the history of the force, each of them more experienced and talented than you and me put together. They did their level best and came up empty-handed. They got pulled out. It happens.'

Now she just sits there, her eyes full of unspoken accusation.

'I spoke to him. Asked him about it. Looked up the records. The dead guy was called Zeke Jakowitz. Wandered off onto Lake Kalingra, chock-a-block full of drugs, in weather like this. Officially death by misadventure. You said you'd heard about it when you were here.'

'Yeah. Once or twice. Nothing I can really recall, though.'

'He lived at the Rapture.'

'Will Montifore come up here now?' she asks, frowning.

'No, Morris Montifore is under internal investigation. That's why he's not here and you are.' Ivan states it, like presenting evidence.

'What?'

'He's under investigation for speaking to the media, to Martin Scarsden. Most likely, he'll be forced into early retirement.' He can see the shock on her face and decides to press the point. 'Do you understand now? All that amazing work he did and he's still getting taken out by the rich and the powerful and the connected. They're out for revenge. The old guard.'

She stares, the horror clear on her face. 'What's that got to do with us?'

'Hopefully nothing. But if we go after Cuttamulla without good cause, it will be us. So let's keep our heads down and find out who killed Jonas McGee.'

Nell's phone pings, then Ivan's, in quick succession.

For a moment, Ivan ignores it, feels compelled to continue: 'We're only one day in. And most murder investigations, the complex ones, work through a process of elimination. Start ruling out the obvious suspects and eventually you get to the perpetrator. That's what we've done today; we've eliminated Stanley Honeywell as a suspect and now we can move on. It's not a day wasted.'

Nell looks unconvinced. She checks her phone, so does he. A message from an unlisted number. *Honeywell and Penuch located and detained. Will bring to FG police station 9 am. Best regards, Cyril Flange.*

'What do you think?' she asks.

'I still want to talk to them.'

She frowns. 'What was the money all about? The twenty thousand?'

'We'll find out tomorrow morning.'

'So what's next?'

'We need to speak to Elsie McGee.'

'I'll do it first thing,' she says, draining her wine. She stands to get another, before thinking of her colleague. 'Drink?' The anger has gone; she's back on an even keel.

'No. I'm good. I need an early night.'

— —

Later, Nell is sitting on her fourth wine, thinking through the day, thinking about Ivan Lucic. She doesn't know what she was imagining when she drove from Bourke yesterday morning, full of enthusiasm. That he was some sort of white knight, a crusader for justice, who would induct her into the inner circle, usher her to her seat at the round table. Instead, he's hard to get a handle on: friendly and collegiate at times, taciturn and removed at others. There are long periods where it's obvious he's running through scenarios, his eyes staring unseeing, or worse, resting on her, when he's calculating possibilities, but doing it internally, by himself, not workshopping with her. And when he does act with consideration, she can see him making an effort; it doesn't come naturally. What is she to him? A colleague or just a grunt, someone to do the paperwork, to apply for the warrants and check police records.

She's thinking of another wine when Trevor Topsoil sidles up.

'Hello, stranger.' His voice is a deep baritone, well remembered.

'Hi, yourself.'

'Having a quiet drink?'

'No law against it.' And she smiles. Trev has always made her smile.

'You should know.' He smiles back. It's a nice smile. She's always liked it. It's relaxed, uncomplicated. What you see is what you get with Trev; no intensity, no inner machinations, no getting shut out. No inconsistencies or mood swings or unfocused staring. 'Can I get you one?' he asks.

Her grin widens. 'Sure.'

'Sauvignon blanc with two pieces of ice, right?'

'That's it.' He remembers. Three years on and he remembers. And she knows there and then she'll sleep with him again. And why not? If Ivan Lucic is going to abandon her, walk off into the night and leave her here, why the fuck not?

— —

Ivan is intending to go straight to his room, to sleep, but the night has cooled, the air losing its malice. It's no longer hot, merely warm, welcoming rather than oppressive. He decides to walk, his mind restless. After only a day, Finnigans Gap is already growing familiar. Here's the cafe where he and Nell had lunch, there's the police station, there's the whitegoods shop, the clothes shop, the motel further along.

He enters the Alpine Cafe, thinking a bottle of water might be a sensible companion to take on his walk. And there, sitting at a booth, hoeing into one hamburger while another waits upon his plate, is the mining magnate, Bullshit Bob Inglis. All by himself.

Ivan takes his water from the fridge in the foothills of the Matterhorn, pays at the counter, then approaches the man. 'Mind if I join you for a moment?'

'Free country,' says Inglis, voice muffled by burger.

Ivan sits. 'I hear that congratulations are in order. The King of Kalingra.'

The billionaire bursts out laughing. 'Fuck. I like that. Mind if I use it? Better than Bullshit Bob.' He takes another bite, chews and swallows. 'I don't know about you, but it's too fucking hot up here to eat during the day. Then it gets to night-time and suddenly I'm ravenous.'

'Burger any good?' asks Ivan, making small talk.

'Fucking glorious.' The big man chortles. 'You know, I spend half my life in these poncy restaurants. Perth and Sydney, London and New York. Wherever. Three hats, five stars, and bottles of wine the price of a second-hand car. And none as good as this.' He wafts the burger before Ivan as if to demonstrate before taking another huge bite, juice running down his chin momentarily before he wipes it away with the back of his hand. He gestures to Ivan with what's left of it. 'The secret is hunger. I'm never hungry in the city. But up here, after a busy day and no tucker, once the sun has set, I could eat a fucking horse.'

'I'll have to remember that,' says Ivan, the pub schnitzel heavy in his stomach. 'So the rare-earth mine is going ahead?'

'Too right,' says Inglis, then eyes Ivan cannily. 'You a gambling man?'

'No,' responds Ivan a little too quickly.

'Very sensible,' says Inglis. 'But this is no gamble. That mine up there at Kalingra will be a printing press. Printing money.' Inglis takes a very satisfied slug of Diet Coke. 'Here's a tip: invest in rare earths. It's a no-brainer.'

'So I've heard. You're going to list it?' asks Ivan.

Suddenly, the shutters come down, the pleasantness is gone and the billionaire is all business. 'Who are you?' asks Inglis bluntly. 'You don't look like a local.'

'I'm a police officer. Detective Sergeant Ivan Lucic. I'm here investigating a murder.'

Inglis nods, calming down again. 'You're up from Sydney? That miner who was crucified?'

'Right on both counts.'

'Getting anywhere?'

'Making steady progress, yes,' Ivan lies.

'Good for you.' Inglis consumes the last of his first burger, wipes his hands and face with a napkin and takes another slug from his bottle of Diet Coke, before looking Ivan in the eye. 'So here's another tip: don't ever ask someone like me for business information. Insider trading is against the law. Got it?'

Ivan realises his mistake. 'Of course. My apologies. It wasn't my intention.'

'So why come talk with me?'

Ivan decides he needs to put his cards on the table before the mining magnate loses all patience. He reckons he's got the man's attention for as long as the second burger lasts, and judging by the way he's demolished the first one, that won't be long. 'The miner who died, his name was Jonas McGee. He was found in his opal mine up on the West Ridge, near the lookout above Lake Kalingra and your rare-earth mine.'

'Go on.' The hostility has disappeared from Bob Inglis's face; the intelligence and focus remain.

'We have reports that a black limousine was seen up there a couple of times in the past week.'

'That'd be right,' says Inglis.

'Were you up there during the past week or so?'

'Why are you asking me that?'

'In case you saw something.'

'Not me.' He looks at Ivan, like a poker player looking for tells. 'If it's the car I'm thinking of, it was rented by Chinese investors. I've been negotiating with them, right up until the early hours this morning. They started out as rivals, they've ended up as allies. But I was never in that car and I haven't been anywhere near Kalingra or the West Ridge for at least a month.' He looks fondly at the remaining burger. 'It's what's under the ground that matters.'

'Do you have contact details for these investors? I'd like to talk to them.'

Inglis nods. 'You have a business card? Give it here. I'll get my people on to it.'

'Thank you.'

'Let's leave it there, Sergeant. I wish you well with your inquiries and hope you catch your murderer, but I have nothing to offer you. Any further approaches should come via my office and my lawyers.' Inglis takes up his second burger and sinks his teeth into it, indicating that the conversation is at an end.

But Ivan perseveres, not ready to be summarily dismissed. 'Just one more question, please. Unrelated.' There is no response from Inglis, apart from chewing, so Ivan continues: 'I read a piece in the *Financial Review* this morning that referred to some long-term rivalry between you and Delaney Bullwinkel from Cuttamulla Coal.'

Bullshit Bob guffaws, spraying half-chewed burger across the table, splattering Ivan. The big man starts coughing and needs to gargle soft drink before he can speak. 'Ancient history, son. Dead and buried.' Then he smiles, convivial once again. 'The trouble with a job like yours, Sergeant, if you don't mind me saying, is that it is forever mired in the past. Who killed whom and when. You're forever playing catch-up. But my job is all about the future. Seizing it, shaping it, owning it. The future, son. It's the future you need to embrace. I don't give a flying fuck about Big Deal Delaney. He's so far in the past that he's become a dinosaur.'

Later, Ivan finds himself retracing the same path he'd jogged that morning, climbing the Queensland road to the low pass between the two ridges, to the lookout facing north across the plain. Up here, he's totally alone, a speck on the land, a mite in the expanse. The night is perfectly clear and moonless. The Milky Way is sprayed across the sky in stunning detail. The black shapes are obvious: the nebulas, large gas clouds blotting out the stars, so clearly defined against the wash of stars they look painted on. He lies on his back on the bench and just looks. Shooting stars streak across the sky, fragmenting, celestial fireworks.

Maybe this is it. The sky is too big, the land is too big. Too many places for secrets. Morris came to Finnigans Gap and got nowhere, just got messed around and frustrated, run around by someone else's agenda. It's where he started to lose his way, started making his own rules. Talking to journalists. Ivan can feel the temptation; he'd love nothing better than to expose the meddling by Delaney Bullwinkel. But he tells himself he won't make the same mistakes as his old boss. He needs to concentrate on finding out what happened to Jonas McGee.

TUESDAY

chapter sixteen

THE FIRST LIGHT, THE MONOCHROME OF PRE-DAWN, CREEPS INTO THE ROOM, insinuates itself into Nell's waking mind. The quiet is emphasised by the call of a lonely bird. She loves the stillness, the silence, the lingering darkness, as if the world itself has decided to delay, to steal a few extra minutes before it all starts again. She nestles into Trevor. She has missed him, missed this. The form of him, the size of him; his heft, his earthy smell.

She hears a car door close, thinks nothing of it. A miner, getting out early to beat the heat. A dog barks, another car door. And suddenly, next to her, Trevor is awake, sitting upright, body tense and alert.

'What?' she asks, voice sleepy.

'Shush!' is all he says, a rough command.

He rolls out of bed, is opening his bedside drawer. And now she is fully awake, trying to interpret his actions in the gloom.

Nearby, there's a sound like an explosion, a door splintering. Men are yelling, 'Police! Search warrant! Police!' And now they're in the room, men in ski masks, guns levelled, torches flaring into her eyes. Yelling, 'Gun! Gun!' And screaming at Trevor: 'Drop it! Drop it!' And she hears the heavy thump as the weapon hits the floor. Trevor raises his hands, looking like he's been hit by a truck.

'You. Hands where we can see them!' It's directed at her; she has instinctively covered her nakedness, holding the sheets to her chest. 'Now. Where we can see them!' She does as she is told, holding her hands aloft, letting the sheet fall.

And past the masked men, standing behind them, she can see Carl Richter, a grim smile on his lips, satisfaction in his eyes.

— —

Ivan doesn't jog. Instead, his sleep is heavy and deep, surrendering only reluctantly to the persistence of his alarm. He shaves, he showers, he dresses. He makes coffee, intermediate strength, feeling so much better for the sleep, realises he must have been running on empty the previous two days. Funny how it's only evident after the fact. The sun is rising. Today will be better. A new day. He can feel it. What was it that Bob Inglis had advised? To forget the past, focus on the future?

Yet when he arrives at the police station, eager to get on, to make progress, there is no one there again, the screen security door locked. Two days in a row. Maybe he needs to ask for a set of keys. He checks the time: past seven on a Tuesday morning. Out on the street there is activity—grey nomads seeking breakfast, miners heading to work, a couple of cyclists lounging outside the Alpine Cafe, morning exertions finished. The town is up; why aren't the police? He rings Nell, but his call goes through to voicemail. He doesn't bother leaving a message. So much for a better day.

He's still there on the verandah when a police car finally arrives. Probationary Constable Garry Ahern gets out and walks through the gate, past the vandalised statue.

'Morning, Constable. Where is everyone?'

Garry stares at him, wide-eyed, not answering immediately.

What is wrong with this guy? 'Where have you been?' he persists.

'Airport,' says the constable. He flicks his head towards the car. A man is climbing out of the back seat, a man in a suit. A suit that says Sydney. Riding in the back: someone who thinks he's important.

'What flight?' asks Ivan.

'PolAir,' says the constable. 'I dropped off the forensic team. He came in on it.' Garry gets the door unlocked and opens it.

Ivan doesn't follow. Instead he waits for the man to walk through the gate and past the busted sculpture. The suit, the walk; there can be no doubt: the man is a detective.

'Morning,' says Ivan, trying to keep his voice noncommittal.

'Sure,' says the man. 'You Lucic?'

'That's right. And you?'

'Nathan Phelan. Professional Standards.' The man doesn't offer a handshake.

Ivan's heart skips a beat. *Feral Phelan, scourge of internal affairs.* 'Right. What brings you out here?'

'You. What else?'

'Me? What for?'

'To talk. Sooner the better. The plane is waiting for me.' He smiles. 'Your stiff is on ice, but the pathologist is getting hot under the collar.' And he offers up a goanna smile: cold-blooded and reptilian.

Ivan thinks of PolAir and the forensic team, forced to wait in the airless terminal. Nevertheless, he can't resist pushing back. 'I'm in the middle of a murder investigation.'

Phelan merely nods. 'And you can't continue it until you speak to me. So let's get cracking.'

He walks on into the station, giving Ivan no choice but to follow.

Inside, Phelan barks to the constable, 'Go buy us some coffees, son.' And then to Ivan: 'Whatcha want, Lucic?'

'Long black. Big one.'

Phelan offers up his bloodless smile. 'Good choice.' He turns to the constable. 'Make that two. Get yourself one while you're at it.' He hands him a twenty. 'Bring the change, bring the receipt.'

The young officer scurries out, not questioning for a moment Phelan's authority to send him on such a menial errand. Such is the power of Professional Standards. *Like the Spanish fucking Inquisition*, thinks Ivan.

They move through reception, Ivan pointing the way to the detectives' room. Phelan takes the chair and desk that Ivan has claimed for his own. Ivan knows it to be deliberate: this is a man familiar with the symbols of power, the feng shui of intimidation; a man who can read body language and facial tics like others might read the police manual. Like a poker player for whom the stakes are never too high.

Phelan slides his MobiPol phone onto the desk. 'I'm recording this, but I want you to know that you are not the subject of this investigation and you are not suspected of wrongdoing—at this stage.'

Ivan feels a sense of relief, despite the coda. 'Glad to hear it,' he says, sounding more assured than he feels.

'So tell the truth, tell me what you know, and I'll be back on that plane and out of your hair, me and the stiff and the forensic wonks. Capisce?'

Capisce? Who does he think he is? Robert De Niro? 'Sure,' says Ivan. 'Happy to help.'

Phelan smiles: all teeth, no warmth. 'For a number of years you have worked alongside Detective Inspector Morris Montifore. I have been tasked with investigating him.'

'Morris? What's the allegation?'

'It centres on your murder investigations in Sydney last year. The high-level corruption.'

'Are you kidding? We got the killer. Several killers. We got commendations.' And to emphasise the point: 'Pay rises.'

'Deservedly so. I've been through the files. You cut a few corners here and there, but no one is going to complain about that. It was sterling work. A masterclass.'

'What then?'

'There is a concern that some ongoing investigations, some prosecutions, may have been compromised—by media exposure.'

'And some investigations and prosecutions wouldn't have happened without that media exposure.' As soon as he's said it, he regrets it. Rule one of being interviewed: don't volunteer information; rule two: don't push back.

Phelan leans across, picks up his phone, examines the screen, as if to remind Ivan that his words can no longer be retracted. Phelan turns the recording off, makes a show of it, examines Ivan. 'Listen. I want to get back on that plane and out of this shithole.

I want you to continue your investigation. And your career. I am not your enemy here. Just answer the questions.' He sets the phone recording again and slides it back onto the desk. 'To your knowledge, did Morris Montifore ever speak to the journalist Martin Scarsden about ongoing investigations?'

Ivan shrugs, trying to appear casual. 'I'm sure he did. Scarsden was an eyewitness. He was there at crime scenes, saw people shot and killed. We interviewed him several times, as we would with any such witness.'

'We? You were always present?'

This time his shrug feels less convincing. 'There may have been times when I wasn't there. Nothing untoward about that.'

'True—provided it was Montifore extracting information from Scarsden, not the other way around.'

Ivan takes this on board. Phelan's assertion is debatable; police often feed information to select journalists, believing it might advance a case. Montifore was skilled at this, and did so with the implicit blessing of the brass.

The Professional Standards man looks pained, as if investigating his fellow officers causes him physical discomfort. 'On any occasion, did Morris Montifore request, either in a formal interview situation or a casual one, that you leave him alone with Scarsden?'

Ivan keeps his gaze steady, resisting the temptation to look away. 'Yes. That's correct.'

'Why would he do that?'

'Because he knows I don't like journalists.'

'Why would that make any difference?'

'I can't speak for the detective inspector.'

Phelan shakes his head, signalling disappointment. 'Take a guess.'

For Ivan there is no avoiding this; this is an interview that doesn't need to follow the normal rules of evidence. And then he realises it: Phelan must already know the answers to these questions; this isn't an interview to gather information, this is an interview to test fealty. 'I imagine he wanted Scarsden to trust him. If Scarsden sensed my antipathy, it wouldn't have helped.'

Phelan smiles, like a dentist who has hit a nerve. He looks down at his file notes, examining them—or pretending to examine them. An old technique Ivan's deployed often enough himself, allowing the pressure and the import to mount.

'Your father, right?'

Ivan nods. This is something he doesn't want to talk about.

Phelan nods back, like a marionette attempting empathy. 'I've read the file. The reporters, they hounded you. You and your mother.'

'Arseholes,' says Ivan, a neat summary.

Phelan presses his advantage. 'So, at any point, did you volunteer confidential information to Martin Scarsden?'

'Me? No, I did not.'

Phelan must hear the anger in his response; he raises his hands, a conciliatory gesture. 'It's okay, son, I believe you. But it's a question that has to be asked.'

Ivan tries to breathe, to settle himself. Phelan is at best ten years older than him; he has no right to call him 'son'. He knows it's deliberate, designed to bait him, but that doesn't mean it lacks impact.

Phelan gives him space, again pretending to examine his papers. 'Why did you join the police force?'

'How is that relevant?'

'Answer the question, Sergeant.'

It's no good delaying; he needs to face this head-on. 'The police, they arrested my father. Rescued Mum and me. And then afterwards, when the media went for us, wrote all the lies, the only people who showed us any kindness and consideration and decency were the police.' He raises his eyes, looks at Phelan. 'That's why I joined. Satisfied?'

Phelan leans back. 'I am, son. I am. I know where you're coming from. A lot of us are like you, you must know that. Tough childhoods, wrong side of the tracks. Some of us have no families and wish we did, some of us have families and wish we didn't.' He pauses. 'You want to know why I do what I do? Internal investigations?'

Ivan just looks.

'It's not an easy job, you know, digging dirt on fellow officers. I walk into a room, the tension notches up. I go to the pub and other cops won't drink with me, worried it will be mistaken as sucking up or, worse, that they're onside, informing on their mates.' He lets that sink in, studying Ivan's face for any reaction. Ivan struggles to keep it free of emotions as the Sydney investigator continues: 'I do it because I'm one of those with no family. The police are my family, my tribe. And I will do anything and everything to protect that family, to protect its integrity. I weed out the corrupt, the weak and the dirtbags. And I weed out those fuckers who sell us out to the crooks or to the media or to the politicians, the low-life who shit in their own nest just to advance their own careers. You ask me, they're not whistleblowers, they're cocksuckers. If they find something wrong, they should come to us, come to me. You hear? Come to me. I'll weed out the dirtbags and the backhand takers and the rats. You're not a rat, are you, Lucic? You wouldn't rat us out to the media, would you?'

'I thought this wasn't about me.'

'Answer the question.'

'No. I would not. I never have and I never will.'

'Glad to hear it.' And some of the steam goes out of the room.

Garry comes in with the coffees. His hands are shaking ever so slightly; Ivan is worried the poor kid will spill them. He must have overheard some of their exchange.

'Thanks,' says Ivan with gratitude. Suddenly the idea of coffee is very appealing.

'That was quick,' says Feral Phelan. He takes a sip, face again pained, as if the coffee is so far below Sydney standards that it requires forbearance to drink it. He waits for the constable to leave the room and close the door before speaking again. 'Okay, so here's a question I want you to consider carefully before you answer.' He emphasises the importance of the point. 'In the final days of the Sydney investigations, in the hours during which the journalist Martin Scarsden was writing his exposés, that same day, did Morris Montifore meet privately with Scarsden?'

Ivan pretends to think, to be searching his memory, but he remembers the day so vividly, there is no erasing it. And then it hits him: Phelan already knows the answer to this question as well. Of course he does. The police car would have tracking data, so would the police-issue phones, his and Montifore's. 'Yes. He did.' He can hear the cracking in his voice, knows what he is doing, but can see no alternative. And he recalls Montifore's own advice: to tell the truth. 'Scarsden was at the Surry Hills police station. So was I. The place was surrounded by media. The detective inspector rang, requested I drive Scarsden out past the media to a nearby cafe.' The words catch in his throat. 'So the detective inspector could speak privately with Scarsden.'

Phelan nods, as if understanding how difficult it has been for Ivan. The Professional Standards man reaches out and takes his phone back, stopping the recording. 'Thanks, Ivan,' he says, using his first name for the first time. He stays seated, his voice moving from the authoritative and official to the friendly and confiding. 'In my opinion, you have done nothing wrong.' He puts the phone in his briefcase. 'But a word to the wise: tread carefully.'

'What does that mean?' Ivan's voice is wary.

'You were Montifore's right-hand man for almost four years. There is a mark beside your name. Not a black mark: a question mark. You need to replace that with a tick.' Phelan stands, sticks his head out the door. He summons the constable, tells him it's time to go, before once again addressing Ivan. 'I'm told you and your offsider have irritated people who have nothing to do with your investigation, nothing to do with the death of the opal miner. So tread carefully. Morris was always very good at that, one of the best. Until he lost his way.'

Phelan is about to say something more, and Ivan is formulating his own retort, but neither man gets a chance to speak. The door from the reception area bursts open, and a phalanx of police come surging in with Trevor Topsoil, who is wearing nothing but boxer shorts and handcuffs. And right behind him is Detective Constable Narelle Buchanan, wild-eyed and half dressed, her wrists also cuffed.

— —

Nell sits in the interview room, staring at the wall, her world collapsing in upon her. There are no longer cuffs, no officer watching over her. Nothing. From time to time, some sound penetrates from the neighbouring interview room, where Trevor Topsoil is getting the third degree. It's as if they've forgotten about her. Perhaps they have. More likely they just want her to stew in her own juice, an embarrassment to them, an embarrassment to herself.

She feels the tears coming, tries to fight them back, wipes her eyes when they insist. She won't cry; she's lost enough dignity. She's not going to let Richter and those other bastards see her in tears. And yet the thoughts still come, the self-condemnation. How could she have been so stupid, so blind? So arrogant? All this time, she thought the antipathy directed at her was because she'd exposed corruption in the station, that she'd ended the career of the station's venerated sergeant, Desmond Ottridge. She'd cloaked herself in righteousness, pretending it didn't matter, that he'd deserved what he got, that her promotion to detective had vindicated her actions, that the powers that be knew she had done the right thing.

But now she knows different. Sure, she helped the Drug Squad close down Paxton Barret and the Longfer brothers, and sure, as collateral damage she ended the career of Ottridge. But now she knows the truth of it, and so do they. Topsoil was her informant, her source, passing himself off as a concerned businessman, a solid citizen. But he was no solid citizen: he was feeding her information to rid himself of his rivals. She'd eliminated Barret for him, opening the way for him to expand his own operations. And that's why, she finally realises, Richter and the others have spurned her and still hold her in such contempt. Not because they are rotten and she is not, but because they believe her to be rotten, resenting her rise, unable to inform on her without revealing their own complicity or implicating Ottridge even further. No wonder Richter hates her.

She puts her head in her hands. What a disaster. Career ending. Being caught in bed with a drug dealer. It can't get worse than that. She needs to resign. She needs to extricate herself. She needs to leave and never come back. But the Drug Squad isn't about to let her walk out of here; they'll charge her, prosecute her, eviscerate her. They won't believe in her innocence; they'll think she played them, that she sicked them onto Barret and the Longfers at Topsoil's behest. And her only defence: to put publicly and categorically on the record that she has been used, fucked every which way by Trevor Topsoil, that she is the world's most gullible, least perceptive and most stupid police officer. Some alternative.

She recalls Topsoil's confident smile at the pub. After she'd already had a drink too many. He probably didn't even remember her favourite drink, just asked the barman. Jesus. How dumb could she be?

The door opens. She takes a deep breath before looking up. But it's not the Drug Squad and it's not Cheryl Pederson. It's Ivan Lucic.

'You okay?' he asks, his voice betraying more puzzlement than sympathy, a kind of fascination, as if she is some sort of exotic zoological specimen.

She feels those laser eyes scanning her face, trying to read her. It's all she can do to shake her head and press her lips tightly together; attempting words would almost certainly release tears.

'Shit,' he says, perceiving her distress. 'What happened?'

She gathers herself, feels a seed of anger, latches on to it, trying to grow it, using it to subvert her misery. Better anger than self-pity. 'Did they tell you?' she asks. 'Were you in on it?'

'In on what?'

'The raid.'

He stands for a moment, as if making a choice, then sits. 'No. I turned up here this morning, there was no one around. All I know is that the Drug Squad is here, and they've arrested Topsoil. Apart from that, they've told me fuck-all.'

'They kept you in the dark?'

He shrugs. 'Why would they tell me anything? Planning raids—especially drug raids—is always highly secretive. You know that.' He's still looking at her, and now she sees the concern on his face as he speaks again. 'I still don't understand what has happened, how you're involved.'

She looks away, stares at a wall, finds it easier to talk when she's not looking directly at him. 'They arrested Trevor Topsoil. A dawn raid. Planned for ages, no doubt. It's drugs. Drugs and God knows what else.'

'What's that got to do with you?' And even as he asks the question, she can see awareness spreading on his face as he checks her clothes, the stupid hoodie of Topsoil's that she's wearing. *Party Animal*, it says in large pink letters. 'Shit. You were there. You were with him.'

'It's worse than that.'

'What? What could be worse than that?' Now his eyes narrow, receptive, his mind working. 'Are you telling me you knew he was dealing drugs?'

'No. *No*. That's it.' And she explains. How Trevor was her source; how he conned her three years ago, used her.

When she's finished, he leans back. 'Faark,' he says, a long and enduring exclamation, not to her, but to the world in general. Then he refocuses. 'When the Drug Squad came through the door, did they know who you were? Did they know you were there?'

She shakes her head, wondering what he could possibly be driving at. 'No. When I told them I was a cop, they didn't believe me. They had backup from Lightning Ridge, one of them knew me. And then that arsehole Richter confirmed it.' The image of him lurking there, full of himself, comes back to her. She again feels the anger and the shame.

'You think you were set up?'

She shrugs. 'Not by the Drug Squad. Not by Lightning Ridge. By Richter? Who knows.'

'What a shitshow,' says Ivan.

'You believe me, don't you?' she says, voice plaintive.

He studies her, unreadable. 'Why do you think you were sent here, to Finnigans Gap, to assist me? Why you?'

She looks at the wall again, his penetrating stare too much. What's he driving at? 'I was junior, not involved in any time-critical investigations. And I'd worked out of here for three years in uniform, they all knew that. It was last minute but it made sense. Why? What are you suggesting?'

'Someone is after us. Setting us up. Me. You. One of us, both of us.'

She frowns. 'What's it got to do with you? Are you sure?'

'No. I'm not sure of anything. But, Nell, I need to get on with the investigation. So talk to the Drug Squad. Tell them everything you know. Don't protect that arsehole Topsoil, not after what he's done to you. If you're innocent, you're innocent. Insist they charge you or let you go.'

She can't believe what he is suggesting. 'You think that's possible? Won't they suspend me?'

'They'll definitely investigate you. Trawl your bank accounts, track your movements, interrogate your phone calls. Same with Topsoil. If you really haven't been here for three years, if you really haven't had anything to do with him, they'll work it out.'

For the first time since Trevor Topsoil's door was caved in, she feels a glimmer of hope. 'You think so?'

'Doesn't mean you'll get off scot-free, but you're not their priority. Not the Drug Squad's. It's Professional Standards you need to be worried about.'

'That's meant to make me feel better?'

'Let me know as soon as you're clear.' Then his voice drops, the veneer of optimism leaving it. 'We need a result here. Both of us.' And he reaches across, places his hand on hers for just a moment, an echo of his gesture on Sunday night. She appreciates it more than she can say. And then his hand is gone, and so is he.

Even after he has left, his words hang in the air. She is not alone. He hasn't abandoned her, hasn't thrown her to the wolves and moved on. Not yet. Maybe because he needs her, needs a result. It may be her only hope. *He* might be her only hope. But what does he mean about them being set up?

chapter seventeen

ONCE HE'S MADE SURE NELL IS OKAY, IVAN GETS OUT OF THE STATION AS quickly as he can. It's not hard to go unnoticed, not amid the swarming Drug Squad detectives, the police seconded in from Lightning Ridge, Cheryl and Richter arguing over something, and Phelan passing silently through them like a shark through bait fish. For a place that was empty when he arrived, it's brimming over now, with police and post-raid energy.

Outside, he gets into his rental, drives through town, up to the lookout. A retired couple have parked their motorhome, extended an awning, set up a collapsible table to enjoy a late breakfast with a view before the temperature grows prohibitive. No matter. They can keep the view; he's staying in his car, air conditioner on. He retrieves his burner, texts Morris Montifore. *Call me.* He still lacks the credit to ring directly, but doesn't dare use his credit card to top it up. Through the windscreen, he can see a wedge-tailed eagle soaring on the thermals, looking down upon the vastness of the world. Ivan feels a tinge of envy; what he wouldn't give for that all-seeing perspective, to be elevated above the saltbush and the boulders. Less than thirty seconds later, the phone starts to chime.

'Ivan. How's it going?' Montifore's voice is light, carefree.

'Nathan Phelan. He's here.'

There's a long silence, and when the senior man speaks the lightness has gone. 'Feral Phelan? What's he doing?'

'Interviewing me. About you.'

'Really?' Another pause. 'Why bother? I'm taking the line of least resistance, told them I'll take a package. I thought it was approved; just needs rubber-stamping.'

'Even before they finish their investigation?'

'The investigation is just window-dressing. They want me gone, I want to go, I'm going.'

'So what's Phelan doing up here?'

'That's what I'd like to know.'

'Maybe he and his sponsors are making sure you don't get a last-minute reprieve. There must be some people in the hierarchy who want you to stay, who will defend you. Who are proud of what we did last year and who are concerned about what sort of signal axing you will send.'

'Yeah. Maybe. What was he asking?'

'All about you and Martin Scarsden last year. The whole investigation, Scarsden's reporting.'

'What about it?'

'They knew that you met with Scarsden in private, right when he was doing all the exposés. They knew that I drove him out of the police station at Surry Hills to meet with you.'

Montifore says nothing for a long while before finally responding. 'It's a long way for Phelan to go, up to Finnigans Gap, to corroborate what they already know, what I'm already willing to concede.'

'What are you thinking?'

'He must be there for some other reason.'

'Like what?'

'Isn't it obvious? For you.'

'Me? What have I done?'

'What did you tell him about what you knew?'

'I did what you advised; I told him the truth. I corroborated it.' He draws a breath. 'I'm sorry I had to drop you in it. But they knew anyway.'

'That's fine, Ivan. Better than fine. It means they haven't got anything on you. But play it safe.'

'You really think he'll go after me as well?'

'If I had to guess, I'd say they're after leverage. To make sure you know your place.'

Ivan considers this. 'Sounds about right.'

Montifore changes the subject. 'How's the case up there going?'

'Pure shit.' Ivan explains about the Drug Squad and Nell. 'It was already looking ordinary, even without that. It seems like our primary suspect has an iron-clad alibi. And we still don't know if the victim was murdered or just keeled over.'

'Will they charge her?' Montifore asks. 'Your constable?'

'With what? Stupidity?'

'So you trust her?'

Ivan doesn't respond straight away. 'I guess I do.' He feels uncomfortable discussing Nell like this, judging her, and decides to move on. 'What do you know about an operation up here called Cuttamulla Coal?'

'Nothing. Why?'

'It's a big mine, about an hour south of Finnigans Gap. Owned by Delaney Bullwinkel.'

This time there is a response. 'Bullwinkel? He's connected. Money, politics, influence. Entwined in that web of corruption we exposed. You must know that.'

'He's powerful and influential. But do we know for sure that he's crooked?'

'No. No more than any of the rest of them. Less so, probably. Isn't he a billionaire?'

'So they say.'

'Well, he's risen above it all then, hasn't he?'

'Maybe not.' He tells Montifore about the run-in the evening before, the call from the deputy commissioner's office after Nell got on the wrong side of Bullwinkel's lawyer.

'Sounds typical,' says Montifore. 'Might explain what Phelan's doing up there.'

'Yeah, he intimated as much. I'll let you know if I hear anything more from him. He should be flying back to Sydney any moment now.'

He ends the call, places the burner in his pocket, wondering what it all means.

His other phone rings, the official one. 'Sorry to bother you, sir. It's Garry Ahern at the station. There's a Raymond Penuch here to be interviewed. His lawyer says they won't wait much longer.'

'I'll be right there.' Ivan checks the time. Nine fifteen. In the madness of the morning, he'd forgotten all about the shift manager.

Driving back down into the Gap, he passes the wedge-tailed eagle, feasting on roadkill.

— —

The detective in charge of the Drug Squad contingent is whippet-thin, cheekbones sharp under unblinking eyes, exuding an electric intensity. Nell thinks she must be a jogger or a gym junkie; someone who has beaten life into shape and is resting her foot on its throat.

Detective Senior Sergeant Faith Basheer looks her in the eye and doesn't smile. 'You remember me?'

'Of course,' Nell replies. The senior sergeant was her contact three years ago, the one who led the busts of Barret and the Longfers.

'You were sleeping with a known criminal,' she says: a statement, not a question.

Nell shakes her head. 'No. I didn't know he was a criminal.'

A raised eyebrow. 'So you're pleading ignorance and stupidity rather than collusion and culpability?'

'If you want to put it like that. Yes.' Nell notices that Basheer is not recording, wonders if she should request it, or if it's better not being on the record.

Basheer doesn't relax. 'I'm going to be frank with you, Constable. Your presence here is a right royal pain in the arse. I want to spend my days and nights chasing bad guys, not wasting my time probing wayward coppers.'

'Yes, ma'am.'

'So what will happen is this: I will write a report, it will go to Professional Standards, and they can determine your fate.'

Nell just looks down at her hands. There is not a lot she can say.

'However, I do need to ask you some questions. Your answers will be recorded, the file will be shared with Professional Standards. You follow?'

'Do I need a lawyer?'

'I don't know. Do you?'

Nell knows what that would indicate, tells herself she has done nothing wrong. Or nothing criminal, at least. 'No, I'm good.'

The senior sergeant starts the recording, stating the time and place and those present. Warns her that her evidence may be used against her.

'Since you were transferred out of Finnigans Gap three years ago, how often have you been back?'

'This is the first time.'

Basheer studies her face. 'You're sure about that?'

'Yes.'

'And Trevor Topsoil? What contact have you had with him since you left here?'

'None. I've had nothing to do with him since I left.'

'No phone calls, emails, social media? Nothing?'

'Correct.'

'Until last night?'

'Until Sunday. Detective Sergeant Lucic and I interviewed him at his workplace as part of the investigation into the death of Jonas McGee. Last night was the first time in three years I was alone with him.'

'So just an extraordinary coincidence? You being in bed with him when we came through the door?'

'Just so.'

The senior sergeant frowns with concentration. Maybe she hadn't been expecting it to be this straightforward. 'Okay, Nell, that's good.' She bites her lip, seems deep in thought, but all Nell hears is the use of her first name and wonders if the detective might be softening. Yet Basheer continues to stare at her, features set hard. 'I want you to carefully consider your evidence here. Your denials are unequivocal. In all likelihood, Professional Standards will go through your personal history with a fine toothcomb. You don't want them finding any nits. They will go back and track your movements, your phone calls, your credit card expenditure, your bank details, everything. So now's the time to tell me about any irregularities. A visit to Finnigans Gap to see an old friend or colleague, nothing to do with Topsoil. Or an uninvited text from him, perhaps. Anything that would raise suspicions, anything that might indicate you're not being completely honest with me now.'

But Nell responds right away. 'I liked him. I was attracted to him. But once I left here, I wanted nothing to do with him or this town. There was no contact.'

'Why not?'

'Sorry?'

'Why didn't you want anything to do with him?'

'He was an emotional dead end. Nothing to offer beyond the physical.' Her judgement sounds harsh, even to herself, but it's the truth.

'Three years ago, he was your source?'

Nell hesitates. Basheer already knows he was, must want it on the record. 'Yes. He was.'

'So you were sleeping with him, back then, partly because he was giving you valuable information.'

'That's not how it started.'

'No doubt.' Basheer leans back. 'Nell, I'm not judging you here. Not in a moral sense. The information you provided was very valuable to us. The case against Barret and his cronies was solid. They were guilty and the evidence demonstrated that. Undercover police officers have been known to do much worse to cultivate a source.'

Nell doesn't say anything.

'However, given what you now know about Topsoil, do you think he was sleeping with you in order to plant information about his rivals?'

'He didn't have to sleep with me to do that.'

'True. You feel used?'

'I feel abused.'

A raised eyebrow, arching with scepticism. 'So he played you?'

Now the moisture has returned to her eyes as she nods. 'I would say so.'

'And you had no idea back then that he himself was involved in the drug trade or other illegal practices?'

'No. I knew nothing of that until this morning.'

The eyebrows lower. Is that sympathy Nell sees in the woman's eyes? Or pity? There's a moment of stillness before Basheer recommences the questioning. 'Do you have any information pertaining to Topsoil or his activities that might be useful to our investigation?'

'No. As I say, I was unaware.'

'Okay.' Faith Basheer folds her papers. 'As far as I'm concerned, you're free to go, to continue your work. But Professional Standards are bound to pursue this. You're not out of the woods yet. You understand?'

'Yes.'

The detective takes her phone, turns off the recording. 'For what it's worth, Topsoil is gloating about how he duped you. Either he's a very good actor or he's a genuine dickhead.' At last there's a smile, some warmth leaking into the senior officer's visage. Basheer rises, prepares to leave. 'Thanks for your candour, Constable. And good luck.'

Nell nods. 'Thank you, ma'am.'

But the senior sergeant isn't quite done. As she goes to leave, she speaks again from the doorway, almost as an afterthought. 'I was the one who recommended you for detective training. Now I'm recommending that there be no further investigation of you in relationship to the drug operations here. I'm putting my neck out for you, Nell. I hope it's worth it.'

'Thank you. You won't be sorry.' She knows she sounds more confident than she feels.

— —

Ray Penuch is huge and surly, his head a cube, bright red hair shaved short on the sides, his beard a more russet tone. Clad in hi-vis, he looks like a Lego character. He's sitting in the interview room, waiting, along with his lawyer. Garry has agreed to sit in with Ivan, more as a witness than a participant, to even up the numbers. The lawyer is wearing a suit, confirming his outsider status. It's Cyril Flange, the same man who humiliated Nell yesterday afternoon, the one who probably put the call in to the deputy commissioner.

Penuch looks like he wants to beat Ivan to a pulp; Flange, by contrast, has the air of a stiletto man, calm and aloof, as if all of this is beneath him.

'Good morning. I'm sorry if I've kept you waiting,' says Ivan.

Flange sneers, Penuch grunts. Garry gets the recording going, and Ivan identifies himself and the constable and the time and location of the interview. 'Please identify yourselves for the record,' he says matter-of-factly.

The lawyer answers. 'I am Cyril Flange, attorney. This is my client, Raymond John Penuch, until recently shift manager at Cuttamulla Coal.'

'Until recently?'

The lawyer ignores the question. 'We are not happy. We informed you last night we would be here. You agreed to meet with us. Not only was there no one to receive us, no one even knew we were coming. What sort of investigation are you conducting? What sort of mickey mouse detective are you?'

Ivan doesn't bother to respond; just looks at the lawyer, expression blank, letting his blue eyes cut into the man's own. Ivan doesn't like him. He doesn't like his five-thousand-dollar suit, he doesn't like his private school vowels, and he doesn't like what he did to Nell. He waits another moment before eventually speaking. 'My apologies.'

'Let's get on with it,' suggests the lawyer.

'Thank you,' says Ivan. 'Is your practice local?' he asks Flange, voice teasing. 'Lightning Ridge? Conveyancing? Parking fines?'

'I am the corporate counsel for Cuttamulla Coal.'

'And what does that entail?'

'I am not the one being interviewed here, Mr Penuch is. Please direct your questions to my client.'

Ivan smiles, but only with his teeth. 'You stated that Raymond Penuch was until recently a shift manager at Cuttamulla Coal?'

'Correct. His employment was terminated this morning.'

Penuch shifts in his chair, mouth zipped tight but head turning redder by the moment, like a thermometer about to pop. The curse of the redhead.

Ivan again addresses the lawyer. 'So if he's a former employee, how is it that you are representing him? He couldn't afford the dry cleaning, let alone the suit.'

'Cuttamulla Coal wants to see justice served. We are concerned about the events involving Mr Penuch and our employee, Stanley Honeywell, and we want to see matters right.'

'I see. So Stanley Honeywell remains your employee?'

'He does.'

'Very noble of you.' Ivan shifts his regard, looks hard into the watery blue pebbles of the overgrown ginger. 'You face serious allegations, Mr Penuch: that you assaulted your fellow worker Stanley Honeywell on Sunday and you abducted him yesterday. You want to tell me what happened?'

Penuch shrugs. 'Yeah. I did it.'

'And did you again assault him yesterday?'

'I'd do it again, the miserable cunt.'

The lawyer closes his eyes, but doesn't interject.

'Is that a yes?' Ivan persists.

'Yep. I beat the shit out of him.'

Ivan sighs, as if there is something tawdry about assault, as if it is a minor thing compared to murder. But internally, he's grateful. The man is going to confess all. 'You want to take us through it?'

'You seen the size of the cunt?' asks Penuch. 'He's even bigger than me.'

'But not so handy with his fists.'

'A complete soft cock.'

Next to him, Ivan can sense Garry bristle, but the constable holds his tongue.

'Tell us what happened,' Ivan instructs.

'He was my assistant at the end of every ten-day shift—payroll.'

'Explain what that means and what it involves.'

Penuch shrugs, is about to answer, but instead looks to Flange for guidance.

'It's okay, Raymond. Tell the officer.'

The man addresses Ivan. 'Some of the lads, they like to be paid in cash. Especially bonuses, allowances, that sort of thing. You follow?'

Ivan does indeed: every red cent a police officer earns is taxed, but that's not always so in private enterprise. 'I get it. Go on.'

'I recruited Honeywell, just to look big and mean while we did the rounds, handed out the cash. In case anyone got any ideas.'

'Seems reasonable. So what happened?'

'I'll tell you what happened: the stupid cunt stole twenty thousand dollars.'

'How do you know it was him?'

'Go ask him. He's admitted to it.'

'Before or after you beat him up?'

There's indignation in the man's voice. 'Before, during, after. Go ask him.'

'You didn't tell management he stole the money? Didn't report it to police?'

'Nah. Fuck that. I knew who took it and how to get it back.'

'So you say.' Ivan gives himself a moment to consider the shift manager's motivation, comprehending it. Penuch was responsible for large amounts of cash; if he reported some of it missing to management or the police, he would inevitably appear negligent, especially if it had been taken by the slow-witted Stanley Honeywell. Much easier to get it back himself, particularly if he was so sure who took it. And if the money was on the dark side of the ledger, the company certainly wouldn't want police involvement. Most likely it was used for more than topping up pay packets. Penuch's official title might have been shift manager, his duties including payroll, but in Ivan's mind a new job description attaches itself to the beefy redhead: bagman. 'Okay, go on.'

'It was Sunday. I checked the safe to see how much cash I would need from the bank to make payroll. I noticed that there was money missing. A lot of money. Twenty thousand leaves a pretty big hole. The blokes don't like hundreds; most of 'em prefer twenties to fifties. I mean, it was pretty fucking obvious it was gone.'

'So why suspect Stanley?'

'There are only three people who know the combination to the safe—or who are meant to know: me, the accountant and the mine manager. And the accountant was on leave. But Honeywell was often there when I was opening the safe. My fault; I didn't think he could count past ten with his shoes on, let alone memorise a seven-figure combination.'

'So you confronted him?'

'That's a nice way to put it.'

'You beat him up?'

'Yes. I did.'

'To make him confess.'

'Yes.'

'And to punish him.'

'Fuck me. He deserved it.'

'What did he say?'

'Oh, he fucking blubbered on. Assured me he still had it, and he'd get it back.' Ray shrugs. 'So I let him go get it.'

'You didn't go with him? You trusted him?'

Ray frowns, as if considering this potential oversight for the first time. 'Yeah. I don't think he was too scared of another beating, to be honest, but as soon as I said he'd go to jail if I reported him, he fell to pieces. Like a total fucking sook.' Another shrug. 'So I let him go by himself. Couldn't bear the thought of him blubbing all the way into town and back.'

'So this is on Sunday night, right?'

'Yeah. Sunday afternoon.'

'Right. But he doesn't come back with the money?'

'No.'

'You know why?'

'I do now.'

'Because he'd put it in the bank, and the bank wasn't open on Sunday.'

'Yeah, I get it. But what fucker steals twenty grand and then puts it in the bank?'

'He didn't tell you?'

'No.'

'Okay. So yesterday, Monday, he's still not back. What did you do?'

'I rang him. He finally answered. I asked where the fuck he was and where was my money.'

'Your money?'

'Cuttamulla's money, but my arse. It was my arse on the line.'

'What did he say?'

'He said the money was in the bank. He was going to get it. I asked what the fuck he was waiting for. He said he was hiding out, that the police were after him. That someone had murdered his mate. It all sounded like bullshit to me.'

'So what did you do?'

'I drove to his place and found him.'

'Just like that?'

'Seriously. The guy is as thick as two short planks.'

'And you beat him up again?'

'Too right.'

'Just for good measure? And trashed his place?'

'I was looking for the money. I still thought he was bullshitting me about the bank deposit.'

'Did he offer any resistance?'

'Not a lot.'

'What next?'

'We drove to the bank and got the money. Turns out he wasn't lying after all.'

'So you got the money and drove him back to the mine. Why?'

'To make sure nothing else was missing.'

'Right. Did you assault him a third time?'

'No. I did not.'

'But you do confess to assaulting him twice, once on Sunday and again yesterday?'

'I told you: he fucking deserved it.'

'So you keep saying.' Ivan is starting to think he dislikes the red-headed thug even more than his smarmy lawyer. 'Why did you hide when you got back to the mine?'

'What do you mean?'

'Security couldn't find you.'

Penuch frowns like he doesn't understand, looks to the lawyer for guidance.

Flange speaks up. 'It's true, Raymond. They couldn't find you.'

The redhead turns back to Ivan. 'You'll have to ask security. We must have been in a blind spot.'

'Must have been,' says Ivan, his tone indicating his disbelief. 'You come into town often?'

'What? Why?'

'Just answer the question.'

'On or off. To the bank. For a beer. For a root.'

'Were you in town last week—say on Monday, Tuesday or Wednesday?'

Now the lawyer is frowning. 'What are you getting at, Sergeant?'

Ivan ignores Flange, keeps his eyes on the bagman. 'The truth, Ray. Answer the question.'

'Nah. Don't think so. I can check. The gate has a record, but nah. Not me.'

'When was the first you heard of the death of Jonas McGee?'

'From Honeywell. He wouldn't shut the fuck up about him.'

'What did he say?'

'All this crap. How McGee had saved him, how much he owed him. Claimed the money was for him.'

'He said that? That the money was for him? The twenty thousand?'

'Yeah, the tool. Trying to blame a dead guy. The gutless cunt.'

'Did he say anything else?'

'No.'

'Thank you, Ray,' says Ivan without a skerrick of gratitude in his voice, and ends the interview.

Once Garry has turned off the recorder, Flange speaks up again. 'My client has confessed to assault. We understand that you may desire to charge him and put him before the court. That is your prerogative. But, of course, should that occur, I won't be able to prevent him pleading extenuating circumstances. Extreme provocation. He will tell the court that Honeywell stole the money. At which point, to protect our corporate reputation, we would need to terminate Mr Honeywell's employment and insist he be charged with stealing the company's twenty thousand dollars. Given his record, he will most assuredly return to prison.'

Now Ivan understands what the lawyer is really doing here: it's his job to make it all go away. To convince them not to charge Penuch with assault, to keep the theft from becoming public knowledge. 'That will be up to Mr Honeywell,' says Ivan. 'He may still want to press charges. I will need to confer with Constable Buchanan before we make a decision.'

'I see,' says Flange, smiling, knowing he will get what he wants. 'You should talk to Honeywell. He's in the town hospital. We brought him in with us. We're paying for it, paying for everything. We want him to get the best possible treatment.'

chapter eighteen

THE INTERVIEW ROOM DOOR OPENS, AND A MAN ENTERS, SOMEONE NELL HASN'T
met before. He's definitely a policeman; the suit says detective.
Although this one is off the rack, with its polyester sheen and
a stained lapel. He must be from Sydney; she knows every
detective within a five-hundred-kilometre radius, and none of
them wear suits.

'Ah, thanks for waiting for me,' he says, pulling up a chair,
placing a thin briefcase on the floor beside him.

'I wasn't aware that I was.'

'No, people seldom are.' He smiles, enjoying his own private
joke. 'My name is Nathan Phelan. You might have heard of me.'

Nell looks at him, unsure why she already dislikes him. 'No. Sorry,
I haven't.' And then, by way of explanation, 'I'm based in Bourke.'

'And doing an excellent job, I'm told.'

'Sorry, but who exactly are you, and what are you doing here? And why should I talk to you?'

Again the smile. Thin lips, nicotine teeth. 'I'm Detective Sergeant Nathan Phelan. Professional Standards.' He pauses, perhaps to enjoy her evident consternation as she connects the name with the reputation. 'And I'm here either to revive your faltering career, or to bury it as quickly and painlessly as possible.'

'You're Feral Phelan?'

'Only to my friends. If I had any.' Again, the thin-lipped smile. 'You can address me as either Sergeant Phelan or sir.'

Nell looks at the clock on the wall. Ten past eleven. If he came up on the plane sent to fetch Blake and Carole, then he would have left Sydney around dawn. Right when the Drug Squad was caving in Trevor Topsoil's door. 'You knew before the raid that I was there? With Topsoil?'

Phelan looks at her intently, as if assessing her. 'No. I didn't, as a matter of fact. I wasn't even aware that the Drug Squad was in Finnigans Gap. So pack up your conspiracy theory and stick it back in its box.' He checks her reaction, making sure she accepts what he says before continuing. 'I'm investigating another matter. But seeing as I'm here, I thought a chat seemed prudent. You were discovered in a compromising situation, in bed with a drug boss. There must be, and there will be, an internal investigation.'

The way he says 'internal investigation' is enough to make her wince. She suspects his choice of words is deliberate, but she's not about to give him the satisfaction of seeing how exposed she feels. Instead, she tries to make the most of the situation. 'I understand, Sergeant Phelan. Thank you for the opportunity to put my position and my recollections on the record. I have done nothing wrong and certainly nothing illegal. I was totally unaware that Trevor Topsoil was involved in any type of criminal activity.'

'So just a good fuck then?' He smiles, with all the empathy of a pterodactyl.

She refuses to take the bait.

He keeps smiling. 'All right, tell me all. How you knew him when you were based here, how you came to be with him last night.'

And so she does, repeating what she has told Faith Basheer, setting out how Topsoil was her source, how their encounter at the pub seemed entirely by chance.

Finally, Phelan seems satisfied. 'All right, here's the situation as I see it. At this stage, there is no concrete evidence of any illegality on your behalf. Stupidity yes, illegality no. Senior Sergeant Basheer, Sergeant Pederson and Senior Constable Richter, as well as your superiors in Bourke, have all vouched for your character and integrity. So for the moment, you are free to go, free to continue with your investigations.'

Nell can hardly believe it. 'I'm not suspended?'

'Is that what you expected?'

'To be honest, yes. Pending investigation.'

'That was my initial inclination. And make no mistake; you will be thoroughly vetted. But for now it makes sense for you to continue your work with Sergeant Lucic.'

'Thank you, sir.'

She can see him considering her. There is no smile now. 'Are you curious to know what did bring me up here, if it wasn't you and it wasn't the drug raid?'

'Sir?' She keeps her demeanour as noncommittal as possible.

'Ivan Lucic.'

'Sir?' This time he must hear the doubt in her voice.

'We don't believe Lucic has done anything wrong, but we need to make sure.'

'Of what?'

'His former superior, Morris Montifore, is about to retire. On a full pension, with honours, a gold watch.'

'I see.'

'I doubt that you do. He is retiring early, at the height of his career, because he knows the alternative. Possible demotion, possible dismissal, possible charges. Reputation in tatters.'

'Montifore? He's crooked?'

Phelan shakes his head emphatically. 'No. Not crooked. Not corrupt. Don't ever suggest that without the evidence to back it.'

'What then?'

'He began to run his own race. Became involved in politics, put his own interests ahead of the police and of the state. Judging people, talking to journalists. That's not the role of police; our job is to enforce the law, nothing more. I'm here to make sure Lucic hasn't been tempted to follow Montifore's example. I have already spoken to him this morning. Like you, he's on probation.'

'Why are you telling me this?'

Phelan lifts his briefcase onto the desk, opens it up, taking his time, leaving her holding her breath. He lifts a phone from the case, pushes it across the desk to Nell. She recognises its function straight away. It's small and cheap and dumb. A burner. Pre-paid and anonymous. 'My number is in it. I need you to tell me if he acts in any way suspiciously.'

She almost laughs, the situation feels so bizarre. 'I don't even know what he's meant to have done. Or what I'm looking for.'

'We've done a preliminary probe. Sergeant Lucic has a problem. Potentially.'

'Potentially?'

'He's a gambler. Poker machines. Sunday night, he dropped almost a thousand dollars at the bowling club round the corner from here.'

'How could you know that?'

'ATM withdrawals.'

'His money?'

'Yes. His money. An inheritance. Or what's left of it.'

'I don't get it.'

'Oh, I think you do. Gamblers get into debt. And debt exposes them. To compromise, to manipulation.' Phelan steeples his hands, as if exuding wisdom, as if passing judgement. 'Montifore had his own motives for taking sides; Lucic may do it for less noble reasons. Pleasing some influential people, irritating others.'

'Is this about yesterday? Me out at Delaney Bullwinkel's coalmine?'

'No. The two of you are investigating a murder. You can interview whomsoever you please. But just make sure it is justified or there will be consequences.'

'Is that what's happening to Sergeant Lucic? Consequences?'

'That's up to him. Just before, when I interviewed him, he was quite happy to do the dirty on Morris Montifore. Gave me chapter and verse on how the inspector was systematically leaking to the media. So Lucic knew all about it, back when it was happening, yet he never once raised his concerns with anyone in authority.'

Nell looks at the burner. 'I'm not comfortable with this.'

'Well, you are not in a comfortable situation—thanks to your own lack of judgement. Now you have to decide whether you are comfortable making an enemy of Professional Standards.' He lets that sink in. 'You let me know if Lucic steps out of line, if he starts running his own agenda. Or if you get even a whiff he's taking money.'

She says nothing.

He stands. 'I need to leave. That plane will be getting hot out on the tarmac. Now go to your hotel and get dressed properly. You're a police officer, a detective. Start behaving like one.'

———

Stanley Honeywell is well and truly damaged, propped up in his hospital bed, freshly bandaged. His face is a mess of cuts and bruising, one eye shut, the other widened with fear. Ivan wishes Nell were here; the big man seemed to like her. 'Stanley, I am a police officer. You remember me?'

Ivan can see he does, recognition evident in that one bloodshot eye.

'People from Cuttamulla mine have told me that you stole money from them. Is that right?'

The man stares at him, frozen.

Ivan sees the reaction, switches tack. 'You won't go back to prison. You tell me the truth and there will be no prison. Understand?'

Relief sweeps the distorted visage. 'Yes,' says Stanley. His voice is rough, but clear enough. He doesn't appear to have lost any extra teeth; he didn't have many to start with.

'Okay. So the truth, remember. Did you steal the cash from the mine?'

Stanley nods, face telegraphing shame.

'Twenty thousand dollars, in cash?'

'Yes.'

'Why? What did you want the money for?'

Now he looks conflicted, uncertain what to say.

'It's okay, Stanley. Just tell me the truth. That's all I need to keep you out of jail.'

'For Jonas,' says the big man, almost blurting it out.

'For Jonas McGee?'

'Yes.'

'Did he ask you to?'

'No. But he needed money. So I got it for him.'

'On your own initiative?' Stanley looks blank, and Ivan rephrases the question. 'It was your idea to take the money?'

'Yes. My idea.'

'Do you know why he needed the money?'

'For Elsie. He said for Elsie.'

'His daughter Elsie?'

'Uh-huh.'

'Why does she need money?'

'I don't know.'

Ivan stares. 'Jonas didn't tell you?'

'No.'

'When did you find out he wanted money for Elsie?'

'When he said I couldn't work with him anymore. He said he needed the opal money for Elsie.'

'So when you went to work at Cuttamulla?'

Stanley frowns. 'I guess.'

'Did he say anything else?'

'He was upset. The opals were running out. He had to find another job.'

'Do you know where?'

'At that other mine. The one by the lake.'

'Kalingra?'

'Yes.'

Ivan remembers what Kyle Torshack told him, the deposits in Jonas's bank account. 'He did carpentry?'

'I guess.'

'Why did you steal the money for him?'

'Because he saved me. In prison. When my brain bled.'

Ivan nods, remembering their last interview. 'And Elsie. You remember Elsie?'

'Yes. Elsie.' He smiles. 'She likes piggybacks. She's my friend.' Then he looks distressed. 'She grew up, she left.'

'You liked her?'

'She was nice to me. Not all kids are nice.'

'Can you remember why she left?'

He shakes his head. 'Sometimes Jonas would cry.'

Ivan considers Stanley. The man isn't beyond lying; he's not that simple. If he could lie about feeding his goat, lie about having lunch when he was really at the bank, he could lie to protect the closest thing he'd ever had to a family. 'Stanley, I want to find who killed Jonas. That's my job. But I need your help.'

'You won't dob?'

Ivan can't follow the logic. 'Dob? Who would I dob to?'

'Ray.'

Ivan smiles. 'No. I won't dob. In fact, I'm going to tell Ray and everyone else at Cuttamulla what a huge help you've been.'

'You will?'

'I will. Provided you tell me the truth.'

Stanley beams through his broken face, teeth like tractor treads. 'Okay.'

'Good. When was the last time you saw Jonas McGee alive?'

The beam fades. Clearly time is not something Stanley is very good at.

'Was it before your last ten-day shift at the mine?'

Still Stanley looks confused.

'Okay. Let's see if I can help. When you stole the money, did you tell Jonas?'

Stanley frowns, concentrating. 'No. I tried. I tried calling. He didn't answer.'

'Was this when you went to the bank?'

'Yes. I didn't know what to do. I wanted to give him the money. I put it in the bank. It would be safe there. That's what the man at the bank told me.'

'Did you go to the opal mine? Did you try and see Jonas, to give him the money?'

'No. No, I didn't.'

'Why not?'

'Jonas told me I wasn't allowed to be there.'

'Why?'

'Don't know.'

'When did he tell you that, Stanley? When he told you there was no more work, when he got you the job at Cuttamulla?'

Stanley is smiling again, as if pleased at connecting two events. 'Yes. That's right. He said I wasn't allowed back.'

Ivan blinks. The excuse is so feeble, it seems strangely believable. 'Stanley, do you have any idea who could have done this? Killed Jonas? Crucified him?'

But the big man's face speaks only of sorrow and grief. 'No. He was good. Always good.'

Ivan ponders the man before him, so large the hospital bed barely contains him, arm in a sling, face battered, head bandaged. 'What will you do now, Stanley?'

'Cyril said I could still work at the mine. Not payroll, a new job. And they'll give me extra money while I get better. He had a name for it.'

'Compensation?'

'That's it.'

'Good for you, Stanley. Good for you.' Ivan stares at him for a long moment, but can think of nothing more to ask. He reaches out, shakes the man's good hand, marvelling at its size. 'And thank you.'

When Ivan goes to leave the hospital, Cyril Flange is hovering near reception. The lawyer looks as out of place as a foie gras stall at Bunnings.

'How is he?' asks Flange. The combativeness has gone; the lawyer sounds concerned.

Ivan doesn't buy it. 'He'll mend.'

'I'm glad to hear it.'

'Says he still has his job. And that Cuttamulla will pay compensation.'

'That's the intention. What do you think?'

'That's your call. I'm not a social worker.' Ivan remembers how this man treated Nell; he's not about to provide an endorsement.

Ivan's brusqueness doesn't deter Flange. 'It's a tricky situation. Normally, if someone stole money, we'd press charges. Of course we would. But the way he is, the way he was treated . . . The boss thought compassion was required, not prosecution.'

'The boss?'

'Delaney Bullwinkel, chairman and CEO of Cuttamulla Coal.'

'He's taken a personal interest?'

'Only because he's here. We arrived yesterday to find the mine manager dealing with the fallout.'

'I see.'

'The boss is in town to see councillors from Lightning Ridge. We donate a lot of money locally. Said he wouldn't mind meeting you. Do you have a moment? He's just having a snack in the Alpine Cafe.'

'Sure.' Ivan's instincts are on edge; he knows people like Delaney Bullwinkel don't request meetings for social reasons: the man either wants something, or wants to volunteer something. And the last thing Ivan wants is to upset him and cop another call from the deputy commissioner's office.

Delaney Bullwinkel is a small man with a large entourage. Unlike his lawyer, he isn't dressed in a suit. Instead, he appears to have bought the Country Road catalogue: beige chinos and a polo shirt. The clothes look brand-new, as if he orders in bulk. He's sitting alone in a stall opposite the Matterhorn; members of his entourage are installed in both neighbouring booths, like a Praetorian guard.

'Senior Sergeant Lucic. Thanks for coming.' He indicates that Ivan should sit with him. 'What would you like?'

Ivan sits. 'I'm good. And it's just regular sergeant. Nothing senior about me.'

'I hear you have been investigating this little imbroglio at Cuttamulla.'

'Indirectly.'

'And it sounds like we have come to a satisfactory outcome.'

'If you say so.'

'Good,' says Bullwinkel, taking Ivan's response as confirmation. 'Thanks for being so accommodating. We've sacked Penuch. Solid enough fellow, from what I understand, but that sort of behaviour, resorting to physical violence, trying to sweep his negligence under the carpet, is beyond the pale. Absolutely unacceptable.'

'You think the police should lay charges?'

'That is entirely up to you. From our point of view, Penuch's dismissal is punishment enough. Our only concern is that the townspeople don't think you have gone soft on him because he was our employee.'

'Why does that concern you?'

'This town is important to us. It's our major supply link. We've contributed money to the hospital, upgraded the thermal pools, spent money on getting the airstrip paved. I feel a sense of responsibility.'

'Yes, it's a good town,' says Ivan, if only to say something.

'I understand you are investigating the death of a local fossicker. From what I hear, a shocking death.'

'I am. His name was Jonas McGee. What interest is it of yours?'

'I hear he was a close associate of Stanley Honeywell.'

'Yes. Stanley used to work for him.'

'That being the case, I wonder if I might ask you something, officer. We are trying to do the right thing by this Stanley Honeywell. We're letting him keep his job, providing him with support.'

'Paying him compensation,' Ivan interjects.

'Indeed. So imagine how terrible it would look if that well-intentioned care came back to bite us.'

'And how might it do that?'

'If he was implicated in McGee's death. It would look like we were sheltering a killer. I don't want that to happen. So I would like you to tell me: is Stanley Honeywell a suspect?'

Ivan considers this, but can see no harm in telling the truth. 'No. Not at this stage.'

'That is a relief. You will let Mr Flange here know if that changes?'

'I'll see what I can do.'

'I hear the murder of McGee was quite brutal. Crucified and left to die like that.'

Ivan shakes his head. 'I can't really discuss details of the case.'

'No, of course not.'

Ivan wants to be the one asking questions, and he changes the subject. 'I hear your old rival Bob Inglis is coming to town.'

Bullwinkel grins, rubs his hands together. 'Indeed. Might liven things up.'

'You don't sound put out.'

'Why would I be? The bloke's a complete arsehole, wouldn't trust him as far as I could kick him. But I wish him well. We might even be able to partner on a few community projects. I paved the runway; he can put some decent air-conditioning in the terminal. I hear it was getting a bit whiffy this morning.'

Ivan looks at the Matterhorn; in the daylight spilling through the doorway, it no longer appears so pristine.

chapter nineteen

NELL WALKS FROM THE INTERVIEW ROOM INTO THE SQUAD ROOM AND HEARS IT go silent around her. She stands there, in her briefs and the ridiculous hoodie with its *Party Animal* slogan, hair a mess, make-up smeared, staring them down. The room has come to a standstill, everyone conscious of her presence, no one prepared to make eye contact. Only Cheryl Pederson, her expression neutral, is looking at her. Nell feels exposed, knows she should slink away, knows that's the expectation—that she should get to the motel, get dressed and spare everyone the embarrassment. But she stands there for a good long time, unflinching. She is barely conscious of what she is doing, but she remains there. Unbowed. *Fuck them*.

Then, something unexpected happens: Carl Richter stands and follows her, catching her as she is pushing through the exterior door.

'Give you a lift,' he says. 'Can't have you walking through town like that. Burn your feet.'

She looks at her bare feet, then up at him, sees the concern on his face. 'Thanks,' is all she says.

The drive to the Golden View Motel is just a few blocks, a couple of minutes. The first words she speaks are directions to her room. Her police car is still parked outside, unblemished by the night's events. Only when he pulls up does she address him. 'Feral Phelan said that you put in a good word. Vouched for me.'

'Yeah. I did.'

'I thought you hated my guts.'

'I think I did.'

'What changed?'

'I got it wrong.'

Thirty minutes later, when she re-emerges, showered and properly dressed, Richter is still there, waiting in his car. She thinks of ignoring him, getting in her own vehicle, driving back to the station. Instead, she walks over, waits as he gets out.

'Buy you a coffee?' he asks.

'Sure.' She knows she should be getting back, that Ivan is counting on her, but she's intrigued. Something has changed in Richter's voice, in his demeanour. If she didn't know better, she'd think it was contrition. Maybe he has something useful to tell her.

'Jump in,' he says. 'I'll drop you back here after. To get your car.'

Again the drive is silent. They pull up across the road from the Alpine Cafe, but before they get out, she sees Ivan standing at its door, talking with the lawyer from Cuttamulla and another man.

'Who's that, Carl? With Ivan and the man in the suit?'

'Delaney Bullwinkel. Owns Cuttamulla.'

In the pocket of her cargo pants, her hand closes on the burner. 'Let's go somewhere else.'

Richter frowns. 'Whatever you say.' He starts driving. 'Cafe at the bowlo?'

'Suits me.'

They drive the few hundred metres without speaking, Nell recalling Phelan's insinuation, that Ivan Lucic may seek money to feed his poker machine addiction. And here he is, briefing Delaney Bullwinkel, a man identified by the journalist Martin Scarsden as a member of a cabal of power and influence. The man who had her humiliated and run off Cuttamulla. To think she's been feeling guilty about not immediately returning to the station, and he's hobnobbing with mining magnates. Her hand grips the pre-paid phone, the urge growing to message Phelan, to let him know. To get in his good books. But it's not something she can do now, not with Richter here.

The bowling club is quiet, air-conditioned and empty, like an airport terminal in quarantine. The cafe isn't really a cafe, just a different corner of the bistro, serving light snacks and coffees while the main kitchen is closed. It has some of the accoutrements of an Italian deli: bags of pasta, four-litre tins of olive oil and loaves of bread that are either made of plaster or so stale they might as well be. Out on the floor, chairs are up on tables, while a cleaner is vacuuming absent-mindedly, earbuds in, giving a little skip every now and then, dancing along to her playlist. Nell feels envious, wishing for a moment that she could swap jobs, revel in the mundane.

She and Richter order coffees and snacks, then take a couple of chairs down and claim a table next to the cafe counter.

Once seated, the senior constable cuts to the chase, as if he cannot bear any more small talk. 'I sat in on the interview this morning, with Trevor Topsoil,' he says. 'They wanted to give him the once-over before they took him to Lightning Ridge—before he could think his story through and lawyer up.'

'And?'

'It was meant to be just a first crack. You know, get what they could on the record. But he caved, didn't hold back. Wanted to strike a deal there and then. Offered to tell them everything in return for leniency.' And then: 'He's a fucking piece of work.'

'So I've come to appreciate.'

'He was gloating.'

She stares at him. 'Do I need to hear this?'

'He said you were clueless. He was boasting about how he'd conned you. Stupid prick.'

She clamps down on her anger. She doesn't want to listen, yet she hears the sincerity in Richter's voice, sees it in his face. 'Yes. It's true. He played me.'

'I should have realised it,' says the senior constable, voice full of regret. 'I should never have listened to Ottridge.'

She thinks of their former sergeant, long gone. 'What's he got to do with it?'

Richter shakes his head, remorse pouring out of him. 'I asked Faith Basheer. She filled me in.'

'On what?'

'On Ottridge. She told me he was the one who stopped you investigating, the one who told us there was nothing to it, who told you not to go to the Drug Squad. I thought he was just slack, that he didn't deserve to lose his job. But Faith says he was taking backhanders from Barret the whole time. He was crooked, Nell. As a dog's hind leg.'

'That's what I suspected.'

'Yeah, but I didn't. He told me, once it was done, that you were in Topsoil's pocket, that Topsoil had you on a lead, handing you kickbacks.'

Nell says nothing, but her face must betray her disbelief.

Richter continues: 'Ottridge didn't just retire; he turned state's evidence. Which meant they protected him, kept it secret what he'd done. He ran out with his tail between his legs. Like a fucking cur.'

'And they didn't tell you?'

'No. Just left me hanging out here, baking in heat and ignorance.'

'You didn't work it out?'

'No. Even while Professional Standards went through my accounts like a dose of salts. I didn't even know they were doing it.'

'And found nothing.'

'No. Just a moron.'

'Well, that makes two of us then. Ottridge played you, Topsoil played me.'

'Can you forgive me?'

She finds herself smiling, doesn't know why. 'I'm not exactly in a position to be judging others right now.'

Richter stares down at his hands. 'I always thought I was a good cop,' he says. 'Now I think I'm just a stupid old man.'

'You are if you believe that.'

'Maybe. Maybe I'm not as tough as you.'

'We'll see.'

The coffees come, with a sausage roll and sauce for Richter and a lamington for Nell. They watch the waitress come and go, happy for the distraction. The vacuumer has finished and is bringing the chairs down from the tabletops.

'Listen,' he says. 'Topsoil had a couple of laptops. We think one of them belonged to Jonas McGee.'

'You sure?'

'Yeah. The Drug Squad has it; they're going through it now, ghosting the hard drive. They know about your investigation. You can collect it when we get back.'

'I will. Thanks, Scaley.'

He smiles at that, the use of his old nickname, before the smile reverts to a grimace. 'And I think you should talk to Topsoil. Well, maybe not you, but Lucic should interview him.'

'Why's that?'

'You know he was a mate of Jonas McGee?'

'Yeah.'

'Well, Faith reckons he's a fence, has been for a long time. Even before moving into drugs. They've had him under surveillance for months, so they know all about him. Word is he was the go-to man for ratters. Selling them lightweight gear, moving their stones for them.'

'Why's that important?'

'He might know who found the body.'

— —

Ivan drives back from his meeting with Bullwinkel. The car park is almost full, but there's no sign of Nell's vehicle. Inside, Garry is at the front counter and the squad room is packed, but their detectives' room is empty, as are the interview rooms. He returns to the counter, where Garry is now dealing with an elderly woman. She's pointing her finger at the probationary constable, a long bony finger with an extended nail, painted blood-red. She looks as if she might eviscerate him with it.

'Hey, Garry, what's happened to Nell?' Ivan interrupts.

'Wait your turn,' snaps the irate woman. 'The constable is talking to me.'

Garry flicks him an apologetic look, even as she ramps up her complaint. 'It's his dog, it's his responsibility,' the woman insists, stabbing her finger again, and Garry edges back. 'Shitting here, shitting there. It's a shitting machine, I tell you. An utter disgrace.'

'I'm sorry, police business,' says Ivan, again interjecting.

'I told you to wait your turn!' snaps the dragon.

Ivan can't believe it. 'I'm sorry, but this takes precedence. I'm a detective.'

'A detective? Good. You can investigate my neighbour and that diarrhoeal dog of his.'

Ivan ignores her. 'Garry, where's Constable Buchanan? Her car's not here.'

'Not doing any police work, I can guarantee you that much,' the old woman says, unwilling to be excluded.

'You want me to arrest you?' says Ivan, glaring at her. 'Shut up.'

'How dare you!' cries the crone. 'Do you know who I am?'

'As if I care.'

'Nell's not here,' says Garry, looking increasingly panicked. 'She's got the all clear. Scaley drove her to the motel to get changed and get her car.'

'Are you ignoring me?' the woman demands of the young constable.

'Not at all, Mrs Tuppence.'

'Thanks,' says Ivan, leaving them to it.

'This isn't the end of the matter,' the crone yells after Ivan. 'Justice will be served.'

He turns left at the corridor, walking down to the squad room. Constable Vince Kantor is at his desk, staring at his computer screen with a look of incomprehension, as if trying to understand the intersection between relativity and quantum mechanics.

'Vince. Any word from Elsie McGee?'

'None. Sorry. I'll give her another try.'

'Good on you.'

'Telstra has come through, though—the phone tracking,' says the constable.

'That was quick.'

'Because there's nothing there. None of the numbers we gave them were on the West Ridge last Tuesday morning. Not before noon.'

'There was a meeting of the miners' co-op,' says Ivan.

'That explains it then,' says Vince. 'They were all in town. Except for Kyle Torshack.'

'Where was he?'

'Up on the East Ridge.'

'Prospecting,' says Ivan, more to himself than Vince.

'I thought it might have been the rain,' says the constable. 'It was heavy throughout the weekend, then started to clear late Monday. They don't like mining in the rain. Jonas's phone is the only one that registers at all before Tuesday afternoon.'

'Show me.' Ivan walks around the desk so he can see the constable's computer screen. The phone log reveals Jonas leaving town late afternoon Monday and heading out to the ridge. 'As the rain was easing,' says Ivan.

'You can see where it cuts out, here.' Vince points at the screen. 'Ten thirty-five Monday night. It just drops out. He must have gone underground.'

'And never came up again,' says Ivan, an observation, not a question. Carole Nguyen never found McGee's phone; whoever took it must have disabled it before returning above ground. 'Strange time to go mining.'

'I asked Telstra if they had traces of any other phones up there. I told them if they had any traces, we could get warrants.'

'Good thinking,' says Ivan, starting to revise his impression of the constable. 'What did they say?'

'Nothing. Just Jonas, and a phone down at the Kalingra Rare Earths mine that didn't move all night. All weekend for that matter. They wouldn't give me a number, but my guess is it's a watchman.'

'Right, thanks. Can you forward what you've got to us, please?'

'Done.'

'Thanks, Vince. Good work.'

And the young man grins.

Ivan is back in the detectives' room when Nell appears ten minutes later. She's showered and dressed in fresh clothes, but he can see the fatigue in her eyes.

'You okay?' he asks.

'I'll survive.'

He can detect both irony and determination in her voice, can see resolve in her stance. 'You're not suspended then?' he asks.

'No. Phelan and Basheer have given me the go-ahead. At least for now.'

'Excellent. We've got plenty to do. First things first, we need to find Elsie, Jonas McGee's daughter.'

'Didn't Vince say she was in Los Angeles?'

'Yeah, he's still trying to reach her. She might be key.'

'That bank cheque, two hundred and eighty-seven thousand dollars—you think it was for her?'

'That's what I suspect. I just saw Stanley Honeywell over at the hospital. He says Jonas wanted money for her.'

'Stanley? Is he okay?'

'On the mend. Cuttamulla has decided to keep him on. Pay compensation. They sacked Penuch instead.'

'Really?'

He can see the incredulity in her eyes; he knows her opinion of Flange. He quickly fills her in: Penuch's confession of wrong-doing, Stanley taking the money, claiming it was for Jonas. But he leaves out his encounter with Bullwinkel.

'I'll check with the bank,' she says once he's finished. 'They were identifying who cashed it. Thought they might know by this morning.'

Ivan notes that her attention is back on the case. Probably a good thing; take her mind off her own problems. He knows they'll still be there, though, lurking beneath the surface.

'One thing,' she says. 'It might be an idea for you to speak to Topsoil. According to Richter, as well as dealing drugs, he's been fencing for ratters and supplying them with equipment. And he was best mates with McGee.'

'You're talking to Richter?'

'If it helps the investigation. He reckons Topsoil might have a handle on who found McGee and rang Crime Stoppers.'

'Good thinking. I'll speak to Faith Basheer, see if I can get access to him.'

'They've taken him to Lightning Ridge. I heard he's spilling his guts, wants to turn state's evidence.'

'Is that right? Maybe he'll agree to talk to us as well then.'

'One more thing. They found McGee's laptop at Topsoil's. Said we can have it.'

'Really?' Without thinking, Ivan reaches for the back of his head. The lump is still tender to the touch. 'So he's the fucker who king-hit me then?'

'Sounds like it.'

'Can you see if they've finished with the laptop?'

'Sure,' she says, but he sees hesitation in her eyes.

'It's okay, I'll get it,' he says.

'It's fine.'

He watches her as she heads out of their sanctuary and turns towards the squad room. She certainly has guts, he'll give her that.

When she returns with the laptop, they open it up. Someone has left a post-it note with the password. He stares at it for half-a-second, recognising it, the memory surfacing of finding it behind the framed photo in Jonas's study. Another memory comes to him: the contract notes recording McGee's share trading. He opens the folder labelled *shares*, shows Nell.

'It's on his bank statements as well,' she says.

'Trading almost entirely in one company, LikeUs. A rare-earth miner, like Kalingra,' says Ivan. 'They must be connected.'

'But how?'

'Don't know. Stanley Honeywell and Kyle Torshack both say he did some work at Kalingra.'

'No reason to get murdered.'

They're left staring at the computer screen. Ivan can feel it wants to tell him something, but for the life of him, he can't see what. He thinks about the rule of proximity, how little it is telling him. The phone records indicate that none of the miners were up on the West Ridge when Jonas died or when he was crucified. According to Telstra, there were no other phones nearby. To him, it suggests premeditation. That someone deliberately left their phone in town. He wonders if it's possible that when Jonas McGee went underground that night, he was planning to meet with someone. Or to hide from them. It makes him wonder who cut the padlock: the ratters who found his body, or someone intent on doing him harm?

— —

Nell sits in the toilet cubicle, staring at the burner. Her pretence has dropped away, her brave face and can-do persona stowed. Her guts are churning. Everyone is being so nice, so supportive: Faith Basheer and Cheryl Pederson and Carl Richter and Ivan Lucic. All of them, taking pity on her. And yet her innards roil. She knows she's being judged, that her career is on the line, that somewhere, in capital city offices, her future is being determined, that Professional Standards are starting to trawl through her past: her phone, her bank accounts, her social media. Her family, her partners, her life. Ringing her colleagues at Bourke, asking all about her, looking for dirt. God knows what they might find; God knows what they might think they are finding. God knows how they might misconstrue the mundane. It's what Carl Richter had done: witnessed innocent behaviour but assumed her to be guilty nevertheless. And that was someone who had known and worked with her for close to three years.

She needs to demonstrate to Phelan that she's a cleanskin, that she's acting in good faith. She can't just wait to be judged; she needs to get ahead of the game, prove her loyalty. It's not in her nature to wait on the deliberations of others; she has always believed in making her own luck.

She thinks of what she has seen: Ivan Lucic chatting cheerily with Delaney Bullwinkel outside the Alpine Cafe. He's recounted his interview with Penuch and his visit to Stanley Honeywell, but omitted any mention of meeting with Bullwinkel. Why? And she remembers what Nathan Phelan said about him: *You let me know if Lucic steps out of line, if he starts running his own agenda. Or if you get even a whiff he's taking money.* It's not as if she owes Ivan anything; she's only known him for two days. She starts typing a text. *Lucic briefing Delaney Bullwinkel.* She studies it, considers it, corrects it. *Lucic met with Delaney Bullwinkel.* That's all she writes. In itself, it's completely accurate, in no way judgemental. A simple statement of fact. She's not claiming he's revealed confidential information or compromised their investigation in any way. But still, she doesn't hit send. She stares at it, and then she starts deleting it, letter by letter. Here she is, hoping that her own actions are not misunderstood, even while she considers feeding Phelan information that could so easily be misinterpreted.

She puts the burner away. She's not a rat, not when there's no evidence. Ivan has done nothing wrong. Just the opposite; he hasn't judged her, hasn't distanced her. He deserves some respect. But that doesn't convince her guts: they continue to stir. This is going to be a difficult day. All the more for knowing her fate is out of her hands. She flushes, puts on her brave face, and heads back into the world.

——

Ivan is frustrated. He feels like he's been treading water, getting nowhere, even as crucial hours pass. Interviewing Stanley Honeywell and Ray Penuch has used valuable time, as has dealing with Cyril Flange and Delaney Bullwinkel. None of them killed Jonas McGee, none of them know who did; he needs to get back on track, needs to work through the most likely leads. He'd thought proximity might be the key; now he's forced to concede he has no idea who was up on the ridge when Jonas McGee died. No one with a phone on them, that's for sure.

He wonders about Buddy Torshack and his son Kyle. Could one or other of them, or both of them, have left their phones behind and travelled up to the West Ridge intending to harm Jonas? It's possible. Maybe he needs to double-check their alibis. Buddy certainly has a motive: the death of his wife, killed when Jonas McGee ran off the road returning from Lightning Ridge. It has to put him in the frame. But something about it doesn't feel right. Why wait eighteen years for revenge? And if Buddy was involved, was he the killer or the crucifier or both?

He considers the son, Kyle. Jonas McGee's nephew. The lad certainly has a chip on his shoulder. But if anything, he seems more resentful towards his own father than towards his uncle. Ivan can't see any real motive for the lad to kill McGee or desecrate the body. If either the father or the son did have a motive, then it must be something Ivan is yet to discover. But he can't rule them out entirely.

Which leaves him with the ratters. Ivan doesn't even know for sure that they exist, that they made the call to Crime Stoppers. But it seems logical. If they were involved in criminal activity, pillaging mines in the dead of night, then it's likely they wouldn't take phones with them. Just the opposite: they'd leave them in town or, even better, have an associate drive them off to Lightning Ridge or somewhere, an instant alibi. Perhaps they aren't just innocent witnesses. For all he knows, they may have been involved in the death of McGee and the desecration of his body. Maybe the Crime Stoppers call was made by one of the crew, someone not directly involved in the crimes, someone with a guilty conscience, someone growing restless as the days passed and the body still hadn't been found.

Ivan imagines a scenario: Jonas is guarding his new find, his new bonanza, and discovers them down his mine. There's a confrontation. They hit him, the blow to the face, and accidentally kill him. They decide there is nothing to be done and continue their pilfering. They return the next night, find the body has been crucified. They freak out and, after much soul searching, call the police. It's possible, but the more he thinks about it, the less likely it seems. If they killed him, left the body there, how likely is it that they would return to the scene, risk leaving DNA or other evidence? He knows opal fever is a strong motivator, and ratters must be both desperate and risk takers, but even so.

It occurs to him that they wouldn't just go down a mine without staking it out first, making sure it was empty. Maybe they saw something during their stake-out? Maybe even the killer, descending the mine? Another possibility plays out in his mind's eye. The ratters are staking out the mine, see Jonas go down, see someone else descend. Then, hours later, only the killer emerges. Days pass, they go down to investigate, find Jonas crucified, ring the police. Playing through possible scenarios focuses his mind. Perhaps that's not how it happened, maybe that's not what they saw, but if they did indeed stake out the mine, note who was coming and going along The Way, who was driving out to the far end overlooking Kalingra, then they may very well possess useful information. He needs to find them, to interview them, to discover how they came across the body.

And Carl Richter has suggested a possible way. It's imperative he talk to Trevor Topsoil, extract what information he has. If the man was fencing for the ratters, as Richter claims, then he must have a good idea who was out pilfering on Friday night, who might have ventured down Jonas's mine. A new realisation comes, hard and fast: Topsoil was supposedly Jonas McGee's mate, but he's also a duplicitous bastard. That much is clear from the way he manipulated Nell. If McGee was getting a good run of opals out of his mine, it's likely he would have been discreet about it, with only the Irishman knowing the value, with the profits poured into buying LikeUs shares. But McGee was a reformed man, an honourable man. Perhaps a trusting man as well. So maybe he confided in his fishing mate, Trevor Topsoil; told him of his run. And Topsoil told the ratters, sent them to do over his mate. Ivan reaches around, feels the lump on the back of his head, decides he very much wants to interrogate Topsoil.

He walks out to the reception area, where Garry is working at his computer. The harridan has left, and the browbeaten constable has returned to his duties.

'Garry, do you have a number for Lightning Ridge? I need to talk to whoever is holding Trevor Topsoil.'

'Sure,' says the constable, writing out the number on a post-it note. He obviously knows it by heart. 'There you go.'

Ivan is about to return to the detectives' room when Vince Kantor appears.

'Progress,' says the constable.

'What have you got?'

'I found out why Elsie McGee isn't answering her phone. She's in transit, returning from the United States.'

'She coming here?'

'Adelaide. She'll get in tomorrow, via Sydney.'

'Who did you talk to?'

'Her husband. He's still in the States.'

'Right. Thanks.'

Nell is back in the office when he returns, working away at her computer.

'Give us a minute,' he says. He rings Lightning Ridge, gets through to Faith Basheer. The Drug Squad officer hears him out, says he's welcome to speak to Topsoil, suggests he should come tomorrow. He thanks her, confirms a time to drive over and ends the call.

'You want me to come?' Nell asks.

'Do you want to?'

'I wouldn't mind watching that arsehole squirm.'

Ivan laughs. 'Sure, come along. You can give me a few tips. His weak spots. But it might be wise if you sit out the interview itself.'

'You don't think I can control myself?'

'I think you're fine. But I don't want Topsoil coming back sometime later, trying to revoke his evidence, claiming malice and prejudice.'

She looks annoyed, but accepts his point. 'Fair enough. They have a video feed over there: I can watch without being in the room.'

'Excellent.'

'Have you seen these reports from Telstra?' she asks. 'Phone records. Metadata for Stanley Honeywell and Jonas McGee. Numbers dialled, call duration, location. The lot. Also, phone tracking for the Torshacks and the other miners Garry canvassed up on West Ridge.'

'Yeah. Vince told me. No phones anywhere near the place, right?'

'Correct.'

'Useless.'

'Not entirely,' says Nell. 'Jonas made two calls that evening.'

Ivan stares. 'Vince didn't mention that.'

'One was to Trevor Topsoil. Topsoil didn't answer. The other was to a mobile number registered to Kalingra Rare Earths. A call lasting almost five minutes.'

'At what time?'

'Just after eight pm.'

'And who had the phone?'

'Don't know. I just called their office here in town. It rang out.'

'Did you call the number?'

'Of course. No answer,' she says, writing the number onto a post-it note and handing it to him.

He calls. The phone rings through several times, then abruptly cuts through to voicemail. *'Not here. Leave a message,'* says a gruff voice, before a short burst of tone.

Ivan identifies himself, asks the man to ring back and ends the call. He shakes his head. 'His last phone call. Why would he be contacting some bloke from Kalingra?'

Nell just shrugs, holds his gaze for a moment, then turns back to the computer.

Ivan realises he's staring at her while he thinks and averts his eyes. She really is sharp, so much better than the gofer he had hoped for on the plane here.

'I'm going up to Jonas's mine,' he announces. 'See if you can find out who has that phone. Talk to Vince. Telstra told him there was a phone active at the Kalingra mine all weekend and into Tuesday. We need to know if it's the same one.'

chapter twenty

IVAN WANTS TO GET BACK UP ON THE WEST RIDGE, TO WALK THE AREA ONCE more, to listen to what it might tell him. He's hoping Buddy Torshack might be up there, or even Kyle, to find out what they know about Jonas's relationship with Topsoil, and what he might have learnt during his time at Kalingra. And he wants to look around the rare-earth mine itself. It hangs in his mind, the knowledge that possibly the last person Jonas spoke to was someone working for Kalingra. The rule of proximity is reasserting itself. The mine site is just down the ridge, walking distance, overlooking the lake. Who was there last Tuesday morning?

But first Ivan calls in on the local court registrar, Humphrey Tuppence. His office is on the highway, just north of the crossroads, between the post office and a pawn shop, HUMPHREY TUPPENCE, SOLICITOR AND FINANCIAL PLANNING. JUSTICE OF THE PEACE stencilled on the window, together with a head and shoulders photograph of a middle-aged man with threadbare hair and a drinker's nose. It looks like an electoral office, as if Tuppence is running for parliament. Ivan probably doesn't need it, but perhaps a warrant for Kalingra is a good idea. That way he can ask to see documents. He knows Jonas received money from the mine, did some work there; he'd like to find out exactly what he was paid to do, why he was still in contact in the hours before he died.

Ivan pushes through the door, is about to speak, but his greeting is stillborn.

'You,' says a woman. It's the same shrew who was giving Garry a tongue-lashing back at the station. She's sitting at the reception desk.

Ivan shuts his mouth, recovers. 'Good afternoon. I'm here on official business. Is your son here?'

Her eyes sharpen, like daggers. 'Do you mean my husband?'

Ivan feels himself redden. 'The registrar. Humphrey Tuppence.'

'Not here,' she says, the flicker of a smile, the flicker of malice. 'Playing golf.'

'In Finnigans Gap?'

'In Queensland. Try later. Through the courthouse. This is his private practice.' And she stands, walks to the door and opens it, ushering him out with the glow of victory in her eyes.

He's just getting back in his car, when a Mercedes pulls up. Nothing new, nothing flash, but a cut above the clapped-out Toyota trucks favoured by the miners.

A man climbs out, dressed in the lairy clothes unique to golfers. Humphrey Tuppence looks even more lived in than the photo on his office window. 'You,' is all he says, obviously recognising Ivan.

'Me,' says Ivan.

'Shit a brick. Can you come back later?'

'Not really, no.'

'Well, don't let my wife see you. She wants to kill you.'

'Too late for that, I'm afraid.'

Tuppence glances nervously towards his office. 'What do you want?'

'A warrant.'

'Fuck me. Search where you like. Come to the courthouse tomorrow, and I'll do it retrospectively.'

'Really?'

'Sure.' Tuppence goes around the back of his car, pulls a set of golf clubs from the boot. 'Ruined a perfectly good round.'

'Me?'

'Her. On the phone.'

'Sorry.'

'Yeah, well, see you tomorrow.' And then, almost as an afterthought, 'Who are you searching?'

'Thought I might take a look at this new mine site over by Lake Kalingra.'

Tuppence stops, lowers the golf bag, its end now resting on the ground. 'What's the basis for the search?'

'In connection with the death of Jonas McGee.'

'Specifically?'

Ivan feels wrong-footed. A moment ago Tuppence was happy to issue a warrant retrospectively, no questions asked, and now he's after details. 'Jonas McGee worked there in the weeks before his death.'

'Is that all?'

'On the night before he died, he called someone at the mine.'

'Who?'

'I don't know. A mobile registered to Kalingra Rare Earths.'

Tuppence frowns. 'So how do you know they were at the mine?'

'It's on metadata supplied by Telstra.'

'Why wouldn't you just ask the company?' says the registrar. 'They can tell you.'

'We've tried. They're not answering their phone.'

'Their office is just down there, next to the bowls club. Try there. Come back tomorrow if you have no luck.' He picks up the golf bag. 'And ring first.'

Ivan decides it's not worth arguing the point.

He's opening the door of his Kia, when Tuppence calls him back. 'Just a minute.'

'What?'

'Have you guys issued a death certificate for Jonas McGee yet?'

'Don't know, I'll have to check with the pathologist.'

'What's the delay?' asks Tuppence.

'What's your interest?' returns Ivan.

'I have his will. But he stipulated that it remain sealed until I see his death certificate.'

'He's dead, all right. You have my word for it.'

'So why the delay?'

'Still determining the precise cause of death. Relax. I'll give it to you tomorrow—when you give me the warrant.'

— ◦ —

Nell is at her desk, stuck in the station, following the list of instructions that Ivan has left her. She'd prefer to be out with him, not in here, where she has to keep up such a front, where eyes turn every time she exits the detectives' room to use the bathroom or the kitchen. It's that dead time in the afternoon, when concentration becomes hard to maintain, when coffee and chocolate become essential. Today, they're not working so well. She's been up since before dawn, was drunk last night and has expended a month's worth of nervous energy.

Her phone rings. 'Hello?' says a tentative voice.

'This is Detective Constable Buchanan. Can I help you?'

'Constable, it's Janelle at the bank.'

Nell immediately softens her voice. 'Janelle. Hi there. I was just thinking of you. What have you got?'

'The information for the bank cheque. It's come through. I've just emailed it to you.'

Nell pulls up her email, sees the message from the bank. 'Yes. I've got it here.'

'It should have everything you need. Call me if there's anything else.'

'Yes. Thank you.'

The call ends and Nell opens the email. There's an explanatory note:

Nell,
The cheque was cashed in Adelaide four days after it was drawn and was deposited into an account connected to a GoFundMe crowdfunding campaign called Save Bess Claremont. See attachment. The account is controlled by someone called Elsie Claremont.
All the best,
Janelle

Nell opens the attachments. The first has the record of the transaction: the cheque number, the time and date, the account details.

Nell googles 'Save Bess Claremont'.

The top hit is a GoFundMe site, a community fundraiser. Nell clicks through. And there it is, set out for her, everything she needs to know. A photo of a young woman, a mother, holding her pretty young daughter, Bess. They have the same eyes, the same curve of the cheek. The girl looks healthy, her skin smooth and her eyes clear, but oxygen tubes lead to her nostrils, and the arm around her mother's neck looks terribly thin. The text spells it out. A terminal disease, no treatment available in Australia. The only hope a radical new procedure, genetically modified bone marrow. In the United States. Los Angeles.

There is a target on the site: $750,000. It's represented by a bar, with a green fill showing how much has been raised so far. Just less than $600,000. Nell can imagine what's happened from those bare facts. Elsie Claremont hasn't yet reached her target but has been unable to wait. She's taken her daughter to America, trusting that somehow she can raise the rest of the money. It explains why she's been in Los Angeles.

Nell rereads the text on the website, comes across an anomaly. The plea for money cites the need for half a million dollars, although the target is clearly more than that. She wonders what that might mean. That Elsie miscalculated, that initially she was too optimistic about what she needed? Or had something changed— the girl's condition deteriorating, perhaps, so that she requires additional treatment?

Nell sits back. It also explains Jonas McGee's sudden desire for money: for his granddaughter's medical expenses. What better reason could there be? Nell checks through the webpage. The appeal was launched six months ago. She runs that against the timeline in her mind. McGee didn't retrench Stanley until three months ago, didn't start his stock market speculation. It makes her wonder: was the grandfather unaware of the appeal, and his granddaughter's illness, for three full months? Was the estrangement between Jonas and Elsie so severe that the mother would not even ask him for help?

It seems unlikely. Surely, under those conditions, you would take money from the devil himself. And yet why else would he use a bank cheque, try to remain anonymous? Why risk making it out to bearer? She checks the appeal. It's tax-deductible. He's donated over a quarter of a million dollars, but is spurning a tax deduction. Even for an opal miner, operating primarily in the cash economy, that's hard to believe.

She thinks of the apprehended violence order, pulling it up on her computer. It prohibited Jonas McGee from approaching his daughter or contacting her in any way, including by post, phone call or electronic means, except through her lawyer. It also restricted him from approaching within two hundred metres of her place of employment and her place of residence for a period of at least one year. And then it hits her: the girl. Bess. She finds the date of the AVO, returns to the GoFundMe website, crosschecks the timing. The court order was issued in the months before the birth of Bess Claremont, when Elsie Claremont, then Elsie McGee, first fell pregnant, aged sixteen. Nell is starting to get a very bad feeling. She feels it rising, as if coming up from the floor, starting to gnaw at her bones. And for a moment, just a moment, she wonders if perhaps Jonas McGee deserved to be crucified. The thought holds her, freezes her, before she shakes clear of it.

She looks again at the apprehended violence order form. It lists Elsie's place of residence as the Rapture, East Ridge. She recalls Ivan telling her that. Her eyes drift lower, to the name of the police applicant: Senior Constable Carl Richter and his signature. Every AVO has one, the submitting officer.

She walks out of the office, through the squad room, oblivious to the attention, sits down at Richter's desk.

'Nell?'

'Howdy, Scaley.' She hands him the printout of the AVO. 'Remember this?'

'Sure.'

'Want to tell me about it?'

'Not a lot to tell. She decided she didn't want anything to do with her father. Said she was scared of him, that he'd tried to physically detain her, lock her up in their house. The magistrate took about two minutes.'

'Was he ever in breach of it? Did he get any warnings?'

'Not that I know of. She left town pretty soon after.'

'It says her residence was at the Rapture.'

'It does?' Richter studies the order. 'Yeah. I'm not so sure about that. They might have just offered her refuge when she escaped her old man's house. Just long enough to get the AVO, get her shit together and leave.'

'Why was Jonas trying to lock her up?'

'Obvious, isn't it? He didn't want her out there with that creep, the Seer. Can't say I blame him.'

'So she was a follower of the Seer?'

'Of some sort. Used to hang out there, go to their parties. Maybe he didn't want her getting messed up with drugs and whatnot.'

Drugs. Nell thinks of the dead man, the one who died out on Lake Kalingra. According to Ivan, he was full of them. And he lived at the Rapture. 'Was she friendly with Zeke Jakowitz?'

'The dead guy?' Richter looks pensive. 'Possibly. Hard to say. They definitely would have crossed paths. But I'm pretty sure she was well and truly gone when he died.' He looks at the AVO, checking the date. 'Yeah. She was gone within weeks of taking this out, I remember that, and Jakowitz didn't kill himself for another year.'

'Kill himself? How do you mean?'

He cracks a smile, as if amused by the intensity of her interrogation. 'I mean he wandered off onto that lake bed in forty-degree heat with no water. In my book, that means he killed himself. Whether he did it on purpose or not is a whole different question.'

'And after she was gone, were there any problems? Jonas venting at the Seer or the Rapture or anything?'

'Nah. Nothing like that. Not that I know of. Be pretty hypocritical of him.'

She frowns. 'Hypocritical?'

'He used to be tangled up with them himself. Back in the day, before the prang and jail.'

Her frown deepens. Ivan mentioned something like this, that the Seer had known Jonas years ago. 'He was up there?'

'Sure. They all were. Him and his missus. Back in those days it was a pretty wild place, if the stories are true.'

'What stories?'

'That it was a full-on cult. Lots of drugs and lots of sex. Orgies. Before it turned respectable.'

'Seriously?'

'Yeah. After the kid died out on the lake, the Rapture withdrew into itself. Hasn't been any trouble since then. But twenty years ago, who knows? If it's consenting adults, there's not that much we could have done.'

She tries to regather her thoughts. It's as if too much new information has landed on her at once. 'Back to Jonas. You're telling me that a couple of decades ago, he'd be up at the Rapture, at their parties. But then there was the car accident and the deaths of his wife and his sister-in-law. That changed him?'

'Too right it did. That and a few years in prison. He saw the error of his ways. I reckon that's why he was so keen to get Elsie out of there, before it ruined her life as well.'

'So, did she take out the AVO because she was at the Rapture and he was trying to force her to leave, or did she take out the AVO and go to the Rapture for sanctuary?'

'Way I remember it, she only went there to get away from him. Same time she got the AVO.'

Nell looks at him, can't help but like him. 'Were you here when it happened? The car accident?'

His face immediately sobers. 'Yeah. I was here. Bloody awful.'

'You were at the scene?'

'I was. We all ended up out there. The car was a total wreck. One woman, Annie McGee, was out through the windscreen, lying there like she was asleep, except for a gash across her head from where she went through the glass. Her neck was broken. Heloise Torshack was still in the car, half naked, but with blood all over her. Jonas was wandering around, raving. Bruised ribs and not much else, but howling at the moon, like a lunatic.'

'What do you think happened?'

'He was pissed and driving. Despite everything else, it was simple as that, I reckon.'

'Despite what else?'

'Well, both women in the front seat like that. One of them half undressed.'

'Jesus.'

'Way we figured it, they were having a fine old time. Dead straight road. He's drunk, sun in his eyes. They get to the Gulch and he goes straight off the bend. End of story.'

'The Gulch?'

'An ephemeral creek out on the road from Lightning Ridge. There was a sharp curve in the road in those days. He went off the outside.'

'He confessed to all that?'

'Not at first. He was gibbering when we found him, blaming everybody but himself. But by the time we got him back here, when he'd sobered up a bit and realised the enormity of what he'd done, yep, he confessed to it.'

'Was the car examined?'

'Nell, he blew three times the limit.'

'So it wasn't?'

'Not unless the Lightning Ridge boys ordered it. There was an inquest. It will be in there.'

'What did the inquest conclude?'

'That he was drunk and ran off the road. That he might have fallen asleep. Although, you know, that seems unlikely.'

She shakes her head. What an awful story. No wonder his daughter couldn't stand him, her mother dying like that. 'Where were the kids? Did they witness any of this?'

'No, thank Christ. Buddy Torshack had them in the back of his car. He came across the scene a few minutes later. Said he'd left Lightning Ridge before the other three, but they'd overtaken him. Way over the speed limit. The kids were asleep. Oblivious. He checked the women, to see what might be done, but by then it was too late. Said Jonas was mad, howling. He didn't want him in the car with the kids, so he got Jonas to calm down and convinced him to stay with the wreck. Then he drove on, got within phone range, and rang it in. He took the kids home, put 'em to bed, looked after them.'

— —

Ivan takes in the landscape as he winds up The Way onto the West Ridge. It looks barren, feels hostile. The rocks are sun-blasted and unforgiving, with only an occasional insinuation of vegetation, most of it stunted, all of it marginal: a twisted cactus, a patch of saltbush, a straggle of box trees. A kookaburra sits motionless on a dead branch, head still, alert for movement, seeking snakes and lizards. He drives past something dead, grey fur matted with red, flies swarming in a black cloud, the taint of death momentarily penetrating the air-conditioning. The sky is blue and merciless, the outside temperature topping forty degrees. It's been mounting all day and now it's reaching its zenith. Where is all this rain they keep talking about? He hasn't seen a drop since Dubbo. A wind is blowing, coming in from the desert, stirring dust and birthing willy-willies. It's a wonder the miners here don't live underground, them and the rest of the community, the way they do down at Coober Pedy in South Australia. It can't possibly be that much hotter there, can it?

The Way slithers this way and that, like a snake, following the ridge, before it forks and forks again, starts to peter out, growing rougher and narrower. Ivan realises he has no real memory of the road that Nell drove on Sunday, but he retains a sense of the location of Jonas McGee's mine, up towards the north-western corner of the ridge. Even so, there are a few wrong turns before he gets there.

He parks his car by Jonas's caravan. The ridge seems forsaken, the blast-furnace wind gusting. There's dust in the air, grit, as if it wants to erase him, to sandblast the memory of Jonas, to return the land to its prehistoric state. Up here, even the flies are sheltering. He walks to the shaft, to the truck, to the caravan. Utterly deserted. He searches inside the van. Nothing. Dirty dishes. Bottles of water, warm and unopened. The smell of something not quite right. Flies. He wonders what he is looking for.

This time he drives to Buddy's mine site. The car is labouring, fighting to keep the air conditioner going with the revs so low, struggling against overheating. It's not made for this landscape, this climate. He wonders if the sand might clog its filters.

There is no one at Buddy's camp site, but the cap of the mine is open. He can hear no machinery operating. Not the diesel generator, not the big blower. But there's a truck parked here, one of the ubiquitous Toyota flat-bed one-tonners. Someone must be here. He climbs down.

Kyle is sitting there, at the bottom of the shaft, drinking beer, leaning against the wall where it opens up into the ballroom.

He has an electric lantern. It casts long shadows on the walls, the outlines of the pine-tree roof props.

'Oh, it's you,' says Kyle. 'I thought it was Buddy.'

'He's not here?'

'Went into town.'

'Right.' Ivan finds a place to sit, an offcut of pine. 'You're not mining?'

'Nah. Been out drilling. Might have found something. An abandoned lease, hardly touched. But it was getting too hot, even for me. Thought I'd come and tell Dad that I'm going out on my own.'

'How'd he take it?'

'Not well.'

'You had a blue?'

Kyle laughs at that. 'Nah. We don't fight. It's more subterranean than that. More intense.' He drinks some more beer. 'So I came down to have a beer or two. Let it all flow out of me. It's cooler underground. Calmer.'

'Quiet too.'

'Like the grave,' says Kyle. He laughs again, a pleasant, carefree sound. 'How's the investigation? Getting any closer?'

'Yeah. We're making progress.' Ivan considers the young man. 'Maybe you can help, Kyle.'

'Sure.'

'Your uncle Jonas. Strikes me he was a pretty complex bloke.'

'You think so?'

'Don't you?'

'More like erratic.'

'In what sense?'

'He could be the nicest bloke on earth sometimes, at other times a complete arsehole. Especially when he got religion.'

'What was his relationship like with his daughter?'

'Shithouse. Poor Elsie really copped it.'

'What happened?'

'The car accident. I told you about it.'

'I remember,' says Ivan. 'Your mother and her mother, both killed.'

'Yeah, sisters,' says Kyle, looking down at his can of beer. 'It was always there. When Jonas was being nice to me, I always felt like it was because he was feeling guilty. Then, when he was being an arsehole, I reckoned it was because I was a reminder of what he'd done.'

'So you never got very close to him?'

'To Jonas? How could anyone? A teetotal bible basher. And it was always there. The accident. All bottled up. I reckon that's why he kept Stanley around the place. Someone who he could love, someone he could care for. Someone who could love him back. Like a dog.'

Ivan can't quite get a handle on what the youth is telling him; what Kyle thought of his uncle. 'Did you hate him?'

That elicits an amused snort. 'Yeah, I did for a while. When I was a kid and he was in jail and I found out what he'd done. I used to have nightmares about him, how he'd get out of jail and come back here to finish us off.' Kyle laughs. 'But then he got out and he wasn't so scary at all. Just a pathetic bastard, haunted by his actions.'

'You forgave him?'

'Kind of. More like he just lost his impact. His relevance.'

'Tell me about Elsie.'

'Sure.' Kyle finishes his beer, pulls another free of the sixpack wrapper, offers it to Ivan. 'They're cold. Coldish.'

Ivan accepts. It's a loose definition of cold.

'She disappeared when he went to prison. Went to Adelaide. We had no contact. Then, when he got out, she came back here.'

'How old were you then?'

Kyle thinks about it, freeing a beer for himself. 'I reckon she was maybe ten, I would have been nine.'

'How was she?'

'She hated it. She'd been down in Adelaide, living the high life with our uncle's family. Our mums' brother. He's a doctor. Loaded. Sent her to a nice school. She used to tell me about it, how the school had trees, lots of them, and that the leaves were so broad and close together that the shade was complete. Like an umbrella. I remember that. And how the house had books everywhere, more books than you could ever read, but they would always buy her another one if she wanted it. Coming back here was tough. Jonas wasn't a reader. Just the bible.' Kyle cracks a new can. 'Our uncle offered to send her to a posh Adelaide boarding school. She wanted to go, but Jonas wouldn't hear of it. He wanted her here. Like she was his possession. All he had left.'

'So she resented it?'

'Too right. He was strict as all fuck. Like he realised how much he'd stuffed up, so she was his chance to get it right.'

'Sounds controlling.'

'That's one way of describing it.' He gulps some beer. 'But you know, we were kids. You adjust. She got used to it. Accepted it. It's not like there was a lot she could do about it.'

Ivan sips a little more from his own can. 'Later, when she was sixteen, she took out a court order, an apprehended violence order against her father. What happened?'

'I don't know for sure. She wouldn't talk to me about it. Neither would he. Then she left. Didn't say anything. Just left.' Kyle stands, extracts a pouch of tobacco from his back pocket and sits again. He starts to roll a cigarette.

'Is that the reason she left? Because he was violent?'

'No. She was pregnant.'

'What?'

'Yeah. So I'd guess that was what the AVO was all about. He was such a fucking puritan.'

'Who was the father?'

'Don't know.'

'It wasn't you, was it?'

And Kyle shakes his head, offended. 'Of course not. We're cousins.'

'I'd better get cracking,' says Ivan, standing. 'Tell me, though. Last Tuesday, you weren't at the miners' meeting? The co-op.'

'Nah. Out prospecting. But now I'm getting my own claim, I guess I'll have to join.'

chapter twenty-one

HE PARKS THE CAR AT THE LOOKOUT TURNING CIRCLE. THE LAKE IS GLOWING, catching the western sun and bouncing it back at him. It seems to have less water today, more salt. Is that possible? To evaporate so quickly, even in forty-degree heat? He climbs out, gets a litre bottle of water to carry with him, leaves his gun locked in the car. The wind has died a little; there's less dust in the air. No flies either, not yet, but he drenches himself in repellent, just in case. He can see the access road winding around the shore of the lake. His eyes follow it, to where it disappears behind an outcrop of rock. He surveys the lake. In the heat, with the sun coming off the salt, it looks so much larger, so much more brutal. It's where Zeke Jakowitz died, alone and disorientated, his crown of thorns no protection from the heavens.

He starts to edge down a spur running from the top of the ridge. He's not following any man-made track, although suggestions of paths come and go, left by the passage of animals. The land is bare, the rocks crumbling underfoot, causing him to slip, then slip again; he's glad he bought the hiking boots. The mine comes into view across an alluvial fan. He stops, drinks some water. There are pegs, revealing a boundary, and signs. STRICTLY NO ACCESS. TRESPASSERS PROSECUTED. And DANGER! UNCOVERED MINE SHAFTS. And DANGER! BLASTING! He wonders at this last. For some reason he had thought the mine would be underground, like the opal pits, not dynamiting above ground.

Over a rise and there it is. A couple of temporary buildings with solar panels, a steel machinery shed, a cinder-block explosives shed. A large diesel generator, cables snaking to the demountables. A composting toilet, an overturned portaloo. A small truck, an updated version of Kyle's. A portable drilling rig, mounted on the back of a full-sized truck—or, more accurately, engulfing it—with TOPSOIL MINING SUPPLIES painted on the side.

He walks towards the demountables. The place is silent, save for some music on the breeze, the whiny sound of a transistor playing country and western.

He tries the door. Locked. He goes to peer in the window.

'Help you?' The voice from behind catches him by surprise, causing him to start involuntarily. Annoyed at his own reaction he turns around, is about to speak. There's a man with a gun, a rifle, pointed directly at his chest.

'Keep your hands up and where I can see them,' says the man. He's an ugly old coot, one tooth protruding over his bottom lip. He leans over, spits into the dirt, like he's chewing tobacco. The country and western music wafts in and out.

'I'm a police officer,' says Ivan. 'Lower the gun.'

'So you say. Keep your hands up.' The muzzle remains pointed at him.

'I'm not armed.'

'Let's see. Hands high above your head. Turn a full circle. Do it slowly.'

Ivan does as he's told, demonstrating his lack of weapons. He can see acceptance on the gunman's face. The tip of the rifle dips towards the ground. Ivan takes the initiative. 'I'm going to get my wallet out, show you my badge.'

The man doesn't speak, but tilts his head in agreement.

Ivan displays his badge. 'You need a closer look?'

'No. I'm good.'

Ivan replaces his wallet, starts to lower his other arm, but the man interjects. 'No. Keep 'em up.'

'I'm a cop. Now you know that, you're breaking the law.'

'Bullshit I am. You've got your badge—where's your warrant?'

'I don't need a warrant. I'm not searching, just looking.'

The man laughs humourlessly. 'Bullshit.' The smile fades. 'I've got my instructions. You can't be here without a warrant or an invitation. Now fuck off.'

'I need to ask you something. Did Jonas McGee ring you? Monday night, last week?'

'What if he did?'

'It was the night he was murdered.'

'Nah. That wasn't until the weekend.'

'No,' says Ivan, arms still aloft. 'That's when they found the body. He died in the early hours of Tuesday morning.'

The man says nothing for a moment. Then: 'Nothing to do with me.'

Ivan eyes the gun, still pointing in his direction. Maybe he should leave. Come back with a warrant. And backup. And his gun. But he pushes on. 'What did he talk to you about?'

The man just shakes his head. 'You're barking up the wrong tree, mate.'

'How's that?'

'It was nothing. He was looking for work. I told him to speak to the office in town.'

'Is that all?'

'Said he might call down, take some photos. Wanted to check some of the work he'd done. Said he was worried the rain might have washed away some of the foundations. Something like that. I told him to ring the office, clear it through them.'

'That was all?'

'Yep. I never heard back. Thought they'd given him the bum's rush.'

'Mind if I lower my hands?'

The old bloke thinks it over, has another spit. 'Yeah. Can't see any harm.'

'Thanks. Is it okay if I have a bit of a squiz around while I'm here?'

'You fucking deaf, mate? Get clearance from the office, or get a warrant.'

'You're doing this wrong,' says Ivan, trying to reason with the man. 'Why piss off a cop when you don't need to?'

But the old bloke is having none of it. He raises the gun quickly, fires into the sky. The sound of the shot echoes off the bluff and washes out across the lake.

'You heard me—piss off. Copper.'

— —

Nell goes online, searches out the coroner's report. There was no inquest, she notes, but the coroner published her findings anyway.

McGee's vehicle was severely damaged in the incident, but investigators found it to have been in a serious state of disrepair prior to this. In particular, all four tyres were bald, to the extent of illegality. There were indications that brake fluid was leaking. These may have been a contributing factor.

She flicks through to the conclusions.

The court finds the deaths of Mrs Annie McGee and Mrs Heloise Torshack were directly caused by the negligence and extreme intoxication of Jonas Wilhelm McGee. A poorly maintained vehicle and the angle of the setting sun may have been contributing factors, but a sober and attentive driver would have been able to compensate for these.

She flicks to the next page, to the coroner's recommendations.

We recommend that Mister Jonas McGee be prosecuted to the full extent of the law. We note that this prosecution has begun.

She rings Ivan, but there is no answer. She types out a text: *Meet you at the pub for dinner 6.30.* She's about to send it when a flashback takes her: she and Topsoil snogging in the corner, the taste of overly fruity wine. She corrects the text before sending: *Meet you at the bowlo for dinner 6.30.*

——

He parks outside the club, deciding against showering and changing, arriving fifteen minutes early. They can eat, exchange insights. He might go back to the station after dinner, start going through some of the paperwork, make sure he has everything he needs for the Topsoil interview.

His phone pings. A text from Nell. *Sorry. I'll be closer to 7pm.* Another forty-five minutes. He thinks of the poker machines. How much damage could he possibly do in less than an hour? He resists, deciding to walk along The Way to the motel, take a quick shower and put on new clothes. But he only gets to the next block, not even to the crossroads. The sign in the window is small, easy to miss. KALINGRA RARE EARTHS PTY LTD.

The office is on the first floor, among a row of professional suites. Downstairs, facing the street, there is an opal dealer and a payday loan place. Upstairs there's a dentist, an accountant, another payday loan joint, a clairvoyant. He passes a man on the stairs, presumably coming from the dentist, prodding cautiously at his jaw with one finger.

But when he gets to the Kalingra office, the full-length glass door is shuttered, with a CLOSED sign. He knocks, just in case. There is no answer, but there is something about the door, the way it has shifted ever so slightly. He gives it a push and it swings open. There's a receptionist desk but no receptionist, two offices but no officials.

'Hello?' he calls, one part of him knowing there will be no answer, another part not wanting to risk another man with a gun. 'Hello?' There is the slightest echo, despite the small space.

Nothing. The place is deserted. There's a set of keys on the receptionist's desk, sitting next to a shredding machine. Photographs are mounted on the walls depicting Lake Kalingra in its many moods: dawn, sunset, a starry night, noon. An aerial shot, showing where the West Ridge ends, the sharp drop down to the mine site and onto the lake itself. He studies it for a moment. There's the turnaround at the top of the bluffs where Kyle took them on their first day here, where Ivan so recently parked; there's the spur he descended; there are the buildings surrounding the mine site and a road winding around the base of the ridge, the access track to the site. Also mounted on the wall: a certificate of incorporation, membership of a mining organisation. Ivan photographs them with his phone. He takes the keys from the desk, tries them in the entry door. Sure enough, they fit. The office has been vacated now that the company has been bought out, the keys left for the landlord. That didn't take long. Ivan smiles, thinking of Bullshit Bob, eyes on the future, closing down the past. There'll be a new office, a shiny big one, not some hokey small-town effort.

He ventures into one of the offices. It too has been cleared out, except for a couple of dead cactuses in pots on the windowsill. A filing cabinet sits next to the window, top drawer still open. It's been emptied, and so have the three drawers below it. He tries the second office. It's much the same as the first: stripped bare. All that's left is a name plate on the desk: PETAL RIMMINGTON—CEO. It's a thorough job; even the wastepaper bin is empty. But one drawer of the filing cabinet in this office remains locked. He tries the keys from the receptionist desk, but nothing fits. A memory comes to him: a training course on executing warrants and conducting searches. He pulls out the drawer below the locked one, pulls it free from the cabinet. He feels around underneath the locked drawer, his fingers finding what he's searching for. He squats, looks inside. Sure enough, there's a key taped to the bottom of the drawer. He remembers the course; the instructor's amusement that the bad guys so often use the same hiding places, stashing cash in the freezer or drugs in the oven, because they saw it in a movie once. Now it's Ivan's turn to be amused: in their hurry to clean out the office, someone forgot where they'd hidden the key. He unlocks the drawer, slides it open, finds it half full with folders, documents and loose papers, not in any order but as if they've been dumped inside. He takes them all out, puts them on the desk.

They're full of mining data. Projections of ore concentrations per tonne, percentages of different metal oxides, height of overburden. A feasibility study comparing initial onsite processing to more distant options. Lots of figures: dollars and metric tonnes. At first, he can't make head nor tail of any of it. He looks at his watch. He's supposed to meet Nell in about twenty-five minutes. Then he finds something that he can make sense of: a folder containing a series of maps. The first is simple enough, detailing the extent of the mining claim. It takes him a bit more time to comprehend the next, until he realises it depicts vertical rise, the surface land climbing up from lake level. Several more maps display cross-sections under the earth, depicting the size of the ore body at various depths. Only a trained geologist could possibly understand what it means. He moves on. There's a series of three maps detailing the planning for a new, all-weather access road, then a chart detailing projected costs. He whistles: who knew a road could be so expensive? Then another, the mining claim overlaid with a series of dots, each of them numbered. He looks at the scale: one dot every two hundred metres or so. He turns the page, and it becomes clearer. There is a table, rows of information, of ore percentages, numbered from one through to one hundred and twenty-nine. He flicks back to the map, understanding the significance: there are one hundred and twenty-nine dots, each dot representing a drill hole, the table detailing the finding from each exploratory core, building up a three-dimensional model of the ore body.

He wonders if the information is of any use to him. It would have been sensitive until very recently, but surely no longer. Bob Inglis must already have this data, obtained it while conducting due diligence before the takeover. Ivan goes to replace the documents in the filing cabinet, then looks around the office. It's been abandoned. Everything here has been left behind. 'Finders keepers,' he whispers. He takes the documents, all of them, and carries them downstairs. He walks back to the club and locks them in the back of his car.

— —

Nell looks for Ivan in the club's bistro but he's nowhere to be found. Maybe he's making a point: she's the one who gets kept waiting, not him. She smiles at the suspicion; she doesn't think Ivan is into those sorts of mind games. At least she hopes not. She returns to the table over by the cafe where she sat with Carl Richter. The cafe is closed now, making way for the bistro proper. It's still early, but already a few people are drifting in, mainly tourists and grey nomads. There is no hi-vis, no miners.

Ivan comes in, looks around, spots her and walks over. 'Something to drink?' he offers.

'Mineral water,' she says with a grimace.

'Good call.'

When he's back from the bar with the drinks they sit and talk. He doesn't mention food and she still doesn't feel hungry. Nell knows she should: she's barely eaten all day, just the lamington with Scaley and some chocolate at the station. But she figures if she were to eat now, she might just about collapse from exhaustion.

'I'm really sorry about today,' she says.

'Nothing to be sorry for.'

'Yes, there is. The whole catastrophe with Trevor. You didn't need that. I wasted a lot of time.'

He shrugs. 'No matter. We're making progress.'

'You think so?'

'Sure. We've eliminated Stanley Honeywell as a suspect. Blake has given us a clear idea of when Jonas died. We know the West Ridge was all but deserted on Tuesday morning. There's a good chance Topsoil can steer us in the direction of whoever found the body. And Elsie McGee is on her way back to Australia.'

'Her kid. She's sick. It's what all the money is for.' And she tells him of the life-threatening disease, the GoFundMe site, Jonas's bank cheque. The pregnancy coinciding with the AVO.

'You see? Progress. Good work, Nell.'

She doesn't feel convinced; she suspects she doesn't sound it either. 'But none of it explains why he was murdered. Or even if he was murdered.'

'Blake will have more on that front tomorrow. With a bit of luck, by lunchtime or so we'll know how he died. And if he was killed, the method might help identify who did it.'

'What if it's natural causes?'

'Let's cross that bridge when we come to it.'

'You'll leave, won't you? If it's not murder?'

'That'd be my assumption. I am a Homicide detective, after all.'

She drinks her mineral water. It tastes good. Much better than wine. She looks around her. She'd thought she'd left this town behind; she'd thought she'd left a lot of things behind. 'Do you think I have a future? As a police officer?'

That captures his attention. 'That depends on you.'

'What does that mean?'

'You've had a golden run, Nell, up to now. You must know that. But now it's different. You've got to decide how much you want it. How resilient you are.'

She considers that. She looks past Ivan, over at the bar. Would she consider throwing it in, becoming something else? She wonders what it might be like.

He speaks, perhaps sensing her disquiet. 'You're very competent. Very can-do. On the ball. I'm sure there are all sorts of things you could turn your hand to and be successful.'

She bristles at that, the hint he's patronising her, even as she realises he's probably just trying to say the right thing.

But before she can respond, he continues: 'No one would blame you if you left. If you let them win.'

'Let who win?'

'The arseholes. The ones who want you to leave.'

'And who are they, precisely?'

'No one in particular, but they're definitely there, just as they're everywhere. Not just in the police. Even if you start a new career, they will always be there, the ones who think the only way to get ahead is to put others down. You can accept it, or you can fight it.'

'Sounds like you're talking from personal experience.'

'Maybe I am.'

'Want to talk about it?' she offers, trying to turn the focus back on to him.

'Not really. But I'm thinking of Morris Montifore. One of the most decent and honourable people I've ever met. One of the best Homicide detectives ever. And yet . . .' He takes a sip of beer. 'And yet he's going on the scrap heap; the arseholes got him in the end.'

'And you're just going to accept it?' she asks.

He smiles at her, a wry smile. 'You're the one who's talking about walking away, not me.'

'I don't walk away from fights,' she says.

'Good. Prove it.'

They stop talking, a kind of stalemate, before Ivan picks it up again. 'Why did you become a police officer in the first place?'

'Why ask me that?'

'Someone asked me the same question today. Feral Phelan.'

'And what did you reply?'

'That I felt I belonged here. That it meant something to me. What about you?'

'Thought it might suit me. Thought I might suit it.'

'Go on.'

She sighs, looks around, figures she can't expect him to be forthcoming if she's not herself. 'I'm the youngest of five kids.

Two brothers and two sisters. You pick up a bit as the youngest. See things, learn things.'

'They bully you?'

'No. Just the opposite. More like they doted on me.'

'Really? A happy family?'

'Happy enough.'

'Lucky you.'

'I guess. But by the time I was turning into a teenager, the older ones were starting to head off. I saw the differences. We lived in the country, or near enough, down along the Murray. The boys went to boarding school, us girls went to the local high school. My parents couldn't afford to send all of us to private school.'

'Were the boys smarter?'

'What do you reckon?'

'No.'

'Of course not. The eldest went into the army, mainly because his marks were too shithouse for much else, despite the fancy school. The other one went to uni, did business. He's an accountant. One of my sisters did nursing, the other is a childcare worker. Married with kids.'

'Not so terrible,' observes Ivan.

'If you say so. Mum and Dad thought I should do something similar to my sisters. Mum was always going on about it. The caring professions, she called them.'

Ivan is smiling. 'Not for you?'

'Stuff the caring professions. I wanted a kick-arse profession.'

Ivan's smile broadens.

'I tried sports. Thought I might become the next big thing. You know: travel the world, get paid a stack, retire at thirty. Too bad my hand-eye coordination is so shithouse. I did martial arts instead.'

Ivan's attention pricks up. 'Seriously? Any good?'

'I can hold my own. Even big guys, guys like Stanley Honeywell or Ray Penuch. They don't frighten me, not a bit.'

'Really?'

'Really. It helps at Bourke. I do a lot with the PCYC. Drop a few fat bastards and the kids really start respecting you. The girls love it.'

'I bet.' Ivan sips more beer. 'So that's why you became a copper. So you could kick arse.'

'Something like that.'

'Well, if you leave now, you're the one who's getting her arse kicked.'

She looks at him. It's not what she really wants to hear right now, but maybe it's what she needs to hear. 'You want to tell me about the poker machines?' She says it without thinking; the words just emerge from her mouth, as if she's hearing them the same time he is.

'What?' is all he can say at first, those laser blue eyes upon her, as if they want to cut through, to sear her core. 'Who told you about that?'

'Small town. Word gets out.'

He continues to stare. 'It's nothing to do with you. Not your business.' His words are icy, distancing, and final. But they're not a denial.

By contrast, her own words are conciliatory. 'Ivan, if you want to talk about it . . .'

'I don't,' he says, standing. 'C'mon. I'm hungry. Let's eat.'

WEDNESDAY

chapter twenty-two

THERE ARE THREE VEHICLES IN THE POLICE STATION CAR PARK BY THE TIME Ivan arrives, including Nell's Nissan Patrol. He's been jogging and feels all the better for it, thinking through the pep talk he gave Nell at the bowlo. He's decided he needs to heed his own advice: don't let the arseholes win. Inside, the station is awake and functioning, a welcome contrast to the previous two mornings. He's feeling positive after a nine-hour sleep and his run. The day feels right to him. The heat is coming, no doubt, but that feels almost normal and to be expected.

Nell is already working in their office, head down, concentrating when he enters. There is a coffee on his desk, still hot.

'Thank you,' he says.

'No probs.'

'You good?'

'Fine, thanks.'

'Sleep well?'

'Ivan, I'm fine. Let's put yesterday behind us.'

'Absolutely,' he says, pleased at her resilience, pleased she doesn't want to revisit the poker machines.

'Here,' she says, handing him a piece of paper. It's a printout from today's *Financial Review*.

HEAT DRAINS FROM RARE EARTHS

By Larry Griggs

Shares in listed rare-earth miner LikeUs Pty Ltd fell by more than 10 per cent in late trade Tuesday as speculators took profits after news broke that mining magnate Robert Inglis has consolidated his stake in the company.

In a statement to the market filed by his private holding company, Bulldust Investments, Inglis indicated he now controls 13.5 per cent of LikeUs, a stake worth around $700 million. It falls well short of the 20 per cent holding that would trigger a corporate takeover.

Inglis is now widely expected to take a seat on the LikeUs board.

'There's no doubt his buying spree has helped drive prices higher. Now he's got what he wants, it's natural that prices should come off in the short term,' says broker Kathryn Eyre of J.B. Were.

Inglis's strategic stake in LikeUs coincides with his imminent acquisition of the privately held Kalingra Rare Earths Pty Ltd, an exploratory-stage company with a highly promising tenement near Finnigans Gap in northern New South Wales.

'He's achieved his twin goals: buying out Kalingra and gaining a seat on the board of listed LikeUs Pty Ltd,' says Macquarie Bank analyst Ponton Lowe.

LikeUs has enjoyed a spectacular year-long run driven by tensions between China and the United States over access to rare earths. Despite yesterday's drop, shares are still up more than 250 per cent in a year.

Day traders and speculators helped drive the price surge during recent months as the market became aware that Mr Inglis, affectionately known in mining circles as 'Bullshit Bob', was building a stake.

Shares in Wide Valley have also come off 5 per cent, the market anticipating Inglis may need to sell some of his holding to fund his stake in LikeUs. He controls 57 per cent of Wide Valley shares, again through Bulldust Investments.

'This is an extremely canny move. He's moving out of the minerals of the past—iron ore and copper—and moving into the minerals of the future—rare earths,' says Macquarie's Lowe.

Both Lowe and Eyre are now of the view that Inglis is satisfied with his position in the market and is unlikely to increase his stake in LikeUs.

'This is an astute play by Inglis. By becoming a board member at LikeUs, he gains access to the insights and knowledge the company has built up over more than thirty years. That will inform his development of Kalingra,' says Lowe.

'LikeUs appears to have welcomed his investment, and is likely to view him as an ally rather than a competitor. The two companies can provide a united front in negotiating with foreign markets, particularly the Chinese.'

Mr Lowe tipped the downturn in the sector will be short-lived. 'Inglis may be out of the market, but the fundamentals of supply and demand remain. There is growing demand for rare earths and serious question marks over the supply.'

'Jonas sold his shares at the peak,' says Nell.

'Lucky him,' says Ivan dryly. 'It's intriguing, but I reckon it's a sideshow.'

They're interrupted by Garry Ahern. 'Sir, there's someone here to see you.'

'Who is it?'

'Elsie Claremont. Jonas McGee's daughter.'

Ivan searches the face for fatigue, for stress, for anxiety, and sees little of it. She's still young, he realises; maybe twenty-four.

'Ms Claremont, we've been trying to contact you.'

'I'm here now.'

'How is your daughter?'

'Bess? She's a fighter. But I need to get done here, get back to her.'

'Of course. It's a long way. Thanks for coming. Detective Constable Buchanan and I appreciate your assistance.'

'I'm not here to assist you. I need a death certificate. Why is there a delay?' There is a hardness in her voice, or at least the pretence of it.

Ivan takes it on board. 'To access his will?'

'That's right. You know about my daughter's condition?'

'Yes. We found the GoFundMe page.'

'So you'll appreciate my need for money. I want to sell my father's house, liquidate his assets. Sell the mine if I can find a buyer.'

'You'll forgive me for the observation, but you don't seem very upset about his death?'

'I'm not.'

Ivan and Nell exchange a glance. He can see the sympathy in the arch of Nell's eyebrows.

And it's Nell who continues, her voice accommodating: 'We will get a death certificate to you as soon as possible.'

'What's the hold-up?'

'Your father's body has been taken to Sydney. They need to confirm the cause of death. We're hoping for it today.'

A frown passes across the unblemished face, a hint of emotion. 'The cause of death? I'd heard he was . . .'

'Yes, he was,' says Nell, 'but we have to make sure that's what actually killed him.'

The young woman says nothing.

Ivan keeps his tone even and non-confrontational. 'We should know soon enough, and then Humphrey Tuppence can make the will public.' Ivan takes a moment, before adding, 'There might not be so much money there.'

'What do you mean?'

'Your father withdrew a hundred and thirty thousand dollars from his mortgage and drained his bank accounts.'

Elsie looks down at her hands, as if to consider her position, before replying. 'I know.' Her voice is not much more than a whisper.

'The bank cheque to the GoFundMe campaign. You knew it was him?' asks Ivan.

'I guessed. Even an anonymous donor wouldn't go to those lengths.'

Nell's curiosity takes over. 'I was looking at the site. Did the amount you were seeking, the target, change—from half a million to seven hundred and fifty thousand dollars?'

Elsie's eyes narrow. 'Yes. That's right.'

'Why? What happened?'

Elsie doesn't answer straight away, as if the police are inquiring into areas that shouldn't concern them. But when she does speak, she responds openly enough. 'We were counting on one of Bess's relatives being a match for the bone marrow transplant. But no one was. Not close enough. So, we need a wider search for donors, for a stranger to match. That costs money. In America, everything costs money. And even with a match, the procedure is likely to take longer, be more complicated. More expensive.'

'Your father? You checked to see if he was a match?'

'A DNA test. Yes. I guess that's what alerted him to the appeal, to Bess's condition. We tested everyone. Me. My father. My uncle, my cousins, my mother's parents. No matches.'

'Who did the testing?' asks Nell.

'My uncle in Adelaide is a doctor. He arranged it. My cousin here helped collect swabs.'

'Kyle Torshack?'

'Yeah. Kyle.'

The two detectives pause, give each other a knowing look. Kyle has kept that to himself. Ivan is sure he asked him if Elsie had been in contact. What was it the young man said? *Only when she wants something*; it was an expression like that. Why didn't Kyle volunteer the information about the DNA testing?

Nell fills the silence, her sympathetic voice disguising the bluntness of her question. 'You were prepared to test your father's DNA, to accept his bone marrow, so why not his money?'

'I was always prepared to take his money. He was the one trying to make it look anonymous.'

'You thanked him?'

She shakes her head, looking contrite. 'No. Not after what he did to me.'

'And what was that?'

Now there is anger in the young woman's eyes. 'Nothing that's relevant any longer.'

To Ivan's ear, Nell is struggling to keep her voice mild. 'What happened, Elsie? What happened back then?'

Elsie says nothing, regarding Nell, unflinching.

Nell presses. 'We know about the pregnancy. We know about the AVO. We know you left. Tell us what happened.'

And now a look of horror, of distaste, crosses the young woman's features, although none of it affects her voice. 'I'm not sure what you are insinuating, but my father had nothing to do with my pregnancy.'

Now it's Nell who looks wrong-footed. 'Then what?'

'I wasn't going to be controlled by him. I wasn't going to live with that puritanical hypocrisy a moment longer.'

'Elsie—'

But that's as far as Nell gets; Elsie Claremont cuts her off. 'What happened back then doesn't matter.' And she stands. 'I wish you well with your investigation, but I know nothing that could possibly help you. I was in Los Angeles when my father died. I haven't had anything to do with him for years, not since I left this place. I just want to get the death certificate and get out of here. Forever.' And then, for good measure: 'I am grateful for his money. His donation. It showed he cared. And I know he would want what remains of his estate to help his granddaughter.'

Nell is about to persist, but Ivan rests his hand on her arm, restraining her.

'We will do our utmost to help you,' he says, voice calm. 'We understand your desperation to return to your daughter. I have your mobile number. I'll notify you as soon as we have the death certificate.'

'Very well,' she says, and Ivan can see her shoulders relaxing, realises how difficult this has been for her. She offers a weak smile, and tells them she's staying at the Golden View Motel.

'Thank you,' says Ivan. 'And our condolences. It must be a very difficult time for you.'

'Sure,' says Elsie Claremont, the carapace back in place.

Ivan walks her to reception, then returns to the detectives' room. 'What do you think?'

'It's like she deliberately doesn't want to know what happened.'

He's about to answer when his mobile rings. He answers it. 'Lucic.'

'Ivan, it's Blake Ness.'

'Blake. What have you got?'

'Murder.'

Ivan takes a breath. This morning is suddenly moving very quickly. 'Are you sure?'

'Sure enough. He died of an insulin overdose. Would have lost consciousness in less than a minute, dead in less than five.'

'Shit.'

Blake continues, even before Ivan can formulate a question. 'There's the possibility it was self-administered, of course. But that would require someone removing the evidence. The needle, the vial. Whoever it was who nailed him up more than four hours later.'

'Self-administered? You mean suicide?'

'There are worse ways of doing it. Not painful. Not messy.'

'Right. And how easy was it to determine that as the cause of death?'

'Not so easy. You have to know what you're looking for.'

Ivan thinks that through. 'So if he hadn't been nailed up, if he'd just been found lying there?'

'If he was a diabetic, then the local pathologist would have looked for it. Probably. If he wasn't, chances are they would have put it down to a heart attack or some such. Natural causes.'

'Okay. Thanks. Anything else?'

'No, that's it. I tried to find a hypodermic puncture wound, but the body is too far gone. Too many insects, if you get my drift.'

'Thanks, Blake. Oh, and if you can, email us a copy of the death certificate.'

'Sure. Right away.'

Ivan finishes the call, looks at Nell. She's sitting perfectly still, eyes wide, having heard half the conversation. He fills her in.

'So, either someone murdered him, or he killed himself,' she summarises. 'Three scenarios. One: someone kills him, using insulin to disguise the murder. Someone else entirely finds him dead, crucifies him. Two: he kills himself, someone finds him dead, removes the evidence of the overdose, then crucifies him. Three: he kills himself, painless suicide, lies down in that pose and dies.

And then, by prearrangement, someone comes down the mine, knowing he will be dead, knowing he will be in that posture, and crucifies him.'

Ivan stares at her, mind whirring. 'Like he wanted to die as a martyr, but without the pain?'

'I'm just putting it out there.'

He shakes his head. 'No. Remember the blow to the face? I reckon someone laid him out cold, then administered the killer shot.'

Nell nods. 'Sounds right. And then what? Laid him out like that, waiting for rigor mortis?'

'No. Doesn't make sense. The whole rationale for using insulin would have been to disguise the murder, to make it look like natural causes. I definitely reckon we're looking at two separate crimes and two separate perps.'

'Sounds logical.'

'Let's chase down the source of the insulin.'

'I'll try Mary at the hospital. Small town like this, she should have a good angle on any insulin-dependent diabetics.'

'Good thinking. I'm going to take the death certificate over to Tuppence. I want to see what's in this will.'

Ivan meets Humphrey Tuppence at the Alpine Cafe, having rung in advance. They exchange greetings. Ivan buys an iced coffee, fetching one of the mass-produced ones from the Coke fridge. He sits, hands Tuppence the copy of the death certificate.

'I'll need the real one, you know,' says the lawyer. 'Or a certified copy.'

'I know. I'll ask the pathologist to mail you one.'

'All good. Provided I get it eventually, we can work from this. I'll let Elsie Claremont know.'

'What's in the will?'

'I've got it here, if you want to read it for yourself. But it's straightforward. He's left everything to her, except the mine. That goes to his nephew, Kyle Torshack.'

'That's interesting. Did he say why?'

'Well, there's what's said and then there's what's not said.'

Ivan feels an inkling of irritation. The solicitor seems to be enjoying this, like it's some parlour game, a tale for recounting up at the nineteenth hole in Queensland. 'You want to explain that?'

'The mine was his life's work. He'd been working that particular claim for years. He was convinced it still held an undiscovered fortune, but he knew that Elsie would simply sell it off. He believed Kyle would work it. Said the lad had been talking about getting his own stake.'

'When was this?'

Tuppence doesn't need to check the document. 'The will was made out just over a year ago.'

'Replacing an earlier will?'

'Not that I know of.'

'You said there was something left unsaid? What was that?'

Tuppence rubs his hands, like a gentleman detective preparing to deliver an insight. 'I think all that about Kyle working the mine whereas Elsie would sell it off, I think that was all correct. But there's more to it. Finnigans Gap is not what it once was. You wouldn't see it, an outsider like you, but the speculative pulse has diminished. Every year, it beats weaker. Fewer and fewer outstanding opals are coming out of the ground. A couple of long-time miners have pulled up stumps, a couple of dealers have left. There's more money coming in from both Cuttamulla and tourists than there is from opals.'

'What's your point?'

'If Jonas had left Elsie the mine, I'm not sure she'd have been able to sell it. She'd have realised just how little his life's work is actually worth. That's the first thing. Second, he wouldn't want Buddy Torshack getting hold of it. He liked Kyle well enough, but there was real animosity towards Buddy. And the third element: guilt. His need for atonement, for recompense.'

'Because he killed Kyle's mother?'

Tuppence looks disappointed, as if Ivan has deprived him of his flourish. 'Correct,' he says.

Ivan sees an opportunity, decides to flatter Tuppence. 'Humphrey, that's enormously helpful. You are clearly very perceptive. A good judge of character.'

'Thank you,' says Tuppence, reinflating. 'I pride myself.'

'So, what do you make of all this intrigue around the Kalingra mine?' asks Ivan, his manner gossipy. 'Quite the coup.'

'Yes. Bullshit Bob Inglis. That'll stir things up. This place could end up like Tombstone. Gunfight at the O.K. Corral.'

'Sorry. You've lost me.'

'Bullshit Bob Inglis and Delaney Bullwinkel. There's bad blood. Surely you've heard?'

'I'd be grateful for your insights.'

'Oh, mate. You don't know? It's a ripper.'

'I saw some reference in the papers.'

'They were partners back in the nineties, over in Western Australia. The Wild West. They'd been friends since uni, apparently. They staked out a big claim in the Pilbara. Inglis was a geologist, had worked for Lang Hancock and Rio Tinto. Knew exactly what to look for. Bullwinkel was an accountant and stockbroker and knew the inside of Perth's big miners like the back of his hand. So they partnered up.' Tuppence stops talking to drink some coffee, or for effect, or both.

'Sounds like a good match,' says Ivan.

'Oh, it was. It was. They got well set up. Private company, owned fifty-fifty, which in turn held a controlling interest in a new public company: Wide Valley Resources. Their timing was perfect. The mining boom was gathering pace, money flooding in from China. They floated Wide Valley and bingo, they were instant multimillionaires. Worth hundreds of millions each. And Wide Valley was flush with capital. They had all the money they needed to develop it.'

'So what happened?'

'Bullshit Bob was spending all his time up at the mine site, overseeing its construction. Delaney was in Perth, gladhanding the money people. And then . . .'

Ivan can't help smiling at Tuppence's theatricality. 'And then?'

'There was a shotgun clause in their company's constitution. The private one. It's a common feature in well-structured partnerships and jointly owned companies—a way of resolving irreconcilable differences. Effectively, party one offers to buy out party two, nominating a price. Then, within a specified period, party two must either accept and sell, or buy out party one for a greater amount.'

'Really? That's brutal.'

'Yeah. It's usually only invoked as a final resort. The ultimate circuit-breaker if no other compromise can be reached.'

'And in this case?'

'Bullshit Bob was up in the Pilbara, and out of the blue, Delaney triggered the shotgun clause, catching Inglis off guard and unprepared. It's widely believed that Delaney was the one who inserted the buyout clause in the constitution in the first place.'

'Hang on. I thought Bob Inglis owns Wide Valley?'

'He does. Or a controlling interest, through his private company.'

'What happened?'

'Bullshit Bob was up at the mine site. It was just a few months before production was set to begin. A cyclone comes in, category four, shuts down Port Hedland and the airports. He's cut off. Delaney pulls the buyout trigger.'

'Sounds like a dog act.'

'All's fair in love and business.'

'So what happened?'

'Bob was a lot brighter than Delaney gave him credit for. He waited until five minutes to midnight, strung Delaney out, then made his counter bid. Ten dollars and a peppercorn more.'

'Seriously?'

'Yeah. It's a famous story in Perth. But peppercorns aren't legal tender, so Delaney only got the extra ten dollars.'

'What was the buyout worth?'

'Oh, Delaney got a fair whack—a couple of hundred million— but nowhere near half the value of the company. That's where he fucked up: he tried to low-ball Bullshit Bob. And that's probably how Bob was able to get finance so quickly: his backers could see the potential of Wide Valley. It's one of the great success stories of the boom, up there with Twiggy Forrest and Fortescue.'

Ivan stares. Suddenly, he's seeing Finnigans Gap in a new light. No longer an opal town, more like a cage fight. Delaney Bullwinkel and Bullshit Bob Inglis back in competition, a quarter of a century later.

'Humphrey, just between you and me, aren't you curious to know what's really going on out at Kalingra?'

'Why? What are you suggesting?'

'I'm suggesting you give me a search warrant.'

'Yes, I see. I'm not sure.'

'I've delivered your death certificate.'

'There is that.'

Ivan can see the man equivocating. And then he has it: the lawyer's love of intrigue, of knowing the backstory, of rumours and secrets and scuttlebutt. Of playing the amateur sleuth.

'You can come with me, if you like. A little on-the-ground detective work. You obviously have a talent for it. I could use your forensic eye.'

And Humphrey Tuppence's face lights up. The Poirot of Finnigans Gap.

— — —

Nell finds Mary in casualty. There's a young child, wailing, arm broken. Mary has just finished setting it and is calming her young patient. The girl is sitting, face red, a drip in her arm, her mother hovering. Mary looks stressed, pinching the bridge of her nose as she steps away from mother and daughter.

'You okay?' asks Nell.

'I'm fine. It's the kid I'm worried about.'

'She doesn't look so bad,' offers Nell, attempting to sound reassuring.

'For now, but it's a compound fracture. Broke through the skin. Took them over two hours to drive her in here, poor kid.'

'Infection?'

'Yeah, that's the danger. I've got her on intravenous antibiotics, and the flying doctor is on the way. They'll take her down to Dubbo. Almost certainly need to operate. Reset the bone, titanium pins.'

'That's hard.'

'Better than the alternative.' Mary smiles. 'Now, what's so urgent?'

'Insulin, Mary. Are there any insulin-dependent diabetics in Finnigans Gap?'

'Sure.'

'How many?'

'There's a couple who have type one. There's no choice: use insulin or die. We have a stack of type twos as well. Too much booze, too much shit food, not enough exercise. Probably a couple of dozen who are insulin dependent.'

'That many?'

'You betcha. It's a national epidemic.'

'Where do they get it from? The insulin?'

'At the dispensary here, or the town pharmacy. It's all routine.'

'Can you give me a list of insulin-dependent locals?'

Mary eyes her. 'What's this about, Nell?'

'In confidence?'

'Of course.'

'Jonas McGee died from an insulin overdose.'

'My god.' Mary looks horrified, then apologetic. 'Nell, I can't just hand over a list of insulin users. Privacy laws, you understand. But I can tell you with certainty that Jonas McGee was not diabetic. Not even pre-diabetic.'

'So he wouldn't have had easy access to insulin?'

Mary shrugs. 'Not legally. Not without a prescription. He'd have to get it off a diabetic. Or maybe online.'

'What about Buddy Torshack and his son Kyle? Or Stanley Honeywell? Are any of them diabetic?'

'No. Not that I know of.'

'Any of the other miners up on the far end of the West Ridge?'

'Couldn't say. I only know them as patients, not where their mines are located.' She considers. 'Nell, I really shouldn't be handing out names, but if there's anyone you suspect, run it past me. I'll see what I can tell you.'

'Brilliant. Thanks so much.' Nell decides the world needs more people like Mary. 'Have you heard of any diabetics having insulin go missing?'

'No.'

Nell tries to think. 'So what does it look like? Insulin. Do diabetics always have it with them?'

Mary smiles. 'Yeah, it's essential. They keep unopened supplies in the fridge, but the vial they're using is stable at room temperature. Typically lasts for several days. They carry their insulin with them, plus a blood sugar monitor and a bunch of single-use needles or an injection pen, plus some jelly beans in case they take too much and need to boost their glucose levels. They take a kit with them everywhere they go.'

And Nell stares, unable to speak. Because all of a sudden, seemingly from nowhere, she knows who killed Jonas McGee. Just like that. She can't wait to tell Ivan.

She pulls out her phone, starts to dial, then stops. No, she needs to make sure. It's only a hunch. But a bloody good one.

chapter twenty-three

HUMPHREY TUPPENCE CAN'T SHUT UP. FOR A MOMENT, THE DISAPPOINTMENT at riding in Ivan's hire car and not a proper police vehicle put a brake on his enthusiasm, but only until they started heading up The Way to the West Ridge.

'Hang on,' says Tuppence. 'This isn't the right direction.'

'Sure it is. We park at the far end of The Way overlooking the lake and walk down the ridge.'

'In this heat?'

'You got a better idea?'

'Sure. We drive. There's an access road that goes all the way to the mine.'

'Round the edge of the lake? Flooded. We'll get bogged.'

Tuppence gestures out the window at that radiant sky, pale and cloudless. 'Last week, maybe. But it hasn't rained since then. We should be right.'

'You sure?'

'Beats walking.'

Ivan reluctantly agrees, although he promises himself he will head back at the first sign that the road is not yet passable. Secretly, he's hoping that the trigger-happy caretaker lets off a few shots above their heads. He can just imagine Tuppence shitting himself. It might even shut him up. Because right now, nothing else seems likely to. The lawyer has embarked on a long story about criminality up at Deadmans Well, with constant rejoinders indicating his own perspicacity: 'But I knew something wasn't right . . .' and 'Most people took it at face value' and 'I wasn't fooled for a minute.' Ivan stops listening to the story and starts counting the self-promoting footnotes instead.

They take the highway south, then turn onto the Old Bourke Road at the roadhouse, heading west. It's a dead straight line of thin, patched bitumen, wide enough for a single car, with gravel shoulders for passing. Ahead, it runs towards the horizon, vanishing in the faux water of a heat mirage. Ivan searches for signs of real water—run-off beside the road or pooling at the base of the ridge—but can't see any. Tuppence might be full of piss and wind, but his assessment of the conditions looks to be on the money.

The road is straight, not so the ridge. It folds back and forth, approaching and retreating, the barren rock rising above the plain. But from below, it looks less than impressive, more an aberration than an Uluru. A wedge-tailed eagle floats into view, rigid black wings with yellow flashes, riding the thermals rising from the rocky outcrop. Imperious, unflustered. Unbothered. But this time Ivan isn't fooled: it's not looking for prey, it's looking for carrion.

Ahead the mirage is starting to grow, the shimmering intensifying. A road sign appears, an arrow indicating the road curves to the left; the first deviation after ten kilometres. Ivan slows and soon sees the reason why: they've almost reached the dunes marking the shores of Lake Kalingra. A fading sign beside the road, paint peeling, states: LAKE KALINGRA YACHT CLUB 5 KILOMETRES.

'Bit optimistic,' says Ivan.

'Apparently still there,' says Tuppence. 'Abandoned, of course. Cinder-block clubhouse.'

'I thought the lake never filled.'

'Not anymore. Not since climate change. Not since the Queensland cotton farmers started harvesting the floodplain waters.'

Another few hundred metres and the thin ribbon of bitumen curves away on its new trajectory towards the south-west. And to the right is a turn-off, a dirt road heading northwards, towards the far end of the ridge. There is a sign next to it. KALINGRA RARE EARTHS PTY LTD—PRIVATE ROAD—NO PUBLIC ACCESS—AUTHORISED VEHICLES ONLY.

'I guess we're authorised,' says Ivan.

'I guess we are.' Tuppence is grinning from ear to ear, holding the warrant in his hand.

Ivan drives cautiously. The road is good, recently graded, but he's uncomfortable on the dirt. He's glad Nell isn't here to witness his tentative driving. At first, the track is lined by saltbush and the open plain, but soon it's being squeezed: on the right is the ridge, folding down into the plain, and to the left are the rising dunes of the lake shore. The road begins to wind, bending to accommodate the landscape, yet it stays firm and dry. Still, Ivan remains wary. He eyes the ridge with suspicion: during heavy rain, the run-off would be considerable; the fact the road is in good shape for the moment is no guarantee it will be passable where the lake pushes it in closer to the base of the ridge.

But they don't get that far. Just before they get to the stony outcrop, with the lake closing in on the left, they reach a fence and a gate. Next to the gate is another sign. KALINGRA RARE EARTHS PTY LTD. NO PUBLIC ACCESS. TRESPASSERS PROSECUTED. But it's not the sign or the threat of prosecution that bothers Ivan; it's the padlock on the gate. 'Looks like we're walking after all.'

'You sure? You don't carry boltcutters?'

'In a hire car?'

'It's still a couple of k.' The lawyer is not sounding keen.

Neither is Ivan, but the thought of the portly lawyer trudging through the heat helps lighten his mood. 'You can stay here if you like,' he says.

He can see Tuppence is torn: the relative comfort of the vehicle and its air-conditioning versus the prospect of participating in a real-life police investigation.

Ivan checks the fence for another way around, but he can't see one. To his right, it tracks away through low bush to the base of the ridge, the rocks climbing directly out of the plain. To his left, there is a rough track shadowing the fence as it heads off into the dunes. In another year, in another season, it would be possible to drive out on the lake bed and outflank the fence, but not now. The track might be passable; the salt pan can't possibly be.

Suddenly, the scowl on the lawyer's face lifts. 'Look,' he says, pointing.

Through the windscreen Ivan can see what has caught the notary's attention: a cloud of dust rising into the clear air.

'Now there's a bit of luck,' says Tuppence. And then, 'I find a touch of luck helps with any investigation.'

'Do you now?' says Ivan. He leans over and opens the glove compartment, retrieving his gun. He's not going to get caught without it a second time.

'Is that strictly necessary?' asks Tuppence.

'Let's hope not,' says Ivan mischievously.

The truck eases to a halt, one of the ubiquitous one-tonne Toyotas, single cab with a tray at back. Ivan sees the driver climb out, the surly caretaker from yesterday.

'C'mon,' says Ivan, 'you don't want to miss this.'

Tuppence complies, but the man is disappointingly accommodating.

'Back again,' is all he says.

'I have a warrant,' says Ivan.

'Good for you. All yours.' The man unlocks the gate, starts to pull it back towards him.

'You don't want to see it?' asks Tuppence.

'Nah. Go for your life, mate.' The man pushes the gate to the side of the track, then goes to get back in his truck.

'Hang on,' says Ivan. 'What's changed?'

'Don't you read the papers, mate? New owner. Gave me two weeks' notice.'

'You're not going to serve it out?'

'Yeah. At the pub.' He climbs back into the truck and drapes the seatbelt over his shoulder in a token gesture of compliance. He advances slowly and stops alongside them, window down. 'I've been out here by myself for three months. I reckon I'm owed.'

And he guns the engine, drops the clutch and snakes his way past them, leaving the policeman and the lawyer eating dust.

'Charmer,' coughs Tuppence.

'One of nature's gentlemen,' says Ivan.

As well as opening the gate for them, the caretaker has done them a second favour. As they approach the mine, Ivan can follow his tyre marks at those points where the road becomes muddy, the last of the run-off. There's a tricky patch or two, but they make it through okay, entering a gap between two spurs and climbing a short rise to the mine site.

'What did I tell you?' says Tuppence, full of self-congratulations as they pull up next to the site office.

If anything, the group of demountables seems more desolate than the day before. Even the country and western wireless has gone, leaving only the sound of the wind. Down the hill, the up-ended portaloo lies on its side. If this is the basis for a bonanza, Ivan can't quite see it.

'What are we looking for?' asks Tuppence.

'See if you can get into the office,' says Ivan. 'Look for any documentation, especially anything with names and contacts. Ownership, investors, contractors. The works.' And then, remembering: 'Your experience as a lawyer could be invaluable.'

'What if it's locked up?'

'We have a warrant, Humphrey. Break in.'

'Of course we do,' says the registrar, smiling ear to ear. 'What about you?'

'I want to check out the drilling.'

'Excellent.' Tuppence beams. 'Just like Bullwinkel and Inglis.'

'What does that mean?'

'I'm doing the paperwork, you're doing the geology.'

Ivan just shakes his head and walks up the incline to the drilling rig: TOPSOIL MINING SUPPLIES. The name irritates him. The mechanism is upright, apparently ready to go, stabilising legs spread out at four corners, supported by blocks of wood, keeping the rig level. Mud has pooled and dried over time. One of the tyres at the front appears half flat. The back has double tyres, but they're looking none too good either. He tries the driver's door. It opens with a rusty shriek. Ivan climbs up. The windscreen is covered in dust, turned to mud and back by the recent rains. The keys are in the ignition. Ivan tries the starter, but is greeted by a *click-clack* and then nothing more. He repeats the action with the same result. The battery is flat. He gets out and heads back towards the car.

Over at the office, Tuppence is struggling with the door, so Ivan detours to the machinery shed, looks about, finds a crowbar. He walks to the office, thrusts the tool into the door and levers it open with a satisfying crack. 'All yours.'

At the car, he gets the folders he took from Kalingra's office in town. He flicks through, finds the drilling assay. At first, he struggles to gain his orientation, but eventually works it out: rows of drilling points, seven abreast, individually numbered, stretching from the lower slopes of the ridge out towards the lake. Closer to the salt pan, the rows are longer: nine holes per row, then eleven. Ivan flicks through from the map, locates information correlating to each drill hole, cross-referenced by the hole numbers. Most of it he can't understand. He's no Bullshit Bob Inglis, that's for sure. But he can make out the references to different ores, or chemicals, or minerals. The concentrations seem higher in the holes towards the lake shore.

He walks down past the office, where he can hear Tuppence laughing to himself like a kid in a candy shop, no doubt rehearsing his account for his golfing buddies. Ivan keeps walking, finds the first line of drilling points, keeps going, gets to another line of drill holes, looks back at the map. He sees it now: the landscape matching the map, the two-hundred-metre grid, covering three kilometres from the base of the bluff to the lake shore. One hundred and twenty-nine holes.

He keeps moving. Another two hundred metres, another row, but beyond that he struggles to find anything. There is no sign the saltbush has ever been disturbed. There should be another kilometre of test holes, five more rows. He keeps moving towards the lake. The heat is really starting to beat down. He passes the bleached bones of a kangaroo, wonders about snakes. The flies come in, a real swarm. Flies. What the hell do they live on, out here? A shadow moves across him; he glances up into the blinding sky, holding his hand to shield his eyes. The sun is almost directly overhead, pouring down upon him. He feels a little groggy, then sees the wedge-tail circling. Like a fucking buzzard. Still he presses on, searching for drill holes. The map says they're here, but that doesn't make it so.

He reaches the dunes, keeps going. They must be ancient, built up over the centuries. He mounts the few metres to their top and is greeted by a view of blinding whiteness, forcing him to squint even through his sunglasses, to again shield his eyes. The heat pours off the expanse, hitting him in the face like a radiator. He stands for just a moment, no longer thinking of Bullshit Bob Inglis or rare earths or anything. The sight has swept away his thoughts even as it has him holding his breath. Out on the white expanse, it must be fifty degrees, maybe more, like the surface of an alien sun. He thinks of the dead youth, Zeke Jakowitz. If it was a day like this, it's amazing he made it anywhere close to the middle of the lake. Ivan reckons a few hundred metres and he'd be finished.

He turns back, one knee almost giving way in the soft sand of the dune. His head is feeling woozy. He wonders why he doesn't have a headache, wonders if it might not be a symptom of something. He mops his brow, is surprised to feel it dry to the touch. Jesus. Ahead of him, the ridge is starting to wobble ever so slightly. An earthquake? He stands still, swaying from side to side, but feels no tremors. He needs to get something to drink, and quickly. And to get out of the sun. It seems to take him forever to reach the first row of drill holes. Now he knows what to look for, they seem obvious. And he's confident this is the last of them; that the map is a fabrication, that there are no exploratory holes out by the lake shore.

At last, he reaches the car, gets his drink bottle. It's half full, but he drains it in two gulps; it makes no discernible impact on his thirst. He chucks it back into the vehicle and heads to the office. There has to be water there. Inside he finds Tuppence behind the desk, guzzling from a bottle and laughing with glee. 'Check this out,' he says.

'Water,' croaks Ivan.

'Over there. In the esky.'

Ivan sees the blue ice chest. There's no ice, but there are litre bottles of water. He cracks one, drinks half, then walks back out onto the riser and tips the rest over his head, experiencing instant relief. He feels the top of his head. Despite the water, his hair is still hot to touch.

Tuppence appears to notice none of this. 'Get an eyeful,' he repeats as Ivan returns inside. 'What a show.'

Ivan rounds the desk, looks at the computer screen. It's a porno: a man dressed as a priest, face masked, has lined up a couple of semi-naked nuns and is screwing them from behind. Tuppence is chuckling like a teenage boy full of hormones and devoid of judgement.

'For fuck's sake, you git,' spews Ivan, unable to remain civil. 'Documents, you idiot. Not the caretaker's wankfest.'

'No, no,' says Tuppence, sounding aggrieved. 'Don't you see it?'

'See what?'

'It's the Seer. From the Rapture. The dirty bastard.'

And Ivan does see: not the pumping flesh and the squirming pinkness, but the faces. And not the Seer, but the nuns, faces pleading, eyes beseeching.

chapter twenty-four

MERV CLAXTON. NELL'S SURE HE'S THE KILLER, EVEN IF THE EVIDENCE IS circumstantial, not so much a smoking gun as a vague whiff of cordite. She races back to the police station with the scene playing over and over in her mind: pulling over the big black Chrysler, Claxton's reluctance to open the boot, trying to bluff her with the nonsense about needing a warrant. The boot opening. His luggage and the guns and the medical kit. It was the guns that drew her attention, the rifle and the handgun, Claxton insisting he was licensed. Of course it was the guns that drew her attention. But if he was licensed, why was he so reluctant to spring the boot? Was it the first-aid kit? She tries to picture it. Small, like a purse, made of some sort of black nylon, but embroidered or stamped with a red cross. Or was there white writing, *First Aid*? She can't quite remember, but there was definitely something branding it as a medical kit. Why else would she think that? What did she think

369

at the time? Her mind was on the guns. Maybe he didn't want to reveal he was working security, and not just as a chauffeur. Was that it? Or did she imagine his reluctance? Did she imagine the whole thing? No, she's convinced: it was a medical kit.

At the station, the detectives' room is empty. She tries ringing Ivan, but he doesn't answer. Still out checking the rare-earth mine, probably. She finds the number for the hire car place in Dubbo, rings it, identifies herself to the receptionist, asks for the manager.

'Hello. How can I help you?' It's a man's voice, sounding hesitant.

'This is Detective Constable Narelle Buchanan calling from Finnigans Gap. I'm ringing in regard to a homicide investigation.'

There's a heartbeat of quiet before the man speaks. 'Are any of our employees implicated?'

'No, they're not.'

'That's a relief. And our company?'

'No. Relax. You're not in any trouble.'

'Thank goodness.'

'Sorry, to whom am I speaking?'

'Oh. Sorry. Peter Langhorne. Managing director. Is one of our clients involved?'

'Yes.'

'Shit. Did they kill someone?'

Nell grimaces. 'I am simply pursuing one of a number of leads. Let's not get ahead of ourselves.'

But Langhorne is sounding excited. 'Does it involve one of our vehicles?'

'It does.'

'The murder weapon?'

'No,' says Nell, tiring of answering questions instead of asking them. 'And almost certainly not used to transport the body. Just answer my questions and you and your company can get back to business.'

'Oh, yes. Quite,' says Peter Langhorne, perhaps hearing the edge in her voice. 'How can I help?'

'I'm inquiring into a large black Chrysler sedan that has been in Finnigans Gap on and off in recent weeks.'

'Yes,' says Langhorne, and recites the number plate to her.

'Correct,' says Nell, 'that's the one.'

'And you're calling from Finnigans Gap police station?'

'That's right.'

'I'll call you straight back,' says Langhorne, and hangs up.

Nell is left staring at her phone. What's the guy doing? Fossicking out some vital piece of information? Packing a bag full of Krugerrands and running for the airport?

The desk phone rings. It's Garry. 'A Peter Langhorne for you.'

'Thanks. Put him through.'

'Constable Buchanan?'

'Yes, it's me. What's going on?'

'I just wanted to make sure you were who you claimed to be. We've had a lot of prank calls lately.'

'Right. Nothing serious, I trust?'

'It's Dubbo. What can I say? Kids get bored.' He gives a nervous laugh. 'Anyway, the black Chrysler. I have the file here.'

'Thanks. First of all, the name of the driver and the dates he hired the car.'

'Sure. The driver's name is Michael Petavitch.'

'Are you sure?'

'What's your email? I'll send it through. The whole file.'

'Yes, thank you.' She gives him her email, and thirty seconds later she has the file. There is a scan of the licence: the name is Michael Petavitch, but the photo is of Merv Claxton. 'Could you wait on the line for a minute, please, Mr Langhorne? I just want to check the bona fides of the driver's licence.'

'Of course.'

Nell opens the program used by highway patrol and mobile units. The licence draws a blank. It's a fake. She gives herself a moment to work through the logic before again speaking with Langhorne. The fake licence would do the trick with a small hire car firm in Dubbo, but it would have been too risky for Claxton to try to pass it off when she pulled him over. If she'd run it through the database using her MobiPol, she would have picked up the forgery on the spot. So he'd used his real licence. And, of course, the gun licences were in his real name.

'Tell me, Mr Langhorne: is your company part of a larger chain, headquarters in Sydney, that sort of thing?'

'Oh no. We're proudly Dubbo owned and operated. My parents, in fact.'

'I see.' That aligns with her thinking: Claxton using a company without an extensive network. 'And are your cars fitted with satnav?'

'The top end ones are. The Chrysler is.'

'And does it track where the cars have been? Record it?'

'They have that facility, yes. If it was turned on.'

'Was it? Can you check?'

'No need. We have a separate geolocation device fitted.'

'Really? Why?'

'Part of the rental agreement. Depending on the type of car, they're not meant to go off sealed roads. Big problem out here.'

'Can you check the record for the Chrysler, please?'

'I'm doing it now. But I can tell you already it was in breach of the agreement.'

'You know that?'

'Yes. We've sent Mr Petavitch an excess bill.'

'Has he paid it?'

There's a brief delay before the manager responds. 'No. Not yet. But we only sent it after he returned to Sydney. He dropped the car at the airport, so we didn't get to ask him about it.'

'Fair enough. Do you have the records of his locations on hand? Can you send them through?'

'I'm not sure. It's proprietary software. You might need it installed to read the file. Can I check something in particular for you?'

'Yes. Last week. I am interested to know if the car was taken from Finnigans Gap up along a road called The Way to an area called the West Ridge. Sometime after about eleven Monday night through to about midday on Tuesday.'

'Wait on.' She can hear Langhorne snuffling and breathing and the tapping of a computer keyboard. Then: 'Yes. Here it is. Is that over towards a big expanse called Lake Kalingra?'

'That's right.'

'Yes. He was up there last Tuesday morning. The early hours. Parked for about thirty minutes.'

Nell can barely breathe. Could it really be this simple? 'I know there's a lookout up there, overlooking the lake. Is that where he was?'

'Hang on. Let me see if I can work that out for you.' More snuffling, tapping and clicking. And then, 'No, I think I see where you mean. I don't think so.'

'Is there any way to make sure? It's important.'

'Yes, it's easy enough. I can tell you this: he drove up there, he stopped for between thirty and thirty-three minutes, then he drove back to Finnigans Gap.'

'At what time on Tuesday?'

'Early morning. Very early. From ten to five to about five twenty.'

She has to force herself to breathe, to steady herself; that is within Blake Ness's estimated window for time of death.

Peter Langhorne continues: 'I'm emailing you the map coordinates of the location where he stopped.'

Nell looks to her computer just in time to see the email arrive. God, if only all witnesses were this helpful. 'Got it.'

'Good. Now feed the coordinates into Google Maps,' Langhorne advises. 'It will show you the precise location.'

Nell does as he suggests, and the mapping app responds immediately. At first, it's hard to recognise the location. She checks the scale on the map: it's zoomed right in; the coordinates are pinpoint accurate. She switches to satellite view and her heart begins to race. She can see what must be Jonas's caravan in the centre, Buddy's camp site on the edge of the screen. The image is old, before this year's rains, but there is no mistaking it. Claxton parked the limo behind Jonas McGee's caravan, out of sight of The Way. She draws a breath, feels a surge of victory. Evidence doesn't come much more damning than this.

'Mr Langhorne, are you still there?'

'Yes. How are we doing?'

'We are doing very well, thanks to you. Now, please listen. This information you have uncovered constitutes critical evidence in an ongoing homicide investigation. Do you understand?'

'Yes.' It's just a single syllable, but Nell thinks she hears a tremor in the voice.

'It's very important you secure the record you are referring to. Make sure it can't be erased or overwritten. If possible, make copies of all the data relating to that car while it was rented by Mr Petavitch, particularly on that Tuesday. Send a copy to me and retain one yourself. Somewhere safe. Also, as soon as possible, put down in writing all your recollections of your dealings with the man who hired your car. Please sign it and send it through to me at this email address.'

'Did he kill someone?' asks Peter Langhorne, and now the tremor is clearly evident.

'Yes, Mr Langhorne, I believe he did.' Nell lets that sink in before asking her final question. 'One last thing: does your company supply clients with a first-aid kit?'

'In the cars? No. Why?'

Nell blurts it out the moment Ivan steps into the detectives' room. 'I know who murdered Jonas McGee.'

He blinks. 'Who?'

'Merv Claxton. Former cop. Driver of the black limo.'

A smile breaks across Ivan's face and for a moment those hard blue eyes light up with something akin to joy. 'And I think I know why,' he says.

She stares at him, and then they are laughing. She's on her feet, throwing herself at him, wrapping her arms around him, squeezing tight as she laughs.

'Hang on, hang on,' he says. But he can't help himself; her joy is infectious. He gives her a quick squeeze back before releasing her. 'Okay,' he says, still smiling, 'you first.'

She tells him of her brainwave about Claxton and the medical kit. She can see the initial scepticism on his face, sees it ease and disappear altogether as she recounts her conversation with Langhorne and shows Ivan the files the Dubbo man has sent through, the pinpoint accuracy of the coordinates, the satellite image of where Claxton parked the Chrysler next to McGee's mine.

'Fuck me, Nell. You treasure. That is absolutely brilliant.'

She beams with pleasure. 'Okay, your turn. Why did Claxton kill him?'

'Because Jonas worked out the sale of Kalingra Rare Earths is a massive scam.'

He quickly takes her through the fraudulent mining assay, the fact that most of the holes weren't even drilled, and his suspicion that the ore samples from the others were faked. 'We know Jonas was desperate for money and we know why. We also know he did some casual work at Kalingra as a carpenter. I reckon he worked out what was going on and threatened the scammers with exposure. So they got Claxton to kill him.'

'So Claxton was in on the scam?'

'Yep. Together with the Chinese investors. I reckon they were actors. Fake competitors, pretending they were keen to buy, sent to force Inglis's hand and drive the price up.'

'So he was the mark?'

'That's right. A whale. Caught hook, line and sinker.'

'That's some scam. Actors, a corporate jet, the limo. A lot of seed money. Any idea who's behind it, who these scammers might be?'

'Just one. Delaney Bullwinkel.'

Nell looks uncertain. 'Based on what, exactly?'

Ivan recounts the tale that Humphrey Tuppence narrated: the two partners who fell out over Wide Valley Resources.

'So, revenge?'

'That would be my guess.'

'That was twenty-five years ago.'

'Best served cold.'

Nell turns to the computer, starts googling. In almost no time she has pulled up half-a-dozen articles detailing Bullshit Bob Inglis's outmanoeuvring of his erstwhile partner. 'It was a huge story in the west,' she says in summary. 'Financial press in the east, but front page in Perth. And the social pages; they take their mining magnates very seriously over there.'

'So I've heard.'

'I agree with your suspicion,' says Nell, 'but how do we stack it up?'

'I need to call Sydney,' says Ivan. 'Claxton is key. We need to arrest him. Suspicion of murder.'

'Will you fly down?'

'Probably. Once they have him. In the meantime, see what you can find out about Kalingra Rare Earths. Who Inglis bought it from, who profited from the scam.'

'You reckon we can find out?'

'I doubt it. If it could be linked to Delaney Bullwinkel, he'd be facing fraud charges. But we have to go through the process, you know that.'

'I'm on to it.'

— —

Ivan leaves Nell working in the office. Outside, a seagull is perched on the broken statue. A seagull, out here, in this vast expanse of nothingness. Maybe a refugee from Lake Kalingra, attracted by the brine when the lake filled, but now lost, seven hundred kilometres from the ocean.

He sits on the verandah, still cool enough in the shade. The flies appear from nowhere, but they no longer bother him quite as much; he's growing used to them. He calls the head of Homicide, Dereck Packenham, in Sydney. He speaks to the superintendent's PA, stressing the urgency. He gets the call back within five minutes.

'Ivan. You're making progress?' Packenham's voice is deep and resonant, even on the limited bandwidth of the phone call.

'I believe we are.'

Quickly he briefs his superior, keeping to the facts, trying to exclude anything extraneous. Packenham hears him out, doesn't interrupt. And then: 'Good work.'

'Thank you, sir.'

'And Constable Buchanan? I heard she might be somehow compromised?'

'I don't believe so.' Ivan explains the imbroglio with Topsoil.

'That's not good,' says his superior. 'Reputationally, if nothing else.'

'That's true. But she has also been instrumental in identifying Claxton as the suspect. That was her work, sir, not mine.'

'I see.'

'I suggest we arrest Claxton, sir.'

'I agree. Leave it with me. But don't mention it to anyone down here. He's a former officer; he'll still have plenty of friends in the force. We don't want him getting tipped off.'

'Thank you, sir.'

'Anything else?'

'Yes. We might need some assistance tracking financial records. It might be sensitive. Politically.'

'Go on.'

Ivan explains his suspicion that Delaney Bullwinkel may be behind the Kalingra scam and therefore ordered the killing of Jonas McGee.

Again, the chief of Homicide lets him set out his case, not interrupting, not commenting until Ivan has finished. 'That's pretty tenuous. Investigating Bullwinkel based on nothing more than a twenty-five-year-old feud and the fact that he owns a coalmine an hour out of town. Is that all?'

'That's not how I'm approaching it, sir.'

'Really?'

'I feel whoever is behind the Kalingra scam must be in the frame for killing McGee. So I want to find out who owned Kalingra, who sold it to Robert Inglis. Constable Buchanan is doing a preliminary search, but I doubt she'll get far. You run a scam like that, you'd want to cover your tracks. We'll need some expert assistance, forensic accountants, to unravel the company structures.'

'So why mention Delaney Bullwinkel?'

'I just wanted to alert you that probing the company ownership might prove to be sensitive. Just in case it does point to someone of standing.'

There's quite a pause. Then: 'That's very perceptive of you. I'll talk to Fraud, see if they can assign a forensic accountant. Maybe someone outside the force, someone not connected. I'll let you know.'

'Thank you, sir.'

'Good job, Lucic. Excellent work. But please keep your investigations confidential. Come to me if you need additional resources—or advice.'

'I will. Thank you, sir.'

Ivan is thinking the conversation is coming to a close. Instead, Packenham surprises him. 'Have you spoken to Morris Montifore lately?'

'Only briefly, sir.'

'So you know he's retiring? Health reasons?'

'So I heard, sir.'

'A pity. A great pity. He has been a remarkable officer.'

'I agree, sir.'

'I know he has been a mentor to you, Ivan. But for all of our sakes, do not discuss this case with Morris under any circumstances.'

'Any particular reason, sir?' The question has left his lips before Ivan can consider its wisdom.

'Yes. Because he talks to journalists. And if what you suspect is true, we don't want the media getting wind of it. That happens and the blowback could be brutal. It could shut down your investigation.'

Ivan finds it hard to respond; he wasn't expecting this level of candour, the head of Homicide conceding his power reaches only so far. 'Absolutely, sir. I understand.'

He's still sitting on the verandah when his phone rings. Not the MobiPol, the other one. The burner. He doesn't want to be seen using it here. He walks towards his car, but it stops ringing before he gets there. He climbs into the Kia and drives out from the car park, pulling in beside the road. He texts Montifore back, telling himself even as he does so that he will reveal nothing to his former colleague of the Kalingra scam and his suspicions surrounding the owner of Cuttamulla Coal.

The phone rings. 'Hi, Morris.'

'G'day. You still in the hellhole?'

'Yeah. Working on my tan.'

'How's it going?'

'Slowly.'

'Right. Better off not telling me now. I'm no longer in the game.'

'Not much to tell,' says Ivan, finding it surprisingly easy to obfuscate.

'I had a few drinks last night,' Morris continues, apparently oblivious to Ivan's reticence. 'You know, some of the old crew, past and present. To toast my retirement.'

'Sorry I couldn't be there.'

'Yeah. You were missed. But there'll be more opportunities.'

'I'm sure.'

'Reg Montgomery came along. Sent his best regards.'

'That's good of him.'

'I told him where you are, up there in Finnigans Gap. Had a good laugh at your expense. And we talked about that case we investigated. You know, the kid who died out on the lake.'

Suddenly, Ivan is all ears. 'What did he have to say?'

'Well, he thought the coroner got it right. Death by misadventure. But that's not why I'm calling.'

'I'm listening.'

'I was always a bit suss about it. I told you that. But after talking to Reg, I realised I got one aspect arse about face. I always thought we'd been sent up to placate the kid's family. That he was connected.'

'So what was the real story?'

'It wasn't the kid who was connected, it was Jonathan Plankten—the brother of our mate the former attorney-general, Jeremy Plankten.'

Ivan says nothing, not immediately. Jeremy Plankten was at the centre of the web of corruption and influence that Montifore and he had exposed the previous year. Them and the journalist Martin Scarsden. 'Who's Jonathan Plankten?'

'He no longer goes by that name. Calls himself the Seer.'

Ivan stares through the windscreen. He can see a woman walking towards him, a shopping bag in each hand, unable to swat at the cloud of flies besieging her. 'The Seer? Out at the Rapture? He's the brother of the former attorney-general?'

'One and the same.'

'You didn't realise that at the time?'

'Plankten wasn't AG back then. He was a backbencher, a committee chair, angling for a ministry. A backroom boy, out of the public eye, but already influential. Reg only made the connection after the Scarsden revelations last year.'

'You got pulled out early. Before you could properly investigate.'

'So it would seem.'

Ivan is staring out through the windscreen, but all he can see is the Seer, half naked, robes falling off him as he screws a nun. He wonders how old the porno is. The local coppers say the Seer and the Rapture behave themselves nowadays, that the cult leader seldom leaves his compound. He wonders if those changes started seven years ago, if the ambitious politician Jeremy Plankten reined in his brother in return for getting the investigation quashed.

'Ivan? You still there?'

'Yeah, sorry. I'm here.'

'I wanted to warn you that the Seer is connected. Jeremy Plankten still has considerable influence. If Feral Phelan has got his eye on you, I wouldn't want you hitting any trip-wires. Not unnecessarily.'

Ivan thinks of Plodder Packenham, his warning to tread carefully. And Phelan, up here doing what exactly? 'Thanks, Morris. But as far as we can make out, the Seer has nothing to do with the death of Jonas McGee.'

'Glad to hear it.'

'Morris, one more thing before you go.' Ivan swallows, remembering Packenham's edict, realises he's walking a fine line. 'Did you ever know a copper in Sydney called Merv Claxton?'

'Not well. Fancied himself as a hard man. Why?'

'I heard he retired.'

'That's right.'

'You know why?'

'Health reasons.'

'Sure. Lot of that going about.'

Montifore laughs. 'Very funny. But I think in his case it was the real deal. We were at the pub one time, another farewell—might even have been for Reg. Anyway, it was quite the afternoon and it was his turn to shout. Stood up and just keeled over. We all thought he'd carked it, heart attack.'

'Shit. I didn't know that.'

'But it wasn't a heart attack. Too much grog on an empty stomach. Turns out he was an undiagnosed diabetic.'

'Is that right?'

'Apparently.' Ivan can think of nothing else to say, and Morris takes it as a cue. 'Catch up soon, hey? When you get back to Sydney. And good luck up there.'

'You bet.'

— —

Nell is on the ASIC website, doing a company search on Kalingra Rare Earths Pty Ltd and getting nowhere fast. Her first search reveals a sole director: Trudy Lampsheet. Her address is listed courtesy of a nominee company in Melbourne. She calls the number, adopts her voice of authority: 'This is Detective Constable Narelle Buchanan from New South Wales Police, investigating a homicide. I'd like to talk to a Ms Trudy Lampsheet, please.'

'I'm sorry, Mrs Lampsheet doesn't work here anymore.'

'Do you have a contact for her?'

'I'm sorry, but Mrs Lampsheet is in care.'

Nell's voice of authority wavers. 'In care? What does that mean?'

'Mrs Lampsheet has advanced Alzheimer's disease.'

'Advanced? When did she leave work?'

'Oh, a good five years ago now, I should think. More. She deteriorated very rapidly.' The receptionist is starting to sound hesitant; Nell presses while she's still talking.

'Has someone taken over her responsibilities? Her clients?'

'Can I ask what it's in regard to? Specifically?'

'We're investigating a homicide, inquiring into a company. She's listed as a director.'

'That's not possible. I know for a fact all her responsibilities were transferred when she first fell ill.'

'Is it possible the ASIC website is out of date?'

'It must be. What's the name of the company?'

'Kalingra Rare Earths.' Nell recites the company's ABN.

'Oh, I see,' says the receptionist, who must have pulled up the ASIC database. 'There must be some mistake. I'll need to get someone more senior to call you.'

'Before you go, tell me one thing. Mrs Lampsheet is the sole director. Does that mean she's the owner?'

'No. Almost certainly not. We're a nominee company.'

'What does that mean?'

'We provide a public face for investors who wish to remain anonymous.'

'So you can't tell me who the owners are?'

'Absolutely not,' says the woman. 'But I can tell you that ninety per cent of our clients are domiciled overseas.'

'You mean in tax havens?'

'More than likely. And many of them are nominee companies themselves.'

'You're telling me I may never be able to identify the owners?'

'That's entirely possible.'

'Thank you,' says Nell. 'You've been most helpful.' She gives her phone number and ends the call.

While she awaits a call back, she probes further into the ASIC website, trawling through historical records. She can see the company was originally called Kalingra Exploration Pty Ltd, and was established twelve years ago. It lists three directors: Phillip Smith, Neil Courters and Wanda Clark. Smith is listed as chairman and general manager. She tries to find him, using the address listed in the ASIC records, but gets nowhere. She googles his name and gets close to two million hits. Just her luck: he has to be called 'Smith'. She tries to narrow it down—'Phillip Smith Kalingra'—but has trouble finding anything recent. She's about to give in and move on to the other two directors when she finds a death notice, five years old.

She reads it. Smith, dead after a long battle with cancer. A mining industry maverick, famed for ambitious projects, more of a prospector than a miner. There's a short list of successful finds, typically developed by others, Kalingra Exploration is not among them.

She searches for the other two directors. Nothing recent in Australia, but when she combines the two names, a bunch of hits emerge, including on Facebook. Courters and Clark are married. Eventually she tracks them down to an address in Fiji. Nadi. An online calculator gives her the time difference: only two hours. She gets a number through directories, rings them.

Neil Courters has a pleasant voice, cultured and calm. Nell pictures him with a gin and tonic, sitting on a wide verandah overlooking a marina. He says he's more than happy to help. 'Yes—we set it up with Phil. We did some exploratory drilling, built a small processing plant, just enough to see what we could find. It looked promising at first, but we were running short on money. And then Phil got sick. He was the real driving force, Wanda and I were more silent partners. Investors. He was the one with the expertise. After that, we mothballed it, let the claim lapse. And then we got this offer out of the blue, about three years ago. A million dollars each. We snapped it up. End of story.'

'If the claim had lapsed, did they really need to buy you out?'

'Probably not. But they wanted to use our plant, so it was fine with us.'

'Did you ever meet with the new owners?'

'No. The offer came through a broker.'

'And your payment. You have a record of it? Who paid the money?'

'I will somewhere. It was an international money order.'

'So that means it can't be traced?'

'Correct.'

'Did the buyer insist on that form of payment?'

'I can't recall. But I believe it would have been beneficial to both parties.'

'You mean for tax?'

'That would be a fair assumption.'

'You know it's been onsold?'

There's a chuckle at the other end of the line. 'So I see. To Bullshit Bob Inglis of all people. Good on them. I hope they got a pretty penny for it. Sometimes you don't see what's right in front of your nose.'

'How do you mean?'

'Rare earths. We never thought of that. Phil was looking for mineral sands.'

'Mineral sands. Is that different?'

'Oh yes. People get them mixed up, I don't know why.'

Almost an hour later, Neil Courters and Wanda Clark are her only successes. The more data she attempts to mine, the harder the rock becomes, the thicker the overburden. She has nothing more to show for her efforts, just a slag pile of useless information.

She's still sitting there, growing increasingly frustrated, when Ivan returns. 'Want to come for a drive?' he asks.

'Where to?'

'Lightning Ridge. I want to speak to your pal Topsoil, remember?'

Nell looks back at the screen, sees nothing there but granite a mile deep. 'Yeah. A drive sounds good.'

chapter twenty-five

TREVOR TOPSOIL LOOKS FORLORN, SITTING IN THE INTERVIEW ROOM AT THE Lightning Ridge police station, picking at his nails, his mouth a grim downward-facing crescent. Ivan studies at him on the video monitor, assessing his mood before entering. When he does, Topsoil attempts to rally, thrusting his chin out in a show of defiance. Ivan just smiles and takes a seat across the table from the prisoner.

'Where's my lawyer?' asks Topsoil. 'She was here before.'

'You don't need one. I'm not here to charge you with anything.'

Topsoil appears puzzled. 'You're that Homicide cop, right?'

'Investigating the death of your good mate, Jonas McGee.'

'I had nothing to do with that.'

'I know you didn't, Trevor. That's why you don't need a lawyer.' A moment for that to sink in. 'That's why I'm not recording this conversation. I'm only after information. Just you and me.' Which is not exactly true; Nell is in an office not ten metres away, monitoring the feed.

'How's Nell?' asks Topsoil. His concern sounds genuine; Ivan tries to leverage it.

'Not good. She's under investigation. Thanks to you.'

The man looks crestfallen.

'But you can help her,' says Ivan.

'I already told the others she had nothing to do with it.'

'That's decent of you. But what she really needs is to make progress with finding the killer of Jonas McGee.'

'So why isn't she here?'

'Because you compromised her. There is no way known she can have any contact with you.'

Topsoil accepts this. 'Yeah. Fair enough.'

'Listen closely. You help me, and I'll put in a good word for you with the Drug Squad. As I understand it, you've already been cooperative. That's been noted. You wouldn't want to ruin that now.'

Topsoil juts out his chin, before reconsidering and withdrawing it again. 'What do you need to know?'

'First up, ratters. The Drug Squad has been intercepting your phone calls for months. They tell me that as well as drugs, you have been involved with supplying equipment and fencing gems.'

Topsoil shakes his head. 'I'm not admitting to anything. I want a lawyer.'

Ivan sighs. 'You can have a lawyer. You're entitled to one whenever you're being interviewed. But right now, you're not being interviewed. There are no witnesses, there are no recordings.' Ivan gives it a heartbeat before continuing. 'This is about Jonas McGee, horribly murdered; it's not about you or any involvement you may or may not have with ratting.'

'Finnigans Gap is fucked.' It comes as a statement of fact and an expression of despair. 'There is no future.'

This is unexpected; Ivan is about to push back, keep the focus where he wants it. Yet he hesitates; the tone of Topsoil's assertion resonates, as if the man is confessing. He decides to go with it. 'How is that relevant?'

'It was meant to be the great boom town. The next big thing. The next Lightning Ridge, the next Coober Pedy. But it's not. It's a fucking ants nest in the middle of nowhere. I thought I was getting a bargain when I bought out the machinery supply business twelve years ago. What a sucker I was; must have seen me coming for miles. Because I forgot one thing, one important thing: opal miners are fucked in the head, either bullshitters or dreamers or both. Optimists, always looking for the strike that's going to set them up, absolutely convinced the mother lode is just a few centimetres further in. But there is no rainbow, there is no pot of gold.'

He looks directly at Ivan. There is something mesmeric in watching this man unravel, the consummate liar suddenly speaking truth. For his words do have the ring of truth to them: not just in their meaning, but in his capitulation, his surrender.

'The opals are almost played out—not that there were many to start with. Everyone talks about the black ones, how amazing they are, how valuable. It's true, and it's bullshit. They're there, all right, but nothing like here at Lightning Ridge. Most of the stones at Finnigans are low grade; good for grey nomads, but nothing that's going to excite collectors, nothing that's going to clear the mortgage in an afternoon's work. Half the businesses in town are only still there thanks to Cuttamulla. The other half depend on tourists and the government.'

Ivan thinks he knows where this is going. 'I'm listening,' he prompts.

'I tried to make a go of it. I really did. My wife and I. Poured everything we had into it. But she could see the writing on the wall; I refused to believe it. So she shot through, and I was left with a pile of debt, an empty house I couldn't sell and a business that would never kick into high gear no matter how hard I worked.'

'So you started dealing drugs.'

'I did. I did. But . . .' He lets it hang.

'But what?'

'But that's not what I was planning. Not when I told Nell about Barret and the Longfers. I was only trying to help her, to impress her. Win her over.' Topsoil stares at the table. 'I was lonely.'

Ivan gives him a moment, knowing there's more to come.

'So I told her. And then she left anyway. Used the information, got the convictions, got the promotion. Off to train as a detective in Sydney. And I was still there. Trapped. Again.'

Ivan is thinking of Nell, watching the video feed, but he can't let that distract him. He needs Topsoil onside. He almost has him. 'Go on.'

'I'd always used drugs a bit. Who doesn't? Nothing serious, just the usual. The occasional party, that sort of thing. It's how I knew about the Longfers in the first place. Then, once they were gone, once Nell had put them inside, it was hard to get anything half decent. You had to drive over here to Lightning Ridge or down to Dubbo. That's how it started.'

Ivan nods, not speaking, not wanting to break the spell.

'The guy in Dubbo, he offered to set me up. I was desperate.' Topsoil shrugs. 'I was weak.'

Ivan puts on his most sympathetic voice. 'I understand.'

'Will you tell Nell? I'm sorry. I never meant to hurt her.'

'Of course.' Ivan gives it a moment, like an actor, letting the audience take in what has just passed before moving on to the next scene. 'But it wasn't just drugs, was it?'

Topsoil looks up; now it's his turn not to speak.

'Ratting. You've been supplying ratters with equipment, acting as their fence. Understandable, given your circumstances.'

But the shutters are up; Trevor Topsoil has left the confessional. 'I'm not going there.'

'And I know why. You've been charged with drug offences. You've been cooperative, admitting to your mistakes. No one has even mentioned ratting. But I'm a Homicide cop; I'm not going to charge you with anything like that. And I've got no interest in telling anyone else. It all depends if you help me or not.'

Topsoil's chin reasserts its defiance. 'So now you're threatening me?'

'Now I'm helping you.'

Topsoil deliberates for a moment and retracts his chin. 'Okay. I'm listening.'

'Jonas McGee's body was down his mine for days before it was discovered. Someone rang Crime Stoppers anonymously. Ratters.'

Topsoil shrugs. 'No ratter would tell me they were doing over his mine. People know that Jonas and I were friends.'

'But it's possible ratters did go down his claim?'

Topsoil thinks it over before replying. 'Yeah. Word was out he was finding gems. It's not as if a ratting crew would ask my permission. They'd do it, just wouldn't tell me where they got the stones from.'

'I want to talk to them, Trevor. That's all. I won't tell them how I got their names, and I won't prosecute them.'

'So you say.' Topsoil spreads his hands. 'People hate them, you know. Detest them. But most of them are just like me. Good blokes who are desperate. Blokes who have gone without a good gem for a year or more. Blokes with wives and kids and mortgages. Blokes who chased their dreams and found nothing but dirt.'

Ivan goes with it. 'Mate, they did the right thing. They called it in. Without them, the poor bastard, your mate, would still be down there rotting, and the killer would be laughing. So I'm not going to bust their balls. Just the opposite; I want to thank them.'

Topsoil stares at him, as if assessing his sincerity. 'Their names?'

'I need to speak to them, Trevor. They may have vital information. There are things about the crime scene that raise questions. I give you my word, I will not prosecute them.'

'Deadmans Well. Know it?'

'Yeah. I've been there.'

'Okay. There's a crew based there. Leader is a bloke called Holgate. He's the one I deal with. I don't know the names of his crew. But I know they were out weekend before last.'

'Okay. That's good. A great help.'

'You won't tell him I gave you his name?'

'You have my word.'

'And don't tell the mayor. Did you meet the mayor?'

'Yeah, I met him.'

'If he finds out that Holgate is involved with ratting, there'll be all hell to pay.'

'Okay. Got it.' He can see Topsoil breathe out, a long release, as if he has just survived some sort of ordeal. Ivan gives him the moment before pressing again, voice gentle. 'Was Jonas McGee ratting?'

This time, there is little resistance. The dam wall is breached, there is nothing to stop the flow. 'Yeah, he was. Selling the gems through the Irishman, pretending they were coming out of his own claim.'

'So how do you know he was ratting?'

'He got the lightweight gear from me.'

'You know why?'

'He was desperate for money. Never was before. For years, long as I knew him, he didn't really give a toss about it. That's why I liked him, why we got on. We'd go fishing and he'd talk about all sorts of things, but never money. It was a relief; all I ever thought about was how to get my hands on it. Going fishing with him took my mind off my own troubles. That's how we became mates.'

'You know why he suddenly wanted money?'

'His daughter, Elsie. She needed it.'

Ivan nods. 'You know where he was ratting?'

'No idea. Last thing I would want to know. From any of them.'

'He ever talk to you about the stock market?'

'Trading shares, you mean?'

'Correct.'

'Just the once. Last time we went fishing. Told me it was a goldmine, said he was making a motza. Reckoned it was foolproof. I reckoned he was talking shit.'

'Why? We think he might have been doing pretty well.'

'Seriously?'

'Yeah. You don't know about that?'

Trevor is shaking his head, but he's smiling. 'He was on about rare earths, to forget about opals, forget about busting your arse. I told him to be careful, that the stock market is just a casino with suits. That everyone wants to believe rare earths are going to turn Finnigans into a boom town, the same way I believed opals were going to make me millions. It's all an illusion.'

'So what do you know about the rare-earth mine at Kalingra?'

Topsoil's head jerks up, eyes scanning Ivan's face. 'Nothing. Why ask me?'

'Because your drilling rig is out there. Because you were commissioned to drill the test holes.'

Topsoil says nothing, but he's alert, sitting stiller, more erect, his eyebrows raised like antennae.

'Your rig's not in very good shape, by the look of it.'

The silence continues.

'No money to get it fixed?'

'What are you on about?' At last, a response.

Ivan retrieves the Kalingra map and unfolds it on the table, a dramatic flourish. 'One hundred and twenty-nine boreholes, Trevor, but less than half actually drilled.'

'Yeah, the rig broke down. I'm getting it fixed. So what?'

'And yet here we have them all completed, their cores analysed.' Ivan places the fraudulent assay next to the map.

Topsoil stares at the document on the desk, but makes no attempt to pick it up, to read it. As if he might get infected. 'That's got nothing to do with me.'

'Of course it's got to do with you. It's your drilling rig.'

The chin comes back out. 'I didn't have anything to do with that,' the big man asserts, flicking his nose at the document in a gesture of disdain.

Ivan leans back, dropping his voice from assertion to agreement. 'No. I don't believe you did. I think you were paid to drill one hundred and twenty-nine holes, but somewhere along the line, maybe after your rig broke down, you discovered they weren't doing a proper analysis on the cores anyway. Right?'

'Nothing to do with me.'

'No. But that's how it happened, isn't it?'

'If you say so.'

Ivan leaves a pregnant pause, eyes boring into Topsoil's own. The big man can't match his gaze. 'Did Jonas know?'

'Know what?'

'That the mine was a fake. A con job.'

Trevor breathes out, looks around the room as if seeking guidance, then stares straight into the video camera hanging from the ceiling. 'Yeah. He knew. I didn't tell him. He worked it out by himself.'

'What did he say?'

'He came into the shop, wanting to know who owned it. Who owned the mine. I told him to forget it, that it was too dangerous.'

'What was too dangerous?'

'Threatening to expose them.'

'He was talking blackmail?'

'Aye. Blackmail.'

'You think that's what got him killed?'

'It's possible. Maybe.'

'How did he work out who owned the mine?'

'No idea. I sure as hell don't know.'

'You sure about that?'

'It was all run out of an office in Finnigans Gap. The manager was Petal Rimmington, but she was just the local front; the real owners were somewhere else. She told me Fiji.'

'You say you don't know who owns it, but you got paid, right? For the drilling?'

'Yeah. For all of it. No questions asked.'

'So who paid you?'

'Petal Rimmington and . . .'

'And?'

'No "and". Just Petal Rimmington.'

'Tell me, Trevor.'

'Petal Rimmington. She paid me. Transferred the money across. You can check my account.'

Ivan stares, gaze unflinching, then reaches around, gingerly touching the back of his head. Topsoil shifts in his seat, no longer able to look Ivan in the eye. The detective lets him sweat for a moment more before homing in. 'Assaulting a police officer is a serious offence.'

'What are you talking about?'

'I was at Jonas McGee's house, checking out his laptop. Some gutless wonder king-hit me from behind. Lucky they didn't kill me. So, aggravated assault. Assaulting a police officer. Assault causing actual bodily harm. Or grievous bodily harm. In fact, with the right prosecutor, it could probably be upgraded to attempted murder.'

'Nothing to do with me.'

'Really? I'm looking at his laptop when I get hit. And the next thing I know, the Drug Squad has found it. At your place. The very next morning. And guess what? There are fingerprints. Three sets: Jonas McGee's, mine and yours.'

'What do you want?'

'Petal Rimmington paid for your services through bank deposits, but someone else paid you cash. Who was it?'

Topsoil hesitates. For a moment he looks like he may deploy the chin of defiance, but then he looks up at the video monitor and folds. 'Ray Penuch. It was Ray Penuch.'

Ivan is almost stuttering with surprise as he asks the follow-up. 'Ray Penuch from Cuttamulla?'

'That's him. Big red-headed prick.'

Ivan glances over at Nell, but she's concentrating on driving, staring straight ahead through the windscreen. Except there is nothing to concentrate on: the road back to Finnigans Gap is dead straight. There hasn't been the slightest curve since they left the turn-off from Lightning Ridge more than ten kilometres back.

'So what do you reckon?' he asks.

He can see her mouth, drawn tight like a purse. 'About Topsoil?'

'Yes. You think he was telling us all he knows?'

'You're asking me to judge his veracity?'

'I'd value your opinion.'

'My opinion?' she says, a touch of anger in her words. 'Given how good I've been at judging him up to now, you mean?'

'Nell.'

She drives on, settling before she answers. 'You were great. Really. Played him like a violin.'

'That's not what I'm asking.'

'Jeez. Take a compliment, will you?' She looks across for the briefest moment, the first time. 'Really.'

'What do you think of Ray Penuch paying him cash to keep quiet about the drill assay?'

'I can't see how he could make that up,' she says. 'Why would he? He wouldn't even know we're aware of Penuch and all that shit with Stanley Honeywell.'

'Not unless you told him.'

Now she turns, stares at Ivan, seething.

'Nell, the road.'

She turns back, correcting the steering ever so slightly. 'No. I didn't tell him anything. Not a fucking word. Not about anything.'

'I believe you.'

'It would be nice if someone did.'

'It makes me wonder, though.'

'Oh, for fuck's sake, what?'

'Think about it. Monday, you're out at Cuttamulla. You want to arrest Penuch. Then, the same night, who should bowl up to you at the pub but good old Trev.'

She doesn't respond, but Ivan can sense the anger radiating off her. Her mouth is drawn sphincter-tight. But at least now he knows the anger is not directed at him.

'The prick,' is all she says.

'So you didn't buy it? His sob story?'

'Oh, I bought it all right. That he didn't shaft Barret and the Longfers planning to replace them. That would take half a brain and more guts than he'll ever possess. The pathetic prick.'

'You don't sound impressed.'

'Why would I be impressed?'

'That his motivation was trying to help you, to give you a leg-up, to impress you?'

Nell hits the brakes hard, as if she intends stopping, but changes her mind and drives on, speaking even as she keeps her eyes on the road, her words spat out. 'He was up to his neck in debt, floundering. But does he think to tell me, the woman he's shagging? To confide? No. It was only ever the big man bullshit, how important he was, how successful, how connected. I mean, fuck me. That big truck of his, and the bloody boat parked outside his shop like that? Who does he think he's fooling? One look at his house and I knew he wasn't Twiggy Forrest. I should have guessed then: just another hopeless man, unable to admit to what he's really facing. Except to another bloke, under duress, in a police interview.' Finally she turns back to Ivan. 'So, no. I wasn't impressed.'

They fall into silence then, Ivan forced to reflect somewhat uncomfortably on his own reticence. Who does he tell his problems to, in whom does he confide? No one. Not even Morris, his long-time mentor. He glances across at Nell. She's right not to feel sorry for Trevor Topsoil. And he realises he did feel sorry for the man, and wonders why. Because it resonated with his own inadequacies, his own parlous finances, his own inability to trust? Because, deep down, he too is pathetic?

'The poker machines,' he says. 'I can control it.' It's not what he wants to say, not how he wants to frame it, but it's out there. He's broached the subject.

She glances across at him. He can't tell what it is he sees in her face: anger, confusion, intrigue. 'Go on then,' is all she says; it's all he needs.

'I received a lot of money. A kind of inheritance. From my father.'

'I'm sorry,' she says. 'I didn't know.'

'He's not dead,' says Ivan.

'What? Then how can it be an inheritance?'

'More like an endowment, let's say.' He's looking straight ahead now, staring out at the featureless road, the words coming out as if of their own volition. 'He's in prison.'

'Jesus. Where?'

'The Hague.'

'What?'

'The Netherlands.'

'The International Criminal Court?'

'The one and only.' He feels the wheels on the road, sees the sun in the sky, knows what must be passing through her mind even before she articulates it.

'A war criminal?'

'Sentenced to forty years,' he says.

She says nothing; she doesn't have to.

'He was born here, in Sydney. Second generation. But when the war started, he left us and went back.'

'Yugoslavia?'

'Croatia. He's Croatian now. Joined the militia, the local police. Committed—' he swallows, forces himself to continue '—atrocities.' He looks across at her. There is no mistaking her expression now: sympathy. Compassion. He continues: 'My mum tried to stop him going, so he beat her up. Abandoned us. I was a toddler.' He draws a deep breath, can feel the tremor just below the surface. 'She was Serbian. Born over there. Wanted nothing to do with any of it.'

The car rockets on, through the heat, through the dust haze, the road unchanging, the horizon so far away, so far away.

'So, what's with the poker machines?' she asks. He can hear the effort in her voice, the effort to be gentle.

'He sent money. Once he knew he was going to get extradited to The Hague. About eight years ago, not long after I joined the force. Money from who knows where. Dirty money.' He pauses. 'I didn't want it.'

'Couldn't you have given it to your mother?'

'She's dead. Killed herself. Couldn't bear the shame.'

'My god, Ivan.'

'I wanted to give it to charity, but I couldn't. It was tainted, blood money. So I started gambling. If I won, then it went to charity; if I lost, it was gone.'

He can feel her eyes upon him as she says, 'You know that doesn't make any sense?'

'Of course.' There's a long hiatus, nothing said, but he can't leave it there. 'It doesn't matter now. It's almost gone.' He sighs. 'Then I can stop.'

They drive in silence. The sun is getting lower, starting to flare. Nell tries the wipers, but the flow of water ignites with sunlight, causing them to squint through it. Then suddenly they hit it, a locust swarm, out here in the middle of nowhere, the hoppers splattering onto the windscreen like a cloudburst, like the heavens are raining insects. The wipers are overwhelmed, smearing the windscreen in an increasingly opaque paste, like raw eggs and sticks. In no time flat, they can't see the road in front of them.

Nell brakes heavily, slowing the car, looking from side to side, trying to keep it aligned by checking through the side windows. There's a slight bump; Ivan thinks they've run over something, or they're off the edge of the bitumen. But no: they've come onto a long concrete bridge, hovering above the floodplain. The car is slowing now, and the worst of the swarm is passing over them. She takes her foot from the brake and the car drifts on, carried by inertia, off the far end of the bridge, momentum easing. She brakes again, bringing the car to a halt off the side of the road. 'Shit,' she says, almost whispering.

'My god. Well done.'

She ignores him.

'Nell, it's okay—we're safe.'

She has her hands off the wheel, is shaking her head, as if in disbelief. 'This is it. This is where it all started. The Gulch. Where Jonas McGee ran off the road and killed his wife and her sister. On the way back from the picnic races at Lightning Ridge.'

They climb out. Nell goes to the back of the car, fetches a couple of bottles of water. She hands one to Ivan. 'Here.' The engine is still running; she starts the wipers going again, and they spend silent minutes pouring water across the glass, gradually clearing the yellow coagulation of dead bugs. Around them, locusts buzz and wheel, outliers from the swarm. Ivan looks back to the bridge, can see the large swathe of green below it, growth generated by the recent rains. Hopper heaven. Emerging en masse, before the predators move in, before the land dries out, before the green returns to brown. Back in the Nissan, Nell checks her mirrors, double-checks, then carves a U-turn. 'It must have been this time of day,' she says. 'Maybe a little later, closer to sunset. Jonas drunk at the wheel. Sun in his eyes. Distracted.'

'But the road is dead straight,' says Ivan.

'It is now. Not twenty years ago. This bridge is new.'

They're back across the span now, moving slowly, Nell with one eye on the road, the other checking the surrounds. The swarm is all around them, clattering as they bounce from the car but no longer smearing the windscreen. She finds what she's looking for: a turn-off to the right. They cross the centre line and she steers onto the track. There's about thirty metres of dirt, then it joins a thin strip of bitumen running parallel to the highway. 'The old road,' she says, bringing the car to a standstill. 'C'mon. You're the one who likes to walk.'

Out of the car, the heat is howling. The insects are everywhere, buzzing and banging into them, oblivious to the two figures walking along the remnants of road, down towards where the creek of the Gulch has so recently been flowing. It's come to a stop now, leaving only waterholes and puddles, baking in the heat, surrounded by an expansive burst of green. Ivan wonders which will last longer: the puddles under the northern sun or the vegetation under attack by the locusts. Another few days of this and they'll both be gone, vanished for years, until the next big rains, the next collision of La Niña, wayward monsoons and cyclonic remnants.

'Here,' says Nell. 'Look.'

The old road has been diverging gradually from the new highway, but running straight enough and at the same level. Now, though, it swings sharply to the left and dips down to where the creek has carved itself into the flood plain, a drop of about ten metres. The footings of the old bridge are still there, emerging from the creek bed, running perpendicular to the new road. Ivan can see the other side, where the old road swings sharply back to the right as it rises up the slope and aligns once more with the direct route to Finnigans Gap.

They stand without talking. Ivan can picture it happening, the crash. McGee drunk, sun in his eyes, distracted by the two women. Maybe at the last, when it was already too late, he would have felt the tyres leave the bitumen, bite into the gravel of the verge. Off the outside of the corner, losing control, the car starting to flip, starting to roll. Too late.

'Not hard to imagine,' he says.

'It's the first curve in the road since Lightning Ridge. Fifteen kilometres. First time he would have used his brakes.'

'He was drunk, Nell. Three times the limit.'

'So he was.'

chapter twenty-six

THE SUN IS TO THEIR LEFT NOW, TURNED A REDDISH ORANGE BY THE RISING dust as the great interior dries and the wind sweeps the sky with silicon. It blows about them, circling, like an escort.

They enter a town grown unfamiliar to Nell. Up past the airport, once associated with commuter flights, not corporate jets. Over on her left, Topsoil Mining Supplies, once a source of comfort, now of angst and regret. Up past the Alpine Cafe to the crossroads, the clock tower stuck on ten-past-ten. In the distance, she sees the cross of St Andrew's, thinks of its green gravel yard and the graves of Annie McGee and her sister Heloise. It's the same town; she's just seeing it with new eyes. She turns right, heading up The Way, heading for Deadmans Well.

*

The mayor is sitting on the steps of his railway carriage, wearing the same tutu as last time she saw him, sucking on a bottle of beer, condensation dripping.

'Who you after this time?' he asks, opalescent teeth glinting with sunset colours.

'Stanley Honeywell,' says Ivan.

She knows it's a lie, that Ivan doesn't want to mention Holgate by name. Topsoil said the mayor hates ratters; the detectives don't want to ignite trouble at the squatter camp. And any man who wears a tutu with impunity in Finnigans Gap is someone to be taken seriously.

'Stanley? Yeah, he's down there, trying to salvage what he can from his place.'

'He okay?' asks Nell.

'Bit rough around the edges, but he'll survive. We look after our own.'

'Glad to hear it,' says Nell.

They find Stanley cleaning up. He appears unsettled when he sees the two police officers walking towards him, perhaps fearing more trouble.

'It's all right, mate,' says Nell. 'We're not here to cause bother. Just wanted to make sure you're okay.'

'Yeah. Good.' Stanley surveys the mess left by Penuch. Then he shrugs. 'No worries. Cuttamulla gave me time off work. Still paying, though.'

'That's decent of them,' she says. 'You need a hand with anything?'

Stanley looks unsure, as if maybe this is a practical joke. She expects he probably cops his fair share. 'No,' says the big man. 'I'm sweet.'

'You heard nothing more of Ray Penuch?' asks Nell.

'No. Why?' There's unease in the voice. 'They sacked him. Said he left.'

'Yeah. That's right. We just wanted to make sure he wasn't back, causing any problems for you.'

'He won't come here,' says Stanley, sounding confident in the assertion. 'The mayor knows what he did.'

'Good,' says Nell. 'Good for the mayor.'

'Top bloke.'

'We'll leave you to it then.'

'See ya.'

Nell gives it a moment. 'Oh, Stanley. Bloke called Holgate. Where can we find him?'

'Just over there. Big canvas tent. Red station wagon.'

'Thanks, Stanley. Take care.'

They're out of earshot, approaching the tent, when Ivan speaks for the first time. 'Well played.'

— —

Ivan sees Holgate before he sees them, the ratter's head in the engine bay of his ancient Holden. The man looks up as they approach, wipes grease from his hands on a rag, his eyes steady.

'What?' says Holgate.

Ivan has his wallet in his hand, flashing his ID. 'Detective Sergeant Ivan Lucic and Detective Constable Narelle Buchanan. Homicide.'

'Homicide? You're talking to the wrong man.'

'Let's go inside,' says Nell.

'Out of the sun,' says Ivan.

'Out of sight,' says Nell.

Holgate looks at her, then at Ivan, then back again, before acquiescing. 'You're not here to search, are you?'

'Homicide,' says Nell.

'Questions,' says Ivan.

'Inside then,' says Holgate.

The tent is big, heavy material, tall enough to stand in, the size of a studio apartment, the roof held aloft by solid wooden poles. There is something old-fashioned about it, like army surplus from a long-ago war. It's baking hot, like a sauna.

'Jeez, why don't you open it up a bit?' asks Ivan.

'Not with the wind up. Too much dust,' says Holgate. 'Later, once the sun is down, once the wind dies, I'll cool it down.'

Ivan looks about. It is remarkably neat, almost obsessively so. The ground is covered by a heavy-duty tarpaulin. It looks like it's been mopped. On one side there's a single bed, neatly made, hospital corners. There's furniture, real furniture, as if perhaps it's come out of a real house. There are trunks lining the opposite wall, more military surplus, next to a bookshelf brimming with serious-looking books: history, biography, science. There's a desk, with framed pictures of a family, suggesting better days: Holgate with a woman, short and smiling. There's a boy between them, holding their hands, and a toddler straddling Holgate's shoulders.

'Water?' the man offers.

'No, we won't be long.' Ivan pulls up a chair, sits, indicates for Holgate to do the same. He does. 'We are in debt to someone who rang Crime Stoppers last Saturday. It was a kind and considerate thing to do. An honourable thing. They reported that Jonas McGee had been crucified in his opal mine.'

'And?' says Holgate, giving nothing away.

Ivan sighs. He feels he needs to reiterate this to every second person he talks to. Maybe he should make a recording. 'We don't care what you were doing down his mine. We're only interested in finding his killer.'

'Sorry. I can't help you.'

'Must have been a hell of a sight, finding him like that,' says Nell, voice placid. 'We know. We saw it too.'

Holgate says nothing, just shakes his head.

'Jonas died last Tuesday,' says Ivan. 'We know the people down the mine on Saturday can't possibly have had anything to do with his death.'

Another shake of the head, Holgate's face resolute.

Ivan keeps pushing. 'We have a suspect. Bloke from out of town. There's a warrant out for his arrest. His name is Merv Claxton.'

'Never heard of him.'

'Drove a big black limousine, a Chrysler.'

Holgate says nothing for a long time, face set stony. But Ivan sees it, the flicker of recognition; the man must have seen the car. The ratter looks Ivan in the eye. 'If you know who did it, why do you need to speak to me?'

'Because knowing is one thing, proving is another,' replies Ivan.

Nothing is said, not for a long time. Whatever is passing through the man's head, Ivan lets it play out. Holgate stands, starts pacing, stops before the table with the family portrait, stares at it for a long moment. He turns back. 'Tuesday, you say?'

'The pathologist has established the time of death.'

Holgate comes back, sits, speaks softly. 'Tuesday. Nailed up like that, like Jesus Christ, like some martyr. He might have lasted a day or two.'

Ivan nods. 'It's been bothering you. It bothers me too.'

But the man has returned to his own thoughts.

'If it's any comfort, he was already dead when he was nailed up,' offers Ivan. 'We have reason to believe his death was quick and painless.'

Holgate says nothing, but there is emotion in his eyes. 'Is that right?'

'It is.'

'Well, that's something, I suppose.'

Ivan doesn't speak. Neither does Nell. It's like someone has called for a minute's silence, out of respect for the dead.

Eventually, Holgate comes to some internal decision, his voice still gentle. 'I was casing the place out. Working out when McGee was likely to be there, when he wasn't. So yeah, I saw the car. It was there Sunday evening, around sunset. The rain had stopped for an hour or so. The car stopped at Jonas's mine, then kept going, up to the lookout overlooking the lake.'

'Thank you. That's very useful.'

'I hope you get the bastard.'

'You weren't casing the place in the early hours of Tuesday? Around five in the morning?' Ivan asks.

Holgate stares at him, mind working. 'No, sorry. I don't think so. Once we determined he was out there for the night, there wasn't much point in hanging around and drawing attention to ourselves.'

It's Nell who takes up the questioning. 'When did you decide it was safe to go down the mine?'

'We checked it when we could. After Tuesday, the access shaft was locked, so we knew no one was down there. At least that's what we thought. We figured he was out of town, that the way was open. We kept checking regularly. The mine was always padlocked.'

'Still sealed when you went down?'

'Yeah.'

'You cut the lock?'

Holgate says nothing, not straight away, as if just catching up with how much he has implicated himself. There's another glance at the table with the family photograph. 'Yeah. Boltcutters.'

Ivan runs it through his mind. If Claxton killed McGee with an insulin overdose, and he was counting on it being seen as death by natural causes, the last thing he would have done was lock the entry shaft. That must have been the next person, the one who nailed McGee up. They climbed out and sealed the entrance, maybe thinking it would be weeks, even months, before the body was discovered. Was that to hide the crime, to let time melt away the forensic evidence, or was it to punish McGee, to make him suffer in some strange way?

'You found the body,' he says. 'What did you do?'

'Got out of there. Covered our tracks and left.'

'Was there anything unusual, anything that caught your eye? Anything that could help us?'

Holgate is staring again. It's a strange reaction if he isn't holding something back.

'Anything,' says Nell. 'No matter how insignificant.'

Holgate stands. 'Promise you will stay here, wait for me. That you won't follow.'

Ivan and Nell exchange a glance. 'For how long?'

'No time. Five minutes.'

'Okay,' says Ivan.

So they wait. Nell walks about, not touching but looking. She checks the books on the shelf, then the family portrait. When she speaks, her voice is sombre. 'I reckon Trev might have been telling the truth.'

'About what?'

'They don't want to do it. They're forced into it. Circumstances.'

'Yeah, maybe.'

Holgate returns. He's wearing gloves, holding what looks like an oversized drill. 'Here,' he says. 'It was down his mine. It's electric. Battery-powered.'

'It was his?' asks Ivan.

'That'd be my guess. That or a supplier in town.'

'What's it for?'

'Ratting. That's what.'

'And where was it?'

'At the foot of the cross. Like someone had placed it there.'

'You took it. Why?'

'He didn't need it anymore.' Holgate looks from one of them to the other and back, then lowers his head. 'I didn't want ratters to be implicated in his death, and he didn't need to be branded a ratter. No one deserves that legacy.'

'Why would he be ratting his own mine?'

'I couldn't say.'

—◆—

Nell has dinner with Carl Richter at the bowlo, a late invitation. She walks in past the sign-in table, the fountain and the artificial greenery, stealing a look at the passage leading off to the poker machines. A group of young men are in the bistro, gathered around the huge screen, watching the cricket. A couple of them are wearing t-shirts—*Cuttamulla Cricket*—and all of them are drinking beer.

Richter is sitting at a table waiting, examining his own beer. He doesn't see her at first. He looks serious. She hesitates for a moment and examines him. He looks older, more careworn, this jovial man who was first her mentor, then her tormentor. And now?

'Hi, Scaley.'

He looks up, reverie broken, and the old Richter is back, smile breaking open like a wave on a beach, eyes creased with kindness. 'Young Nell.'

He insists on buying her a drink, a soft drink, and then paying for the food. He has a steak, a T-bone, she has the chicken-and-leek pie. It's not bad. It's not good either; she wishes she'd ordered the steak.

'I hear congratulations are in order,' says Richter, once he's made sufficient inroads into his meal.

'How's that?'

'I heard you have a firm suspect for the murder of Jonas McGee.'

'Yeah, we do. We've got a warrant out. Ivan will probably head down to Sydney tomorrow to interview him.'

'So not a local then?'

'No.'

'That's a relief,' says Richter, cutting off another hunk of meat. 'It'll make the healing easier.'

'I guess.'

Richter chews his food, and then, as if he's made a decision, rests his cutlery on his plate. 'Nell, I wanted you to know: that bloke who was up here, Detective Phelan, he's been asking around after you.'

So that's why Richter wanted to catch up; not just to repair their relationship, but also to warn her.

'I know. They need to vet me. He said you vouched for me, remember?'

'He was asking all about your past. How you performed when you were here. The sarge wasn't around back then, so she passed him on to me.'

'What did you say?'

'The truth. You're an excellent cop. But he was all over the arrest of Barret and the Longfers. You using Topsoil as an informer. Asking whether you and Topsoil were in cahoots.'

'I see,' says Nell. She looks down at her chicken pie, losing all appetite. She too lays her cutlery down.

'I tried to set him right,' says Richter. 'I'm not sure he believed me.'

Nell looks at him. 'Thanks, Scaley. I've done nothing wrong, so I've got nothing to fear. Right?'

'Right,' says Richter. But he doesn't look convinced, and she doesn't feel it. She'd thought Phelan was interested in Ivan and Morris Montifore, not her. 'Did he ask about Ivan?'

'He wanted to know how you two were getting along. Whether you're close.'

'In what sense?'

'I didn't ask. I just said you both seemed to be highly professional. Not sure it's the answer he was looking for.' And Richter smiles. It's a good smile.

'Okay. Thanks for the heads-up, Scaley.'

'Listen, Nell, the guy has it in for Lucic. I spoke to a mate in Sydney. Way he tells it, Morris Montifore had already agreed to fall on his sword before Phelan came up here. So it can't be Montifore in his sights; it must be Lucic.'

'What are you saying?'

Richter grimaces. 'I don't know, really. But maybe you should keep your distance from Lucic. Don't get too close. You don't want to become collateral damage for a second time.'

——

Nell is eating with Carl Richter, and Ivan is tossing up whether to go for the better food at the club, and risk the poker machines, or opt for the dubious food of the pub instead. But the pub has pokies as well. And that's when he has a better idea. He has a quick shower, changes into more casual clothes. Time to give the black jeans a run. He walks down to the crossroads and onto the main street, to the Alpine Cafe.

It's already gone eight, the sun long dipped behind the West Ridge but still bathing the heights of the East Ridge with golden light. The town is starting to breathe, the heat lifting as the shadows grow.

Inside, he orders coffee at the counter and asks if the big man has been in for a burger, Bullshit Bob Inglis. Not yet, they say. But if he's in town, he comes every night.

So Ivan slides into a booth opposite the Matterhorn, sits on his coffee. It's not hard: it's possibly the worst he's ever had, bitter with burnt milk. He should have gone for the bottled stuff instead. He gives up on it, leaving it to grow a skin.

Before him, a steady line of locals come through the door, many picking up phoned-in orders. He can see the chalkboard menu, studies it more closely as the odours coming from the grill start to elicit hunger. There are all sorts of offerings, from fish and chips through pies to soup of the day, but people are ordering one thing and one thing only: hamburgers with the lot.

He can't resist; he returns to the counter and orders one himself, including beetroot but not pineapple, winning a nod of approval from the counter staff. 'I'll bring it over, love.'

A few minutes later, he takes his first bite and his mouth fills with pleasure. The meat is succulent, the bun is Turkish bread, firm and tasty, and there's some sort of homemade sauce, a kind of relish, slightly spicy. It might be the only food worth eating for two hundred kilometres. He's just savouring it when Bob Inglis strides through the door. The big man goes straight to the fridge, extracts a two-litre bottle of Diet Coke, then moves to the counter. Only after he's ordered his two burgers—with beetroot, hold the pineapple, chips on the side—does he look around for somewhere to sit and spies Ivan, sitting by himself with his burger.

'A convert,' says Inglis.

'Bloody good,' replies Ivan. 'Thank you.'

'Mind if I join you?'

'Please do,' says Ivan. *Perfect.*

Inglis sits, cracks the Coke, takes a long slug straight from the bottle. 'How's your investigation going?' he asks, with all the interest that one might use to inquire about the weather. 'Found the killer?'

'Making good progress,' replies Ivan. 'We have a suspect. There's a warrant out for his arrest.'

'Good for you.'

'Bloke called Merv Claxton. You heard of him?'

Inglis frowns. 'No. Should I have?'

'He's a driver and bodyguard. Been driving potential investors up along the West Ridge so they can take a look at the Kalingra Rare Earths mine. A big black Chrysler. Asian clients.'

Inglis places the bottle of Coke back on the table, screws the lid tight. The ease has left his face, replaced by focus and concentration, his body rigid. 'You already asked me about this two nights ago. Remember?'

'About the car, not the man.'

Inglis thinks for some time before answering. 'I know the bloke you mean. I never spoke to him. I have my own transport, or use Kalingra's. He was driving the Chinese.'

'You said they were now your allies. Something like that. You cut a deal with them?'

'I outbid them.'

'So why weren't they more upset?'

'Who says they weren't?'

'My colleague saw you together at the airport. You went to the effort of saying goodbye. I'm told it was smiles and bowing all round.'

Inglis says nothing for a moment, studying Ivan's face before speaking. 'We signed a memorandum of understanding. The minerals will be processed at their plant in China.' Inglis raises a single finger of warning. 'And that really is commercial-in-confidence. Don't breathe a word of that to anyone.'

Ivan takes a bite from his burger, thinking about how to get to where he wants to go. In the end, he barrels in. 'This mine up at Kalingra. You own it now, right?'

'Come midnight I will.'

'How closely have you checked it out?'

Inglis raises an eyebrow, intelligence working. 'Why?'

'I'm not sure it's all it's cracked up to be.'

'Go on.'

'I think some of the assays were faked. Maybe all of them. A lot of the drill holes were never completed.'

Inglis stares at him, forehead creased. 'I thought you were a Homicide detective.'

'True.'

'So I would be grateful, very grateful indeed, if you were to stick to your knitting.'

Ivan takes another bite of his burger under the scrutiny of Inglis before speaking again. 'You don't want to hear what I found?'

'No, I do not. You need to keep your theories to yourself.'

'Sure,' says Ivan. 'Nothing to do with me.'

Inglis doesn't respond, just keeps staring at him, as if to take his eyes off him might risk Ivan doing something unexpected. Only when the billionaire's own twin burgers arrive does the man deign to look down.

Ivan speaks. 'We believe the dead man, Jonas McGee, may have discovered the true state of the rare-earth mine.'

'I doubt that very much,' says Inglis, and takes a huge mouthful of burger.

Ivan suspects the man is in denial, doesn't want to hear he's been comprehensively taken. He pushes on. 'Did McGee ever get in contact with you? Offer you information in return for money?'

Inglis had been about to take another bite from his burger, but now he holds it hovering before him. A line of juice has flowed down his chin, but he makes no move to mop it up. There is no pleasure in his face; his mind is elsewhere. 'I believe he might have done so. Someone contacted my office, said they had valuable information about the mine, but they would only talk to me. Whether it was him or not, I don't know. I brushed it off.'

'When was this?'

'A couple of weeks back. Last time I was up here.'

'Is there any way of checking?'

'Of course. I'll ask my staff to see if he left a number.'

'Thank you,' says Ivan.

Inglis resumes eating. Another portion of burger is taken, chewed, swallowed. 'Are we done?' the billionaire asks through his chewing.

'Who are you buying the mine from?'

'That should be easy enough for you to find out.'

'We're having difficulty.'

'Commercial-in-confidence. Sorry.'

'No one would know how I found out.'

'Why do you want to know? How is it relevant?'

'I think Jonas McGee believed the mine is a fraud. An elaborate con job, with you as the target. He tried to warn you. For money. You blew him off, so he went to the owners. Attempted blackmail. So the scammers killed him.'

'Good theory. I'll make sure my people get back to you. Apart from that, I can't see how I can help.'

Ivan takes a bite of his own burger, then sips some coffee. It tastes no better. 'I don't get it. I'm telling you that you're being conned, scammed out of God knows how much, and you don't seem the least bit interested.'

'I'm not.'

'Claxton must have been working for someone. Unless he's some sort of serial killer who wanders around killing people at random.'

Inglis harumphs. 'You don't believe that for a minute.'

'No, I don't.'

Bullshit Bob takes a massive mouthful, a slice of beetroot slithering out and landing on his plate with a splat. It's the last of the first burger, gone in mere minutes. One down, one to go. It takes him a good thirty seconds of chewing, juices leaking, before he can speak again. 'I'm going to help you,' he says.

'How's that?'

'Let me speak to my lawyer. See if we can tell you who we're buying the mine from.'

'Is it too late to pull out?'

'Technically, no. I'll be taking your information on board, rerunning our own figures against their assays before midnight.' And then he smiles, as if making a private joke, a self-deprecating aside. 'But figures never were my strong point. I'm a geologist.'

'I see.'

'So thank you. If what you say is true, then you may have saved me considerable money. And embarrassment.' Inglis wipes his hands on a pile of napkins, then finishes the job by wiping them on his pants. He pulls out a wallet and extracts a business card. 'This is my lawyer. He'll be in touch.'

Ivan is just reaching forward to accept it, a word of thanks on his lips, when a movement catches his eye. He looks to the doorway. Nell is standing there, eyes wide and mouth open.

— —

She walks. The sun has set, not just behind the West Ridge but down below the rim of the world. The sky has moved through its evening palette, from blue and white, to blue and pink, then clouds flaring orange, to the muted tones of mauve, violet and purple. Now only a glow remains, and the first stars are emerging in the eastern sky. An owl swoops low, huge against the street lighting.

She walks the streets, so familiar and yet changed, the houses and buildings filled with more meaning than the innocent facades of her uniform days.

She's tired, but she realises she's resisting returning to the motel. The burner is there, the phone that Phelan gave her. It's in the drawer in the dresser next to the bed, still fully charged, still available, still insistent. Richter was right, she knows. Her career is still in the balance; nothing has changed. A stay of execution, that's all. She's receiving the benefit of the doubt over her entanglement with Trevor Topsoil. One strike. But she's entangled with Ivan Lucic, her fate bound to his. A second strike. And now? Now she is remembering Phelan's riding instructions, that she should notify him—*if you get even a whiff he's taking money*. She has seen Ivan first with Delaney Bullwinkel, and now with Bullshit Bob Inglis, the billionaire's wallet open, Inglis handing something to Ivan. And on neither occasion has he informed her that he was meeting with the tycoons. Once could be coincidental, but two occasions, two separate billionaires? Her choice is stark. If she doesn't tell and Phelan finds out, then that's it: strike three. Her career over.

Ivan has confessed to gambling, to throwing money away on the poker machines. She believes his story, the awful endowment from his father, that he wants to rid himself of it. But what else did he say? Not to worry, that the money was almost gone. Almost. And what then? When it has all gone, what does a gambling addict do to feed his habit? Of course she feels sorry for him. And he's trusted her with this secret of his. But surely she needs to put herself first, inoculate herself.

She wonders why she is even hesitating. What does she owe Ivan Lucic? She hadn't even met him until three days ago. Richter was right in saying that their relationship is a professional one: cooperating on their assignment, aware that a successful prosecution has the potential to extricate each of them from their respective predicaments. And yet, for all his silence and all his stoicism and his secrecy, it has grown beyond the purely professional. She has to acknowledge that. He has let his guard down. First, when she was gone for all money, sitting in the interview room in her underwear and that ridiculous hoodie, dejected and hopeless, he stood by her. She remembers him putting his hand on hers, resting it there for a heartbeat, letting her know he was with her. At a time when it would have been in his own best interest, a cop who was himself under scrutiny by Professional Standards, to have distanced himself from her. And then, on the drive back from Lightning Ridge, confessing to his gambling addiction, explaining it. Was that simply to engender her sympathy, her collaboration? No. She doesn't believe that. She can't believe that.

And so she decides in this moment that she won't inform Phelan, that she won't rat. Not yet. The least she can do is talk to Ivan first, ask about the clandestine meetings. And if his responses aren't satisfactory, then she can always notify Phelan.

She stops walking, breathes deep, feels the relief rising from her shoulders. She feels like she has made the right decision. The air smells sweet: dust and not much else, the settled air of the inland.

She realises she has walked to the edge of Finnigans Gap on the highway north, the road to Queensland. She remembers that there is a lookout, up where the road tops the rise, before its descent towards the Sunshine State. She keeps walking, and now it feels good. Good to be out of the heat, to be out of the car, to be out from under, if only for a time. The road begins to curve to the left, then back to the right, flattening before sloping down towards the border. She stops, turns back to look at the Gap. The crossroads are laid out before her, the clock tower illuminated and clear, with no trees of any size to obscure the view. Cactuses don't grow that high. Beyond the crossroads, the streetlights end, and there is little more than the flickering lights of the occasional house. Down on the southern approach, the roadhouse is bathed in its own oasis of light. And beyond it, the plain, vast and dark, melded with the sky. Except the sky has stars and light and vitality; the plain is entirely black and inscrutable. She sees a set of headlights appear on the East Ridge, winding down towards the town. She watches, transfixed, as they drop in and out of sight. She wonders where the car is heading: the cafe or the pub, the bowlo or the roadhouse. There's not a lot of choice. The pub wins.

She continues around the curve, which is just as she remembers it, a plateau before the road heads down again. She passes a large sign, flicks on the torch app on her phone. SCENIC LOOKOUT. 100 METRES ON RIGHT. She keeps walking.

There are no cars at the lookout. Little wonder: there is nothing to see. Just the sky, shimmering treasure above the dark secrets of the earth. Not that you always need something to look at; Trevor had brought her up here once. She lets that memory go; it's not something she wants to dwell upon. She walks towards the wall, wondering if her memory is correct, that there is a bench over here, somewhere to sit and look, somewhere to contemplate the vast nothing.

She is almost there when she hears it: a whimper, a sob. She stops, listens. There is someone here, someone on the bench. Another sob, then a cry, from someone in genuine pain. A woman's voice, a woman in distress. She flicks on her torch app, its reach surprising in the darkness of the night, her other hand on the stock of her gun. A couple is sitting on the bench, backs to her. Not fighting, not struggling: the man with his arm around the woman, comforting her, the woman leaning into him. Their faces turn: Elsie Claremont and Kyle Torshack, eyes wet.

Nell flicks off the torch. 'Sorry,' she says, as if speaking to the night, the young cousins no longer discernible. She leaves them to their grief, and starts the walk back down the hill.

THURSDAY

chapter twenty-seven

HE PACKS HIS BAGS, CHECKS OUT OF THE MOTEL, NO TIME FOR JOGGING. WORD
has come through: they've located Claxton, know where to pick
him up. They're doing it right, taking no chances: the house under
surveillance, a dawn raid. He'll be in custody by the time Ivan
gets to Sydney. The call came at midnight, Dereck Packenham
himself, telling him to be at the airport by eight. They want him
in the city to lead the interrogation of the former policeman. Ivan
is feeling a mixture of excitement and trepidation, going head-
to-head with an experienced detective. Claxton will know all the
tricks of the trade, know exactly what Ivan is attempting. And he'll
have a lawyer. With such big money involved, it will be a good
lawyer. Not a corporate suit, but a case-hardened defence attorney.

Ivan doesn't drive straight to the airport. First, he needs to meet
with Nell, brief her. And thank her. She should be happy. If the

prosecutor accepts the case against Claxton, it will be a feather in her cap, not just his. The win that both of them need.

She should be happy, but when he enters the Alpine Cafe she looks nothing like it. It could be the coffee, or it could be the pastries. They look sad and depleted. When were they baked? And where? Lightning Ridge? How can a place that makes such glorious burgers stuff up everything else so comprehensively? He acknowledges her with a tilt of his head and plucks a plastic bottle of iced coffee from the display fridge. At the counter he orders raisin toast; surely they can't bugger that up.

'Morning,' he says, taking a seat in the booth across from the snow-covered summit.

'You look cheery,' she says.

'So should you. We're about to nail Merv Claxton.'

'And those he was working for?'

'One thing at a time. We get him, we're one step closer to his masters.'

The raisin toast arrives. Just like that. Almost instantaneous. It's white sliced bread, with raisins and butter smeared across its surface. The bread is warm, but with no sign of being toasted. Possibly microwaved. He looks at the retreating server, at the counter staff, sees no evidence of irony or a practical joke. He takes a bite: it tastes like butter and raisins smeared on a slice of microwaved bread.

'You want to tell me about Bullshit Bob? You two looked pretty cosy last night,' she says.

Ivan can hear the accusatory tone. He lowers his bread. 'You know why.' He opens his iced coffee, takes a swig. 'I reckon Delaney Bullwinkel is attempting to swindle Bob Inglis. Jonas McGee worked it out, tried approaching Inglis and was killed by Claxton to shut him up.'

'You already suspected that.'

'I wanted to confirm it with Inglis.'

'And did you?'

'Not really. He's a cagey old bastard. He said it was possible.'

'And when were you going to tell me you were interviewing him?'

Ivan feels his irritation rising. It's his investigation, he's the lead investigator, he should be concentrating on Claxton, not answering her insinuations. But he doesn't want to leave on a sour note. 'This morning. Right now. If you want to know who controlled Claxton, Bullwinkel is still my best guess.'

But Nell looks in no way placated. 'I saw you here the other day. Tuesday. With Delaney Bullwinkel, the man himself.'

'My god, Nell. What are you implying?'

'That I don't know what's going on. That you're keeping me in the dark.'

'Bullwinkel was trying to snow me. That's what I think now. Pretending to be concerned about Stanley Honeywell, sacking Ray Penuch to show what a modern and enlightened employer he is.'

'And it wasn't worth telling me?'

'Look, I'm sorry. At the time, I thought it was inconsequential. I'm sure I would have told you, but by then things were a little messy.'

'You mean me and Topsoil? That sort of messy?' Now he can hear the seeds of anger in her voice, not just accusation.

'You and Topsoil, Feral Phelan arriving out of nowhere, me getting king-hit by your boyfriend. That sort of messy.'

'He's not my fucking boyfriend.'

Ivan is riled, thinking he should tell her plain and simple she is out of line. He's saved by the waitress, back to check on them. 'Everything okay?' she asks. 'Anything I can get you?'

'No. All good,' says Ivan.

'How's the raisin toast? Our own interpretation.'

Interpretation? What is this, *MasterChef*? 'Excellent,' he offers. 'Unique.'

Nell waits until the waitress has returned behind the counter before responding. 'Jesus, you're gutless. You can't even tell the waitress the truth.'

He stares at her, temperature escalating. And bursts out laughing. 'Yeah. You're right. It's shit raisin toast. *Guinness Book of Records* bad.' He can see the glimmer of a smile, and the effort she puts into suppressing it. 'Nell, listen.' And now his voice is calmer, non-confrontational. 'I'm the lead on this investigation; it's my responsibility. But when I get to Sydney, I will make it known far and wide that Merv Claxton is your bust. That it was your hard work, your intuition and your corroboration.'

'Right.'

'Now, can you give me a lift to the airport? I'm going to drop off my rental.'

'Sure,' she says. 'Sure.' But to his ears, she doesn't sound sure at all.

He leaves her there, together with his breakfast, and heads out to return the car. But when he emerges from the garage some minutes later, it's not Nell waiting, it's the probationary constable, Garry Ahern.

They drive to the airport. Ivan feels bad. The sense of anticipation he awoke with has deserted him. This should be a pivotal day: the arrest of Merv Claxton, the interrogation, laying the charge of murder. Justice for Jonas McGee, vindication for Ivan Lucic, absolution for Nell Buchanan. But he feels no elation. It should be her driving him to the plane; they should at least have the chance to settle any differences before he flies out. He likes her, admires her focus, her quick intelligence and her slow humour. Maybe more than he is willing to confess.

'You get pulled out early?' asks Garry. The tone suggests the young constable is just making small talk, feeling uncomfortable with Ivan's brooding. Yet Ivan can't help but feel there is some sly implication in the question, some second-hand observation the young constable has picked up on and is innocently repeating.

'No. The investigation is ongoing. I'm pursuing a strong lead in Sydney.'

'That's terrific,' gushes the young constable. 'Will you be back then?'

'Possibly. Depends on how it pans out.'

'I hope so,' says Garry. 'It's so good to have a couple of real detectives about the place.'

Ivan smiles, suspicions allayed, his mood lifted a little by the enthusiasm of the first-year constable.

The airport terminal is locked. The manager mustn't have been informed of the unscheduled PolAir flight. It's not too hot yet, but the wind is rising. Ivan wants to get inside, away from the dust. There's a notice in the window, a mobile number for the manager.

He calls it and the man answers. A minute later he appears, wearing a stained robe, thongs and a three-day growth.

'Morning,' is all he has to offer. He unlocks the door, enters, opens the door leading onto the tarmac, then shuffles away again without another word. Inside, the terminal is stuffy and airless.

Twenty minutes later, Ivan is inside, laptop out, working on the evidence against Claxton, working through potential lines of interrogation, when his phone rings. The screen gives the warning: it's coming from Homicide in Sydney.

'Ivan Lucic,' he answers, voice low and official.

'Morning, Sergeant. It's Dereck Packenham.'

'Sir?'

'Where are you, Ivan?'

'Finnigans Gap airport.'

'You haven't left yet?'

'Just waiting for the plane to arrive.'

'Well don't. Claxton is dead.'

Ivan says nothing. There is nothing to say. He stares at his laptop screen, the half-formed questions, the useless thoughts.

'Ivan? You still there?'

'What happened?'

'At first glance, it looks like an unintentional insulin overdose. Claxton was a diabetic. Insulin dependent.'

'At first glance?'

'Forensics have been tasked with going over it with everything they've got. Dying just a few hours before being arrested and charged with murder is just too much of a coincidence.'

'What are you thinking?' asks Ivan.

'More importantly, Sergeant, what are you thinking?'

'I agree. The coincidence is too great. It's possible he did it deliberately. Learnt that he was about to be arrested and took the easy way out. Or he was murdered to shut him up.'

'Easy to say, difficult to prove. You have any evidence to support that?'

'The manner of his death. As you know, we believe he killed Jonas McGee the same way: an insulin overdose.'

'So why would anyone use the same method to kill Claxton? A bit clumsy, surely?'

'To send us a message.'

The Homicide boss doesn't respond straight away. 'You're suggesting intimidation?'

'Or confidence. A sense of impunity.'

'Tell me what you know, Sergeant. What you suspect.'

'I have a working theory, sir, but now Claxton is dead, it will be hard to substantiate. He was the key.'

'You still think Claxton was working for Delaney Bullwinkel?'

'I do. And I suspect Bullwinkel ordered Claxton's death.'

There's a whistle at the other end of the phone, a small chuckle, dark humour. 'Shit a brick. What have you got on him?'

'Not a lot, sir. I told you how I thought Bullwinkel was scamming Inglis. I've been able to establish that Jonas McGee was aware the rare-earth mine was a con. Inglis thinks McGee may have tried to approach him, to warn him.' Even as he continues to explain, he's aware the theory is good, but the proof is thin. Paper thin.

The head of Homicide is no fool, picking up on the paucity of evidence straight away.

'So, is there any record that McGee approached Robert Inglis?'

'Not at this stage, sir. Inglis is checking with his people.'

'Did Delaney Bullwinkel own Kalingra or stand to benefit from the acquisition by Inglis?'

'We haven't been able to verify that, sir.'

'What, then?'

'We know that a man named Raymond Penuch, who was a bagman at Bullwinkel's coalmine up here, Cuttamulla, paid a machinery supplier to keep quiet about what was really happening with test drilling at Kalingra.'

'Is that it?'

'Pretty much.'

'And where is this bagman?'

Ivan swallows. The air is dry. 'I don't know his whereabouts. He was sacked this week for an unrelated incident.'

'So who's making this claim of hush money?'

'The machinery supplier. Name of Trevor Topsoil.'

'Is he credible?'

'No, sir.' Ivan explains that Topsoil is in the Lightning Ridge lock-up, charged with drug offences and awaiting a bail hearing.

'Hell, Ivan. You've got fuck-all.'

'That's why Claxton was so important.'

'Right. Any reason for you to come back here immediately?'

'No.'

'Agreed. I want you to stay there. If someone has taken out Claxton, whether it's Bullwinkel or anyone else, it's important that we aren't seen to be running up the white flag. Pursue this, Ivan.'

'Yes, sir. Thank you, sir.'

Another bitter chuckle. 'I'm not sure why you're thanking me. Without Claxton, it sounds like you're up shit creek.'

'We'll do our best, sir.'

'Very good. But listen, Ivan. Take care. And reach out if you need backup. If these people are prepared to take out a former cop like Claxton, they won't hesitate to kill a serving officer.'

'Sir.'

'And, Ivan? I probably don't need to tell you this, but any investigation of Bullwinkel must be by the book. Keep it discreet, tread carefully, record everything.'

'Understood, sir.' Ivan can feel the conversation coming to an end, takes the opportunity before it's too late. 'Sir, I should tell you that Professional Standards has been probing. Detective Sergeant Nathan Phelan has been here.'

'I am aware of that. I'm sorry, Sergeant, but there's not a lot I can do about it.'

The call ends and Ivan sits for a few minutes, thinking of possible options and coming up with precious little. He rings Blake Ness.

The pathologist answers on the third ring. 'Ivan. You still heading down?'

'Not much point now, is there?'

'No. Not really.'

'So you have the job? Investigating Claxton?'

'Yeah. Me and Carole and a cast of thousands. You have my word, if there is anything to be found, we'll find it.'

'Is there any doubt about his status as a diabetic?'

'None. Type two, but insulin dependent.'

'Time of death?'

'An hour either side of midnight.'

'Is that usual? Taking a shot at that time of night?'

'Not really, but it's not conclusive. Insulin use is determined by blood sugar, not the time of day. What he was eating, or intending to eat.'

'Which was what?'

'Haven't got to stomach contents yet. Carole's team is scouting out what he might have been intending to eat.'

'First impressions?'

'Highly fucking suspicious.'

'Blake, is there any way of making a match? The batch of insulin used to kill Jonas McGee and that which killed Claxton?'

'Sorry. Wouldn't think so. No.'

— —

Nell is in the detectives' room, feeling useless, a spare wheel. Ivan is on the plane to Sydney. That's where the action is: Merv Claxton. She feels flat. She should have driven him to the airport, parted on better terms. She feels a surge of antipathy towards Feral Phelan, getting into her skull, planting suspicions, seeding anxiety.

The phone rings. An officer out on the floor transfers it through.

'Detective Constable Narelle Buchanan.'

'I was hoping to talk to Detective Sergeant Ivan Lucic.'

'Sergeant Lucic is flying to Sydney. Can I help you?'

'You work with Sergeant Lucic?'

'That's correct.'

'My name is Mark Gavel, personal assistant to Robert Inglis. He has requested I pass on some information to Sergeant Lucic. May I send it to you instead?'

'Of course. I'll see it gets to him.'

The man asks for her email address. She supplies it, and Ivan's for good measure.

Shortly after the call has ended, the email arrives. The first thing she notices is the sender: a completely anonymous gmail address, just a series of random letters before @gmail.com. A one-off account. Untraceable. The subject line says *Kalingra*, and the body of the email simply says *attached*. There are three attachments, all pdf files.

She opens the first file. It's a company register for Kalingra Exploration Pty Ltd, the company that was owned by Phillip Smith, Neil Courters and Wanda Clark, similar to what she found on the ASIC website. It details the sale of the company and its assets three years ago, confirming what Courters told her from Fiji: the windfall offer of a million dollars each for him and his wife.

She clicks on the second pdf. It details the renaming of the company to Kalingra Rare Earths Pty Ltd and identifies its sole director: Trudy Lampsheet. Three years ago, two years after Ms Lampsheet retired and entered care, suffering from Alzheimer's.

She clicks on the third pdf. It's a contract, specifying the sale of land and assets to Bulldust Investments Pty Ltd for ten million dollars. The date of the transfer is today's date, with the transaction recorded as taking place at one minute past midnight. The principal officer of Bulldust Investments is listed as Robert John Inglis. So he went through with it, bought the mine despite Ivan's warning. She can't understand why. He really must be an obstinate old goat. And yet here he is helping them, sending the history of transactions, detailing how he bought a company fronted by a woman with advanced dementia, owned by untraceable offshore investors. It makes no sense.

Nell goes online, searching for news of the transaction. She finds a fresh report, posted just fifteen minutes ago. The *Financial Review* again. She reads it with astonishment, rereads it.

RARE EARTHS CARNAGE
By Larry Griggs

Shares in listed rare-earth miner LikeUs plummeted by a massive 25 per cent at the opening of the market Thursday, coming on top of a 10 per cent decline late Tuesday.

The company has issued a statement to the stock market, stating it is unaware of any factors that may have caused the sell-off. 'The fundamentals of our business remain robust and unchanged,' the statement reads.

Macquarie Bank analyst Ponton Lowe says LikeUs is attempting to calm the horses before panic selling can set in and algorithmic trading drives share prices even lower. 'This correction is long overdue and not unexpected. Shares in LikeUs have risen some 300 per cent over the past year. Those sort of increases are simply not sustainable over the long term.'

However, Mr Lowe says he is surprised by the severity and speed of the sell-off.

'A lot of speculators and day traders are taking profits while they can. The market has been ramped up by acquisition, largely driven by Bullshit Bob Inglis and his Wide Valley Resources. But news he has achieved a board position on LikeUs and is set to take control of his own venture in New South Wales, Kalingra Rare Earths, has investors believing his appetite has been sated.'

According to sources within the broking community, the sell-off is potentially disastrous for Mr Inglis, at least in the short term, with the value of his investments dropping by upwards of $100 million overnight.

Nell is wondering what all this means, when the door opens. It's Ivan Lucic, out of his suit and into street clothes. 'You're back,' is all she says.

'I am. Did you hear?'

'What?'

'Claxton is dead. Insulin overdose. Before they could arrest him.'

She can feel her eyes expand, her jaw drop. 'No way,' is all she can summon.

'He either suicided, or someone ordered him murdered.'

'Jesus. What now?'

'I spoke to Packenham. He wants us to press on. He's not happy about a homicide investigation being derailed.'

'How did they know that we were arresting him?'

'Someone must have talked.'

'Shit.'

Ivan sits and sighs. He unpacks his laptop and opens it, but he just stares at the computer screen and doesn't turn it on.

'Hey,' she says. 'I'm sorry. About this morning at the cafe. I shouldn't have said those things.'

'Don't worry about it.' And then he adds, 'I'm sorry too. I should have kept you in the loop. My discussions with Bullwinkel and Inglis.'

'Speaking of which, have you seen this?' She brings up the news story, the one detailing the fall in LikeUs shares.

Ivan scans it quickly. 'That's crazy,' he says. 'He's walked into it with his eyes wide open.' He rereads it. 'I told him last night. Warned him it was a scam. He still went through with it.'

'It's very fast,' says Nell. 'This sell-off. Abrupt.'

'Meaning?'

'It's almost like someone has been waiting to drive the price down.'

'You think? Is there any more?' He flicks his head at her monitor.

She runs another search, and sure enough there is. The *Sydney Morning Herald*, just ten minutes ago:

WIDE VALLEY SHARES CRASH
By James Zimmerman

Shares in Western Australian iron ore and copper miner Wide Valley Resources have fallen by almost 20 per cent in early trading as the market comes to terms with an unprecedented sell-off in the shares of rare-earth major LikeUs, now down almost 30 per cent this morning after a 10 per cent fall on Tuesday.

'The market is now anticipating Wide Valley's chairman and majority shareholder Bob Inglis will be forced into a significant selldown of his holdings to finance a recent spending spree that has seen him acquire a 13.5 per cent stake in LikeUs and complete a takeover of Kalingra Rare Earths,' Macquarie Bank analyst Ponton Lowe has told *The Age* and the *Sydney Morning Herald*.

Rumours are rife within financial circles that Mr Inglis, widely known as 'Bullshit Bob', is severely overextended and is now facing margin calls in a falling market.

A margin call occurs when a bank calls in a loan when the underlying assets, or collateral, fall below a certain level.

'If Inglis is forced to sell LikeUs and Wide Valley, then that could in turn force the market even lower, triggering fresh margin calls, catching Inglis in a vicious downward spiral,' explains Lowe. 'Should that happen, Inglis will almost certainly lose his board position at LikeUs and loosen his grip on Wide Valley, and it will cost him a good slice of his fortune. He's looking at losses of hundreds of millions of dollars. It's a bloodbath.'

Market insiders believe that Bob Inglis's balance sheet has been further weakened by the overnight purchase of an unproven rare-earth mine near Finnigans Gap, close to the New South Wales–Queensland border. It's believed the site cost in excess of $100 million, and will require three times that much again to become operational. Without access to the capital required to finance it, the mine is in danger of becoming a white elephant.

Nine Newspapers are seeking comment from Mr Inglis.

Nell finishes reading first, scrutinises Ivan's face as he completes the article, his face a study in concentration. 'It's not true,' she says as his eyes leave the screen and meet hers.

'What bit?'

'I established the chain of ownership. Inglis paid ten million for Kalingra, not more than one hundred million.'

'How did you work that out?'

'Inglis's office. They sent the sale documents through. It was definitely ten million.'

'So where does the hundred million dollars come from?'

'Fake news,' says Nell. 'Someone backgrounding the journos in order to accelerate the sell-off.'

'Fuck, you really are clever,' says Ivan. 'C'mon. Let's go.'

'Where?'

'To find Bullshit Bob. To find out what this bullshit is all about.'

But they're too late. By the time they get to the motel, the mining magnate has checked out. Gone.

'What now?' asks Nell.

'Look,' says Ivan, pointing skywards. She follows the trajectory of his arm: a jet, coming in low and at speed. 'Let's go. Before he gets away.'

Nell doesn't hesitate. She runs to the Nissan, has the engine fired up by the time Ivan makes it into the passenger seat, is accelerating fiercely even as he struggles to buckle his seatbelt. She has the lights flashing, the siren blaring, pushing the big car into and out of the crossroads roundabout at alarming speed, Ivan hanging on to the Jesus handle with grim intensity.

They arrive at the airport even as the jet is taxiing to a stop on the tarmac. The airport manager, still dressed in his bathrobe and sandals, is opening the gate to let a couple of four-wheel drives out onto the airfield. Nell gets the car there first, coming in to stop between them and the opening gate, blocking their access. Only as she stops does she recognise her mistake. The two cars: white Range Rovers.

'Ivan, it's not Inglis. It's Delaney Bullwinkel.'

He stares at her for just a moment, those intense blue eyes. She feels them run over her face, knows now that he isn't even looking at her, that his mind is elsewhere. 'Even better,' he says. 'Come on. Let's put the wind up the bastard.'

--

When they get out of the car Delaney Bullwinkel is standing with his lawyer, Cyril Flange, by his side. Bullwinkel has ditched the casual wear and is dressed for the city, while Flange looks like an advertisement for lightweight wool. They look unbothered and confident; Ivan feels woefully unprepared.

'Fancy seeing you here,' says Bullwinkel over the pitch of the jet engines, as if being cut off by a police car—tyres squealing, lights flashing and siren sounding—is an everyday occurrence. 'I'm in a bit of a hurry. Busy day. How can I help you?'

'We're looking for Ray Penuch. Can you tell me where to find him?'

Bullwinkel smiles, taunting: *Is that all you've got?* 'No, I can't. The man is a disgrace and no longer an employee of Cuttamulla Coal. Cyril, do we have a forwarding address?'

'I can certainly check,' says the lawyer, his own smile reptilian.

'Are you selling off shares in LikeUs?'

Bullwinkel gives a grim little smile. 'Walk with me, will you? Hand your phone to Cyril first.' To Nell he says, 'Sorry. Just the detective sergeant. You can move your car.'

Ivan looks at Nell. He can see she's looking on with eyes full of doubt, knows how she feels about him dealing with these moguls, but he figures if the coal baron wants to talk in confidence, she'll just have to wear it. He can square it with her later. He hands the phone to the lawyer.

Bullwinkel walks off, Ivan following. The billionaire stops halfway between the cars and the planes. The jet engines are idling, but generating enough noise that Ivan has to strain to hear Bullwinkel. Even if he had his phone, even if he was wearing a wire, it's unlikely any recording would work. Bullwinkel speaks clearly, but he isn't about to shout, forcing Ivan to lean in, close enough to smell the man's cologne, mingled with avgas and dust.

'I wish you well with your investigation, Ivan, but there is no connection to me, my companies or our financial transactions.'

'Are you selling off LikeUs?' Ivan repeats the question, anger growing.

'I am. I am in the process of completely ratfucking Bullshit Bob Inglis. He will be rooted, good and proper. But that is no concern of yours.'

'You're behind Kalingra. The scam. You can't expect to get away with that.'

'I have never had any financial interest in Kalingra, and I will instigate defamation proceedings against anyone who suggests it.'

'Why would that be defamatory?'

'Because the mine is worthless and Bullshit Bob has been conned.'

'I think ASIC will want to investigate, don't you? I might give them a call.'

Bullwinkel smiles. 'No, you won't. Wouldn't matter if you did; there's nothing for them to find. But my advice? Don't mess with things you don't understand, okay? You don't want to end up like Morris Montifore.'

'What does that mean?'

'Work it out, genius.' Bullwinkel smiles, extends his hand, offering to shake Ivan's. Ivan declines; Bullwinkel's smile remains unaffected. 'Now I really must get going. And, Ivan, just to show there are no hard feelings: wait until Tuesday morning, then start buying Wide Valley. They'll be falling until then. Plummeting. After that, I suspect the shares are in for a bit of a run. My guess would be sometime Wednesday afternoon.'

And with that, Bullwinkel removes himself, climbs the stairs of his corporate jet, even as the Range Rovers ease to a stop beside the plane and flunkies start unloading bags. An entourage of staff, led by Cyril Flange, make their way towards the plane. There is nothing left for Ivan to do but accept his phone back from the lawyer. He sorely wants to arrest Bullwinkel, charge him with attempting to bribe a police officer. He knows exactly where that would get him.

Nell pulls up in the police car. He shakes his head, climbs into the passenger seat.

She drives them back through the gate. 'Didn't go well then?' she says.

'You might say that.' He remembers the awkwardness between them at the cafe, decides he needs to confide. 'He threatened me and tried to bribe me.'

She cracks a smile; it looks forced. 'So nothing useful?'

He shrugs. 'He admitted he was behind the stock market sell-off, but denied any involvement with the Kalingra con.'

'What was the threat? End up like Claxton?'

'No. End up like Morris Montifore.'

'Jesus. What do we do now?'

'Hang on,' says Ivan. Someone has opened the door of the terminal and is waving to them. 'Who's that?'

Nell squints. 'Bullshit Bob.'

chapter twenty-eight

FOR A MAN HAEMORRHAGING MILLIONS, BULLSHIT BOB INGLIS APPEARS CHIPPER, bouncing from one foot to the other with barely concealed energy. He hurries them into the terminal, where his team appears to have taken over. There's about six of them, all on laptops, all huddled.

'So you've seen the bastard off then?'

Ivan and Nell look about, see the team, feel the electricity in the air.

'What's going on?' asks Ivan.

'Let's sit over there, by the windows,' says Inglis. 'Let my people work. They've got a lot on.'

They take a seat amid the rows of terminal chairs. Inglis sits with his back to the floor-to-ceiling window, as if to show his contempt for Bullwinkel's Learjet and the twin Range Rovers. Ivan and Nell sit opposite him. The big man looks solid, backlit by the glare and heat haze of the tarmac. Behind him, the Range

Rovers are coming off the runway and the plane is starting its taxi.

'This is my colleague, Detective Constable Narelle Buchanan,' says Ivan.

'Good to meet you, Nell. Didn't realise the thin blue line was blessed with such lookers.'

Ivan can feel Nell bristle and quickly moves the conversation on. 'You seem very relaxed. We're reading stock market reports that you're losing your shirt.'

'True. Tens of millions, maybe hundreds of millions of dollars,' says Inglis, face serious but eyes twinkling. He winks at Nell. 'Bullwinkel is shorting me for all he's worth. LikeUs and Wide Valley both. He'd be shorting Kalingra if it was listed.'

'You went ahead with the purchase of Kalingra,' states Ivan. 'You got the documents?'

'Yes, thank you,' says Nell.

'Ten million dollars. Bargain of the century,' Inglis says with a grin, clearly enjoying himself. Then, like the turning of a switch, he becomes serious. The bonhomie disappears and Ivan can see the steel in the man's face, the hardness in eyes that no longer twinkle. Ivan gets the sense he's seeing the real man for the first time. Through the window, the Learjet has reached the end of the runway and has turned into the wind.

'Do you understand what shorting is? On the stock market?' asks Inglis.

It's Nell who answers. 'You make money when the price of shares fall.'

'Correct,' says Inglis. 'But do you know the mechanics of it?'

'Why don't you tell us?' says Nell.

Ivan can hear the slightest niggle in her voice, but Inglis seems oblivious.

'It works like this. Say, for example, I think the shares in a particular company are going to lose value. I borrow a million shares for a month and immediately sell them on market, let's say for ten dollars each. So that's ten million in the back pocket. And with a bit of luck, merely by selling them, it might have helped the price come off. Depends on the size of the company. But at the end of the month, I have to return the shares. So I buy back the million shares on market, but by now the price has fallen to eight dollars a share. I pay eight million dollars, return the shares and pocket two million. All for a month's work—if you can call that work.'

'Why would anyone lend you shares like that?' asks Ivan.

'Well, people say lend and borrow, but of course it's a commercial arrangement; you pay for them. It's more like you're renting the shares for a month, or whatever the time period is. Longer the period, higher the rent.'

'People do that, rent out their shares?'

'Sure,' says Inglis. 'The big investment funds, superannuation and the rest, they hold investments for the long term, for decades. Shares in the big banks, the big miners, the big industrials. For them, it's easy money. Another revenue source.'

'Low risk for them,' Nell summarises, 'but dicey for those doing the shorting.'

'Sure can be,' says Inglis. 'But the potential for gain is enormous. That two-million-dollar profit I mentioned? That's not made from an outlay of eight million dollars or ten million dollars. It's generated off the amount the shorter paid to rent the million shares.

So if they paid a hundred thousand dollars, that's a profit of two thousand per cent in a month. Understand?'

Ivan isn't so sure of the arithmetic, but Nell looks like she's across it. 'But it could just as easily go the other way, right? If the shares rise in value, say to twelve dollars, the shorter would need to buy them back on market and lose two million dollars. That's a loss of two thousand per cent.'

Inglis's blue eyes are twinkling once more. 'Brains as well as beauty,' he says. 'You're correct. That's why shorting is the province of hedge funds, running multiple shorts balanced by other strategies, assisted by computer-generated models and algorithmic trading. And, many would argue, market manipulation, intervening to make sure the shares fall. One entity selling to an associated entity, forcing the price down, that sort of thing.'

'Isn't that illegal?' asks Nell.

'Yes. But almost impossible for the regulator to establish, let alone prove.'

'So why are you so relaxed?' asks Nell, cutting to the chase. 'The way we see it, you've bought a useless rare-earth mine, and Delaney Bullwinkel is destroying your fortune through shorting. You even risk losing control of Wide Valley Resources.'

'That's a fair summary of what's happening.' Now he's rubbing his hands together gleefully. 'Or what that bastard Bullwinkel *thinks* is happening. What he is trying to *make* happen.'

'And what's your perspective?' asks Ivan.

'Well, he is most certainly shorting both LikeUs and Wide Valley, and manipulating the market down to maximise his profit. But you have to ask yourself this question: where is he renting the shares from? He thinks it's a collection of superannuation funds and the like.' And he smiles a wicked smile.

'He's renting them from you?'

'Yes, he is.' Inglis grins.

Nell is frowning, shaking her head. 'But that would be chicken-feed compared to what you're losing. Way less than one per cent, surely.'

'Yes. Just a side hustle, a little light entertainment.'

'A side hustle to what?' asks Ivan, starting to feel irritated by the magnate's glee.

Perhaps Inglis picks up on it, again turning off the twinkle and bringing back the steel. Outside, Bullwinkel's jet is accelerating down the runway. 'As the entity renting shares to Bullwinkel, I know when the shares need to be returned. I expect by that time, the price of both companies may well have been halved. But—and it's a very big but—shortly before that, when he has sold almost all his holdings and is moving to buy the shares back, I will make an announcement to the market.' He leaves a theatrical pause, knowing they must respond. In the distance, Bullwinkel's jet becomes airborne.

'Announcing what?'

'That I have found an investor for my holding in LikeUs. It's a very sizable holding, you realise. A very strategic holding in a producer of very strategic metals. I have a real investor, not like those actors from Hong Kong Bullwinkel had parading about in their crass limousine. A real investor, from the United States, with the backing of the CIA, the Pentagon and the State Department, keen on balancing the Chinese domination of rare earths. And paying me a very large amount of money to do so, at a price that's already above where the market sits today. The share price of LikeUs will rebound, most likely to record levels.'

'Bullwinkel will need to buy the shares back on market,' observes Nell.

'And the renter is not about to cut him any slack,' adds Ivan.

'Precisely,' enthuses Inglis.

'Jesus,' says Nell. 'How much will he lose?'

'Hundreds of millions of dollars. Won't know what hit him.'

'So, you'll be out of LikeUs with a huge profit, Wide Valley will be secure, and Bullwinkel will be struggling for years,' says Nell.

'I won't give him years. I'll have a war chest, thanks to the Yanks, and he'll be wounded. I'll launch a hostile takeover for Cuttamulla.'

Ivan and Nell say nothing, not knowing what to say.

'Not that I'm interested in coal. That's the past; I'm looking to the future. As soon as I control Cuttamulla, I'll sell it on.'

'So the whole purpose is to screw Bullwinkel?'

'Correct. And to fund my next stage of development and growth.' He's turned serious again, the mercurial switching of personas. 'Don't feel sorry for him. He deserves everything he gets.'

'So that's why you went ahead with Kalingra, even knowing it's worthless. You didn't want him to suspect that you were on to him.'

And now, just like that, the twinkle is back, but Ivan can see the accumulated malice underneath, Inglis's detestation of Bullwinkel. 'That's true. But make no mistake, I want Kalingra for itself.'

'But it's worthless,' says Ivan. 'The drilling assays are fraudulent.'

'Yes. Concocted by Bullwinkel.' And he smiles, leaving room for their next inquiry.

Ivan racks his brain, but can't see where this is going. He looks at Nell, but she looks just as flummoxed.

'Can you explain it for us, please?' she asks, seemingly over any offence the miner has caused her.

'This is the good bit,' says Bullshit Bob. 'The Kalingra scam is a paper fraud. It's all based around fabricated documentation—the ones you seem to have discovered, Ivan. But Bullwinkel forgot one thing: long before I was a businessman, long before the boardrooms and the banks, I was a geologist. I'd go out there, camping in the middle of nowhere, getting my hands dirty. I was the one who identified the deposits at Wide Valley, who saw the potential. He was only ever a backroom boy, a financier, a paper shuffler.'

The contempt that Inglis distils into the word 'financier' almost makes Ivan smile.

'There are no minerals of value at Kalingra. Not rare earths or anything else. But it's the only piece of high ground anywhere near Lake Kalingra. Flood proof. With a supply of permanent water. Artesian water. The dam there is always full. Unlimited. It will be easy enough to run power from the grid along the West Ridge and down to the site, although we'll be generating plenty of solar and wind. The end of the West Ridge is perfect for wind; the whole place is good for solar.' Outside, Bullwinkel's jet is just a dot on the horizon. 'I've staked a mining claim for the whole of Lake Kalingra. I just want the rare-earth site to build a processing plant.'

'The lake?'

'The lake. You've seen the surrounding plain, how green it is after all this rain, but the lake bed itself remains dead.'

'It's full of salt,' says Nell.

'And the salt is full of lithium. Potentially worth a couple of billion.'

'Lithium?' asks Ivan.

'Batteries,' Nell says. 'Everything from mobile phones to electric cars to home solar to grid batteries.' She turns to Inglis. 'Right?'

'On the money.'

'Wow,' she says, voice now full of admiration. 'Wow. So you get to keep Wide Valley, you sell out of LikeUs at a massive profit, you destroy Bullwinkel, *and* you have all the money you need to develop a lithium mine at Kalingra,' she summarises.

'It's locked in.'

'Why tell us? Isn't that a risk? We could tell Bullwinkel.'

'I don't think you will,' says Inglis, again serious. 'He ordered the execution of your opal miner, Jonas McGee. You know that now. If you help him, you betray everything you stand for.'

Ivan is motionless. Beside him, Nell is still, her mouth drawn and grim.

'Listen,' says Inglis, 'I heard what happened to the driver. Claxton. Assassinated. I don't need to tell you who ordered it. Bullwinkel has blood on his hands. But it's all at arm's length, you'll never get close enough to prosecute, to build a case against him. I swear, if I could help you get that evidence, I would. I'd love to see the little fucker in prison. But I just can't see it happening.'

'What are you saying?' asks Nell.

'I'm saying this is as close as you're likely to get to justice. You can witness his demise and draw whatever satisfaction you can from that.'

And now there really is nothing more for Ivan and Nell to say.

Inglis considers them soberly, perhaps understanding their discomfort.

'The price of LikeUs will dip for another two weeks or so, before massively rebounding when I announce the sale to the Yanks.'

But Ivan is shaking his head, and beside him Nell Buchanan is doing the same.

— —

Nell sits in the four-wheel drive, staring out the windscreen. The windows are up, the air-conditioning on, the outside temperature rising. In the passenger seat, Ivan is silent. They watch as Bullshit Bob Inglis's Cessna Citation comes in to land. She wonders if it's been up there the whole time, circling over the horizon, waiting for Delaney Bullwinkel to leave. Probably. It swoops in, fast and sleek and kick-arse, landing on the airstrip built and maintained by Cuttamulla Coal. She can only imagine the satisfaction that must give Bullshit Bob Inglis.

And now the man himself and his entourage are walking out across the tarmac, the big man walking among his staff, a spring in his stride. The four-wheel truck from Kalingra Rare Earths has arrived from somewhere to ferry their equipment to the plane. They get in, the roar of the engines intensifies and the plane moves off, taxis to the far end of the airstrip as if savouring the moment, then accelerates down the runway, lifts its nose and climbs into the air, turning as it does so, heading west towards Perth. Soon it is nothing more than a speck, and then it's gone altogether.

'I feel dirty,' says Nell.

Ivan reaches across, places his hand on hers, just for a moment. That same touch. 'We've done nothing wrong.'

'Don't,' she says, withdrawing her hand, then sighing. 'Do you think we helped him? Inglis?'

'By distracting Bullwinkel? Maybe. But we weren't the ones who killed McGee and Claxton.'

'Do you think he's right? That we'll never get the evidence we need to go after Bullwinkel?'

'Maybe. Probably.'

And they sit there for minutes longer, with nothing to see, nothing to say, nothing to do, watching as the airport manager shuffles past, locking the terminal, closing the gate.

And then Nell's phone rings and suddenly there is too much to say, too much to do.

chapter twenty-nine

IT'S GARRY, VOICE URGENT AND TREMBLING. 'THERE'S A GUNMAN. WE NEED backup.' Nell can hear the rumble of a car; Garry is on the move.

'Where are you? Where's the shooter?'

'I'm with Scaley. We're heading up onto the East Ridge. There's someone with a gun at the Rapture. Shooting. That's all we know.'

'Where's the sarge and Vince?'

'Lightning Ridge.'

'Shit. Okay. We're on our way. You call Lightning Ridge, I'll call Bourke.'

She looks at Ivan; she can see the word 'shooter' has seized his attention. 'Up at the Rapture. Garry and Richter are on their way. I'll drive. Can you call Bourke?'

'Will do.'

Nell fires the engine, gets the siren and lights going, mind racing ahead even faster than the car as she speeds back along the airport road towards town.

Beside her, Ivan ends his call to Bourke. 'They're on their way,' he says. 'Two hours, more like two and a half.'

'Might be all over by then,' she says.

'Let's hope not.'

She knows what he's saying: it's unlikely to end quickly without people dying. The best outcome would be to stabilise the situation, negotiate a surrender. That takes time. Garry said that there was shooting, not just a man with a gun. Her stomach turns. Ivan is on the phone again, alerting Sydney, assuring them he'll get back to them as soon as he's onsite, as soon as he can assess the situation. If it's bad, if there is still gunfire, or if it's a siege, the tactical response team will be in the air within the hour. They might even be on their way to the airport now, preparing to fly, awaiting his word. There's a chance they'll beat Bourke here, but it will still be at least two hours.

So for at least an hour it will be just the four of them: Richter, Garry, Ivan and her, until Lightning Ridge can get here.

'You armed?' she asks.

'Yes. You?'

'In the back. And my tactical vest.'

'Good.'

She's through the crossroads, winding up The Way. Her phone rings; Ivan takes it. It must be Garry. She can't hear what he says, only Ivan's response. 'We're just heading up onto the ridge. Fifteen minutes tops. I've alerted Sydney.' He ends the call, turns to her. 'It's bad. More firing. Probably people dead. Garry says take it easy when we get close. They're under fire. We'll be a target.' And then he's back on his phone to Sydney. 'Yeah. Send them. There's a gunman in there, others returning fire. A regular shootout.'

She glances across, sees her own fear mirrored in his face. They're racing into a gunfight armed with handguns and one lightweight armoured vest. He's staring at his phone, call finished, as if struggling to comprehend his own words. She tries to remember her basic training in the academy, the refresher courses. She recalls the overarching rule: *Don't get killed; don't endanger yourself, don't endanger fellow officers, don't endanger the public.* And, of course, the other rule: *If you shoot, shoot to kill. Central body mass.*

They roar past the corrugated-iron church, spraying tourist cars with pebbles, get to Deadmans Well, head right at the fork. As The Way fractures further, so does the quality of the road. She loses the back end, corrects, almost careers off the road, back sliding out the other way, corrects again just in time, wonders why she is going so fast, driving so quickly into danger. Because Garry is there, and Carl Richter, and innocent people. She doesn't ease off the accelerator.

'Slow down, Nell. We're getting within range.'

He's right. They round a curve, come over a slight rise, and there are people on the road, like refugees in a war zone. She brakes, sounding the horn, sliding to a stop. She has the door open.

'Down there, at the Rapture,' says a young man, breathing hard, blood smeared on his face. 'Inside the Seer's house. A lunatic. He's shooting.'

'Who is it? Who's the gunman?' demands Nell.

'Not one of ours. A miner. People are dead. Others sheltering—trapped—in the dorms.'

'Okay. Get to Deadmans. Take refuge there.'

And she closes the door, trades a grimace of disbelief with Ivan. He has his Glock out, checking the magazine. She drives on. Another two minutes and she can see the gates to the compound, Richter's car pulled up to one side, Garry crouched behind it, service pistol in his hand. She pulls in hard behind him, is about to speak when the windscreen explodes. She has her door open before she can think, launching herself out, can sense Ivan scrambling after her, out of the vehicle and into the dirt. He lands half on top of her as they put the car between them and the compound.

'You good?' he asks.

'Yeah. But my gun's in the back.'

'Leave it for now.' Ivan is up, running in a crouch behind the vehicles, his own gun out. Like a movie, she thinks. Like a fucking movie. She scrambles after him as he joins Garry.

'Thank God you're here,' says the probationary constable, eyes aghast and staring.

— —

Ivan looks into the young man's face, sees the panic rising, the effort to understand, the struggle to remain composed. He knows he can't afford to show his own weakness, his own fear. When he speaks, his voice sounds calm, measured, his hand coming to rest on the youngster's shoulder. 'It's okay, mate. Is your safety on?'

Garry looks at the pistol in his hand, as if he's forgotten he's holding it. 'Shit.' He re-engages the safety.

'Where's Scaley?' asks Nell.

'Out there,' says Garry, and the words put a tremble through him. 'Shot.'

'Jesus,' says Nell. 'Alive?'

'Yes, but he's bleeding bad. Shot in the leg. Near that fountain. He'll know you're here.'

Now Ivan understands why the young man is in danger of losing it. 'So he has cover?'

'Yeah, he does now. He walked out there, arms up, gun stowed. Trying to talk them down. And that mad fucker shot him.'

'Who? The Seer?'

And now the panic is close to the surface, threatening to overwhelm him, Garry's voice rising. 'He's shot! He's out there! Bleeding. We can't get to him, we can't help him.'

'Okay, mate. Not your fault. Got that? Not your fault.' Ivan lets the words penetrate. 'Now, settle down. I need you calm and collected. Carl Richter needs you calm and collected.'

That seems to do the trick. Garry eases back from the brink, swallows. 'Yes, sir.'

'Who has the gun, mate? Who is it?'

'Buddy Torshack. He's got a rifle, possibly a shotgun as well. He's in the house. He's yelling that he wants the Seer. If he doesn't get him, he'll shoot more people.'

'Buddy Torshack? You sure?'

'Saw him with my own eyes.'

Ivan looks to Nell, sees the reflection of his own surprise and lack of comprehension. Buddy Torshack at the Rapture, turned homicidal. Why?

It's Nell who returns first to the task at hand. 'More? You said more. How many has he shot?'

'Don't know. But some, for sure. There were people sheltering here with us, trying to get away, out of the line of fire. Scaley sent them out of here, running.'

'How?'

'Me and Scaley, we opened up. Covering fire. They ran.'

'Good work. We saw them on the road. They're safe.'

'There are more, over on the other side there. In the bunkhouse. They fired too, forced Torshack back into the house. They've got at least one gun. They know we're here.'

Ivan sums up the situation, taking a quick glance through the vehicle's windows, remembering the layout of the compound from his visit. He questions Garry, establishes that Torshack appears to be barricaded inside the grand house, the McMansion at the far left of the semicircle of buildings, that others are trapped in the dorm building, separated from the house by the church and hall. It's not clear where the Seer is, but he's not in the house; most likely he's sheltering in the bunkhouse. And at least one person has a gun in there, meaning Torshack can't just walk across the open ground. So it's a stalemate, a three-sided one. If anyone moves into open ground, they're going to get shot.

'Garry, is it just Torshack shooting at us from the house? Or are we getting targeted from the dorms as well?'

'Just the house,' says Garry.

'Right, here's what we do,' says Ivan. 'Our first priority is to get Richter out of there, without getting shot ourselves. After that, it sounds like a hostage situation. We try to calm it down, wait for reinforcements.'

Nell nods, Garry nods. He's about to speak again when another shot breaks through the wind. There's nothing to indicate where it's come from, what it signifies, until, many seconds later, a long, wailing cry comes from the house. Jesus. He knows that cry. It's not one of fear or terror or even pain; it's one of grief, of despair.

People are dying here, and the police are powerless. Two hours before Bourke and Sydney get here, almost an hour for Lightning Ridge. Hopefully they'll have superior body armour and rifles, but that's not going to advance things much. They need the professionals, with the full kit, and the trained negotiators. But they're too far away, the situation is too volatile. This will be over long before that.

'Fuck me,' says Garry. 'Behind us. Look.'

Ivan looks. And can't believe what he sees. For careering along the road towards them, trailing dust and spewing black smoke, emitting a roar like a dinosaur on heat, comes the armoured personnel carrier from Deadmans Well, dragging a clothes line and tarpaulin, the barbecue still welded to its side.

'Holy shit,' says Nell.

'The cavalry,' says Ivan, startled at the absurdity of his own comment.

Buddy Torshack has seen it as well, and bullets start rifling past them, filling the air with the keening of ricochets as the bullets rebound from the APC's steel plates. The engine might be old, but the armour is still good. The three police officers cower, even as the carrier comes to a standstill beside them, facing the compound. The back door opens, and out comes the mayor, wearing a blue frock and a flak jacket, followed by a woman, packing twin revolvers in holsters, like Lara Croft with a pot belly, then Stanley Honeywell, brandishing what appears to be a grenade launcher. Last out, wearing jeans and a black singlet, the only half-normal-looking one among them, comes Holgate, carrying a hunting rifle, complete with scopes. Ivan recognises it: the real deal. And he sees the tattoo he missed the first time around, the insignia.

'Tell me,' he says to Holgate.

'Commandoes,' says the man. 'Sniper.'

'You up for this?'

'Yeah, I'm up for this. But I need to get set, find a stable base. The range is a piece of piss, but the wind is a nightmare.'

'Meaning?'

'If the target's in the open, even if they're not, if there's a clean shot, I can take them. But if they're with others, hostages, using them as shields, it's no go. Too risky.'

'How long since you fired that thing?' asks Nell.

'Years. Not something I'm fond of,' replies Holgate, voice steady, eyes challenging. 'But not something you forget.'

'We believe the shooter is a man called Buddy Torshack, probably working alone. You know him?'

'Yeah, I know him.'

Ivan looks Holgate in the eye. 'You do not have the authority to shoot him. You got that? Not unless it is to save your own life or the lives of others.'

'Fine by me,' says Holgate, voice firm and eyes steady. Ivan realises with silent gratitude that the man is solid.

Ivan looks at Stanley, cradling the grenade launcher. 'What the fuck is that?' he asks the mayor.

'RPG,' says the mayor, flashing an opal-toothed smile. 'Bought it for shits and giggles. Took out a few fast-food billboards one night outside Moree. Don't know if it still works.'

'Okay. We're not using it,' says Ivan. 'Too dangerous. Too many innocents about.' He turns to Stanley. 'You got that, Stanley?'

The big man nods, eyes like saucers.

'We brought this along,' says the woman, indicating her shopping bag. 'It's a drone. We can send it up high, get the lay of the land.'

'Or send it in low,' says Nell. 'Get a message to the others, the ones sheltering in the bunkhouse. Give them our phone numbers.'

Ivan looks about him, feels all the eyes on him. He realises that they're deferring to him, even the mayor, even the former commando, that he is the leader, by virtue of his rank, his position. He represents the law, like some Wild West marshal with a thin tin badge. He regards the woman. 'Who are you?'

'Lydia. Mayor's wife.'

'Right.' He looks at the bag in her hand. 'How much charge has it got? How long can you keep it in the air?'

'Twenty minutes.'

'How do you control it?'

'Smartphone. Records vision on board, but you can see what it sees on the phone screen.'

'Excellent. So here is what we'll do. Lydia: stay here with us, get the drone set up. Holgate, you get ready to fire. Doesn't have to be perfect. The bonnet of one of these cars. When we're ready, I want the drone up, buzzing the house. Try and draw fire from Torshack. Holgate, prepare to put a few rounds in close to him. Suppressing fire. Above head height. The mayor and I will take the armoured car. We need to drive it in there, get Richter out. We need to coordinate it, get Torshack off guard, so his focus is on us, and he doesn't simply start threatening hostages, or worse.'

He looks them in the eye, one by one, as they reach unspoken agreement. Lydia gets to work setting up the drone, attaching propellers, hooking her phone up to the machine's controller.

Holgate is loading the gun, laying out ammunition, attaching a lightweight tripod. But before they are ready, two things happen rapidly, one after the other. First, a car comes rocketing over the rise from the direction of The Way, a sedan, travelling fast, dust billowing. Then, from the compound, a shot, followed by another.

Holgate is on to it: he stands behind the bonnet of the police car, lifts the rifle to his shoulder and fires twice in quick succession. The shooting from the house stops long enough for the car to reach them in safety. Ivan can see its windscreen has been shot out; Buddy Torshack isn't messing about. Out from the side door comes Elsie McGee, tears in her eyes and anguish on her face as she crouches low and runs to them.

'You should not be here,' says Ivan angrily. 'You cannot help.'

She ignores the admonishment. 'Is it true? It's Buddy Torshack?'

'Yes. It's true.'

'I can talk to him,' she says. 'Calm him down.'

'No, you can't,' says Ivan. 'There's a policeman lying seriously wounded out there. He was shot trying to do just that.'

Elsie says nothing, but the words have stopped her. She looks around as if seeking an answer and finding none.

'Hey. Over here! Over here!' The voice comes, urgent and cracking.

'Shit. It's Scaley,' says Nell.

'Fuck, look at this,' says Holgate.

Ivan raises his head once more, peering through the windows of the police car, signalling everyone else to stay low. What he sees fills him with dread. A door in the dorm building has opened and, with an armed man on either side, the Seer emerges, dressed in long flowing robes, white, like a prophet from central casting. His hands are held high, his eyes to the heavens, his voice beseeching holy intervention.

'Torshack will kill him,' says Holgate. 'I can't stop it.'

And yet there is no firing. The Seer starts walking into the centre of the compound, chanting as he goes. And out from the house comes Buddy Torshack, armed with a shotgun.

'He wants it up close and personal,' states Holgate.

'If he brings the gun to bear, shoot him,' says Ivan.

'Will do,' says Holgate grimly.

The inevitable starts to unfold in slow motion, the scene scripted, the players unable to change what is about to happen. Lydia looks at her half-constructed drone, knowing there's no more time; the mayor looks longingly at the troop carrier, as if wishing he could somehow intervene; Stanley looks distressed, still holding the RPG. Ivan too watches it unfold, Buddy smiling as he walks towards the self-proclaimed holy man, coming to a standstill, starting to raise his gun.

'Fuck, no,' swears Holgate.

'What?' demands Ivan.

'Jammed. The fucking thing is jammed,' says the former commando, dropping into a crouch, starting to strip the weapon.

Ivan stands, gun in hand, knowing he's going to have to go out there, do what he can.

But he's too slow, a step behind. Elsie McGee is ahead of him, running out into the compound, into the line of fire, yelling as she goes. 'Buddy! No! Don't! Don't do it!'

It's enough to distract the gunman's attention. He delays, looking at her. Sneering at her, 'Why the fuck not?'

'I need his marrow. I need to suck out his fucking bone marrow!'

Ivan realises his mouth is open. He looks at Nell. She returns his stare; he can see her struggling to grasp the implications. Bone marrow. His mind flickers and shunts an image into his consciousness: the porno at Kalingra, the Seer in rut. He must be the father, the father of Bess. Her last hope.

Buddy starts laughing. Like it's a mad joke, as if the world is a mad joke. 'You can die as well then, you bitch.'

Ivan looks to Holgate, who's starting to reconstruct the rifle.

And now, out from behind the vehicles, steps Stanley Honeywell, grenade launcher mounted on his shoulder, walking calmly out into no-man's-land, moving slowly, as if he realises how important every second is. He walks towards the woman he once piggybacked around her home, the young girl who made him a birthday card, who brought light and joy into his damaged world. Torshack lets him come, as if to savour the moment. The gunman sidles sideways, putting himself behind the Seer and Elsie, denying Holgate a clear line of fire.

'Let's go. The APC. Let's get in amongst it,' says the mayor to Ivan, adding without irony: 'You're shotgun.'

But it's too late; it's all too late.

There's a blast, gunfire. One shot. And Stanley Honeywell falls, silently. Torshack steps sideways, bringing the gun to bear on Elsie, his second shot. Even from this distance, Ivan can see he is smirking.

But before the shotgun can speak again, there is a cracking retort next to Ivan. Holgate. Buddy is stopped dead. Ivan is sure he's heard the bullet thwapping into the miner's chest. Holgate fires again. Buddy Torshack crumples and falls.

He's dead; it's over.

For a moment, no one speaks, no one moves. There's just the wind, the Seer spewing incantations to the heavens, and keening coming from the house.

Ivan looks skywards. Up above them all, carving through the blue dome at altitude, a corporate jet is marking its presence with a long thin vapour trail. Like a dog pissing on a tree.

chapter thirty

IVAN FINDS KYLE TORSHACK UP AT THE TURNING CIRCLE AT THE FAR END OF the West Ridge. The youth is sitting, smoking a roll-your-own cigarette, looking out over Lake Kalingra, dressed in a t-shirt and jeans and work boots, his hat beside him. It's late in the day, the sun hovering above the horizon, the view astounding. As the clouds above the sunset glow with pink and orange, mauve and yellow, the salt reflects it back, so the earth and the sky are united in colour. A few last birds take to the air. There is so little water left now, the lake is almost empty, the drought reasserting its dominance, returning the expanse to salt.

The young man hardly seems to notice as Ivan sits down next to him; he gives just the slightest tip of the head, the barest acknowledgement. They sit unspeaking for a long time, watching the view.

'I'm sorry to have to tell you this,' says Ivan at last, 'but your father is dead. He was shot this morning out at the Rapture on the East Ridge.'

'He's not my father,' says Kyle. 'Never was.'

Ivan feels the tension within himself ease ever so slightly; after speaking with the traumatised Elsie Claremont, he'd been hoping for something like this, some sort of confession. 'When did you find out?'

'Sunday before last. Elsie rang me from America.'

'Two days before Jonas was killed.' Ivan offers the observation, hoping for a reaction, but not getting one.

'If you say so.'

'So, it was the DNA tests that confirmed it? For the bone marrow transplant?'

'Yeah. She discovered she wasn't a compatible donor for her daughter. Needed to test her wider family. Enlisted my help. We tested me, as her cousin. And Jonas, as her dad.'

'He volunteered?'

'Sure.'

Ivan scans Kyle's face, searching for emotion, but the youth is staring at the lake, face revealing nothing. 'So who is your father? Jonas?'

'No, not him.' Kyle looks him in the eye. 'The DNA test, the first one. It showed that I'm Elsie's cousin, through our mums. That's what we expected. But it also showed I was related to Bess's father.' Kyle takes a drag on his cigarette, lets the smoke linger on his lips before exhaling, as if to slow time. 'Elsie worked it out. Or guessed. Whatever. The Seer. We tested him, got the results yesterday. Confirmed it. Tested Buddy as well, to make sure he wasn't.'

'Wasn't what?'

'My father. That he wasn't a compatible donor.'

Ivan takes a moment to understand what Kyle is saying. 'They agreed to be tested?'

'No way. But we only needed some saliva. I got Buddy's. A girl at the Rapture, a maid at the house, she helped get the Seer's sample for me.'

There's more silence. There is a peace here, a quiet, a tranquillity. After the blazing sun and dust of the East Ridge, up here the earth has calmed itself. A light breeze is blowing in from the south-east; not much, but enough to take the edge off. The sun is touching the horizon now.

'When did Buddy find out?'

'I told him last night. That he wasn't my dad and neither was Jonas. That it was the Seer. I thought I owed him that much.' The youth takes a toke on his cigarette.

Ivan remains quiet, letting the questions ask themselves, sensing that Kyle will get there, all in good time.

'He just gaped, unable to talk. It shocked him.' Kyle looks across at Ivan. 'Want one?' He has a sixpack at his feet, with four beers left.

'Sure,' says Ivan, accepting the beer, cracking the can, taking a sip. It's warm and yeasty and bitter. But it's wet. And it gives him time to think. Jonas and his wife Annie and her sister Heloise were followers of the Seer twenty years ago, or at least attended parties up at the Rapture. Ivan recalls the porno he saw at the mine site, feeling a chill pass through him despite the heat. More than just parties then. And now, two decades on, Kyle revealed the truth, telling Buddy that he'd been cuckolded by the self-proclaimed prophet. The old miner must have stewed on it overnight, his rage building, before taking his guns and his humiliation and seeking revenge. Ivan returns his attention to Kyle. 'Did Jonas know any of this?'

The youth shrugs. 'No. Why would he? The tests showed he was Elsie's father, no doubt about it.'

'But not a compatible donor?'

'No. The bone marrow needs to come from the father's side; that's where the fault lies. Jonas and Elsie weren't any good. I was a closer match, but still not good enough. Jonas died without knowing any of that.'

'We know who murdered him.'

That sparks interest in the youth, the phlegmatic attitude falling away for just a moment. 'Murdered? I thought he'd just carked it. Heart attack or something.'

Ivan fixes his gaze upon him, bringing all the intensity of his blue eyes to bear. 'We haven't told anyone about that, the circumstances of his death. That it would have looked like natural causes. Everyone else thinks he died on the cross.'

Kyle says nothing.

'Was it you? Did you crucify him?'

There is a long sigh from the young miner, but no real hesitation, no attempt at denial or deflection; he answers matter-of-factly, as if describing what brand of tobacco he favours. 'Yeah. I nailed him up.'

'He was already dead?'

'Yeah. All stiff, a smile on his face, like he was happy about it. Happy about what he'd done to me, done to all of us. His arms were out, already in that position. Like he was asking for it.'

'You made the cross?'

'Sure. Not difficult. His carpentry tools were down the mine, in the box at the bottom of the ladder.'

'So it wasn't planned? You didn't head out there intending to do that to him?'

'No.'

'But you left your phone up on the East Ridge. Why?'

'Because I was coming up to beat the living shit out of him. For all that he'd done.' And now, for the first time, there is a hint of emotion, the suggestion of anger.

'Can you explain that?'

'The damage he did. All those years, all those people,' says Kyle. He's not looking at Ivan but out across the lake, as if he's explaining his actions to the landscape, not to a policeman. 'But he was already dead, and I just hated him. It was so unfair. And he still had his fucking ratter's gear with him.' Kyle looks at him. 'You understand? He was ratting our mine, the arsehole. He'd already taken so much from us. And there he was, going through the gap, stealing our opals.'

'I thought the mine was played out. Isn't that what Buddy thought?'

'Yeah. I don't think he was bullshitting when he said that. He just didn't know.' Kyle breathes in more smoke, a kind of punctuation. 'Jonas must have found a lucrative pocket of opals right up against the boundary, realised there might be more on our side. But instead of telling Buddy, he was sneaking in there, plundering it. The old cunt.' Kyle takes a last toke of his cigarette and flicks the butt away, watches as it bounces on a rock. 'He was just lying there, like a fucking saint, when I found him. A martyr. He'd escaped everything, his responsibilities, his comeuppance. I came up here wanting to hurt him. It was too late for that, but I had to do something. So I crucified him.'

'But why? You didn't know he was ratting until you found him. What had he ever done to you?'

'Fuck. You still don't get it, do you?' says Kyle, another hint of anger breaking through the studied insouciance. He turns away, starts rolling another cigarette, paper on his knee, threading the tobacco between his fingers. It's like a meditation, calming himself before recommencing his explanation. 'When I was a kid, Jonas was always so kind to me. Almost doting. A better dad than Buddy, by a long shot. It was only later, much later that I worked out why: Jonas reckoned he was my dad. And I reckon Buddy suspected the same thing, the way he treated me, how he'd lay into me, beat me black and blue, call me worthless, call me a bastard. I always thought it was just a word, you know. Bastard. Everyone uses it. But now I think he meant it. I reckon they both thought that Jonas was my father. They were both wrong.'

Ivan thinks of the will, Jonas leaving his mine to Kyle. It makes sense. 'But you can't know they thought that for sure.'

'Yes, I can.' Kyle lifts the cigarette to his lips, licks the edge of the paper, seals the tube of tobacco. 'Jonas was always so nice. Until Elsie and I got to about sixteen. We'd hang out together. I was keen on her. She's pretty. Beautiful, really.' He turns to Ivan, checks his reaction, before returning his attention to the lake. The sun has gone now, but its light endures, splashing the underside of the clouds. 'It's allowed, you know. Cousins. You can marry. Law says so.' He lights the cigarette with an old-fashioned zippo, draws deeply, letting the smoke linger as it curls from his mouth.

'He got so angry. Warned me off. Said it was unholy, could not be allowed. Started spouting scriptures, being a shit. Cruel and nasty and ugly. Just another old cunt. Just like Buddy.

'But he never told me straight out, like he told Elsie. Even when I was collecting his DNA, when he knew it might reveal the truth. She told me last night; it was the first time I had it confirmed, after we'd found out about the Seer. Jonas had warned her, back when we were teenagers, that we couldn't be together. He told her that there was a good chance we weren't just cousins, but brother and sister as well. Swore her to silence. Told her that it would be too painful for me, to think of my mother like that.' Kyle stares, breathes deep, as if trying to calm himself down, the emotion welling, trying to get out. 'The fucking coward. Hiding behind my dead mother. He should have told me what he told Elsie. Or he and Buddy could have had the guts to get us tested. It could have been so different. None of it would have happened.' The anger in his face has been joined by regret and sadness.

'You've lost me, Kyle. What wouldn't have happened?'

Kyle looks back across the lake. He drinks some more beer. 'Buddy thought I was a bastard, Jonas thought I risked incest. Elsie had been warned off. I had no one to turn to. So, I started going to the Rapture. The Seer was chill, had his act together, was kind to me. Compared to all the other adult men I knew, he was like a saint. Let me stay there. It was fun. There were parties and girls and the rest of it.'

'You mean drugs and sex?'

'Yeah.' He looks at Ivan. 'You blame me?'

'No. Not really.'

Kyle leans down, pulls a beer from the sixpack for himself. Cracks it open, takes a long draught. 'Here, look.' He points to the sleeve tattoo on his arm, the solid band of ink. 'I even got their tattoo. The cross. That's what all this is. To cover it.' He draws on his cigarette. 'Elsie started coming as well. Her life was almost as shit as mine. I introduced her, thought we could be together over there, away from Jonas and Buddy. Live our own lives, do what we wanted. I thought I could win her over. But that was never going to happen, not after what Jonas had told her. Pretty soon, she was into it as much as me. And that's where she met him. Zeke. And then they were together, an item.' Another draught of beer. 'I fucking hated it, man, those two, so into each other. I was so lonely and so jealous and so fucking miserable. But I swear, if I'd known why she'd brushed me off, it would have been different. If I'd thought she was my sister as well as my cousin, I would have helped them. None of it would have happened.'

'Zeke Jakowitz and Elsie were together?'

'Yeah.'

'What happened?'

'Jonas saw my tattoo, realised we were both going over there. He was fucking livid. He bashed me, he bashed her. Told us we couldn't have anything to do with the Rapture, forbade Elsie from going there again. I've never seen someone so angry.'

'That's because he knew what happened at those parties,' says Ivan. 'When Jonas was young, he used to go there too. With Elsie's mum. And your mum,' says Ivan. 'I guess he never told you that, either.'

Kyle turns from the landscape, stares deep and long and hard into Ivan's eyes. 'No. But if the Seer is my father, that makes sense.'

'Is that why Elsie left? He was hitting her? We know about the AVO.'

'Yeah. That and she was pregnant. With her girl, Bess. She needed to get away, get somewhere safe.'

'Nowhere safer than Adelaide,' says Ivan.

Kyle cracks a weak smile. 'Yeah. I guess.'

'The Seer. He was the father of Elsie's child?'

Kyle frowns. 'No. What makes you think that?'

And now Ivan is confused. 'Elsie wants his bone marrow. For her daughter.'

Kyle is still frowning. 'That figures. But the dad was Zeke. That's what Elsie told me.'

It takes Ivan a moment to understand the scene out at the Rapture, Elsie pleading with Buddy not to kill the Seer. 'Zeke was *his* son? The Seer's?'

'Yeah. My half-brother.'

And Ivan is silent for a while, making the connections. Initially, Montifore said it was the dead lad, Zeke, who was well connected. Later, after talking to Reg Montgomery, he'd asserted it was actually the Seer who wielded influence. Now Ivan understands the confusion: they were linked to each other as well as to the future attorney-general, Jeremy Plankten. What a web.

'She left in a hurry,' says Kyle. Now he's started talking, he sounds like he wants to get it all out. 'She had to. She rang when she got to Adelaide. Sent me an email. She couldn't get in touch with Zeke. There are no phones at the Rapture; they're not allowed. I went over, but they told me he'd been sent into a religious retreat, incommunicado. More like solitary confinement. Elsie was getting desperate. Finally I got a message from him. A letter from Zeke to Elsie. Here.' He stands, pulls a beaten envelope from his back pocket, hands it over.

In the fading light, Ivan reads the letter.

Darling Elsie

I can't leave. They are holding me. I can't get to a phone.

I said I was leaving, that if he didn't let me go, I was going to tell all. The drugs, the videos, the unpaid labour.

He is making me pray all day and all night. No sleep. Weird drugs. But I'll get out. I'll be with you.

All my love. All of it forever.

Zeke XXX

'You never sent it to her,' says Ivan.

'No. I hated him. Hated him for getting her pregnant. Didn't understand her wanting the baby. I wanted to be with her. I still loved her. I didn't know anything about what Jonas and Buddy thought, their false belief she was my sister as well as my cousin.'

Ivan knows more is coming. He drinks some beer, waiting, barely tasting it. Out across the lake, the colour is starting to drain from the sky.

Kyle continues: 'I copied his handwriting. I sent her a letter, pretending to be him. Said it was over, he was devoted to the Rapture. After she got it, she rang me, crying. I told her I'd heard from people we knew there; he'd taken an oath of abstinence, of celibacy, was purifying himself.' He looks to Ivan, eyes imploring. 'If I'd known, it would have been so different.'

'I believe you.'

'And then he was dead out there, on the lake, a couple of months later.' Kyle takes a gulp of beer, holds it in his mouth, before swallowing. 'We saw it. We saw it happen. And we did nothing.'

'What?'

'I was with Buddy, down the mine. He was being his usual fucking arsehole self. I was sixteen. I'd had enough. I'd been saving money, ratting his mine to get a few dollars together. His mine and Jonas's. I was almost set. I was heading to Adelaide to be with her. I came up the shaft, and I could see Jonas, standing up here, up at this lookout, overlooking all of this.' His arm sweeps wide, encompassing the vista. 'I was curious. It was a blazing hot day. Forty degrees easy. He wasn't even wearing a hat. I couldn't work out what could be so interesting that Jonas could be up here, just standing. So I walked up. Not next to him—I was over there, by that little tree. But I could see what he could see. There was a car down there, stopped on the road to the new mine site at Kalingra. And there were two men out in the dunes. It was so hot up here, on the ridge, but down there, on the salt pan, who knows? Like the surface of the sun.

'I could recognise the car, see who it was. The Seer and Zeke. Then Zeke started walking out towards the middle of the lake. I couldn't work it out, what was going on, why the Seer would let him do that. Then the Seer turned and walked back to the car, stopping once to drink some water and check that Zeke wasn't following. And then he got in his car and drove away.' Kyle has tears in his eyes now; the emotions held back for so long are beginning to assert themselves. 'I looked across at Jonas, he looked at me. Then he went down his mine and I went down ours.'

'His own son?' says Ivan. 'The Seer killed his own son?'

'His only begotten son.' A weak smile. 'Or the only one he knew about.' Kyle looks across at Ivan, cheeks shimmering wet in the setting sun. 'I could have saved him. I would have saved him. I just didn't know.' He goes to drink beer, but stops, not putting the can to his lips. 'He was my brother.'

'And the Seer: he didn't see you? The two of you standing up here?'

'Don't know. There would be so much glare down there, maybe he didn't. Or maybe he just didn't care.'

Ivan nods, letting the moment breathe, waiting for the incipient evening to calm them. If Kyle is looking to him for some sort of absolution, he's not about to give it. 'Will you testify?' he asks instead. 'If we charge the Seer, will you testify?'

'Yes. Against him. Against Jonas. Against Buddy. Against myself. You can charge me with anything you like, anything I deserve. I'll plead guilty.'

'Just spell it out for me. Last Tuesday. Elsie had told you a day or two before that Jonas was not your father. You left your phone on the East Ridge, came out here intending to beat him up. Why?'

'Because he stopped me being with Elsie. Because he caused me to stand between her and Zeke. Because I let my own brother walk out into the lake and die. He ruined all of our lives: him and Buddy and the Seer. All these cruel old men. I wanted to hurt him. I wanted to hurt him so bad. So when I found him lying there, looking so peaceful, so fucking righteous, I couldn't let it stand. I made the cross; I crucified him.'

Ivan looks out across the darkening lake. He'll get his murder conviction after all; not for the death of Jonas McGee, not for the death of Merv Claxton, not for the death of Stanley Honeywell, but for the death of Zeke Jakowitz. It doesn't seem much; it doesn't seem enough.

But Kyle isn't finished. 'I remember it, you know. The accident.' He drains his beer, crumples the can, throws it away. He lifts another from the sixpack, thinks better of it and places it gently on the ground. A shudder runs through him, and Ivan finds himself sitting absolutely still, as if something is telling him that this is important.

'We were coming back from Lightning Ridge. It was such a grand day. Picnic races. I remember the horses, they were so big, their hooves so loud, their breath like steam trains. I'd never seen a horse before. Or so many people. And there was fairy floss. Elsie and I had some; never had that before either. She was so pretty, such fun, in her dress that her mother made her. Jonas was being funny, kind of silly. He was drunk, but I didn't know that back then. Buddy kept giving him drinks.'

Kyle's voice has had a faraway quality to it, almost dreamlike, but now it turns darker, the joy leaving it. 'Elsie and I were asleep in the car, together on the back seat. We stopped and I woke up. There was a dog howling. That's what I thought. A dog. But it wasn't a dog. It was a man; it was Jonas. It was night-time and he was howling, like in a nightmare. I could smell smoke. The headlights on Buddy's car were making beams through it, and I knew something bad had happened. Then the howling stopped. I could hear them talking, men's voices above the sound of the engine. Not what they were saying, just the urgency in the words. Then Buddy was getting back in. I closed my eyes, pretended to be asleep when he checked. Then we were driving again, off into the night, leaving Jonas and whatever it was behind us. And all the way back, all the way to Finnigans Gap, Buddy was laughing. Laughing like he'd heard the biggest joke in the world. Laughing because he'd killed them.'

'You can't know that.'

'Yeah, I can.'

'How?'

'Last night. When I told him that Jonas wasn't my father, that it was the Seer.'

'He confessed?'

'I said it to him. I told him I knew what had happened, that he'd murdered them. And he nodded.'

And now the young man loses it, the years of practised nonchalance falling away, leaving the shell of the five-year-old, weeping for his mother, mourning for the future that was taken from him, his shoulders heaving, his body consumed by the physicality of emotion.

Ivan says nothing, but he reaches across, places a hand on Kyle's arm. The boy-man reaches across, places his other hand on Ivan's.

The sky is almost dark, its palette reduced to monochrome. Ivan tries to think of something more to say, some words of comfort, but they fail him. Instead he looks out into the expanse and ponders the thoughts of Buddy Torshack. It explains why he went gunning for the Seer. Not just because he'd been cuckolded by the preacher, but because Buddy had blood on his hands; he'd killed Annie and Heloise and tried to kill Jonas. All because of the Seer.

Ivan turns to Kyle. 'Time we went to town. Time we started to set things right.'

'If you say so.'

FRIDAY

chapter thirty-one

MIDNIGHT HAS GONE, BUT THEY'RE STILL AT THE PUB, OUT IN THE BEER GARDEN where the air is cooler and the night is quiet. The bar closed at eleven, but they're allowed to stay, at the publican's insistence, beers on the house. Ivan is at one table, drinking silently with Nell and Cheryl and Vince. At the next table, the mayor, Lydia and Holgate are sitting with Garry, chatting as they drink. There's a couple of forensic staff at another table, but Carole and Blake are still working, twelve hours on. Stanley Honeywell is dead, Buddy Torshack is dead. Three of the Seer's disciples are dead. Carl Richter is in hospital on the Gold Coast, out of surgery and out of danger. The media have arrived, have started to swarm, like flies, like locusts, but for now the pub is a no-go zone.

'You think he will?' asks Vince. 'The Seer? Donate his bone marrow?'

'Hope so,' says Nell. 'Maybe some good will come out of it.'

Cheryl drains her beer and stands. 'I'm calling it a night. C'mon, Vince. We'll need to be up early. Prisoners to feed, prisoners to transfer.'

The Seer is in the lock-up and so is Kyle, guarded for the moment by officers from Lightning Ridge. Cheryl and Vince are on the early shift.

Over at the other table, the calm is broken by a wave of laughter. It's Garry, recounting the day. His voice is high, pitched to mimicry. 'Don't kill him! I want to suck out his fucking marrow!' More laughter.

'He's done well,' says Nell to Ivan.

'Yeah. Learnt a few things.'

'Steep learning curve.'

'Isn't that what life is? A learning curve.'

'That's very philosophical,' she says.

'I'm not just a pretty face.'

'Ha. Don't get carried away.'

They fall into silence once more, happy to sit and catch snippets of conversation from the other tables.

'What will happen to Kyle?' she asks after a moment more introspection.

'That'll be for the courts to decide. And the prosecutor's office.'

'Poor fuck,' she says. 'Seriously messed up. Needs help.'

'He should get it. They'll want him in good shape if he's going to testify against the Seer.'

Nell shakes her head. 'Not for his own sake.'

'Does it matter? Provided he gets it.'

'I guess not.' She looks about her, taking in the pub. 'It shits me. We'll get the Seer for murder, or for manslaughter. Whatever. Kyle for interfering with a crime scene, desecrating a body. All of it. Even Holgate will get the third degree. And meanwhile, Delaney Bullwinkel gets away scot-free. The murder of Jonas McGee, the murder of Merv Claxton. No blowback. Untouchable.'

'Well, if the cards fall the way Bob Inglis says, he'll be up shit creek.'

'It's not the same. You know it's not the same. He should be in prison.'

'There'll be an inquest. We can testify, tell the court what we believe happened.'

'Yeah? Wouldn't be surprised if it was a closed court. Suppression orders.'

'We'll see.'

She takes a drink. 'You tempted?'

'By what?'

'The stock market. LikeUs. Wide Valley. There for the taking.'

He shakes his head emphatically, not quite believing what she's suggesting. 'No. We cannot go anywhere near that. You know we can't.'

'It would help, though. If you have any debts.'

'No, I'm good. No debts. Not much else, but no debts.'

'What about the rest of your father's money?'

He considers his drink, then turns to her. His gaze rests lightly upon her face, catches the concern in her eyes, before he looks away again. 'I'm giving what's left to the fund for Bess Claremont.'

'You no longer feel it's tainted?'

'No. I reckon we've done enough to give it a good rinse.'

She smiles, almost teasing. 'I wouldn't tell, you know. The stock market. If you needed it.'

'Don't even joke about it, Nell. We can't go there. Not and remain police officers.'

'Well, good for you.' And now it is Nell who reaches out, who places her hand on his. 'Let me know if I can help.' It's a small gesture, a gesture reciprocated, but he feels its warmth flow through him.

His phone rings, cutting the moment. He glances at the screen, shrugs. 'Feral Phelan. Doesn't sleep.'

Nell smiles. 'Vampires don't.'

He takes the call.

'Ivan, it's Nathan. I hear congratulations are in order.'

'Thanks,' is all he can muster.

'You have the Seer in custody, so I hear. Charged with murder.'

'You hear right.'

'You know who he is then? Jonathan Plankten. Brother of the former attorney-general, Jeremy Plankten?'

'Are you telling me to back off?' Ivan's voice is clear and calm and resolute.

'No. Do what you feel is right. I'll back you. You're a policeman, you're one of us. We decide who gets arrested and who gets charged, not some network of powerbrokers.'

'Glad to hear it,' says Ivan, although he is thinking of the corollary: that it's people like Phelan who are also deciding who doesn't get charged and prosecuted. Nevertheless he keeps his voice neutral. 'I appreciate that.'

'One favour, if I may.'

'Go on.'

'If anyone does try to dissuade you, discourage you, you'll let me know who they are?'

'Absolutely.'

'Well, good luck with it then.'

Ivan ends the call, looks across at Nell. 'He sure knows how to play the angles, that lad.'

'How do you mean?'

'He sits there collecting dirt on people. Leverage.'

Nell's face is sombre. He thinks maybe she's recalling her own encounters with Professional Standards.

Ivan's phone rings again. Not the MobiPol, the burner, vibrating in his pocket. He takes a look at Nell, then brings it into the open, answers it. Trusting her.

'Morris. Howdy.' Across from him, Nell is staring, taking it all in.

'I've just been watching the news. Channel Ten,' says his old boss. 'A Doug Thunkleton exclusive.'

'You're kidding. Is he up here?'

'Apparently. He's reporting that you've arrested the Seer for the Zeke Jakowitz death.'

'We did. For the death of his son.' And now he's smiling, and, to his relief, so is Nell. He watches her listen as he recounts what they found. Finally, he recaps. 'You know, Morris, if you didn't take down the AG, you and Martin Scarsden, if Plankten was still in office, then I wonder if we'd be able to prosecute.'

'Not just Scarsden and me—you too, Ivan,' says Morris Montifore across the ether. 'You were part of that as well. The good guys are winning, the old guard are retreating.'

'So how come it doesn't feel like we're winning?'

'What does that mean?'

'We know who killed the miner up here, but we can't do anything about it.' He lays out their suspicions: Claxton killing McGee at Bullwinkel's behest, then Claxton himself eliminated.

'Give it time,' says Montifore. 'There's always the inquest.'

'You believe that?'

There is no answer.

'Morris, I need a favour. Send me Scarsden's number.'

Again there is no response, not for a long time. 'You sure?'

'Just send it through.'

The call ends. Nell says nothing; he can't read what she is thinking. The laughter from the other table is growing; mourning is starting to meld into celebration. The mayor's wife, Lydia, gets to her feet and raises her glass, holds it high, bringing a sombreness back to proceedings. 'Stanley Honeywell,' she declares, and the others stand and echo the toast. Ivan and Nell raise their own glasses skywards and drink to the big man. Contemplation overtakes them, even as the revelry recommences at the other table.

Then, at last, Nell puts words to the question that is hanging between them. 'Scarsden. You're going to rat?' Except it's not really a question, it's more of a statement.

'I'm not dobbing on police; I'm not compromising investigations.'

'That's what Montifore said. Look what happened to him.'

He can hear the concern in her voice. 'You were the one who said Delaney Bullwinkel shouldn't be allowed to get away with it.'

'We're police officers, Ivan. We're not judges or juries or journalists. It's not up to us.'

'Isn't it?'

'Phelan will gut you if he finds out.'

Ivan raises his glass again in a mock toast. 'Fuck Feral Phelan.'

'Nice alliteration,' she says dryly, but doesn't raise her own glass. 'Promise me you'll think it through. Don't go off half-cocked.'

'I promise.'

And they leave it there.

— —

Nell feels a kind of sadness, sitting in the beer garden, the air warm around them. They've achieved something, she and Ivan. Maybe not enough, but something. Brought justice to some, resolution to others. She looks across at her partner and realises that she likes him. At last, she likes him. Understands him, respects him. Maybe even admires him. A good man, trying his best.

She gets up, walks towards the Ladies, goes inside. She stands at the basin, examines her face in the mirror, a face that is somehow older. Here, she knows, is her opportunity. Ivan Lucic talking to Montifore on a burner phone. Ivan asking for Martin Scarsden's number. All it would take now is one call to Phelan and she would be out from under, her association with Topsoil erased for all time, her career back on track. She looks herself in the eye and smiles. Then she takes her own burner and throws it in the bin.

Acknowledgements

FINNIGANS GAP IS NOT A REAL TOWN, BUT IT IS LOOSELY BASED ON LIGHTNING Ridge in northern New South Wales. None of the characters are based in any way on Lightning Ridge locals.

A huge thanks to opal miner Fred Mallouk, who took me down his mine and explained some of the basics to me, and to Tony 'Kingy' King, former NSW detective, who outlined some practices of police investigations. All the mistakes, inaccuracies and exaggerations are mine, not theirs.

Huge and enduring thanks to:

- Everyone at Allen & Unwin, including marketing, sales and publicity.
- The editorial A-team that has guided all my books: Jane Palfreyman, Christa Munns, Ali Lavau and Kate Goldsworthy. The best of the best!

- Publicist extraordinaire Laura Benson.
- Designer Luke Causby for yet another eye-catching cover.
- Photographer and mate Mike Bowers, for the author photographs and publicity shots.
- Artist Aleksander Potočnik, for again making my imaginings real with another incredible map.
- Australia's best literary agent Grace Heifetz of Left Bank Literary, and her co-conspirators, Felicity Blunt in London and Faye Bender in New York.
- Audio book narrators Dorje Swallows and Rupert Degas.
- All the team at Wildfire in the UK, notably editors Kate Stephenson and now Jack Butler, as well as Jo Liddiard and Caitlin Raynor.

I also want to thank the brilliant translators, who have worked so diligently to bring my books to non-English speaking markets. Such very fine work—thank you!

Thanks also to all the amazing booksellers in Australia and beyond.

And, of course, thanks to my family: Tomoko, Cameron and Elena for their love and support.